# THE SCHOLAR'S BLADE

## Chris Emmett

The Scholar's Blade

By Chris Emmett

ISBN-13: 978-988-8769-44-5

© 2023 Chris Emmett

FICTION / Historical

EB191

All rights reserved. No part of this book may be reproduced in material form, by any means, whether graphic, electronic, mechanical or other, including photocopying or information storage, in whole or in part. May not be used to prepare other publications without written permission from the publisher except in the case of brief quotations embodied in critical articles or reviews. For information contact info@earnshawbooks.com

Published in Hong Kong by Earnshaw Books Ltd.

For S, JJ and VSM

# EPISODE I

## THE HEAVENLY KINGDOM

# 1

## Yongan City, South China – 1848

In the pantry, the darkness was complete. Meng hugged his knees and pressed himself against the wall, wishing he could become part of it. His breath rasped fast and shallow. Sweat prickled his brow. He squeezed shut his eyes and whispered a prayer to *Ne-Zah*, the God of protection.

Beyond the pantry door, footsteps scurried across the scullery floor. Meng recognised the tread of the mission steward, Da Fan. He held his breath but that made his heart beat so hard he was sure Da Fan would hear it. The pantry's door latch rattled and a strip of light appeared.

'Boy. *Boy!*' The steward's voice was harsh. 'Come out now or the Reverend will beat you, and I will beat you for displeasing him.'

The door opened wider and the glow of an oil lamp crept into the pantry. Da Fan peered around the doorjamb. He held the lamp high and squinted into the gloom. He wore loose-fitting black britches and a jacket of white linen. By the emperor's decree, he dressed his hair in the Manchu-mandated style: shaved above the forehead and bound tight at the back into a heavy queue.

'*Aiiyah*,' he cried, 'there you are, you devil's imp.'

Meng squeezed back into the corner. He tried to speak but his tongue was like dried leather. Da Fan reached into the pantry and grabbed Meng's tunic. He dragged him from the pantry and pushed him to a table where a tumbler of milk stood on a tarnished tray.

'You are a little demon disguised as a boy,' Da Fan snapped. 'Now take this to Father Petrus.' He clapped his hands. 'Hurry boy, the Reverend has asked for you specially.'

From somewhere, Meng found a small voice.

'Please, Master Da. *Please.*'

The steward made shooing motions with both hands. 'Go, go now or I will throw you into the street and you can fight the dogs for your next meal.'

Meng reached for the tray. His hands trembled and milk sloshed over the brim of the tumbler. The steward rolled his eyes. Meng grasped the tray with both hands and backed from the kitchen.

He found himself in a dim corridor. A fusty carpet softened his tread and high on the wall, pictures of saints looked down with mournful eyes. As he climbed the staircase, the steps creaked beneath his feet. At the head of the stairs loomed a heavy door. Meng pressed his ear against the wood and hearing nothing, he tapped at the door. There was no answer. He backed away, then remembered the steward waiting in the kitchen. He took a deep breath and knocked again, this time harder. From beyond the door, a harsh voice answered in the local dialect.

'Enter.'

Meng pushed the door ajar. He eased the tray through the door, placed it on the floor and turned to scurry back down the stairs.

'Stop. Come in. Let me see you.'

The door swung open and Meng stood in the doorway feeling small and alone. The room was large and smelled of dust and old polish. Its ceiling was lost in shadow. In the middle of the room, a European priest sat reading in a sagging armchair. On a table beside him, a lamp threw hard shadows across the walls. The priest peered at Meng over the top of his spectacles.

'Ah yes,' he said, 'the new one.'

He looked old but in fact, he was only middle-aged. He had a large head topped by a shock of silver hair. His lips were thick and he had watery eyes. He beckoned Meng closer.

'Come,' he said. 'Do not be afraid.' The priest did not speak the local dialect well and to Meng the words sounded harsh and crude.

Meng took a step forward and stood with his eyes on the carpet.

'Do you know my name?' the priest asked.

'You are the Reverend Father, Father Petrus.' Meng wanted to sound brave but could not raise his voice above a whisper.

'Yes, I'm Father Petrus. And how old are you?' The priest tried to look into Meng's eyes but Meng turned away his face.

'I... I'm not sure Reverend Father,' Meng stammered. 'Twelve I think. Yes, maybe I'm twelve.'

The priest gave a warm chuckle. 'Twelve eh? What a wonderful thing it is to be twelve. And what is your name?'

'I am Meng, Reverend Father.'

'Meng, Meng,' the priest mused. 'An ugly name; a heathen name. We must find a proper name for you.' He chewed his knuckle. 'For you it must be something special.' He paused for a few seconds. 'Yes I have it. You shall be Joseph. Joseph had a wonderful coat of many colours. He was very beautiful, in fact he was so beautiful his brothers became jealous and threw him into a deep pit.' He clapped his hands. 'So, Joseph it is. But don't be afraid, I shan't let your new brothers throw you into a pit.'

Father Petrus laid his book on the table. He stood and moved closer to Meng. Meng shuddered. Something about the priest's closeness made him want to shrink away. The priest's voice was

## THE SCHOLAR'S BLADE

a soft growl.

'So Joseph, speak your new name for me.'

He cupped his hand to Meng's cheek but Meng flinched and took a step back. Father Petrus' lips curled, showing yellowed teeth. His hand snapped forward and he grabbed a fistful of Meng's hair.

Meng cried out. He tried to twist away but the priest's fingers were like talons.

Father Petrus wrenched on Meng's hair, forcing back his head. The skin of Meng's throat stretched tight. His spine felt ready to snap. His strength drained away and he dropped to his knees.

Father Petrus put his face close to Meng's and Meng gagged at its whisky smell. Shadows cast by the lamp turned the priest's eyes into dark sockets.

'I will ask again,' Father Petrus purred. 'What is your name?' He tightened his grip, forcing a gasp from Meng's mouth.

'Please Reverend Father.' Meng screwed shut his eyes. 'I know nothing of holy men and pits. My name is Meng.'

'That was your heathen name,' the priest snarled. 'Tell me your good, Christian name.' He leaned closer. 'Try it in English. Say after me. My... name... is... Joseph.'

Meng thrust out his chin. 'I am Meng,' he croaked. 'I have always been Meng. I will always be...'

Father Petrus silenced him with a slap.

Meng's cheek burned. Tears stung his eyes.

The priest's breath was hot against Meng's face. His voice was soft in Meng's ear.

'Your name, child, is Joseph.'

He backhanded Meng across the face and pushed him down to the carpet. He stood with his legs straddling Meng's body. He licked his lips. They glistened, moist and fleshy. He pointed a trembling finger at Meng's face. His voice rose to a shout. 'You are defiant; defiant and Godless.'

Meng tried to stand but Father Petrus knelt on his chest, driving the air from his lungs. The priest pinched Meng's cheek in a mockery of affection. He put his mouth close to Meng's ear. His voice was a hard whisper. 'Yes, you are Godless. But fear not, for I am an excellent teacher.'

He ran a finger along Meng's neck. His eyes shone and there was a quiver in his voice. 'This is a house of love,' Father Petrus rasped. 'Are you ready to receive my love?'

'I am not Joseph,' Meng answered but his voice was so small he knew that Father Petrus had not heard. The priest's lips were wet on Meng's neck, his hands explored Meng's body.

In the downstairs corridors, people stopped their work. From the room at the top of the stairs, Meng cried out again.

But no one moved to help him.

### Sishun Village – Southwest of Shanghai

One-eared Wu scratched his backside and eased himself down onto a rock beside the stream. The water chuckled over stones lying just below the surface and there was a glint of silver as a perch darted for the safety of reeds growing by the far bank. He laid his burden beside him, rolled his britches up above his knees and dipped his feet into the water. He sighed as the current tugged at his ankles.

Some said One-eared Wu was well past his fiftieth year but no one knew for sure. There were silver streaks in his queue and deep lines scored his face. But his eyes were a puzzle, they were not the eyes of an old man, they shone with mischief.

He pulled a fishing line from the folds of his jacket, baited the hook with rancid pork and dropped it into the water. He tugged at the line and began to half-sing, half-hum a song.

Behind him, there was a rustle in the undergrowth and a

## THE SCHOLAR'S BLADE

bird twittered into the air. One-eared Wu stopped his song and his eyes narrowed. He took a slow breath and reached down to touch the slim bundle beside him. Satisfied it lay within reach, he continued with his song and began to reel in his fishing line.

There was a footfall on the grass and a shadow moved into the edge of his vision. There was the scurry of feet. Something thudded against his back, driving the wind from him. Two arms wrapped around his neck.

'I'm a bandit come to take your head and eat your liver,' a voice piped in his ear.

One-eared Wu took gentle hold of the arms grasping his neck and chuckled.

'Indeed, my little friend,' he said, 'if you were a forest brigand, I'd be on my knees begging for a quick end.'

The boy laughed and untangled his arms from One-eared Wu's neck. He stood before the older man and cocked his head to the side.

'You promised to tell how you lost your ear,' he said. His eyes widened. 'Was it fighting brigands?'

One-eared Wu pulled a sour face. '*Chehh*,' he snorted. 'Is there a brigand in all China who can best One-eared Wu?'

'Then how?'

One-eared Wu glanced over his shoulder.

'It was *Yan Luo*,' he said in a loud whisper. 'Yes, *Yan-Luo*, the master of all demons.' He fixed the boy with an earnest stare. 'The trickster tried to steal my soul as I slept,' he continued. 'But I was too fast for him. I would have beaten him but he took me in a bear's grip and bit off my ear.' He took on a look of injured pride. 'He'll not be so lucky next time.'

The boy pursed his lips and placed his hands on his hips.

'My father says there's no such person as *Yan Luo*,' he snorted.

'Does he indeed?' One-eared Wu said. He pointed to his missing ear. 'Then how does our excellent doctor explain this?'

The boy grinned. 'You're impossible,' he said.

Not for the first time, One-eared Wu marvelled at the boy. To some he was a fearsome sight. When they saw him, children hid behind their mothers and old women mouthed silent charms. One-eared Wu did not think him at all fearsome, he had become used to the boy's golden hair and blue eyes.

'Why are you smiling?' the boy asked.

'Your Chinese, it's so clear,' One-eared Wu answered. 'I swear, in the dark you'd pass for a local boy.' He fixed a frown to his face. 'Shouldn't you be at school? I hear Master Yau visited your father's clinic yesterday. If the doctor finds you've been truant, he'll be angry.'

The boy lowered his eyes. 'It's boring,' he said. 'And... and the other boys laugh at me. They say my eyes are the colour of a funeral lantern and my hair is pale, like a demon's.'

One-eared Wu dropped to one knee and took hold of the boy's shoulders.

'Who said these words?' he asked.

'It was Chan-yu,' Mark said. 'He thinks because he's the oldest and his father is a landowner, he can say what he wants.'

One-eared Wu gave a slow nod. 'I have known such people,' he said. 'When next this Chan-yu teases you, say you are Mark Falchion and punch him as hard as you can. Give him no warning, just remember to strike with all your strength.' He stood and dusted off the boy's gown. 'Do this and he will trouble you no more.'

Mark Falchion's voice became small.

'You won't tell my father I missed school, will you?'

'Education is important,' One-eared Wu growled. 'But so are friends. I will say nothing.'

# THE SCHOLAR'S BLADE

Mark grinned his thanks then scuffed at the grass with his feet.

'But it's true,' he said. 'Blue is the funeral colour. Why do I have blue eyes?'

One-eared Wu shrugged.

'Why is the sparrow not like the camel? The Gods have decreed it and they are cleverer than I.'

Mark knelt and touched the package at One-eared Wu's feet. It was long and slim and wrapped in grubby linen.

'What is it?' he asked, all the time exploring it with his fingers. 'Quick, tell me,' he pleaded.

One-eared Wu's eyes sparkled. 'Why not open it and see?'

Mark tugged at the bindings and the linen fell away to reveal a bright sword. The blade was narrow where it joined the hilt but broadened along its length before tapering to a fine point. The hilt guard was round, like an oversized coin, dark leather covered the grip. Mark gawked, never had he seen anything so beautiful. He brushed the blade with his fingertips. It felt like iced silk.

'Have you been teaching the soldiers?' he asked, his voice hushed.

'I have, but I don't teach them very well.' One-eared Wu gave a wicked smile. 'Someday, we people of *Han* will free our land from the Manchu invader and restore our Chinese Ming emperor.'

Mark glanced around and lowered his voice.

'You talk like a... a...'

'Which name do you prefer?' One-eared Wu growled. 'Heaven and Earther, or triad?' His eyes became sad. 'Once, to be of the brotherhood was to be a man of honour, but now...' He shook his head.

For a while, the only sound was water bubbling over the

stream bed, then Mark took the sword's grip in both hands and raised the blade to eye level.

'Death to the Manchu,' he cried. His arm trembled and the point dropped back to the turf. 'It's heavy,' he grumbled.

'Don't fight the blade,' One-eared Wu chided. 'Let it do the work for you. Here, watch me.'

He took the sword from Mark and sucked in a heavy breath. He swung the sword in a slow arc then snapped his wrist. The blade sighed through the air then quivered as he brought it to rest. He ran his palm along the flat of the blade. '*Ahh,*' he sighed. 'The *dao* broadsword, there's no finer weapon under heaven. Sharp enough to split a hair, heavy enough to take a head.'

Mark's eyes were wide, his voice pleading.

'You must teach me, Uncle. I must learn.'

'You'll need a bit more muscle in that arm,' One-eared Wu chortled.

'I'll exercise,' Mark said, clutching One-eared Wu's hand in both of his. 'I'll exercise and practice, I promise. You must teach me, Uncle, you must.' He was jumping up and down and tugging at One-eared Wu's arm.

'You are a buzzing gnat,' One-eared Wu snapped. 'Do you think to become a swordsman overnight?' He softened his voice. 'A swordsman must exercise until his bones ache and his muscles are on fire. And when the pain becomes unbearable, he must work all the harder.'

He glared at the boy.

The boy gazed back.

'Books are more important than steel,' One-eared Wu insisted. He flashed a smile. 'An Imperial magistrate can steal more in a day than a swordsman can in a lifetime.'

Mark pressed his hands together as if in prayer.

One-eared Wu turned his face to the sky.

'You are indeed a gnat,' he muttered. 'Maybe after a few lessons you'll get bored and leave me in peace.'

A grin split Mark's face but One-eared Wu held up a hand.

'Hear me,' he said. 'If I learn you've been truant again, I'll teach you no more.'

Mark nodded.

'And you'll not touch this or any sword, not until you prove yourself with a quarterstaff.'

Mark sniffed and lowered his eyes.

One-eared Wu pressed his index finger against Mark's forehead and twisted it like a drill.

'First the brain, then the body,' he growled. 'A quarterstaff will teach you the four virtues: discipline, speed, grace, power.' His brows furrowed. 'Show me these and I'll think about training you on the *dao*.' His eyes twinkled. 'Maybe I'll teach you some secrets, secrets of the true brotherhood.'

Mark tried to speak but joy swelled in his chest, choking off his words.

One-eared Wu tried to look stern but could not keep a smile from his lips. *The boy is a firecracker,* he thought, *full of joy and energy. Aiiyah what task have I set myself?* He shouldered the broadsword and turned to go.

'We begin tomorrow,' he barked.

Mark Falchion clasped his hands at his chest and bowed. 'I will be ready, *Master* Wu,' he called.

The schoolhouse had mildewed walls and cobwebby rafters. The teacher had a reedy voice and his gown hung from bony shoulders. His face would have better suited a cadaver than a living man, and behind his back, the pupils called him Skull Yau.

'This afternoon, we examine the work called, *The Mandate of Heaven*,' the teacher intoned.

There were groans and behind Mark, a voice whispered, 'The barbarian knows about heaven, he even has eyes of death.' The voice belonged to Chan-yu, the oldest boy in the class.

'Who spoke?' Master Yau snapped. 'Falchion, was it you?'

Chan-yu put down his head and sniggered. 'It was the barbarian, Master Yau,' he chimed. 'I heard him. You should punish him.'

Mark stood. 'I said nothing, Master,' he answered.

The teacher pointed his cane at Mark. His voice shook and the end of his cane quivered.

'How dare you lie,' he shrieked. 'You will stand by my desk then we shall see how proud you are.' He strode to Mark and gave his ear a twist. Mark bit back a cry as the teacher dragged him to the front. 'Now everyone can see your defiance,' he said, his voice imperious. 'Stay here until your shame is expunged.'

Mark thought the afternoon would never end. At length, Master Yau took a sip of tea from his flask.

'Today's class is over,' he announced.

The pupils filed from the classroom, taking care to stifle their yawns. In the yard, Chan-yu stood taller than the other boys. When he saw Mark, he whispered to his companions and they laughed.

Mark fixed his eyes on Chan-yu and the smile fell from the older boy's face.

'Why do you stare, Funeral-Eyes?' Chan-yu called. 'You should take care.'

Mark's heart bounded as he crossed the schoolyard. He stopped before Chan-yu and bunched his fists.

'I am Mark Falchion,' he said. He summonsed every fibre of strength he possessed and punched Chan-yu square in the face.

Chan-yu staggered back and fell hard onto his backside. Blood flowed from his nose. His mouth worked like a landed

# THE SCHOLAR'S BLADE

fish. He put a hand to his face and stared uncomprehending at the blood on his fingers. In an instant, the other pupils gathered round, laughing and chattering.

'*Falchion*.' The teacher's voice cut through the clamour and all became silent. Footsteps hurried towards them and a bony hand grabbed Mark's arm.

'You are truly a barbarian,' Master Yau cried. 'You will *kow-tow* and beg Chan-yu for forgiveness.'

'I am Mark Falchion,' Mark cried. 'I *kow-tow* to no one.' He wrenched himself free and stepped closer to Chan-yu, who shrank down and covered his head with both arms.

'Do you hear me, Chan-yu?' he shouted. 'I am *Mark Falchion!*'

Master Yau's voice quivered with rage.

'You will *kow-tow*,' he screeched. He brought his cane down on Mark's shoulder.

Mark flinched but would not cry out.

Master Yau aimed a backhanded cut but Mark backed away and the blow whistled past him.

Mark turned and ran from the schoolyard. At the gate, he paused.

I am Mark Falchion,' he called again. 'And I *kow-tow* to no one.'

And this time, there was joy in his voice.

The seasons turned. The nights cooled. The daytime heat became less muggy. It was at this time the rice growers burned incense to the divine farmer, *Shen Nong*, and gathered in their harvest.

At the Sishun village school, Chan-yu took care not to anger Mark Falchion. Instead, he drew the other boys close to him. When they saw Mark, they would point and whisper and laugh.

As for their teacher, Master Yau, it seemed Mark had become

invisible. Mark's raised hand was always ignored; his questions went unanswered. He drew deeper into himself. He spoke to no one and no one spoke to him. His days became dark and empty.

Except on every third day. On every third day, he met One-eared Wu in the clearing by the stream. Mark would drop his school bundle and old Wu would throw him a staff of *Hongmu* hardwood.

'*Aiiyah,* you grow so quickly,' Old Wu chided. 'The staff will soon be too small,' He pointed off to Mark's left. 'Look, I have prepared a longer one for you.'

Mark turned his head and instantly felt a sharp blow on his shoulder.

'Never turn away from a man holding a weapon,' One-eared Wu growled. 'Now, take the guard position I taught you.'

Mark took the staff in both hands. He moved his right foot back and bent his knees. He angled the staff upwards so the tip was at eye level and the trailing end was close to the ground.

'Good,' One-eared Wu said.

He stepped forward and aimed a light blow at Mark's head. Mark parried the blow and the two staffs met with a solid *clack*. Then, with the speed of a civet taking a bird, One-eared Wu pivoted on his heel, dropped to one knee and landed a stinging blow on Mark's thigh.

Mark yelped and moved back, his leg numb. He shot Wu an angry glare then bent to rub feeling back into his thigh. A blow to his midriff doubled him over. He dropped to his knees, retching and clutching his belly.

One-eared Wu stood over Mark, the tip of his staff resting on the ground.

'Three blows,' he barked. '*Three!*'

He reached down, grasped Mark's hand and pulled him to his feet.

'In a fight, trust no one,' he snapped. 'And do not expect your opponent to follow the rules of your training. Be ready for anything.' He smiled and ruffled Mark's hair. 'Did you learn anything useful today?'

Mark massaged his belly. 'I learned not to trust anyone who claims to know *Yan Lou*,' he answered. Despite himself, he grinned. 'Can we work with the *dao* next week?'

One-eared Wu laughed a long rolling laugh.

'Only if you do not mind losing a body part,' he said. 'But in time, my young friend, in time. You have courage and you are stubborn. Soon enough we will work with the training swords.'

Mark clasped both hands to his chest and bowed. 'I will look forward to that time, *Master* Wu,' he said. He picked up his bundle and as he left the clearing, his step was lighter.

Spring was a time for planting and for renewal but for the school teacher, Master Yau, it was a time of decline. His face became even more skull-like; his skin became sallow and brittle, like dried paper. He took on an assistant, a young scholar named Jeung Dak who came from a nearby village.

It was rumoured that Jeung Dak had taken the civil exam and failed only by the thinnest of margins. He had a broad, open face and was quick to smile. He played little part in classroom activities and to Mark, he seemed no more than Master Yau's servant.

Spring gave way to steamy summer and Master Yau took to his bed. Three days later he died. He had never been popular but he was a man of learning and so deserved a proper funeral. He had no relatives and no one called him friend so the village head appointed two men and two women to act as mourners. They hung a blue lantern by Master Yau's door and, clad all in white, they held an overnight vigil by his body.

The next day, everyone gathered outside the village shrine where a Taoist *doashi* incanted prayers for the old teacher's soul. Ceremony done, the *doashi* led a procession to the burial place, a good distance from the village. With the burial over, they all returned to the village, discarded their white robes and went back to their daily routine.

A week later, Jeung Dak became *Master* Jeung Dak, the village school teacher. On his first day, he walked slowly and with much dignity, to the front of class. He took the cane from the corner of the classroom. He scowled and shook the cane at the class.

There was silence.

Two dozen pairs of eyes fixed on the cane. Jeung Dak took the cane in both hands. He bent it into steep arch and kept bending it until it splintered and broke.

At first the children gawked at him, slack jawed and wide-eyed. Someone laughed. Another clapped. Then they were all clapping, laughing and chattering. It seemed that after years of darkness, the classroom shutters had been thrown open to the sun.

In the following days, the children arrived early for class and lingered after the end of lessons. On the second week, after lessons had ended for the day, Jeung Dak called Mark to him.

'I have heard stories of you, Mark Falchion,' Jeung Dak said.

Mark lowered his eyes,

'They say you are a fighter. A disruptor.'

Mark squared his shoulders. 'I will not *kowtow* to bullies,' he snapped.

'Nor should you,' Jeung Dak said. 'But have you asked yourself why they bully you?'

Mark shook his head.

Jeung Dak looked into the young Westerner's eyes. 'They fear you,' he said. He raised a hand to silence Mark's response. 'Yes, they fear your fists.' He gave a soft chuckle. 'And so they should. But they also fear your intellect.'

Puzzlement furrowed Mark's brows.

'Take your calligraphy,' Jeung Dak said. 'It is still a little crude but it is far above the standard of the others and your understanding of the Confucian classics is well beyond your years.' For while, he was silent. 'You learn not only his words but you seek their inner meaning,' he continued. 'I see in you, great potential Mark Falchion,' he said. 'What are your ambitions? What do you see for your future?'

Mark shrugged. 'I love the poetry of the great teacher's work,' he said. 'But I'm not sure... My father wants... he wants...' He turned away. 'It's silly.'

Jeung Dak's voice was soothing.

'What does he want? Tell me. Maybe I can help.'

'He wants me to study the classics and become a great scholar,' Mark blurted.

Jeung Dak's eyebrows arched.

'A scholar is it? And how do you feel about that?'

Mark's voice became small. 'I don't know,' he said. 'It feels odd.'

'A blue eyed, golden haired scholar of the Chinese classics.' Jeung Dak mused. 'That would be odd indeed.'

Mark chewed his lip. 'Confucius teaches us that a son must always obey his father,' he said. 'But still, I don't know if it's the right path for me.'

'Do not give up your studies,' Jeung Dak answered. 'There are many opportunities for a man of learning who has the courage to grasp them. When you are old enough, bind your hair into a queue and adopt Chinese dress. Take the teachings of Confucius into your heart. Become a man of *Han*.'

'What's the point?' Mark sulked. 'Sishun Village is tiny. It is a dot. It is nothing.'

'Perhaps,' Jeung Dak mused. 'But in Soochow, there is a Confucian master called Wang Shi.'

'Yes,' Mark said, his eyes brightening. 'My father knows him, he has visited our mission.'

'Then you are fortunate,' Jeung Dak said. 'Wang Shi's students occupy some of the highest ranks in government. They also work in prestigious seats of learning in Soochow and other great centres.' His lips twisted in a wry smile. 'Sadly, I was a grave disappointment to him.'

'But you can take the examination again,' Mark said. 'I hear there are old men who return year after year.'

Jeung Dak shook his head. 'I was happy to have failed,' he said. His voice became a low growl. 'To be a low ranking official is to constantly kiss the backside of your senior. You must pretend not to see their self-seeking greed and corruption. You may even have to take part in it.'

He laid both hands on Mark's shoulders. 'Then what? If you are lucky and you kiss the right backsides, there is advancement. But then there is another backside to kiss and more greed to deal with. And when you are an old man, you will retire to your native place, sit in the sun and see that nothing has changed. The rich are still rich, the poor are still poor and those who govern are still corrupt.'

Mark's shoulders slumped. 'So what's the point?' he asked. 'Why should I study? Why should I become... become... Chinese?'

Jeung Dak let out his breath in a long sigh. 'You are a clever boy,' he said. 'But you have much to learn.'

He clapped his hands together and his voice became crisp. 'For now, practice your calligraphy and study the great sage.' He leaned closer to Mark. 'But remember,' he added. 'Always listen to your heart.'

As Mark stepped into the sunlight, his mind was a fog of contradictions. Of course he would study the works of Confucius. In those passages there was wisdom and beauty. But was Doctor Falchion's chosen path for his son really that hard? And what did it mean, to listen to your heart?

Mark's step lightened as he remembered that today was the third day, the day for his lesson with One-eared Wu. The talk with his teacher had made him late so he quickened his pace and hurried to the clearing by the stream.

## Hwangli Village South of Yongan

The village was a place of toil and poverty. The dwellings had sagging roofs, dark mildew streaked their walls. The central square was packed earth that during the rains, would turn to clinging mud. Dominating the square was a grain store with an ironbound door. The people were much like the buildings, joyless and without colour. They moved about the village in silence, heads down, gait shuffling.

'Come child, don't dawdle,' the woman snapped. She was in her late twenties, but years of fieldwork under the South China sun had toughened her skin and etched lines into her face. 'Please Mei,' she pleaded. 'We must not be late.'

The girl, whose given name was Mei, was small for her age, but that was normal in these times of shortage. She was slim and her hair was cropped short. She had fine features but it was her eyes that struck most people. They were large and seemed to be forever questioning. Today they were dark and troubled. She was ten years old, the eldest of five children. The others were boys. Even at ten years old, Mei understood the problem. Four boys and one girl. Boys grew into strong men, strong enough to till the earth and harvest the crops. Girls were a burden and in time, there would be a bride price to pay.

So now, they were here.

Mei tugged at the woman's hand.

'But mother,' she said. 'I don't want to...' She cast down her eyes and fell silent.

The mother dropped to her knees and placed her hands on Mei's shoulders. Her voice became soft.

'You will be *mi-jeh*,' she said. She pulled a grubby paper from her tunic and unfolded it. 'Look.' She pointed at a line of neat characters. 'This is your future.'

To Mei, the characters were just ink scratches.

'I do not understand that... that writing,' Mei sulked. 'Only boys learn those things.'

Her mother sighed. 'I know, child. I know,' she said. 'But teacher Wu read the words to me.' She held the paper close to Mei's face as though that would make everything clear. 'The magistrate has asked for you specially. He will take you as his *mi-jeh*, his adopted daughter. You will live in a fine house with the best food, the finest clothes.'

She cuffed a sudden dampness from her cheek and put her arms around Mei. She held her so tight, Mei thought she would never let go. Then she stood and smoothed down the front of her tunic. Her voice became firm.

'You will be *mi-jeh*,' she said. 'It is a rare privilege. Now come, we must not be late.'

They made their way along narrow levees separating rice paddies where workers waded thigh deep, planting rice stems in the ooze. Before them, a grand house sat on a low hill. The outer wall was rendered in crimson, broken only by a gate of ironbound teak, which stood open.

A man lounged against the gate jamb. He wore loose britches and a dark tunic buttoned to the neck. A heavy queue hung down his back and around his brows was a broad band of white cotton. His eyes were small and pockmarks scarred his face. He carried a staff, as long as he was tall. At their approach, he drew himself to his full height and moved to block the gate.

'What business have you here?' he demanded.

The woman lowered her gaze. She held the paper towards the man, making sure not to raise her eyes from the ground.

'Here, Excellency,' she wheedled. 'These are the words of your most honourable master. He commands our presence.'

The man snatched the paper, glanced at it then handed it back. He jerked his chin towards the gate.

'Go,' he growled. 'The master is expecting her.' As he spoke those words, he laughed.

Mei looked at the man, not understanding why his laughter troubled her. When he saw her watching him, the man scowled and made a half lunge towards her. He laughed again and a chill clutched at Mei's heart.

Mother and daughter passed through the gate and into a garden where willow shaded a path that meandered through a confusion of shrubbery. There was birdsong and the perfume of Azalea. A gardener stood aside to let them pass. Mei smiled at him but he turned away and would not meet her eyes.

They came to a pool, edged with dressed stone. The water's surface was thick with the pink blossom of water lotus. An arched bridge led to an open-sided pavilion with a glaze-tiled roof supported by crimson pillars.

Then they were before the main house. The walls were white lime-wash and the roof tiles were green glaze. The hooked eaves were gilded dragons. There was a low porch leading to folding screen doors of dark timber. The screen doors were open, allowing a cooling breeze to enter the house. They stepped onto the porch and paused. The woman squinted into the gloom of the house interior, unsure what to do next.

'*Wei?*' she called. Even to her own ears, her voice sounded small. She moved closer to the screen doors. '*Wei?*' she called again. 'Is anyone there?'

'No beggars.' A man was scurrying across the reception room towards them. He wore a gown of grey cotton and a skullcap of dark velvet. He had a narrow face and bulbous eyes. 'How did you get into this place?'

From behind her mother's legs, Mei peered up at the man and for the first time, he noticed her.

'Ah,' the man said. 'You have brought her.' He pulled a leather pouch from the folds of his gown. It jingled as he thrust it at Mei's mother. His voice became imperious. 'Take this and go.' He took a step towards them and made shooing motions with his hands.

'Let me say my farewell, Excellency,' Mei's mother pleaded. 'She is my only daughter.'

'No time for that,' the man said. 'Go, go, go.'

Mei screwed shut her eyes and shook her head. She clung tight to her mother's legs.

'Mama. Please don't...'

The mother's voice was shrill and pleading.

'Please, Your Worship... *Please.*'

The man's grip was hard on Mei's arm. 'Come child,' he snapped. 'We will have no nonsense.'

Mei tried to twist free but the man's grip was unrelenting as he pulled her into the house. She had a fleeting impression of high backed chairs and willow pattern vases as tall as a man. There was the smell of camphor mingled with incense. She looked back towards the entrance door where her mother stood, silhouetted against the garden, her arms outstretched.

The man dragged Mei along a corridor lined with carved

## THE SCHOLAR'S BLADE

wooden panels. A door opened and they were in a scullery. The smell of herbs drifted from hessian bags hung from the rafters. A clutter of earthen and iron pots stood on shelves pinned to stone walls. There was a table of rough-hewn wood where a woman was chopping at a slab of meat with a heavy cleaver. A servant girl stopped her labours and gawked at them.

The man shoved Mei from him, sending her sprawling against the table.

'Mistress Loo,' he snapped. 'Here is the girl. Instruct her well.' Without waiting for an answer, he turned and left the way they had entered.

The woman had heavy features and narrow eyes. She wore a blood-spattered apron over a gown of coarse cotton. She hammered the cleaver into the chopping board and walked around Mei, looking her up and down like a side of fresh killed pork.

'Well, what have we here?' the woman asked. She prodded Mei's ribs and squeezed her arm. 'She seems strong enough,' she added. 'But is she obedient?' She put her face close to Mei's and her voice became a growl. 'Well, *girl*? Are you obedient?'

Mei squared her shoulders, threw back her head and tried to sound brave.

'You are mistaken,' she said. 'I am Ping Song-mei. I am the *mi-jeh*. I am the master's adopted...'

The slap seemed to come from nowhere. It sent Mei reeling back against the table. She stared, uncomprehending at the woman.

The woman planted her fists on her hips. 'I am the *mi-jeh*,' she mimicked and let out a hard laugh. 'You are *nothing*,' she snapped. '*Mi-jehs* are *nothing*.' She spread her arms, encompassing the scullery. 'This is now your world.' She levered the cleaver from the chopping board and shook it at Mei. 'This is your whole world and here I, Mistress Loo, rule. Here you will work, eat and sleep but mostly, you will work.' She let out a sharp breath. 'You,' she barked, pointing the cleaver at the servant girl.

The girl hunched her shoulders and scurried forward.

'Yes, Mistress Loo.'

'Show this one her duties,' Mistress Loo ordered. 'And be quick. There is much to do.' She turned and went back to her work.

Anger burned Mei's neck. She balled her fists and took a step towards the woman but the servant girl stepped between them.

'Take care,' the girl whispered. 'This is no place to be brave.' She steered Mei to a corner. 'And speak softly,' she said. 'Mistress Loo beats us only when she is angry.'

Mei rubbed her cheek, still stinging from the blow. 'I think she might be angry all the time,' she said.

'*Hush!*' the girl hissed. 'Come, we will fetch water.'

The girl collected an ironbound bucket and together, they slipped through the door into a kitchen garden. A stone path led between rows of *baak choy*, *choy sum* and *tatsoi*. Chickens scratched the ground inside a fenced area.

The servant girl was Cha Saang-lin and as they emerged into the sunshine, her step became jaunty.

'We get pork from the village and sometimes there is fish,' she said. 'The master owns the rice paddies, so there is no shortage.' She scowled and lowered her voice. 'At least for Mistress Loo there is no shortage.'

'You don't understand,' Mei said. 'I am not a servant girl, I am *mi-jeh*. I should have my own sleeping chamber and fine clothes.'

Saang-lin's lips formed a bitter smile.

'*Mi-jeh!*' she snorted. 'This house has known many *mi-jeh*.' She cast her eyes around the garden and lowered her voice. 'I have been *mi-jeh* here for five years,' she said. 'I sleep on the kitchen floor and I eat what is left from Mistress Loo's meals. Sometimes there is enough.' She shrugged. 'Most times there is not.'

They came to a hand-cranked water pump. Saang-lin worked the handle and water sloshed into the bucket.

'I am sixteen years old,' she said, 'and soon I must go.' Her shoulders slumped. 'The master will sell me.'

'Sell?' Mei asked. 'Why? To who?'

'Why?' Saang-lin answered, her voice suddenly scornful. '*Why*? Because I am too old. The master likes his *mi-jeh* young.' She turned away her face. 'I will be sold,' she said again. 'There are flower boats and music palaces. I think they are places where men sometimes go...' She put a finger to her lips and nodded towards the house.

A man had entered the garden and was watching them. He was of middle years but to Mei, he looked old. In the fashion of officials who scorn manual work, his fingernails were long. To Mei, they looked like claws. A wispy beard did little to disguise heavy jowls. He wore a robe of dark green that stretched over an ample belly. A silken square, chased with crimson and gold thread, graced his chest. At its centre was the image of a white egret.

'Is he the master?' Mei asked.

'Do not stare,' Saang-lin hissed. 'Do not even look at him.' A small muscle throbbed on her jaw. 'To stay safe, you must obey Mistress Loo but heed me carefully.' She stared into Mei's face. It was a stare that held Mei as if she were bound by strong twine. 'You must never be brave,' she whispered. 'And...' She scooped up a handful of dirt and smeared it on Mei's cheeks.

Mei tried to push her away but Saang-lin knocked aside her arms.

'And, most importantly...' Tears filled Saang-lin's eyes. Words tumbled out in a sob. '...Most importantly, you must never look pretty.' She gripped Mei's shoulders. 'Do you hear me? You must never, ever look pretty.'

Then she picked up the bucket and made her way back to the house.

# 2

## Kwangtung Province, South China – Five Years Earlier

In late autumn, the women of Kwanlubu Village took the bed quilts from their lofts and hung them outside to air. 'Winter's coming,' one would say with a frown.

'I hate the winter,' another would answer. 'It's always grey.'

Within weeks, the winter monsoon came. It plucked the leaves from the trees and scattered them about the village lanes. Frigid winds swept down from the northern steppes and collided with the humid South China air, making thick cloud that stretched from mountain peak to mountain peak.

The Year of the Rabbit came on such a day and in Kwanlubu, people cast off the gloom and celebrated the New Year. Kwanlubu's little square was a jam of people. There was the crackle of firecrackers. Impromptu street kitchens served up steamed rice balls, noodles, savoury dumplings and baked fish.

Bundled in padded jackets and britches, children sang New Year songs and clustered round the grown-ups, laughing and demanding red packets stuffed with money.

A crowd thronged around a storyteller who, with much flourishing of arms and pulling of face, told of the wise sage who banished the terrible monster *Nian* from a village much like the village of Kwanlubu.

There were tumblers and a troupe of dancers. There were

singers, magicians, and even a Western priest telling of the Christian God's glory.

Among this clamour, there walked a man and a woman. Their breath misted the morning air and they hunched their shoulders against the chill. The man was tall and heavyset but his tread was light. His jaw was square and he had high cheekbones. There were flecks of silver in his hair but his eyes were those of someone younger. They were bright and alert to all around him. A heavy sword hung from his belt.

The man's appearance was striking but it was the woman who drew most attention. She was not beautiful, in fact some might call her plain. She was short and stocky. Her shoulders were as broad as most men's and she walked with a quiet assurance uncommon in women. Bouncing against her hip was a quiver of birchwood arrows. Slung across her back was a Mongolian longbow.

The storyteller grimaced as he invoked the name *Nian*. At the sound of the demon's name, the woman reached behind her and touched the strip of ox horn fixed to the inside edge of her bow. The horn gave the bow extra power. Some said a Mongolian bow could down an elk at five hundred paces but the woman did not believe it. For her, it sufficed that it could down a deer at one hundred paces. Her prey was mostly deer or wild pig but sometimes there was other quarry.

'I'm hungry,' the man said. 'Do we have money?'

'Enough for a day or two,' the woman answered. 'It's a shame the wild pigs were hiding. Just one would have bought food and maybe a little wine.'

Two soldiers shouldered their way through the crowd. They wore short tunics of deep blue and black britches tucked into stout boots. On their heads were brimless caps of black felt.

The man's lips became a thin line. His hand moved to the hilt

# THE SCHOLAR'S BLADE

of his sword.

The woman touched his arm. 'Be still,' she hissed. 'Do not draw attention.' She gave a half smile. 'They do not know you here.'

'I hope not,' the man growled. 'But watch them close, the emperor has a long reach.'

The aroma of savoury beef drew them to a food stall where a vendor stood over a pot of steaming noodle soup. The vendor smiled and nodded as they counted copper coins into his hand. He piled noodles into two large bowls and ladled in generous helpings of braised beef, black beans and savoury soup stock.

At last replete, the man and woman took time to watch the tumblers and the dancers. Then they moved to where the Western priest was addressing the crowd from a raised platform.

'I don't understand the barbarian tongue,' the man said.

The woman laughed and punched his arm. 'He's speaking Chinese, you dolt,' she said.

'Chinese?' The man shook his head. 'It's not any Chinese I know.'

'*Hush!*' the woman chided. 'Let's listen, just for while.'

'I will not *hush*,' the man grumbled. He nudged the woman and nodded to the platform. 'Who is the Chinese man beside him?'

Standing to one side and slightly behind the priest was a young Chinese. He was slim and had a smooth face with even features. He wore a quilted jacket over the simple cotton robe of a scholar.

'That is the village school teacher, Master Hoong Hsiuchuan,' the woman answered. 'He's sat the government's civil examination so many times, they say his shoes could walk to the examination centre all by themselves.' She leaned closer to the man and lowered her voice. 'Everyone thinks he's mad but still, they trust him to teach their children.'

'He looks sane enough to me,' the man said. 'In what way is he mad?'

'*Aiiyah!*' the woman chided. 'Am I a madhouse keeper who knows the ways of madmen?' She cast around her eyes as if wary of eavesdroppers. 'I know only that he claims to have had a wondrous dream. Now, he seeks out the company of these foreign priests and often speaks nonsense, even to those close to him.'

The man barely heard her words. He felt Hoong's eyes on him. The young man's gaze was unrelenting but somehow unchallenging.

'He is calm,' the woman said.

'No,' the man answered. 'Not calm; he is serene.'

The priest lifted a leather bound book above his head. His voice rose to a crescendo. White spittle flecked his beard. Then he fell silent and stepped back.

'He's drunk,' the man snorted. 'He can hardly stand.'

The young Chinese, named Hoong Hsiu-chuan, stepped down from the dais and moved through the crowd. He held a velvet bag into which people were dropping coins. With each donation, the young man smiled and bowed.

The woman touched the man's arm. 'Come,' she said. 'I don't want people to see we have no coins.'

'Wait,' the man replied. His brow furrowed as though he was seeking an answer that eluded him. 'He... he intrigues me.'

The woman hissed her frustration and seemed about to speak but the man stared her into silence.

Hoong Hsiu-chuan moved closer until he was standing before them. He clasped his hands together at his chest and bowed to the woman. His voice was soft but it carried an underlying resonance.

## THE SCHOLAR'S BLADE

'Madam Yen Lin,' he said. 'I wish you a happy and a prosperous New Year. It is good to see you back in our village at this special time.'

The woman returned the bow. 'Thank you Master Hoong,' she said. 'Please accept my best wishes for your continued health and prosperity.'

'Indeed,' Hoong replied. He turned to the woman's companion. 'And this must be the noble Kong Liu.' He smiled and lowered his voice. 'Or should I say *Captain* Kong Liu, late of the emperor's Banner cavalry.'

'You are mistaken,' the man snapped. 'My name is Wang Lon. I know nothing of the *emperor*.' He almost spat the last word.

Hoong fixed the man with an unblinking gaze. 'I know of you,' he said. 'You served the emperor but refused to oppress the people.' He shrugged. 'You are Kong Liu. That is that.'

The man gripped his sword hilt and put his face close to the younger man's.

'How do you know this?' he demanded. 'Who else in this rat hole knows this?'

'Here, only three people know your story,' Hoong replied. 'You, Yen Lin and of course me, Hoong Hsiu-chuan.' He half closed his eyes. 'There is another but he is not here.' He smiled. 'He is not here and yet he is everywhere.'

'*Pshaw!*' the man called Kong Liu snorted. 'It is true. You are mad.'

Hoong Hsiu-chuan gave a throaty chuckle. 'So they say, my friend,' he said. His eyes gleamed and Kong Liu again found himself drawn into his gaze. He grasped Kong's arm. His voice hardened. 'But soon I will embark on a great mission,' he said. 'And when I do, Kong Liu, you will follow me.'

Then he became the affable schoolmaster. He spread his arms in a gesture of embrace and smiled, showing a row of even white teeth.

'Indeed, you must both come,' he said. 'Kong Liu the soldier and Yen Lin, the archer.'

Kong could not help but smile. 'And why would we follow a mad school teacher?' he asked.

Hoong shrugged. 'There is only one who knows the answer to that,' he said. 'And he is the one who is not here.' He pressed his forefinger to his lips and his voice became a whisper. 'But he is the one who is also everywhere.' He took a step back. 'Just before dawn,' he said. 'You will meet me on the road leading south.'

'I will not,' Kong Liu scoffed.

'Yes, you will,' Hoong answered. 'And then I will tell you a most wondrous secret. Do not be late. I cannot wait for you.' He turned and walked away.

Yen Lin waited until Hoong was out of earshot.

'I told you he was mad,' she said.

'Is he?' Kong mused.

'Of course he is...' Yen Lin took in a sharp breath. Her eyes widened. 'Surely, you don't mean to...'

'We can't stay here,' Kong answered. 'He's utterly mad but if he knows who I am, then others must also know. There are soldiers about. It's not safe.'

'Very well,' the woman sighed. 'We will embark on this *great mission* but only for as long as it serves us.' She gave a hard laugh and shook her head. 'But tomorrow, there will not be one mad person on the road south, there will be three.'

Dawn was a grey line against the hilltops. On the road leading south from Kwanlubu, Kong Liu stamped his feet and hugged himself against the cold.

'He's late,' Kong grumbled. 'I knew this was a fool's idea.'

'Then who is the fool who suggested we be here?' Yen Lin snapped back. 'Wait, someone's coming.'

From the gloom, two figures appeared. Their hair hung loose about their shoulders and at first, Kong thought they must be women. As they drew closer, he saw they were men. One spoke.

'Captain Kong Liu; Yen Lin. I knew you would come.'

Yen Lin clasped her hands to her breast and bowed. 'Master Hoong,' she said. 'You must take care. The soldiers will beat you if they see you have unbound your queue.'

'The queue is a symbol of our slavery,' Hoong replied. 'I will have no more of it. Kong Liu, you should follow my example.'

'Enough,' Kong grumbled. 'I want to be gone from this place.'

Hoong moved closer to Kong. Mischief sparkled in his voice. 'Do you not want to know our mission?' he asked. 'Are you not curious about my wondrous secret?'

'If it will hasten our departure, then tell me of this *great mission.*' Scorn was heavy in Kong's words.

'I mean to raise an army,' Hoong answered. He took hold of Kong's arm. His grip was hard and insistent. 'With this army, I will bring down *Yan Lou*, the master of all demons. The demon king has many names. The foreign barbarians call him Satan. We Chinese sometimes call him...' For a moment he was silent then his voice grew firm. 'We sometimes call him *Dao Guang.*'

Kong brushed away Hoong's hand and took a step back.

'*Dao Guang?*' he gasped. 'You mean to bring down *Emperor* Dao Guang?' He gave a barking laugh. '*Ha!* You and this...' he waved his hand towards Hoong's companion. 'This... what is he? A scholar? A scribe? No soldier that's for sure.'

'Forgive my poor manners,' Hoong said. 'This is Feng Yun-shan, my cousin. He is a good man.' He smiled. 'We have cousin Feng, we have you, and we have the archer Yen Lin. How can we fail?'

'We'll need more than this four,' Kong snorted.

Hoong softened his voice as if speaking to a child.

'Ours is a mission to save mankind,' he said. 'We will crush the Manchu's earthly kingdom and establish our own heavenly kingdom. In the tongue of the Peking overlords, ours will be a *Taiping Tien Kwoh* – a Kingdom of Heavenly Peace.'

'Such a grand plan,' Kong scoffed. 'We need only a mighty army, trained and equipped to defeat the emperor's forces. I expect you have one in your backpack.'

'Ah, but I have not told you my wondrous secret,' Hoong said. 'My father will protect us.'

'I hope he's a warrior,' Kong retorted.

'Oh, he is far greater than that,' Hoong said. 'Our holy book says that the Lord God sent his only begotten son Jesus to cleanse our sins.'

'And this Jesus will raise our army?'

'No,' Hoong answered. 'The Lord Jesus has finished his task. This mission will be completed by God's second begotten son.'

'And where may we find this second son?' Kong demanded.

'Why, he is here,' Hoong answered. 'He is with you now. His name is Hoong Hsiu-chuan.'

Hoong's eyes gleamed. His breath became harsh. His voice became deep and guttural. His eyes bored into Kong's.

'I am the second son of the Lord God Almighty,' he said. He spread his arms, tipped back his head and called out to the sky. 'Hear me Lord. I am your second begotten son and I will crush the demon army of *Yan Lou*.'

For a moment all was still, then Hoong Hsiu-chuan and his cousin, Feng Yun-shan, turned to the south and went in search of *Yan Luo's* demons.

The soldier, Kong Liu and the archer Yen Lin shook their heads and sighed.

# THE SCHOLAR'S BLADE

Then in silence, they followed.

That year, the rain season ended early and the road was hard and dusty. Sometimes, it took them to towns where the people listened in polite silence. Elsewhere, the townsfolk jeered and spat at them.

They were a curiosity. The one named Hoong Hsiu-chuan talked of free will and everlasting life. His gaze had the power to hold people fast, as if in some rapture. His voice was at the same time calming and inspiring. In time, Hoong's fame preceded him. They arrived at villages to find people had come from the countryside and nearby hamlets just to hear him speak.

The seasons turned. The path became steep and the evenings cooled as they journeyed into the Kwangsi mountains. They traversed the upper passes and there, at the town of Sigu in Guiping County, they rested.

Old Hwang was a stick-like man well past his middle years. He had a bony face and a wispy beard but his eyes were bright. They found him standing before the spirit wall that shielded his house from passing demons.

'Welcome, nephews,' he called, spreading his arms in greeting.

Hoong Hsiu-chuan leaned on his staff and bowed.

'It has been many years since we last met, Excellency,' he said. 'I hope this traveller does not intrude.'

'You must treat this house as your own,' Hwang said. 'And pray, do not be so formal, I am your uncle.'

'You know my cousin, Feng,' Hoong said.

Old Hwang nodded and smiled.

'And these are my new companions, Kong Liu and Madam Yen Lin,' Hoong added.

Hwang stood aside and ushered them into a small courtyard. Eucalyptus bushes gave off their perfume and paper lanterns cast soft shadows. Hwang guided them up a few steps into a reception chamber. The furnishings were dark rosewood. Hanging at the walls were silk scrolls bearing poetic scripts. Blue-glazed vases stood on carved tables and the scent of incense drifted from a small shrine.

'Sit, sit,' Hwang invited. He clapped his hands. 'Ah Soo,' he called. 'Where is that girl?'

A teenaged girl came into the chamber. She stood with her eyes cast down and her hands by her side.

'Ah Soo, tea for our guest,' Hwang ordered. 'And pork dumplings.'

Minutes later, the girl returned bearing a tray on which there was a pot of tea and several fist-sized dumplings. She poured the tea and set down the tray. For a moment, her eyes met Hoong's then she lowered her gaze and bowed herself from the chamber.

'Your servant is bold,' Hoong said.

Hwang gave him a pained look.

'My daughter,' he said. 'Actually, she is *mi-jeh*. Her parents were poor so I took her in. She's a pretty child, but wilful.' He was silent for a moment then he smiled. 'You disapprove?'

Hoong gazed at the ceiling and spoke as if to himself. '*Yan Lou* resides in beautiful women,' he muttered. 'They befuddle the senses and divert men from their duty.' He sipped his tea. 'Forgive me, uncle,' he said. 'You are most generous. I hope the girl appreciates your kindness.'

'Tell me of your travels,' Hwang asked. 'Have you news of Canton? Are the barbarian factories still there?'

Hoong nodded. 'Yes,' he said. 'But the owners stay behind their factory walls. The city is not safe for foreigners.' His voice became harsh. 'There are some missionaries, but they are blinkered.'

'These foreigners are nothing but trouble,' Old Hwang

grumbled. They make life impossible for the coastal pirates.'

'Then they are to be commended,' Kong Liu said.

'Commended by the coast dwellers, maybe,' Hwang snorted. 'But not by us. The brigands have moved inland and now infest *our* roads.'

'Does the emperor's army do nothing?' Hoong asked.

Hwang gave a barking laugh. '*Ha!* The bandits take only our purses. The soldiers would have our entire rice crop.'

For a while, there was silence.

'We need our own militia,' Hwang grumbled. 'But who will lead it? I am old and our young men are simple farmers. We need a man with spirit, a man with education.'

'Uncle... I...'

Hwang raised his hand, silencing Hoong.

'Now is not the time,' he said. 'I will not take advantage of your fatigue,' He clapped his hands and the girl stepped back into the chamber. 'Ah Soo,' he said, 'prepare rooms for our guests.' He turned to Hoong. 'I do not live in a cocoon,' he said. 'Your fame grows, or should I say your notoriety?'

Hoong lowered his eyes.

'We shall leave, Uncle,' he said.

'You will do nothing of the kind,' Hwang replied. He slapped his hand onto the arm of his chair. 'A young man needs connections,' he said. 'You are the son of my brother and I will be your sponsor. Go into the countryside and tell the people of your strange God. If they believe you, more fool them.' He closed his eyes and for a time, there was silence. 'My brother's son feigns humility,' he said at last. 'But I can see there is iron in those thin shoulders.'

He stood and smoothed down the front of his gown. 'So, nephew. Preach your sermons and let your fame multiply. Soon your very name will draw the people here to my militia.' He smiled. 'But not now. Now this old man will retire to his bed. And you will eat and then you will rest.'

They rested, then took their message to nearby towns and villages. In time, so many came to listen that Hoong had to take on disciples to marshal his congregations and help with the washing of sins. Across Kwangsi, the teahouses and inns buzzed with tales of a wondrous mystic who dared to unbind his queue and who offered everlasting life.

Hoong and his growing band of followers crossed the Chian River and journeyed through Huali to Jintian on the slopes of Thistle Mountain. There, the cousins parted. Feng Yun-shan embraced Hoong Hsiu-chuan and promised to spread the message through the mountain ranges.

Kong Liu and Yen Lin followed Hoong back into Kwangtung. They were now part of a sizeable troop. Eventually, their travels led them back to Kwangsi province and the house of Old Hwang in the village of Sigu.

The seasons turned and turned again. Then in autumn of the Year of the Dog, 1850 by Christian reckoning, the soldiers came.

They came in the afternoon. They were not many, just a few dozen Imperial regulars. They marched in disciplined lines and carried heavy infantry spears with broad blades that gleamed in the morning sun. At their head was a mounted officer. He was young and had smooth features. He sat straight in his saddle and had about him an air of cool detachment.

Hoong Hsiu-chuan was standing at the rim of a hollow that formed a natural amphitheatre. Below him, a hundred worshippers knelt with their hands clasped in prayer. Hoong spread his arms.

'The injunctions were given,' he intoned.

## THE SCHOLAR'S BLADE

'And the heavenly commandments are...' The congregation's voices tailed away as the troops closed on the gathering.

'The injunctions were given,' Hoong said again, his voice taking on an edge.

The soldiers split into two files and broke into a run, flanking the hollow. Their helmets and weapons were stark against the sky. Their eyes were hard. Their faces betrayed nothing.

Hoong rounded on the officer.

'Who dares interrupt our saviour's word?' he snapped.

The officer ignored him and walked his horse down into the hollow, pushing people aside. He reined to a halt and looked about as though committing every face to memory.

'By the emperor's decree, this assembly is unlawful!' he cried.

Hong's voice resounded around the hollow. 'You think to curb God's word? Does the worm challenge the plough?'

Bright spots burned the officer's cheeks. 'I speak for the emperor,' he roared. 'You will tremble and obey.'

'I tremble before none but the Almighty,' Hoong answered.

'You speak true, Master Hoong,' Yen Lin called. Her voice was a blend of defiance and mockery.

The officer turned to the woman. 'Name?' he snapped.

Yen Lin placed her hands on her hips. 'My surname is Yen,' she answered in an even voice.

The officer looked her up and down. 'And your given names?' he demanded.

'You may call me Madam Yen,' she answered. A smile touched her lips 'Or better still, *Lady* Yen.'

Laughter spread through the congregation.

Yen Lin walked up the side of the hollow and stood beside Hoong Hsiu-chuan. 'Before whom do we tremble?' she called.

'Only unto the lord our God,' a man answered.

In seconds, others took up the chant.

'*Only unto God. Only unto God.*' They advanced on the officer. They were an ever-tightening circle. '*Only unto God. Only unto God. Only unto God.*'

The officer paled. He spoke but the chanting drowned his words. The people pressed closer. They pulled at the officer's thighs and plucked at his tunic. He drove his heels into his horse's flanks and the animal plunged forward, tossing people aside.

The soldiers moved down from the rim, slipping and stumbling on the hollow's slopes. An old woman moved to block a soldier's path. He cuffed her aside. The chanting stilled. A group of young men tried to scramble up the bank but the advancing line of soldiers forced them back. An Imperial blade flashed, then another. There were screams and blood. People clustered at the hollow's centre as the soldiers pressed in on them. Some fell to their knees and begged for mercy. Others prayed. A few fought and were cut down. The soldiers pressed closer, hacking and stabbing. The hollow was a jam of people and flashing blades.

Screams. More blood.

Strong hands gripped Hoong's arms. Above the clamour, Kong Liu's voice was loud in his ear.

'We must go,' he cried.

Hoong tried to fight free but Kong was too strong.

Yen Lin added her voice to Kong's. 'We must go *now*,' she shouted.

Numb, Hoong Hsiu-chuan watched the scene before him. Then, with the screams of his congregation filling his ears, he turned and ran.

They ran to the east: Hoong Hsiu-chuan, Kong Liu, Yen Lin and a handful of followers

Sometimes there were troops on the road, then they hid in the scrub. At night, they slept shivering under the stars, too fearful to light a fire. Whenever they stopped to rest, Hoong sat apart from the others, silent and brooding.

Kong chewed on a strip of dried beef and nodded to where Hoong sat alone. 'What do you think is on his mind?' he asked.

Yen Lin shrugged. 'Who knows?' she said. 'Perhaps he's just unhappy. Unhappy and afraid. He doesn't have our stomach for bloodshed.'

'You're wrong,' Kong said. 'See how he rocks back and forth. See how his fists are always clenched. There is hatred in his eyes. That's a man who is plotting revenge.'

Yen Lin took a moment to watch Hoong. 'Yes,' she said. 'You're right.'

'Anger is a poor planner,' Kong said. 'I hope his anger doesn't see us all dead.'

The next morning, two brothers came down from the hills and joined them. They were unshaven and their hair was unkempt. Each had a curved dagger tucked into his belt. Their arms were bare, displaying tattoos of mythical beasts and triangular patterns.

Hoong spoke to them in whispers and the brothers departed in silence. Three days later, they returned with others.

Kong drew Hoong aside. 'Did you not see their tattoos?' he snapped. 'They're not converts, they're Heaven and Earthers. *Triads!* They seek only plunder.'

Hoong smiled. 'All are my father's children,' he said. He laid a hand on Kong's arm. 'You, me, Yen Lin, the newcomers. All are one and one is all. Each has their role.' He fixed Kong with an unblinking gaze and Kong could only turn and walk away.

They crossed back into Kwangsi as the autumn winds turned northerly, blanketing the South China skies with cloud.

It was on such a day that the soldiers came again for Hoong

Hsiu-chuan.

The soldiers were grumbling. There were twenty of them and they had been on the mountain track since dawn. The track was steep and they walked, heads down and sullen. They carried spears, which they now used as walking staffs. They were low on water and some had eaten all their rations.

Their captain was in his fortieth year, old for a captain. He was a dour man with a lined face and small eyes. He was short of stature but broad of body. He was a man of frequent bad moods, but today he was particularly unhappy. The path was unsuitable for horses, forcing him to walk with his men.

He signalled a halt and scanned the way ahead. He did not like what he saw. There was a sheer drop on one side and on the other, heavy scrub covered a gentle slope up to a rocky ridge. The path curved away to the left and the slope obscured his view forward. He listened but could hear no telltale noises of men waiting in ambush: no clink of weapons, no scuffing of boots on gravel. He prepared to give the signal to march but the clatter of a stone stayed him.

He reached for his sword. '*Stand to!*' he hissed.

The soldiers dropped to a half crouch and levelled their spears.

Two men and a woman emerged from the scrub and stepped onto the path, blocking the soldiers' way. One of the men was slim. His hair hung loose about his shoulders. His expression was serene. The man at his side was tall and big-boned. The woman held a Mongolian bow and at her hip, arrow flights showed bright against the dull leather of a quiver.

The woman drew an arrow and nocked it to the bowstring.

The captain gave the strangers a cool look. 'You're a long way from anywhere,' he said. 'Are you local militia?'

# THE SCHOLAR'S BLADE

The serene stranger answered. 'Ours is a special militia,' he declared. 'A militia of peace, in the Mandarin tongue you would say it is a *Taiping* militia.'

'Do not play games,' the captain barked. 'Answer me, what brings you out here?'

'We're looking for brigands,' the taller man answered. His lips parted in a wicked smile. 'It seems we're lucky enough to have found some.'

The captain grinned. 'Lucky? Oh I think not,' he said. He drew his sword. 'Tell me your names so I may report them to my colonel when I give him your heads.'

'I am Hoong Hsiu-chuan,' the serene stranger said. He gestured towards his companions and spoke as though he were introducing friends to a family gathering. 'My companions are Kong Liu and Yen Lin.'

'A woman and two madmen,' the captain said. 'Today there's triple the sport.'

The soldiers laughed.

'More than triple,' Hoong Hsiu-chuan said. 'There are many in these parts who do my father's work.'

Along the column's length, the scrub rustled as men stood and showed themselves. Some held swords but most carried sickles, billhooks or axes. All had unbound their queues.

The Captain's lips twisted in a sneer. 'You're the Christians the peasants speak of,' he scoffed. 'Who else would ask farmers and women to do this work?'

Hoong Hsiu-chuan shrugged. 'Do not women hold up half of heaven?' He said.

He gave a short nod and Yen Lin's bowstring sang. There was the thud of steel on flesh. The captain gave a small cough. His eyes bulged and he toppled forward.

The soldiers crouched. Their faces paled. They levelled their weapons and stepped back until their boot heels found the path's edge.

Hoong Hsiu-chuan raised his arm then dropped it in a chopping motion. His followers let out a rolling cheer and streamed onto the path like an avalanche.

And like an avalanche, they swept the soldiers into the ravine.

# 3

SUMMER PASSED and the Kwangsi farmers gathered in the final rice harvest. The winds veered from the north and at Sigu village, Hoong Hsiu-chuan's followers prepared to celebrate the birth of Jesus.

Old Hwang looked up at the skies and pulled his jacket tight about his shoulders.

'You should not have attacked the patrol,' he grumbled.

Hoong shrugged. 'It is my sacred duty to destroy *Yan Lou's* lackeys,' he replied.

'They say Imperial forces have crossed the Shun River,' Old Hwang said. He frowned. 'They've looted grain stores and are putting up earthworks. They won't leave until they have you in chains. Do you know what soldiers do to people who attack them?'

Hoong Hsiu-chuan nodded. 'My spies report Imperial infantry on the roads and cavalry moving into the mountain villages,' he said. 'They're getting close.'

For a while, Old Hwang was silent. Then he touched his nephew's arm. 'You're not safe, my boy,' he said at last. 'Your militia is strong but it can't withstand an Imperial campaign.'

'I'll take them into the hills,' Hoong answered. 'My cousin has a base at Jintian, on Thistle Mountain.'

'I remember him well,' Hwang said. 'They say his community has grown.'

Hoong's mood brightened. 'We'll join our militias together,' he declared. 'Let the Imperials come, we will throw them back down the mountain.'

Hwang shook his head. 'If you take Sigu's young men, who will prepare our spring planting?' he said. 'They're farmers not soldiers. If they leave, Sigu will die.'

Hoong sucked in a long breath then nodded. 'You're right uncle, I must go and the young men must stay.'

'I will burn incense and beg *Kue Hsing* to grant you safe journey,' Hwang said.

'I will offer prayers to my father,' Hoong answered. He gave the old man a sad smile. 'I hope His grace is all we need for the journey.'

'May your Gods and mine go with you,' Hwang said.

'And may they also stay with you, Uncle.'

Hoong bowed to his uncle then walked to where Kong Liu and Yen Lin were waiting.

'Do we stand or run?' Kong asked.

'We run,' Hoong answered.

'A sad choice but a sensible one,' Kong said. 'I'll tell our people to prepare for the road. When do we leave?'

'We leave now,' Hoong said. 'Take only what you can carry.' He turned away and for the last time, looked into the face of his uncle.

They travelled at night along the backways to the mountains. In the day, they hid in the scrub or paid silver to farmers who let them bed down with the pigs. At last, they came to Jintian. People came from their houses to gawk at the road-soiled travellers.

A man stepped into the street. Flanking him were others with drawn swords. He raised his hand. 'Hold,' he said. 'Stand and identify yourselves.'

'Do you not know me, cousin?' Hoong asked.

Feng Yun-shan squinted at the strangers.

'Hsiu-chuan? Cousin, is it you?' he asked. He spread his arms and rushed forward then stopped and wrinkled his nose. 'Has pig farming become more profitable than saving souls?'

He shrugged and threw his arms about his cousin. 'You're famous in these parts,' he said. 'Everyone talks of you.' He frowned. 'They say you ambushed an Imperial column and that's why the soldiers have come.'

Hoong lowered his eyes. 'If our presence endangers you, we will move on,' he said.

'Rubbish,' Feng snorted. 'You are my teacher, my cousin and my closest friend. You will be safe enough here. Now you must eat and rest.' He smiled and made a show of holding his nose.

'But first, you must bathe.'

The Jintian militiaman crouched below the gully's rim where the Imperial soldiers could not see him. He winced as a twig snapped beneath his foot. He counted to one hundred then, satisfied no one had heard, he scooped up a handful of mud and smeared it onto his face. He lay on his belly and crawled up to where he could look down into the village.

Below him, the soldiers moved from house to house, dragging people into the open. One man had resisted and now his head stood on a stake outside the ancestral hall.

A line of smoke rose from a house, then another. Flames crackled at windows and soon the village was ablaze. Smoke burned the militiaman's eyes. He palmed tears from his eyes and pulled his tunic up to coverer his mouth and nose.

The soldiers gathered the villagers in the market square and used their spears to herd them onto the road. The women pulled their young ones close. They fell to their knees and begged the soldiers to spare the children. But the soldiers made no move to harm them. They stepped aside and pointed to the hills.

The villagers obeyed. They bent their backs, shouldered what possessions they had salvaged and moved north.

To Jintian.

Jintian was a snarl of clogged roads and blocked lanes. New arrivals squatted in the town square, in the alleys and even on the rice paddy levees. There was no pork, no beef, not even bean curd. A handful of rice cost an ounce of silver.

And still people arrived. There were care-worn peasants and bewildered gentry. From the hills came gangs of unwashed and bearded men. They carried daggers, swords and longbows. They bared their chests and arms to display the now familiar tattoos of mythical beasts and triangular patterns. They strutted around the market square and lanes. Wherever they went, people lowered their gaze and stepped aside to let them pass.

Hoong Hsiu-chuan set up a command centre in the town's ancestral hall. All day runners came and went. They carried supply lists, manpower rolls and intelligence briefs. Each intelligence brief contradicted the one preceding it.

Kong Liu clenched his fists and spoke to the ceiling.

'Paper, paper, paper,' he growled. 'Battles are won with steel not paper.'

'Be calm,' Yen Lin said. 'The enemy is strong. We must prepare.'

In the middle of the hall, a map lay unfurled on a trestle, its edges weighed down with stones. Hoong Hsiu-chuan called Kong and Yen Lin to him. He tapped the map.

'My spies report the Imperial forward base is here, five miles to our south,' he said. 'They're forcing people from their homes and sending them here. They can bring what they can carry, but no food.' He gave a grudging nod. 'Their commander is clever. We will starve before we can fight.'

## THE SCHOLAR'S BLADE

Kong Liu turned down the corners of his mouth. 'Not so clever,' he countered. 'He's swollen our numbers with thousands of desperate people.'

'Can we break out?' Yen Lin asked.

'Hard to say,' Kong answered. 'With our force, plus the Jintian militia, the triad brethren and the displaced newcomers, we can perhaps muster twenty thousand fighters.'

'I don't trust the triad brotherhood,' Yen Lin grumbled. 'And the others are just farm boys. What's the Imperial strength?'

Kong took a slow breath. 'Scouts report a full *gūsa*,' he answered. 'Over seven thousand men, each one a regular.'

'When will they come?' Hoong asked.

Kong shrugged. 'Who knows?' he answered. 'They might be on the way now.'

Hoong clasped his hands together.

'I have consulted my heavenly father,' he said.

'Is he sending cannon?' Kong snorted.

'No,' said Hoong, his tranquillity unruffled. 'But he gives us a holy trinity. Look.'

They bent over the map. There were three low hills and behind them, the land fell away to form a shallow hollow.

'*Yes!*' Kong said, stabbing down on the map with a finger. 'We put a few men on the summits to draw the enemy's attention while our main force assembles in the low ground.'

Yen Lin flashed a grin.

'From the Imperial line, our main force will be invisible,' she added.

'When we attack, they'll think our forces have sprung direct from hell,' Kong chortled.

Hoong massaged his temples.

'But are we ready?' he sighed. 'It is a huge risk.'

'Of course it's a risk,' Kong snapped back. 'It's war.'

Hoong tipped back his head and spread his arms. 'Make us ready, Father,' he cried. 'Today your younger son continues the work of the elder. Today *Yan Lou* will know your wrath. Today, *Yan Lou* will tremble.'

The Imperial cavalry was first across the river ford but the force commander, Colonel Ikedanbu, did not intend to waste them on a band of religious lunatics. He ordered the infantry forward, then he advanced to where the river ran fast and wide, protecting his right flank. There he halted.

A half mile to his front stood a low hill. At its peak, the rebels clustered around a banner of imperial yellow. The colonel smiled. Yellow was the emperor's colour and it was death to anyone who usurped it.

There were two other hills, one to the north, the other to the south. On the southern summit, a red flag showed. On the northern summit, the flag was black. Ikedanbu almost laughed out loud. Not only had the enemy divided their meagre forces, they had isolated those forces from each other. There was the thud of hooves and an officer drew up alongside.

'Report,' the general snapped.

The officer grinned. 'One thousand on the central peak, sir,' he said. 'The other two peaks are hardly manned at all.'

The general frowned. 'The enemy must see the odds against them yet they don't withdraw,' he mused. 'What arms do they have?'

'A few spears. A sword or two,' the officer replied. 'But mostly just farm tools.'

The general rubbed his chin.

'I'll keep the cavalry in reserve,' he said. 'Half the infantry should be enough.' He drew his sword and rested the blade on his saddle. 'The other half can watch my back.' He raised his sword and pointed to the central peak. 'Now give the order,' he snapped. 'I want that yellow banner.'

From the central peak, Kong Liu watched the Imperial advance.

'See how they march in orderly lines,' he said to his standard-bearer. 'And look how high they hold their banners. That's pride.'

He ran his eyes over his own men and sighed. Their weapons were billhooks, chain-flails and machetes. They wore no uniforms. Most were bare-chested and many had no shoes. All had unbound their queues so their hair hung loose and wild.

'Is all ready?'

Kong turned to the sound of Hoong Hsiu-chuan's voice. He gasped. In the manner of the Ming emperors, Hoong wore a gown of imperial yellow embroidered with lotus patterns and five-clawed dragons. Behind him, Yen Lin wore a tunic and matching britches of yellow silk. Slung across her back was her Mongolian bow.

Kong Liu hesitated then gave a grudging bow.

'All is ready... Excellency,' he said.

'Is the enemy close enough?' Hoong said.

'They are,' Kong replied.

'Then unfurl the flags and give the signal,' Hoong ordered. He stepped forward and before him, one thousand men dropped to one knee.

Hoong's voice resonated across the hilltop.

'Rise, my soldiers,' he cried. 'For today, hell's demons will know there is a new kingdom in China.' He spread his arms in a gesture of embrace. 'Henceforth this land will be called the Kingdom of Heavenly Peace.'

He switched to the ancient tongue of the Ming emperors.

'Today is born our *Taiping Tien Kwoh*. Stand, my soldiers, and in the eyes of God, make ready to crush the lackeys of *Yan Luo.*'

The one thousand stood. They raised their weapons and let out a thundering cheer. They turned their faces to the enemy.

And as one, they began to sing.

Colonel Ikedanbu's horse snorted and skittered sideways. The beast could sense the coming conflict and was eager to meet it. The colonel stroked its neck and made soothing noises, calming it. He beckoned a dispatch rider to him.

'Order a slow advance,' he said. 'I don't want to tire the men.'

The dispatch rider spurred away. Now, the colonel could see the enemy clearly. They were indeed a peasant rabble. He frowned, his men would have little plunder for this day's work. A figure appeared on the central hilltop and again, the general almost laughed. The man wore an emperor's robes.

On the summit, the rebels paid brief homage to their leader then stood. They began to sing. Their voices swelled. Their song rang off the hillsides and rolled across the plain.

Then, from beyond the central hill, there were other voices. Ikedanbu stood on his stirrups but could see no one. As he watched, a band of men ran from the valley separating the central and southern hills. At their head flew a red banner. Behind them came more men. Now there were hundreds of screaming, running men. Still they came and the hundreds became thousands. The red banner fighters bypassed the advancing infantry and circled behind Ikedanbu, cutting him off from his rearguard.

From the northern valley, thousands more streamed onto the plain. Their banner was black. They brandished chain flails, scythes and pitchforks. To the colonel's front, the black banner attackers piled into his infantry like an axe into beancurd. They flailed, cut and killed. Officers tried to organise a defence but the rebels split the column into small pockets and hacked them

# THE SCHOLAR'S BLADE

down.

Ikedanbu watched his disciplined force disintegrate. He wheeled his horse about and drove hard for the river ford. He risked a backward glance as a band of rebels broke from the fighting and gave chase. His horse slowed. He tried to urge it onward but this close to the river, the ground was marshy. The horse stumbled. Its hindquarters went down. It toppled onto its side, eyes wild, hooves thrashing. The colonel kicked free of the stirrups and rolled clear. His helmet was gone and he scrambled in the mud for his sword.

Then the rebels were on him, kicking, punching, stabbing, cutting. Ikedanbu fell to his knees and covered his head with his arms. A scythe sliced into his shoulder. A hayfork punctured his neck, turning the mud crimson. He gasped. His eyes bulged. He pitched forward and the last sounds he heard were the cheers of rebel victory.

All was quiet but for the *cawl* of crows as they hopped from corpse to corpse. Hoong Hsiu-chuan came down from his hilltop where, under a sky heavy with cloud, knelt row upon of row of Imperial prisoners. Behind them stood the rebel host, their faces grim.

'So, my loyal Kong Liu,' Hoong said. 'Tell me again, how went the battle?'

'More than eight hundred enemy dead,' Kong cried in a voice that carried to every rebel soldier. 'And three hundred prisoners. The rest have fled. They have abandoned their camp and left us a gift of their equipment.' His eyes shone. 'We have armour, swords, horses, even a few cannons. It is a wonderful victory.'

A cheer washed over the plain. The rebels shook their weapons at the sky and embraced their comrades.

Yen Lin raised her Mongolian bow above her head.

'Today is born our Kingdom of Heavenly Peace, our *Taiping Tien Kwoh*,' she cried. Her voice was rich and strong. 'And a heavenly kingdom needs a heavenly king. A king of ten thousand years.'

'Hoong Hsiu-chuan, Heavenly King!' a voice shouted from the ranks.

'Hoong Hsiu-chuan, king for ten thousand years!' another answered.

In seconds, the chant swelled and became rhythmic. Caught in the moment, Kong Liu chanted loudest of all.

'Loyal Kong Liu,' Hoong called. 'Today, we are all noble. Will you take the title of Loyal Prince?'

Kong cast down his eyes. 'I'm no prince,' he growled. 'I'm a simple soldier and proud of it.' He scratched his head. 'I want no titles. Give them to someone else.'

'Yen Lin, then.' Hoong gave a mocking bow. 'I mean *Lady* Yen, today you never left my side. I declare you Taiping warrior of the first grade.'

'What of the prisoners?' Kong Liu asked.

'Kill them,' Hoong snapped.

'Kill them?' Kong's face paled. 'All of them? But...'

Hoong rounded on Kong. 'You question *me?*' he snapped. 'Did you not hear the people? Am I proclaimed king or not?'

Kong gawked at Hoong. When he found his voice, his words sounded cracked and uncertain.

'The... the people have indeed acclaimed you king... *Sire*.' He hung his head and turned to go.

Hoong's voice became shrill. 'Do not presume to turn your back on me, Kong Liu. Not unless you want your head to join those of my enemies.'

Kong turned to face Hoong.

'Sir...' He lowered his voice. '*Sire*...' He squared his shoulders

## THE SCHOLAR'S BLADE

and drew himself to his full height. His voice firmed. 'It is true you have been proclaimed king of ten thousand years, but surely our first act should be one of mercy.'

'Mercy?' Hoong growled. *'Mercy?'* His voice dripped scorn. 'If you lack the stomach for the task, there are others who do not.'

For a moment, Kong was silent then he nodded slowly. 'Very well,' he sighed. 'If it is to be done, it is best done in a soldierly manner.'

Hoong placed a hand on Kong's arm. His voice softened.

'It is good that you see things clearly,' he said. He drew Kong closer and embraced him like a favoured son. He released the embrace and his brow furrowed. 'The Manchu demons will be back,' he said. 'I doubt their next commander will be so easily tricked. Can we defend this place?'

Kong shook his head. 'We'll need earthworks and stockades,' he said. 'They'll be on us before we finish building. We need a city; a fortress city.'

Hoong beckoned an aide who spread a map on the ground before them. Hoong, Kong Liu and Yen Lin squatted on their heels and examined it in silence.

Kong traced his finger along a blue line marked, 'Meng River.' He tapped a spot on the map shown as a crenulated square.

'Yongan,' he said. 'Sixty miles north of here.' He set his mouth in a frown. 'But you can't march an army on dreams. We'll need money and supplies.'

'Empty the grain stores. Strip the fields. Squeeze silver from the gentry,' Hoong said.

'But... but the villagers,' Kong sputtered. 'How will they survive the winter?'

'They will come with us,' Hoong replied. 'They will burn their houses and destroy anything they can't carry. We leave nothing for the enemy.'

'And the sick, the old, the feeble?' Kong asked. 'We cannot leave them?'

Hoong's eyes narrowed. 'How did the Israelites survive the wilderness?' he asked. 'The Heavenly Father fed them on His manna.' He made fluttering motions with his fingers. 'It drifted from heaven and lay on the ground. Our father will not let the people starve.'

Kong seemed about to speak but Hoong raised his hand.

'*Enough!*' Hoong snarled. His eyes gleamed. His lips were a thin white line. 'I am master of our Heavenly Kingdom and you will obey.' He gazed at Kong and Kong's resolve fell away.

Then Hoong was his old affable self. 'Think, loyal Kong Liu; think *Lady* Yen Lin. Think of what we can achieve. Not tens of thousands, but hundreds of thousands all under our banner. Good men, strong men, and their families.' He drove his fist down onto the map. 'We go to Yongan.'

Hoong stood and his voice rolled across the plain.

'Soldiers of *Taiping Tien Kwoh*,' he called. 'I go in search of our heavenly kingdom. Will you follow?'

The army roared its assent.

Kong Liu shook his head. 'And where is this heavenly kingdom, Sire?' he asked.

Hoong fixed him with a hard stare. For a heartbeat, the gentle schoolteacher was gone, replaced by something dark and brutish. Then he smiled and in an instant, the gentle teacher was back.

'Kong Liu,' he chuckled. 'You are the most loyal of all. How else could one so bold keep his head?' He turned to his aides who answered with dutiful laughter.

Kong bowed and turned away. There were orders of march to prepare, stores to gather and wealthy landlords to squeeze. But first, there was a grimmer duty.

First, there were executions to be done.

# 4

## SISHUN VILLAGE, SOUTHWEST OF SHANGHAI - 1851

DOCTOR JAMES Falchion had a face made for smiling, or so the ward orderlies said. Strands of silver flecked his hair which, like his son's, had once been golden.

He dropped his suturing needle into his bag and stepped back from the bed where an old man lay.

'Your grandfather's had a nasty fall,' he told the woman hovering beside him. 'I've given him something for the pain, but you must keep the wound clean and make sure he rests.'

The woman bobbed her head.

The doctor turned to the young man standing beside him.

'Have I forgotten anything, Mark?' he asked.

'Feed him plenty of leafy vegetables,' Mark Falchion added. 'It will build up his strength.'

In his fourteenth year, Mark Falchion was nearly as tall as his father. He was slim and long-limbed. His features were strong and regular, his hair thick and the colour of sun-bleached straw. On market days, the village girls would brave their fathers' wrath to smile at him. Sometimes, they would comment on his looks and Mark would delight in their embarrassment when he answered them in the local dialect.

Mark Falchion's fluency in their language should not have surprised them. The young Westerner was a regular visitor to the local market where his bargaining skills were the talk of the store holders. With the passing years, fear of his blue eyes had faded. His smile and easy manner made him a great favourite with the villagers. Some even believed that touching his golden hair would bring good fortune.

The woman spoke. 'Will... will my grandfather be strong enough for the autumn harvest?' she asked.

Doctor Falchion frowned. 'Let's hope so,' he replied.

Mark drew closer to his father.

'The old man will be laid up for weeks,' he said. 'Even when he's up, he'll not be strong enough for farm work.'

'Perhaps they have relatives,' Doctor Falchion offered.

'They have no one, father. They'll starve.'

Mark spoke to the woman. 'We'll visit during the harvest,' he said. 'If your grandfather's not fit, I'll help you.'

The woman grasped Mark's hand with both of hers. Tears welled in her eyes. 'I will burn incense and beg *Kwan Yin* to reward your kindness,' she said.

Doctor Falchion coughed. 'It's time we went, my boy,' he said, picking up his medical bag.

Mark moved to the door and collected his staff. It was as tall as Mark and as thick as a man's thighbone. Together, father and son ducked under the lintel. A dog raised its head to watch them pass and chickens scurried about their feet. They walked along a path that led from the farmhouse and skirted paddies, lush with the final rice crop.

'You give too much of yourself,' Doctor Falchion grumbled. 'I've plans for you, my boy, great plans, and they don't include you wading about in a rice paddy.'

Mark Falchion replied with a shrug.

'Your spoken Chinese is flawless,' Doctor Falchion continued. 'Far better than mine. How's your calligraphy coming along?'

## THE SCHOLAR'S BLADE

'I practice,' Mark sighed. 'But there's so much to learn.'

'You're young,' Doctor Falchion said. 'There's plenty of time.' His mood brightened. 'The riverboat from Soochow dropped off the Confucian texts I sent for,' he said. 'Have you had chance to look at them?'

'Yes father. And the mathematics, and law, and the sciences, and...'

Doctor Falchion interrupted him.

'And I know you still see your old bandit. It's time to put him aside and focus on your studies.'

'He's not a bandit,' Mark answered, his voice sulky. 'Well, not any more he isn't. But look, I'm really coming on.' He trotted a few paces forward then stopped. 'Watch,' he said. He windmilled his staff and it cut the air with a soft moan. He changed hands and tossed it, still spinning, above his head. He snatched it from the air and with a snap of his wrist, brought it to rest.

'Impressive,' Doctor Falchion said, his voice sour.

Mark's eyes gleamed.

'Soon, I might start with the broadsword,' he said. 'Master Wu says I have promise.'

'*Master* Wu?' Doctor Falchion growled. 'When did that old reprobate earn the title *Master*?'

'Good morning, Excellencies!'

The voice belonged to a man who stood blocking the path. He wore a patched tunic and torn britches. His skin was grimy and his queue was unkempt. Tucked into his belt was a curved dagger.

Doctor Falchion made a small bow.

'Forgive my manners,' he said. 'My mind was elsewhere. Please let me pass.'

'Please let me pass,' the man mimicked. His voice hardened. 'You may pass if you pay the toll.'

'Toll?' the doctor asked. 'What toll?'

'My toll,' the stranger answered.

Mark leaned on his staff. 'We've nothing to give you,' he said, surprised at how calm he sounded. 'But I have something to show you, *brother*.'

'Easy, Mark,' Doctor Falchion warned. 'I'll give him some coins to see him on his way.'

Mark took a step closer to the stranger. He placed his free hand in front of his body then extended his fingers and tucked his thumb into his palm.

The man gave a harsh laugh. '*Ha!* Should I heed a barbarian whelp who mimics a sign of the brotherhood?' He fingered the dagger at his belt but his lips had become thin and pale.

'You'll give me your coin or...'

He's uncertain, Mark thought. 'Or what, *brother?*' he growled. He took a firmer grip on his staff and moved closer to the stranger.

The man dropped to a crouch and pulled the dagger from his belt.

Mark Falchion's heart pounded slow and heavy. His muscles tightened. 'If you doubt me, step closer,' he said. His voice was calm, cajoling. 'Step closer and I'll recite the phoenix code.'

Doubt clouded the stranger's face. He held the dagger straight-armed before him. He edged closer.

'If you mean to fool me...'

Mark flicked the staff forward, fast as though swatting a fly. It connected with a *tack* and the man staggered back, clutching his brows. Mark followed and dropped to one knee. He swept his staff across the man's legs, lifting his feet clear of the ground.

The man went down hard. His breath exploded from between clenched teeth. The dagger clattered beyond his reach. He made to get up but Mark placed a foot on his chest and pressed the staff's tip against his windpipe.

'You'd best find honest work,' Mark growled. 'You're too slow for this job.' He jabbed down hard, then stepped back.

The man rolled onto his side, retching and massaging his throat. He tried to stand but his legs buckled and he sank to his knees.

'Are... are you truly of the brotherhood?' he croaked.

'I'm no brother to your kind.' Mark's voice was hard and guttural. 'I made the sign so you'll know we have guardians in this place.' He grasped the man's arm and hauled him to his feet. 'Now go,' he ordered. 'Or I'll break your skull.'

The man backed away. He muttered an obscenity then turned and ran.

Doctor James Falchion looked at his son as though seeing him for the first time. 'Mark... my boy... I'm astonished,' he stammered.

Mark rested the staff against his shoulder and looked at his hands. They were trembling. A nervous laugh bubbled in his throat.

'Astonished father?' he said. 'Frankly, so am I.'

Doctor Falchion shook his head.

'What was it for,' he asked. 'I have a few coins. He had a knife. You could have been killed.'

Mark's cheeks flushed. His mouth became a thin line.

'I am Mark Falchion,' he growled. 'And I submit to no one, particularly the likes of him.'

'There's wildness in you, my boy,' Doctor Falchion sighed. 'Your mother had it and so do you.' His voice softened. 'Hear me, if you do not tame that wildness, it will destroy you.'

Mark seemed not to have heard. Above them, the clouds were thickening. A gust of wind ruffled the trees.

'I think it might rain,' Mark said. 'We'd best get back to the mission.' Without waiting for a reply, he turned and strode down the path.

Doctor James Falchion groaned, rolled his eyes and followed.

The next day was the third day; the day for Mark's meeting with One-eared Wu. In the clearing near the stream, One-eared Wu greeted him with an impish smile.

'I have a surprise for you,' he said. He nodded to a hessian bundle lying on the ground beside him.

'What is it?' Mark clamoured. 'Quick, tell me.'

'*Aiiyah!*' One-eared Wu chided. 'You are still a child who clamours after mysterious bundles. Open it and see.'

Mark fell to his knees and pulled at the bundle's fastenings. There was the dull gleam of steel. He opened the bundle to reveal two *dao* broadswords. They were poor things. The metal was without lustre, the edges were blunt and rough twine bound their grips.

'What is... is *this?*' Mark muttered.

'They are for practice,' One-eared Wu answered. 'Their weight and balance are the same as a true combat blade.'

He retrieved one of the practice *daos* and exercised a slow cut to the left. He snapped his wrist and drove the blade in a fast upward slash.

Mark picked up the other *dao*. 'It's a toy,' he snorted.

'Toy, is it?' One-eared Wu chortled. His eyes narrowed. He darted forward and laid the flat of his blade on Mark's shoulder. 'If this was a combat blade, I'd have taken your head,' he growled. 'And what did you do? *Nothing!*'

'It's not fair.' Mark snapped back. 'I wasn't ready.'

One-eared Wu pulled a face. 'Not fair?' he chided. 'You weren't ready? Tell that to someone who seeks your death.' His lips twisted in contempt. 'Stupid swordsmen do not live long.'

Mark's cheeks burned. His breath became fast and shallow.

# THE SCHOLAR'S BLADE

'*Ah!* You do not like cruel words,' Wu chuckled. 'If you had spirit, you would punish me.' He spread his arms wide. 'But it seems you lack a backbone.'

It was as if a string of firecrackers had exploded inside Mark. He raised the practice *dao* and charged. He sliced the blade down hard towards One-eared Wu's skull.

The old swordmaster sidestepped and Mark hurtled past him.

'*Pshaw!* You think yourself a swordsman?' One-eared Wu called. 'More like a coolie.'

'Damn you,' Mark roared. He charged again, thrashing the blade left and right.

One-eared Wu swung his *dao*, knocking aside Mark's blade.

Mark attacked again. One-eared Wu sidestepped, ducked and parried. The more furious Mark's attacks became, the more the old swordmaster laughed and the more cruel his jibes became.

Mark's attacks slowed then stopped. His sword point dipped. His breath came in ragged gasps. He glared at One-eared Wu through sullen eyes.

Wu smiled and wagged a finger. 'Anger is a tool but you must control it,' he said. 'It must be cold and focussed. Think of it as a spear point. A spear point made of ice.'

Mark lowered his eyes. 'I will remember this lesson well,' he sighed.

One-eared Wu's flashed Mark a wry smile. 'In combat, anger is just one of the emotions,' he said. 'The other is *fear*. You must master and guide them both, just as you would master your sword.'

'I will try,' Mark answered.

'Try?' One-eared Wu snapped. 'You will do more than try.' He stepped back. 'But that is for another day. For today's training you will practice the forward descending cut.' He raised the practice *dao* above his head and shouted *'Shaaa!'* At the same time, he took a step forward and chopped down, hard and fast.

He turned to Mark. 'Now, you will repeat that one-hundred times.' His voice hardened. 'And when we next meet, you will learn about fear.'

Summer passed into early autumn. Soon it would be the Mid-Autumn Festival of the Moon. There would be family feasts of pumpkin and hairy crabs, taro and treacly moon cake. But as the celebrations drew near, storm clouds gathered over the Eastern Sea.

On the banks of the Huangpu River, near the village of Sishun, the sky darkened. Noon became twilight and the first raindrops *thwacked* against the farmhouse roofs. Then the storm struck in its full wrath. Rain swept in, flooding paddies and washing away the vegetable crop. It battered the levees and turned roads into rivers.

The Huangpu rose and became a ferment of eddies and crosscurrents. On the river, a boat battled upstream. The men on the sweeps gritted their teeth and dug their oars into the river. The helmsman, a veteran of many such battles, leaned on his steering oar and squinted through the rain. The boat shivered as a crosscurrent caught it on the beam. Lighting flashed blue-white and lit a figure standing at the prow. The man wore a scholar's gown of grey cotton but his white beard showed he was no student. The gown was sodden and the wind thrashed at the man's beard.

'Uncle, get below!' the helmsman shouted.

The man cupped his hands to his mouth. 'Can we make Soochow?' he called.

The boatman hung onto the steering oar as an eddy threw spray over the freeboard and forced the boat to swing in the

## THE SCHOLAR'S BLADE

current.

'Not in this,' he called back. 'We'll have to put in and wait it out.'

The river frothed about the hull. The bank showed as a dim mass. Rain glistened off the sweepmen's backs.

'Pull!' the helmsman roared to the sweepmen. He leaned hard on the steering oar but the boat shuddered and turned side on to the current. The deck tilted and brown water poured over the railing. It swilled around the deck and battered open a poorly secured hatch. The hull groaned against a rock and the boat went over on its side, tossing everyone into the river. A roar filled the helmsman's ears. Water filled his nose, mouth and ears. He did not know which way was up, which down. His head broke the surface and he sucked air into his lungs. The boat tumbled, showed its keel and was gone. For an instant, lightning turned everything white. The helmsman had a fleeting glimpse of silver hair and a scholar's gown near the bank. Then the current dragged him down. It crushed the air from his lungs and dashed him against rocks lurking beneath the surface.

And like his boat, he was gone.

For two days, the rain battered the coast from the Yangtze delta in the North to Hangchow Bay in the South. It left behind ruined fields and the bloated carcasses of livestock.

In the Falchion mission, the sick and injured filled every cot, they lined the broad verandas and queued in the mission grounds. Doctor James Falchion moved about the injured with his son and the ward orderly, Tong Shu.

'Mark,' Doctor Falchion called. 'Check the jetty. If by some miracle the supply boat arrives, it must be able to land.'

Mark hurried to the jetty but found it broken and half-submerged. Shattered stumps showed where the storm had torn away the stanchions. Reeds and debris covered what remained.

The river was high and running fast. A tree branch sped by. A bloated pig carcass showed its belly then disappeared downstream. Mark tugged at a clump of reeds then gasped and took a step back. The reeds had concealed the body of an old man. He lay face up, his body swinging in eddies close to the bank. Blood matted his hair and mud clogged his beard. His skin was white and his lips were blue. Mark splashed into the shallows. He took the old man's shoulders and dragged him to the shore.

'Rest easy, Uncle,' Mark said.

He took the old man's hand. The skin was cold and his fingers were like brittle sticks. Mark laid him on the grass and stood for a moment with his head bowed. The old man's body lay cold and unmoving. Then an eyelid fluttered. Mark dropped to his knees and put his ear close to the old man's lips. He felt a hint of breath on his cheek.

'Father!' Mark shouted. 'Tong Shu! Anyone!'

Doctor Falchion strode onto the mission porch. He called to someone inside then hurried to the jetty. Tong Shu and another orderly followed. Doctor Falchion knelt and looked into the old man's face. His eyes widened.

'Master Wang!' he called. 'Wang Shi. Old friend, talk to us!' He massaged the old man's hand, trying to rub some warmth into it. He beckoned the orderlies forward. 'Get him inside,' he snapped. 'Take him to my private quarters. Hurry now.'

The orderlies made a cradle of their arms and carried the old man into the clinic. Doctor Falchion followed with Mark scurrying beside him.

'Who is he, father?' Mark asked.

'Someone I've not seen for a long time,' the doctor said. 'Someone who's been a good friend to many, me included. And,

God willing, someone who will change your life.'

In the coming days, Wang Shi drifted, hovering between life and death. Sometimes he spoke, but the words were garbled and indistinct. His fever broke, then returned, then broke again. Mark knelt by his cot, sponging sweat from the old man's body.

After a week, his eyes opened and he tried to sit up but Mark pressed him back onto the bed.

'Lay still, Uncle,' he said, bringing a lantern closer. 'We thought we might lose you.'

Wang Shi gave a wan smile.

'The Gods take only the good and the wise,' he croaked. 'They leave men like me to ponder our foolishness.'

Mark propped up the old man's head. He held a soup bowl to his lips but Wang Shi pushed it away.

'How long have I been here?' he asked. 'I have important business in Soochow.'

'Nothing is as important as getting you well,' Mark said.

'I have a student,' Wang Shi croaked. 'He will soon take the civil examination. I promised...' A coughing fit cut off his words.

Mark put aside the bowl and placed a towel across Wang Shi's brow.

'Easy, Uncle,' he said. 'There's still some fever and there was a nasty head wound. Do you remember your name?'

'I am Wang,' the old man answered. 'I am a simple teacher.'

Doctor Falchion came close to the bed.

'Are you feeling stronger, Master Wang?' he asked.

The old man arched his eyebrows.

'Is that the most excellent Doctor Falchion?' he asked. 'Still trying to steal our medical secrets, I see.'

'Mark,' Doctor Falchion said. 'May I introduce China's foremost Confucian scholar, Master Wang Shi. It is Master Wang who has been sending the texts for you to study.'

Mark cupped his right fist in his left hand.

'Master Wang,' he said. 'How may I serve you?'

'You can tell me how you became so adept at our language,' Wang Shi said, his voice little more than a whisper.

'My son's a clever young man,' Doctor Falchion chuckled. 'I often think it's a shame only true men of *Han* may sit the civil examination.'

'It was ever so,' Wang Shi mused. 'And will likely remain so.' He beckoned Mark closer. 'Your teacher is Master Jeung Dak, yes?'

'He is, Master Wang.'

'Did he tell you he was once my student?'

'He speaks of you often and with much fondness,' Mark answered.

Wang Shi sighed and lay back on his pillow.

'Another clever young man who showed great promise,' Wang Shi said. He smiled and nodded to himself. 'But he was rebellious. He could never prosper as an official.'

'He is a fine teacher,' Mark offered.

'Ah yes, and so we come to another matter. Do you know he sent me examples of your work?'

'He did?' Mark blinked back his surprise. He and his father exchanged glances.

'Your calligraphy is quite superb,' Wang Shi said. 'But more importantly, your insights into our culture and the writings of the great sage are most incisive.' He beckoned Mark to come closer. His voice was a whisper. 'I have long thought to spread Confucian wisdom beyond our borders,' he croaked. 'There are Westerners who can translate the sage's words but words alone do not impart his deeper wisdom.' He grasped Mark's forearm. 'But now we have you; you who truly understands.' He gave a soft chuckle that became a hacking cough.

'Now is not the time for talk,' Doctor Falchion chided. 'Come Mark, leave Master Wang in peace.'

Wang Shi's grip on Mark's arm became firmer. 'Your father speaks true, you are clever,' he said. 'But to advance in life, even a clever young man needs connections.' A smile lingered on his lips. 'Bind your hair into a queue,' he said, 'When the time is right, come to Soochow. We will study together and at the same time build your connections. Connections that will see you advance.'

Doctor Falchion touched Mark's shoulder and nodded towards the door. In the corridor, the doctor laid his hands on Mark's shoulders.

'Do you realise what just happened?' he asked.

Mark shook his head.

'You've been invited to study at the college of Master Wang Shi,' Doctor Falchion said. 'His past scholars sit at the highest levels of government, of learning and of the arts. In China, success is all about patronage. This is a wonderful boost to your prospects.'

'But father...'

Doctor Falchion raised his finger. 'Do not squander this chance,' he cautioned. 'You must waste no more time with your bandit.'

Mark bristled. 'He's my friend,' he said. 'One day, I'll be a fine swordsman.'

Doctor Falchion cupped his hands together as though holding a great treasure. 'Mark, you have within your grasp a most wonderful gift. You must not throw it away.'

Tong Shu's voice echoed along the corridor, 'Doctor, come quick.'

Doctor Falchion backed away. 'I must go,' he said. 'Think on what I've said. I know you'll do the right thing.' He turned and hurried down the corridor.

Mark watched his father leave. *Soochow!* It all seemed so far away. He pictured himself in the gown and cap of a first ranked scholar. He looked at his hands, imagined the skin soft, the nails long and ink-stained. They might even be covered with jewelled nail guards. The corridor stretched away from him, dark and empty.

And for the first time in his life, Mark Falchion felt completely alone.

In the clearing beside the stream, Mark and One-eared Wu took up their practice *dao* broadswords and faced each other.

'Today, we learn defence,' One-eared Wu declared. 'In the right hands, the *dao* becomes a circular shield. It has four parts. First quarter: the heart.' He swept his practice *dao* in a slow, graceful sweep to the left, carving a broad quarter circle covering his heart and shoulder. 'Second quarter.' He repeated the move to the right. 'Third and forth: protect the belly and legs.' His blade traced two more quarter circles, low to the left then to the right.' He rested the blade on his shoulder and signalled Mark to repeat the drills.

'One-hundred times?' Mark sighed.

'Not this time,' One-eared Wu answered. 'Just show me you have the basics.'

Mark gripped tight to his practice *dao* and repeated the moves.

'Good,' One-eared Wu called. 'Now again, this time faster.'

With each practice Mark's confidence grew. He swung his blade faster and faster. The practice *dao's* weight carried each move seamlessly into the next. It was as if sword arm and sword had become one. Sweat beaded Mark's brow. His breath became deep and heavy. Joy swelled in his chest.

'*Enough!*' One-eared Wu called. 'Now I will test you.' He

# THE SCHOLAR'S BLADE

knelt to return his practice *dao* to its hessian wrapping. When he stood, he held another *dao*. Its blade gleamed. The sun sparkled off a honed cutting edge. The air *whushed* across the steel as he executed a scything cut to the left. He dropped to one knee and rotated his wrist. In an instant the blade swept to the right. He stood and his face hardened. His eyes narrowed. His voice was a half-whisper.

'Defend yourself!'

Mark raised an eyebrow. 'You mean to test me with your combat *dao*?' he chuckled. 'Now I know you're mad.'

One-eared Wu did not answer. His blade flickered forward and sliced though the fabric of Mark's sleeve. A trickle of blood seeped into the cotton.

'I said, *defend yourself!*'

Mark's heart bounded. His mouth dried.

'Wait... ' Almost too late he saw One-eared Wu's blade sweeping towards his neck. He dropped to a crouch and the cut whispered over his head. He took a step back. His heel connected with a stone and he fell hard on his backside. The practice *dao* clattered away from him.

Mark stared up at One-eared Wu. The old swordmaster's eyes gleamed. He raised his *dao* above his head then sliced down, hard and fast.

Mark Falchion's world slowed. He could not move, could not speak. He could only watch the blade arcing down towards his brow. He screwed shut his eyes. He waited for the flash of pain that would end his life.

There was no pain.

Mark opened his eyes. One-eared Wu's blade hovered a finger's width from his forehead.

'Anger is easy to control,' One-eared Wu said. 'It requires only discipline. But fear? Controlling fear is the hardest of all disciplines.' He took Mark's hand and pulled him to his feet.

Mark cast down his eyes. 'I... I have failed you,' he said.

One-eared Wu softened his voice. 'There is more to swordsmanship than a strong arm and a sharp blade,' he said. 'A swordsman's spirit must be as strong as his steel.' He brought his fingertips together like a rosebud and brought them to his forehead.

'The first is the spirit of the mind,' he said. He moved his fingertips to his chest. 'The second is of the heart.' He touched his belly. 'The third is here, in the core.' He cradled the *dao* with both hands and held it like an offering. 'And finally, it is here in the *dao*. All four must be in harmony. Without one, the others mean nothing.'

Mark turned away. 'I am not good enough,' he said.

One-eared Wu rested his hand on Mark's shoulder. 'You have the spirit,' he said. 'I have seen it. Together, we will train your mind, heart and core to master the anger and the fear. When you can channel those feelings into the *dao*, then you will be a fine swordsman.' He brought his hands together in a loud clap. 'But now you will practice the circular shield.'

'One hundred times?' Mark groaned.

'One hundred times,' One-eared Wu answered.

Mark retrieved the practice *dao*. He took the defence position and executed a slow, arcing parry to the left. As he exercised, his movements became faster and more fluid. Mind, body and blade became one. There was no Master Wang Shi; there was no Soochow college. There was only the steel and a growing sense of spirit.

And a surge of joy that swelled in his breast.

# 5

WHEN IMPERIAL soldiers returned to Jintian, the crows were pecking the flesh from the heads lining the road. The soldiers honed their spears and swore they would have blood. They moved into the mountain villages but found only ruins. The fields were scorched and bare. There was no rice for the men, no grain for the horses. The force withdrew to its forward base and divided into two columns. One ranged east, the other west but it was as if the land had swallowed the Taipings.

Then came word of movement on the Meng River. Scouts converged on the reports and saw barges loaded with weapons, supplies and men. On each riverbank women trudged, bent under the weight of blankets and tents. Children drove carts loaded with grain and household wares. And there were fighters, a ragtag band of thousands.

The scouts spurred back to their commanders, but by the time the Imperials gave chase, they found only riverbanks churned to ooze by thousands of feet.

The Taipings were a nation with no home. Some carried spears and swords but most bore only scythes and rice flails. At their rear, trundled three cannons.

It was harvest time and by the banks of the Meng, farmers raced to gather in their crop before the Imperials could seize it or the Taipings could burn it. From dawn to twilight, they bent to the task but stopped to watch the approaching lines of longhaired men who sang as they marched.

It was the spring of 1851 and the Taiping host was on the move.

The boy called Joseph stood on Yongan's southern rampart and watched the Taiping force wrap itself around the city. Joseph thought them an odd-looking army. They did not march like soldiers, they ambled like farmhands. Their hair was long and wild. They carried their weapons on their shoulders. Some wore breastplates, others shoulder guards, but none among them had a complete set of armour. Those with helmets wore them at jaunty angles. Their feet threw up clouds of dust and to Joseph, they seemed without number.

'Will they attack?' he asked the soldier standing beside him.

The soldier turned down the corners of his mouth. 'The question is, can we defend?' he snapped. His voice fell to a whisper. 'They say there's been a great killing at Jintian. By the looks of this host, the reports are right. You'd better find somewhere to hide.'

'I'm eighteen,' Joseph said, throwing back his shoulders. 'I can fight.'

'You're fifteen,' the soldier growled. He looked the boy over. He wore baggy britches and an oversized tunic that made him look skinnier than he was. He was tall for his age, tall and gangling but there was something about his eyes. They were dark and angry.

The soldier gave the boy a grudging smile. 'Yes,' he said. 'You're only fifteen but I think you can fight.'

Further along the rampart, there was the bang of a musket.

'Waste of powder,' the soldier snorted. 'They're well out of range.'

'How will we know they're ready to attack,' asked Joseph.

## THE SCHOLAR'S BLADE

'Oh, we'll know,' the soldier answered.

Before the gates, the Taiping ranks parted and men dragged three cannons to the front. Behind each one, a gun captain squinted along the barrel and made frantic hand signals to his crew who pushed and nudged the guns into alignment. Satisfied, the gun captains stood back and each raised an arm.

'They can't get in, can they?' Joseph asked.

The soldier laid a hand on Joseph's shoulder, this time his voice was kindly. 'Go home, boy,' he said. 'Go home to your priest.' He hefted his spear and stepped up to the parapet. He gave a harsh laugh and beckoned the boy to stand beside him. 'Come and look, Joseph,' he said. 'They've sent a troop of women to...'

There was the *thump* of an arrow strike. The soldier staggered back, clawing at an arrow shaft embedded in his chest. He coughed a wad of blood then crumpled to the battlement walkway.

There was a hard bang and the stone under Joseph's feet shuddered. A cheer swelled from the Taiping ranks. The boy called Joseph turned towards the mission. The soldier was right, now was the time to be with Father Petrus.

He put down his head and began to run.

The gate at Yongan shattered like a rice paper screen and Taiping fighters streamed in. Others brought up scaling ladders. They clambered onto the city ramparts. They screamed their war cries and cut the defenders from the battlements. They ran cheering through the city. There was no plan, no mercy, just war cries and killing.

Trapped in the streets, alleys and lanes, the defenders fought like men who knew there could be no surrender. The clamour of war cries mingled with defenders' screams. The Taipings cleared the city, street by street and house by house. As the morning passed, the war cries grew louder; the screams became fewer.

In a lane near the city wall, Kong Liu had steel in his fist and the battle fury in his heart. His chest heaved; his eyes glittered; blood soaked the sleeve of his sword arm. He paused to catch his breath and to cuff sweat from his eyes. His men took the chance to rest. Their faces were blood spattered and sweat smeared. Some were leaning on their weapons. Others dropped to their knees and gasped for breath.

'Call yourself fighters,' Kong chided. He beckoned them with his sword. 'Follow me. I'll make men of you.'

'Captain Kong,' a man called. 'Wait. We nearly missed it.' He pointed to an arch that led to a courtyard. 'That house hasn't been cleared.'

Kong dropped to a crouch. 'Be careful,' he snapped. 'You,' he pointed to a man. 'Take your troop right. The rest, follow me to the left. Ready?'

There were tense nods.

'*Move!*'

The men sprinted through the gate. Half of them fanned right. Kong led the rest left. They found themselves in the courtyard of a grand house that rose three stories. Above the entrance hung a wooden cross. The men pressed their backs against the courtyard wall, their eyes flicked from windows to door and back to windows, searching for movement.

'First troop, secure the ground floor,' Kong snapped. '*Go!*'

A man put his boot to the door and it crashed open. He darted through and his troop followed. Moments later, his face appeared at the door.

'Clear,' he called. He stood aside as Kong shouldered past him.

They were in a dim corridor. A worn carpet covered the floor and pictures of mournful saints looked down from the wall. A staircase led to a broad landing. Kong winced as the bottom step creaked under his weight. He climbed the stairs, his sword thrust out before him.

At the top of the stairs was a door. He put his ear to the door but could hear nothing. He tried the handle and it yielded with a soft click. He stepped into the room and there, in a sagging armchair sat an old European. His eyes bulged. His mouth gaped as if in shock. Fresh blood spurted from a gash at his throat. His clothes were dark with blood. Blood pooled on the floor.

Behind the chair stood a youth. His eyes gleamed. His chest heaved. In his hand was a kitchen knife.

Kong held out his hand. 'Easy, boy,' he said.

The youth let out an animal snarl and leapt at Kong. Kong sidestepped and rammed his sword pommel into the youth's midriff. The youth fell and rolled into a ball. His face twisted in an agony.

Kong dropped to one knee and prised the knife from the youth's hand.

The youth rolled away. He sprang to his feet and stood facing Kong, fists clenched, teeth bared.

'Easy,' Kong said. 'No one will hurt you. You're a brave boy. Now, tell me your name.'

The youth's eyes blazed.

'I am not Joseph,' he snarled. His voice rose to a shout. 'Do you hear me? I am not Joseph. My name is Meng. *I am Meng.*'

Kong Liu ran his eyes over the Yongan defenders' barracks.

'Their sergeant wants his arse kicking,' he grumbled. 'This pig's mire looks like it's never been inspected.'

Standing with Kong were a young man and a youth. The youth was Meng, who had once been named Joseph. The other was a young fighter. He wore a Manchurian breastplate and had a rice sickle tucked in his belt. Years working the fields under the south China sun had darkened his skin and calloused his hands.

'We kicked his arse, right enough,' the young fighter chuckled. He grinned, showing strong teeth. 'Did you see how we beat them, General?'

Kong shot him a sour look.

'What did you say your name was?' he growled.

The young fighter's cheeks reddened. 'It's... it's Yan, General,' he stammered. 'Yan Bing.'

'Well, Yan Bing,' Kong snorted. 'The men we fought today were city watch. The banner infantry won't be so easy.' He frowned. 'And I'm no general,' he added.

Yan Bing looked crestfallen. 'Then what are you?' He gave a sheepish smile, like one caught in a practical joke. 'Of course you're a general,' he scoffed. His voice became uncertain. 'Aren't you?'

Kong Liu shook his head. 'I don't suppose you've secured the armoury,' he said.

Yan Bing grinned. 'I have, sir,' he answered. 'I've ordered all enemy weapons collected and I've posted guards at the treasury. It's quite a haul.'

Kong gave a grudging nod. 'Well done,' he said. 'Now let's see how their officers lived.'

They crossed the barracks and climbed a flight of steps leading to an upper corridor. Here, the floor was polished maple and the walls were lime-washed to a dazzling white. Kong swept aside a crimson drape and stepped into a large chamber. In the centre of the room, a rumpled quilt covered a low divan. The quilt and surrounding floor were sticky with blood.

'Is this where you found the garrison commander?' Kong asked.

'It is,' Yan Bing answered. 'He must have opened his veins as we breached the gates.'

'Pity,' Kong said. 'With persuasion, he might have told us of Imperial strength and deployment.'

He walked to a mahogany cabinet that rose from floor to ceiling. Scrolls and leather bound books jammed every shelf. He chose one and passed it to Yan Bing.

'What's this?' he asked

Yan Bing's eyes widened.

'It's treasure,' he said. 'Imperial flag codes.'

Kong plucked another scroll from its shelf.

'And this?'

'Discipline rules,' Yan answered.

Kong snatched back the scroll and tossed it aside.

Yan Bing took a third scroll from the shelf and unfurled it.

'By all the Gods,' he gasped. 'It's the standard battle order.'

He laid the scroll on the floor and knelt beside it. He beckoned Kong to come closer.

'Look,' he said, running his finger over diagrams and lines of text. 'See how the infantry are arrayed: weakest units forward to blunt the first charge. And here, safely at the rear, the strongest kept safe for the final push.'

The youth, Meng, laughed. 'All the soldiers look the same,' he said.

'Of course they do,' Kong snapped back at him. 'They're in uniform.'

'He has a good point,' Yan Bing said. 'In the confusion, how do their commanders know which unit's which?'

A rebuke sprang to Kong's lips but he stayed silent. He studied the scroll as though seeing it through fresh eyes.

'You're a clever man, Yan Bing,' he mused. His voice became brisk. 'I need a clever man at my side,' he said. 'From now on, you stick with me.'

Yan Bing's eyebrows arched. 'But... sir... I'm no commander,' he stammered.

'And I'm no general,' Kong chortled. 'We are all comrades here,' he said. 'Comrades and brothers.' He flashed a rueful smile. 'But some of us have to do the planning.'

He moved back to the cabinet and selected a scroll at random. He tossed it to the young fighter.

'Consider yourself part of my inner group,' he said. 'Now, start reading, we have an army to build.'

Yan Bing's first duty was to set up a training camp beyond the city wall. From first light, Kong's men cleared the ground, pitched tents, built cooking kilns, dug latrines, and stacked their weapons. All day they toiled. Sweat etched dark streaks through the work grime caked to their bodies. By dusk, the work was complete. That night, they sang and drank until their campfire was just a pile of embers. Two days later, the quartermaster arrived with a wagon laden with supplies.

'Do you have them?' Kong demanded.

'I do,' the quartermaster said.

Kong called men forward and together they pulled hessian sacks from the back of the wagon.

'Pass these out among the men,' he ordered Yan Bing. 'Then report back to me.'

An hour later, Kong Liu stepped from his tent and tied a scarf of white silk around his brow. He smoothed down the front of a sky-blue tunic.

Meng glared at him and scowled.

Kong spread his arms and turned full circle.

'Well, my boy?' he asked. 'What do you think of our uniforms?'

'I'm not a boy,' Meng grunted back. 'And you look unlucky.'

# THE SCHOLAR'S BLADE

'How so?' Kong demanded.

'Why do you have blue tunics?' Meng asked. 'Blue is a death colour.'

'Indeed it is,' Kong replied, tugging the tunic straight. His mouth split in a broad smile. 'When we advance, our enemies will see their death approaching.' He glanced at the bronze mirror hanging by the flap of his tent. 'And it's not just any blue, it's the colour of the sky. It looks good with the black britches. I think it suits me.'

'Well, I'll not wear it,' Meng said, sulking. 'Yip's men have crimson and Wong's unit is plum.' He rolled his eyes. '*Blue.*'

Kong pointed to a scroll lying on his campaign table. 'Read me the day's training schedule,' he ordered.

'I want to be a soldier, not a clerk,' Meng snapped back. 'You read it.'

Kong's cheeks reddened. 'I, *er*...' He lowered his voice. 'When I was a boy, I didn't get much schooling...' he shrugged. 'Please, Meng, read me the training schedule.'

A sly smile cracked Meng's lips. 'I will if you let me train with the men,' he said.

Kong bristled. 'I'll not be blackmailed,' he snapped. 'Read me the damned training schedule.'

Meng snatched up the scroll and made a show of reading it. 'My my,' he said in mock horror. 'You'll never believe what they want you to do.'

'You can run dispatches,' Kong grumbled. He glowered at Meng. 'If you're any good, I'll think about putting you in the ranks.'

Meng thought for moment then nodded. 'It will have to do for now,' he said. He dropped the scroll back onto the table. 'Today you practice moving from turtle formation to swarm attack.'

Kong groaned and repeated the order as if he were a bored

child.

'Turtle to swarm. Turtle to swarm.' He scowled and his voice became a low growl. 'These are Imperial drills. What is the point in using them when we beat the Imperials in every fight? In our army, there are just three lines of attack.' He raised his hand and counted off the points on his fingers. 'One: find the Imperials. Two: kill the bastards. Three: find more Imperials.'

Meng raised his forefinger to his temple. 'I almost forgot,' he said. 'The uniforms were not the only thing the quartermaster delivered.' He ducked into the tent and returned carrying a hessian package.

'What are you grinning at?' Kong snapped.

Meng pulled a bundle of blue silk from the package. He laid it on Kong's campaign desk, unfurled it and took a step back. It was a square banner of sky-blue. Embroidered at its centre was a single character picked out in yellow. The character read, '*Kong.*'

Kong gasped. 'Now, there's a word I can read.' He traced his finger along the character. 'My name on a battle flag. Who would have believed it?'

Meng laughed. 'I believe it,' he said. 'Can I be your standard bearer?'

'You'll be the target of every archer in the enemy ranks,' Kong answered. 'No, my boy, you stick to being a dispatch runner.'

'Do I need training to carry dispatches?' Meng asked.

Kong flashed him a wicked smile. 'Now that you mention it,' he said. 'I believe you do.'

The mare stamped its hoof and gave Meng a mournful gaze.

'Will it bite?' Meng asked, backing away.

'If it does, bite it back,' Kong chuckled.

Kong's troopers were smiling and nudging one another. They were wearing their new uniforms of sky-blue and black. Each had a broad strip of white cotton tied around his brow.

Meng thought how the uniform had changed them: they stood straighter, their laughter was more free, some had even bathed.

'You didn't say I had to ride a horse,' Meng grumbled. 'You said I would be a runner. Aren't runners supposed to run?'

Kong rolled his eyes and made a stirrup of his hands. 'No more talk,' he said. 'Get up there.'

Meng put his foot into Kong's hands and grabbed onto the saddlebow. The saddle creaked as Meng hauled himself up.

'It's a long way down,' he said. 'What if I fall?'

'You won't fall,' Kong said. 'Give her a nudge with your heels then remember what I told you.'

Meng dug his heels into the mare's flanks. She shook her mane and walked forward. He tugged on the right rein and the mare turned right. He pulled on both reins and she stopped.

'You were right,' he said, a grin spreading across his face. 'This is easy.'

'Try a trot,' Kong said. 'Give her a firmer kick.'

Meng stretched out his legs and kicked the mare as hard as he could. The mare shot forward, throwing Meng against the back of the saddle. He let out a cry and gripped tight with his knees. He pulled hard on the reins but the mare tossed her head, fighting the bridle.

She put down her head and lengthened her stride. Meng leaned forward and made small pleading noises. Then he felt the animal's power flow into him through the saddle. The *drubdrubdrub* of hooves on turf matched his heartbeat. The wind brought tears to his eyes. It was as if the horse's strength had become his strength. Never had he felt such joy. He let out a whoop and kicked the mare again. He tugged the reins to the right and the mare circled back to the camp.

Ahead of him, Kong's soldiers formed a line, waving their arms. They jumped up and down and from side to side.

Meng put his head against the mare's neck. His heart swelled. 'Fly, strong one,' he shouted. '*Fly.*'

He charged through the soldiers, scattering them like leaves. He laughed and eased back the reins. The mare slowed to a walk then stopped. Meng kicked his feet free of the stirrups and vaulted to the ground.

Kong ran to him, his eyes wide, his lips white. 'Are you alright?' he panted.

'I'm fine,' Meng said. His cheeks glowed. His eyes sparkled. 'We're both fine.' He grabbed a handful of grass and mopped sweat from the mare's shoulder.

'Here,' Kong said, thrusting a red scarf into Meng's hand. 'If you're to ride like a madman, best keep your hair out of your eyes.

Meng tied the scarf around his brows and stepped back for Kong's approval.

'And you'll need one of these,' Kong added, handing Meng a short-bladed sword.

Meng cradled the sword in both hands. The blade was two feet long. The steel was chipped and dull. He grinned and gave a trial cut.

Kong raised his arms in mock surrender.

'Hold, boy, hold,' he chuckled. He grasped Meng's shoulders. 'Now you are every bit the Taiping warrior. There remains only one thing. Our ruler demands your baptism.'

Meng shrugged away Kong's hands. His eyes flashed. 'I was baptised once before,' he snapped. 'Baptised and named and...' He turned away, his eyes puffy.

Kong's voice became gentle. 'I suspected as much,' he said. 'You have suffered what no man should suffer.' His lips tightened.

'Nor any child.' He tried to look into the youth's eyes but Meng would not meet his gaze. 'That life is no more,' Kong declared. 'Know this: I, Captain Kong Liu, swear to be your protector.'

Kong backed off a few paces then turned and walked away. He stopped to exchange words with Yan Bing, the newest member of his inner circle. The two of them laughed together.

Their intimacy troubled Meng, it was if a best friend had found a new companion.

Meng watched the other soldiers move about the camp. They walked with easy confidence, laughing and swapping banter. Meng screwed shut his eyes but it seemed he could see them all the more clearly: pointing, whispering, laughing. Shame burned his neck. His breath became deep and harsh. They know the truth, he thought.

They know it all and they despise me for it.

Yongan's official *yamen* was a sprawling compound with broad verandas and latticed galleries. Pillars of dark wood supported a roof with tiles of glazed orange. Gilded hooks decorated the eaves.

In the main audience chamber, soldiers had chopped up the fine furniture for their cooking fires. The remnants lay scattered across the maple floor. A breeze drifted through screen doors leading to a garden. Meng stepped into the sunlight and walked along meandering paths. An arched bridge spanned an ornamental stream and beyond that stood a pavilion with crimson pillars and glazed roof tiles. Behind him, there was the sound of heavy footfalls. He turned to see Kong striding towards him.

'Do we have orders?' Meng asked.

'Our Heavenly King, Hoong Hsiu-chuan, is with his toadies,' Kong growled. 'Why should he bother with us?'

'But you've been gone hours,' Meng said. 'Surely you saw him.'

'I waited. I waited some more. I left. Now I'm here,' Kong snapped. 'Come, I need exercise.'

They walked back through the audience chamber and into a courtyard where a groom stood with two horses. They pulled themselves into the saddles and clattered through the streets of Yongan. They rode past the shattered gates and into the countryside. Once clear of the city, Kong kicked his horse into a brisk trot.

Meng whooped for the sheer joy of it. He dug his heels into his mare's flank and she bounded forward. He lay flat against the mare's back as she lengthened her stride.

'Meng, wait!' Kong cried. 'You'll wear her out.'

Meng twisted in his saddle and laughed. 'Afraid?' he shouted. 'Follow me. I'll make a horse soldier of you.' Then he was head down and slapping his horse with the loose ends of his reins.

He almost missed the warning. It was just a glint of steel amongst the trees but it was out of place. He sawed back on the reins and the mare skidded to a halt.

Ahead, a line of Imperial infantry emerged from the trees. In their padded armour, they were slow and stiff-legged. From a distance, they looked like children playing at being soldiers. Meng tugged hard on his reins. The mare snorted, tossed its head and wheeled about.

Kong was galloping towards him, his eyes wild and his hair streaming behind him. 'Come lad,' he called. 'It's time to go home.'

Meng risked a glance over his shoulder but the Imperials showed no sign of pursuit. Laughter bubbled in his throat as he urged the mare on. Then a bolt of fear jolted him. Ahead, another line of infantry ran into the clearing, cutting off their escape.

## THE SCHOLAR'S BLADE

Meng pulled on his reins and the mare skidded to a full stop. Its nostrils flared and it showed the whites of its eyes. Indecision tugged at Meng: forward or back?

Kong trotted back to him. 'No time to dither, boy,' he said. He drew his sword and pointed to the Imperial line. 'That's the way home, now *move*.' He slapped Meng's mare with the flat of his blade and she bounded forward.

Then they were side by side, driving hard for the Imperial line. The Imperials held their ground, spears level.

Kong leaned low over his saddle. His sword swept in a glittering arc. An Imperial fell and Kong was through.

Meng cut at an upturned face but missed. The mare shuddered as the weight of her charge hurled another Imperial aside. She staggered and almost fell. Then she recovered her stride and Meng was through.

Off to his left, Imperial archers nocked arrows to bowstrings. Something whickered past his head.

Meng flattened himself against the Mare's back. 'Fly. *Fly*,' he shouted. The mare tossed its mane and lengthened her stride.

There was a sound like tearing silk and a blow like a hammer slammed into Meng's ribs. He looked with disbelieving eyes at the arrow embedded in his side. His strength drained away. He slumped onto his saddlebow. The shortsword slipped from his fingers. He could not catch his breath. White mist drifted before his eyes.

Then all was dark.

There were faces, pale and blurred. There were voices, hushed and far off. There was darkness, there was light. There was pain and there was the soft smell of opium. For a week, Meng drifted on the margins of death. Then one day he awoke. He lay on a narrow cot. A gnarled old man bent over him and lifted his head from the pillow. A bowl pressed against his lips. He sputtered as bitter fluid trickled into his mouth.

From somewhere a familiar voice said, 'Welcome back.'

Meng tried to sit but pain seared through his side. There was a touch on his shoulder. 'Lie still, boy,' the voice said. 'Lie still and grow strong. Your comrades need you.'

Calm wrapped itself round Meng like a goose down quilt. He smiled and closed his eyes.

Then he slept.

By week's end, Meng could take solid food and walk to the tent flat. After two weeks, he took a few steps in the open air. On the third week, he felt strong enough to join the others who had gathered in the central training ground. As he came closer, the babble of conversation died. Smiling faces turned towards him. There was a table and on it was a flask of wine, a chalice and a dagger. Kong stood before the table. He beckoned Meng forward.

'This boy...' he corrected himself. 'This *man* took an Imperial arrow destined for me.'

He poured a measure of wine into the chalice then gripped the dagger by its blade and raised it above his head. He squeezed the blade until blood trickled from his fist and soaked his sleeve. He dropped the dagger onto the table then raised his open palm, turning full circle so all could see the wound. He made a fist and let his blood flow into the cup as if from a bloody sponge. He turned to Meng and said, 'Come forward, Comrade.'

Meng stepped up to the table and Kong grasped his wrist. Meng winced as Kong sliced the blade across his hand. He held Meng's hand over the chalice, mingling their blood with the wine.

Kong took the cup in both hands and held it aloft as though making an offering to the skies. He turned his face to the north. 'To the north,' he cried. 'I, Kong Liu, pledge this man my friendship.' He brought the chalice to his lips and drank. He turned to the east. 'To the east, I pledge to be his faithful comrade.' He drank and turned again. 'To the south, I promise to be his protector against all adversity.' He drank once more, then turned to the west. 'And finally, to the west and in the presence of you all, I make this man... my son.'

He thrust the chalice into Meng's hand. 'And you, Meng, will be my friend, my comrade...' His voice became a whisper. '...Will you be my son?'

Meng took the chalice and drained it down. The wine burned his throat. The blood was hot and sharp on his tongue. He upended the chalice and held it aloft. He turned full circle, showing everyone it was empty.

The soldiers raised their weapons and their cheers filled Meng's ears.

Kong draped his arm across Meng's shoulders and held him close.

'You lost your sword,' he said. 'A soldier is nothing without steel.'

Shame burned Meng's cheek but Kong beckoned to a soldier who stepped forward cradling a sword.

Meng's mouth fell open at what he saw. The sword had a bronze hilt, flecked green with age. Golden silk covered its grip and the pommel was a disc of pure obsidian. The scabbard was purple velvet. A mother-of-pearl dragon ran its full length. Kong drew the sword from its scabbard. It had a slim blade and the same dragon motif ran in fiery gold from hilt to point.

'I once met a Manchu noble,' Kong said. 'He had a good eye for weapons.' He gave a short laugh. 'Lucky for me, he was a poor swordsman.'

He sheathed the sword and thrust it into Meng's hand.

'You have the courage to own such a blade,' he said. He pointed to one of his soldiers. 'That man is Cho Lung. He is our best swordsman and he will give you the skill to wield it.' He smiled and gave Meng a light punch on the chest. 'Heed him well. If you do not, then take care because he will give you good cause to pay better attention.'

Cho Lung was older than the others. Deep lines etched his face. His shoulders and chest were heavy with muscle. His hair was piled into a topknot, like the warriors of ancient times. A broadsword nestled in a plain scabbard slung across his back. He walked around Meng, looking him up and down like prized livestock.

'He'll do,' he said. Then he returned to his place with the others and stood, eyes hooded, arms folded across his chest.

Meng's hands shook as he clipped the sword to his belt. He could not speak; could not move. He could only look into the eyes of the man who was his friend, his comrade.

And his father.

They killed a pig and roasted it in a clay kiln. They ate and they drank. They told impossible yarns and they laughed. As the sun sank below the western hills, they danced like pagans.

Kong Liu draped an arm across Meng's shoulders. His eyes were puffed and his face was flushed. His breath reeked of wine.

'Not a word about the wine,' he cautioned. 'Our Celest... Celest...' he took a deep breath. 'Our ruler vows to have the heads of opium smokers, fornicators and drinkers.' He raised a cautionary finger. 'Not a word,' he said and reeled away.

From the shadows, Meng watched Kong challenge Yan Bing to a drinking game. Yan Bing won the game and Kong quaffed a flask of wine as forfeit. Both men laughed and embraced each other.

# THE SCHOLAR'S BLADE

To Meng, the embrace was like a dagger thrust. It chilled his heart and filled his mouth with ashes.

Yan Bing put his wine flask to his lips and tipped back his head. The wine ran down his chin and dribbled onto his tunic. He belched, wiped his sleeve across his mouth then staggered into the shadows.

Meng followed, taking care the others did not see him.

Away from the firelight, Yan Bing fiddled with his britches. He gave a contented sigh as a stream of urine splashed into the undergrowth.

Meng stepped up behind him. 'He doesn't love you,' he said.

'What?' Yan Bing turned to the sound of Meng's voice. 'Oh, it's you,' he said, relaxing. 'Damn, I've pissed in my britches.' He gave a sheepish grin. 'What did you say?'

'I said, our captain doesn't love you,' Meng answered.

Yan Bing shrugged. 'Yes he does,' he said. 'He loves us all.'

'He can't,' Meng said. There was ice in his voice. 'He loves only me. He proclaimed it.'

Yan Bing spread his arms in embrace and tottered towards Meng. 'We all love you, my boy,' he slurred.

'I am not your boy,' Meng snarled, drawing his sword.

The smile fell from Yan Bing's lips. 'Put away your sword, *boy*,' he growled.

Meng dropped to a crouch. 'I am *Meng*,' he growled. 'And I am a man.' He darted forward and thrust the sword into Yan Bing's belly.

Yan's eyes bulged. He made mewling noses and clawed at the blade. He dropped to his knees. Meng put his foot on Yan Bing's chest and pulled the blade free. Yan gasped and fell onto his side.

'He loves only me,' Meng hissed. He wiped the blade on Yan Bing's britches, sheathed his sword and walked back to the firelight.

# 6

THEY BURIED Yan Bing along with evidence of the night's feasting. Kong tripled the guard but everyone knew the killing was not the enemy's work. Soldiers went about their duty in silence. Men who had been comrades since the start, cast sideways looks at one another, each wondering, each doubting.

Later that day, Kong ordered the men to pack their gear and move back to the city. He set up his headquarters in an old storehouse and listed Yan Bing as missing, believed captured or killed.

Then came orders. Kong was to seek out nearby lands owned by Imperial sympathisers. He was to empty their grain stores and lay waste to all that might be of use to the enemy.

At first, the prospect of action gladdened the soldiers, but their cheer turned sour as they yoked a muscular buffalo to a cart. The beast regarded them with sad eyes and refused to move. With one soldier tugging at its ear and another slapping its rump, the beast lumbered forward but neither coaxing nor threats would make it move faster.

Meng walked at Kong's side but instead of sky-blue, he wore a tunic and britches of black cotton.

'You should wear my uniform,' Kong grumbled.

'It's unlucky,' Meng answered. 'You should wear mine.'

They travelled in silence. The sun burned down on their heads and the road's dust clogged their throats. As the sun arced to its noon high, they came to a village that did not show on their maps. Surrounded by rice paddies, it was no more than a collection of dwellings clustered around a single storehouse. On a low hill overlooking the paddies stood a grand house. Its surrounding walls were rendered in crimson. Tiles of green glaze topped the roof. The hooked eaves were gilded dragons.

Kong ordered a halt. A breeze stirred dust from the road and somewhere, a shutter banged.

'Where are the damned workers?' Kong growled. He called Cho Lung forward. 'Take three men and look around,' he ordered. 'And be careful. If it doesn't smell right, get back here.'

The men moved into the village. They went door to door, probing and searching but they found nothing. They approached the storehouse and used their spears to prod open the door. It swung open and for an instant, a face showed in the shadows.

The soldiers pressed their backs against the wall and levelled their spears. Cho Lung looked to Kong and raised his arm.

'Move up,' Kong barked. The rest of the soldiers moved into the village, covering the buildings and village approaches.

Cho Lung and his three soldiers moved into the storehouse. Moments later, they emerged dragging with them an old man. He wore the faded tunic and britches of a worker but his skin was pale and soft.

They released him and he dropped to his knees. Tears tracked through dust clinging to his cheeks. He clasped his hands together, as if in prayer.

'I beg you, Excellency,' he pleaded. 'Spare this old servant.'

'*He lies!*'

The voice belonged to a girl. She had followed the men from the storehouse and now she stood to one side, watching them. She was slim and to Kong she looked to be in her mid-teens. She wore her hair short, like a boy. She had fine features but it was her eyes that struck Kong most, they were large and without fear. She thrust her chin towards the old man.

'He's the landowner,' she said. She waved her arm, encompassing the village and surrounding paddies. 'All this belongs to him.'

'Do not listen,' the old man pleaded. 'She is my daughter.' He lowered his voice. 'The child is touched.'

'I am not your daughter,' the girl snarled. 'I am *mi-jeh*, your house slave.'

'Where are the people?' Kong demanded.

'Gone, Excellency, all gone,' the old man sobbed. 'The Imperials came...'

Kong grabbed the old man's tunic. 'Imperials?' he snapped. 'When? How many?'

The old man cowered down. 'How many?' he whined. 'Who can tell? Very many, I think. Just two days ago, or was it three? They stripped the village clean. My... the workers... they've fled.' He pointed to nearby hills. 'They have coin and they have grain. If you hurry, you might catch them.'

Kong pushed the old man away and he sprawled on the road.

'Where's that damned girl?' Kong growled, looking round.

The girl squared her shoulders and looked up at Kong.

'I have a name,' she declared. 'I am Ping Song-mei.' She lowered her eyes and her voice became small. 'But everyone just calls me Mei.'

Kong placed his hands on the girl's shoulders. 'Mei,' he mused. 'That means "pretty." But you're more than pretty. I think you're clever. I bet you know how many soldiers there were.'

Mei raised her eyes to Kong's. 'Twenty,' she said. 'I couldn't understand their language but I remember one had a blue flag.'

Kong stepped back.

'Banner infantry,' he said. 'Imperial regulars. They're a long way from base. We'd best get back and report it.'

'What about these two?' a soldier asked.

'Leave them,' Kong said. He turned away but the girl ran after him.

'Wait,' she called. 'Take me with you.'

Kong looked down at her. 'Take you?' he chuckled. 'Would you be a soldier?'

'I'm strong,' the girl chimed. She stood with her fists on her hips and her feet apart. 'And I'm brave,' she said.

There was a ripple of laughter. 'Take care, Captain,' a man called. 'She'll have your command within the week.'

Kong leaned closer to her. 'Stay here, little one,' he chided. 'Without you, who will look after your father?'

The girl's cheeks burned. 'He's *not* my father,' she cried. 'I am *mi-jeh*. My mother...' she stifled a sob. 'My mother... sold me to him. I work all day and at night...' she lowered her eyes. 'He... he sends a servant to bring me from my sleeping place...' Her voice tailed away.

Kong raised his arm. 'Form on me,' he bellowed. 'Meng. Where are you?'

'Here Father?' Meng snapped back.

'You've the youngest legs,' Kong said. 'Get back to Yongan. Tell them we have reports of Banner Infantry less than a day's march from the city.' He glowered at Meng. 'Well?' he said. 'Why do you wait? Run. *Run!*'

Meng turned and was off like a hare, down the road to Yongan.

There was a tug at Kong's tunic. Kong knotted his brows and glowered down at Mei.

Mei stared back at Kong.

'You're a girl,' Kong said. 'There's no place for a girl in the army.'

'There's one place,' Cho Lung called. 'Lady Yen's mounted

archers are always looking for new blood.'

Kong looked the girl up and down. 'She couldn't lift a bow,' he chortled, 'never mind shoot one.'

'Give her a chance,' another soldier said. 'Bring her along.'

There was another tug on Kong's tunic. He looked down to where Mei stared silently up at him.

'You are a flea, an annoying insect,' Kong growled. He rolled his eyes then grasped Mei around the waist and swung her onto the cart's riding board. 'Sit there and say nothing,' he snapped.

Mei's eyes shone. She grinned and her cheeks dimpled. She opened her mouth but Kong raised a finger.

'Nothing,' he growled. 'Not a single word.'

Then he turned away before Mei could see him smile.

The barrack had high ceilings and a stone floor. Lime-wash peeled from the walls, showing the crumbling brick beneath. Running the barrack's length was a scattering of rush sleeping mats. A woman stood in the centre of the barrack. She was short and heavyset. She wore a tunic and britches of yellow silk. Tied tight around her brows was a turban of the same yellow silk.

'I am Lady Yen Lin, your commander,' the woman snapped. 'For some strange reason, you've been sent to me. Have they assigned you a sleeping place?'

'Yes, Madam,' Mei answered. 'It's in the scullery. But...'

Yen Lin looked Mei up and down. 'Show me your hands, child,' she ordered.

Mei held out her hands and Yen Lin gave a grunt of approval. 'You've the hands of a coolie,' she said. 'What were your previous duties?'

'Scrubbing, sewing, gardening, fetching,' Mei answered. She shrugged. 'I did whatever they told me to.'

'Good,' the woman said. 'Because here, your duties are

exactly the same.'

'But Lady...'

Mei reeled back from a stinging slap to her cheek.

The woman looked hard into Mei's face.

'Who am I?' she demanded.

Mei lowered her eyes.

'You are Lady Yen,' she answered.

'And what am I?'

'You are my commander,' Mei answered in a small voice.

'And don't forget it,' the woman snarled. Now get a broom and start work.' She strode from the room leaving Mei alone in the barracks.

A great sadness filled Mei as she looked along the line of mats marking the archers' sleeping places. The slap burned her cheek as had the slap on that first day in the grand house at Hwangli village.

I was *mi-jeh* then and I'm *mi-jeh* now, she thought.

'Have you time to daydream?'

Mei turned and her breath caught. Framed in the door was a woman like none she had ever seen. She was young, in her late teens, Mei guessed. She had high cheekbones and full lips. She was tall and straight. She wore a suit and turban of yellow silk. Slung across her back was a longbow. At her hip was a quiver of arrows. An ivory handled dagger hung from her belt. She stepped into the barrack and it struck Mei that she did not walk like a woman, she had the straight-backed, square-shouldered gait of a soldier.

The woman cast her eyes about the barrack and gave a snort of disapproval. 'Lady Yen's getting soft,' she said. 'My first job was digging latrines.'

'Are... are you a soldier?' Mei stammered.

The woman arched an eyebrow. 'As are we all,' she said.

Mei's voice was resentful. 'I want to kill Imperials, not sweep barracks.'

'Ah yes,' the woman answered with a cold smile. 'I can see you now, charging into battle, scattering enemies with your arrows.' The smile dropped from her lips. 'Can you ride a horse?' she asked. 'Have you ever seen a horse?'

'I'll learn,' Mei answered. 'How hard can it be?'

'Can you shoot a bow?'

Mei shrugged.

The woman unslung her bow. 'Catch,' she said, tossing it to Mei.

Mei winced as she fumbled and almost dropped it.

Mei ran her hand along the bow's length. It was as tall as she was, but it weighed almost nothing. The wood was pale and smooth. From a rawhide grip, two perfect arches tapered away to tips that curved forward against the bow's natural shape. Bonded to the inner curve was a strip of horn. The string was sinew interwoven with silk. It sang like a harp when Mei plucked it.

'It's Mongolian,' the woman said. 'It will drop a man at two hundred paces.' She stood beside Mei. 'Grip it like this,' she said. She made a fist and crooked her left arm as though holding a bow.

Mei copied the grip.

'That's it,' the woman said. She knelt beside Mei, checking her position. 'Now, show me how strong you are. Pull back on the string and at the same time, push against the bow.'

Mei raised the bow. The string bit into her fingers and her muscles strained against the combined tension of wood and horn. She could draw the string only a few inches. She eased off the tension then gritted her teeth and tried again. Her strength gave out and she let the bow drop to her side. She massaged

## THE SCHOLAR'S BLADE

her shoulder and turned away so the woman would not see her cheeks redden.

'That's why you sweep floors,' the woman said.

Mei's voice was flat. 'Will I ever be a soldier?'

The woman squeezed Mei's biceps as though testing a chicken.

'You're strong,' she said. 'But pulling a Mongolian bow takes special training. It's going to take time.'

Mei cocked her head to one side. 'Who are you?' she asked.

'I'm Jade,' the woman answered. 'And it's my sorry duty to see if you've the makings of an archer.' She pointed at the broom. 'But not today. Today you sweep.'

In the coming weeks, Mei chopped wood and hefted logs. She filled sacks with grain and carried them on her back to the stables. She groomed the horses and raked out their stalls. She swept the barrack floor and cleaned the unit's weapons. At night, she worked with a half-sized training bow.

Draw, release. Draw, release. Draw, release. She worked until her fingers bled and her muscles burned.

Each morning, Jade plumbed the depths of blame. There was grime on the barrack floor, cobwebs in the eaves, rust on the window hinges, the stable straw needed changing, the saddlery was dull. Then one day, Jade stood at the door and cast her eyes about the barrack. At length she turned to Mei.

'It's not perfect,' she said. 'But it must suffice. Now, show me how strong you are.'

Mei retrieved the training bow and made ready to draw back the string.

'Wait,' Jade ordered. She pulled a metal cylinder from her tunic. 'Put this on your draw thumb, it will protect the skin.'

Mei pushed the ring onto her thumb then brought up the

bow, exerting steady pressure. Her arms quivered. She gritted her teeth and pulled harder. She felt the bowstring caress her cheek. She let out a whoop and released the string. It sang and the bow shivered.

'Not bad,' Jade said. She smiled and her eyes shone. 'Now it's time to make an archer of you.'

Jade showed Mei how to brace the bow against her foot and flex it just enough to set the bowstring. Then they went to the stables and Jade led a mare out into the yard. She helped Mei clamber onto its back. With Mei clutching its mane, Jade walked the mare around the yard's perimeter.

Every day, they practiced. Mei learned how to guide the mare and how to fit its saddlery. A week later, they rode together along Yongan's narrow streets. A week after that, Mei slung the training bow across her back and they rode through the gates and out into open country.

Jade sat as straight as a spear.

'Keep it at a brisk trot,' she called to Mei. 'The horses can trot for hours without tiring.'

As the sun reached its highest point, they crossed a meadow then reined in beneath a Ginkgo tree. Autumn was approaching and Mei shivered as a breeze ruffled the grass and shook the branches.

Jade swung her leg forward over the saddlebow and dropped to the ground.

'Come,' she said. 'I've a test for you.' She pointed to a tree, thirty paces away and pulled an arrow from her quiver. 'Remember what I told you,' she said.

Mei unslung the training bow and slipped the bow ring onto her thumb. She took the arrow and nocked it her bowstring. She brought the bow up and sighted. She held her breath but her arm began to shake, making the arrowhead move in wide circles. She loosed the arrow and watched it fly away into the undergrowth.

'You waited too long,' Jade said. 'The bow will steal your strength if you let it. Watch me.'

She unslung her own bow and nocked an arrow. Her eyes narrowed. She drew in a breath and in a fluid movement, raised the bow, drew back the string and let the arrow fly. It hit the tree with a solid *tump* and stuck there, quivering.

Jade plucked another from her quiver and handed it to Mei.

'Don't waste too much time on the aim,' she said. 'Align the shaft with the target, then *think*. Think of the arrow striking home.' She took Mei's shoulders in both hands and looked into her eyes. 'Let that thought control everything.'

Mei nocked the arrow and fixed her eyes on the tree. Around her, all became still. She focussed on a section of trunk. Her vision narrowed. She could see every seam of its bark. She raised the bow and drew back the string. The arrowhead swung up into her sight line. Tree and arrowhead became one. She released and, as if in a dream, the arrow floated away. It thudded home, breaking the spell.

Jade grasped Mei's shoulder. 'I knew it,' she cried. 'I saw it from the start. Most archers just see the target. But not you, you *feel* it.'

Mei stared at the bow then at the arrow, still quivering in the trunk.

'I did,' she gasped. 'I really felt it. What does it mean?'

Jade lay her arm across Mei's shoulders and put her mouth close to Mei's ear. 'It means, little sister, you're an archer.'

Jade walked to the horses and pulled a strip of yellow cotton from her saddlebag. She tied it round Mei's brows.

'There,' she said, adjusting the knot. 'Now you're an archer.' She smiled and wrinkled her nose. 'Albeit a little one.'

Mei touched the scarf and thought her heart would burst.

They rode back to Yongan in silence and later, after the curfew bell had sounded, Ping Song-mei went to her sleeping place in the scullery. She unfurled her bed mat and lay down. She forgot her faded clothes. She forgot her menial duties. She touched the yellow cloth still tied around her brows and imagined herself not in the scullery, but in the barracks of Lady Yen's mounted archers.

As the year turned, the Imperials set up camps to the east and south of Yongan. They raised earthworks and palisades. They ventured close to Yongan's walls but withdrew when the Taipings came out to meet them.

In the city *yamen*, Hoong Hsiu-chuan paced the floor while Kong Liu and Meng bent over their maps. Hoong rounded on them. 'How many soldiers have we?' he demanded.

'Twenty thousand, Sire,' Kong replied.

'And the *devils*?'

Kong scratched his chin. 'Reports are sketchy,' he mused. 'Anything between thirty and fifty thousand.'

Hong's eyes glittered. 'Damn your reports,' he growled. 'You are supposed to know.'

Kong shrugged. 'I send out scouts but they don't return.'

'Then send out more,' Hoong snapped. 'Scouts are expendable.'

For while he was silent, then he moved close to Kong and Meng. He draped an arm over each of their shoulders. His voice softened. 'Noble Kong Liu,' he said. 'We have been together from the start.'

For the first time in months, Kong saw a hint of the openhearted young scholar he had met on that chilly morning in Kwanlubu village.

'I have been speaking with my Heavenly Father,' Hoong continued. His voice became animated. 'He told me of a garden of learning and culture.'

'Did he?' Kong replied, trying not to sound sceptical.

'He did,' Hoong said. His eyes gleamed. 'He has opened a book that any wise man may read.'

A sly smile played on Meng's lips. 'And may we also read it?' he asked.

Kong flashed Meng a warning glare. To Hoong he said, 'We are simple soldiers, Sire, not wise men.'

'There is a city,' Hoong said. 'It is a place of learning and culture. It is home to philosophers, past and present. It is the spiritual home of our nation.'

'Does it have strong walls?' Kong snorted.

'Indeed it does,' Hoong answered. 'It was once the seat of the Ming emperors.'

Kong squinted at Hoong. 'Surely Sire, you don't mean...'

Hoong grinned and clapped his hands.

'*Yes*, my loyal captain,' he chuckled. Where else but the ancient capital? Where else but Nanking?'

'*Nanking?*' Kong gasped. 'That's seven hundred miles from here.'

'Yes, seven hundred,' Hoong said. 'A short journey, given the prize.'

Kong shook his head. 'Seven hundred miles with our women and children,' he said. 'Not to mention the sick and the lame.'

Hoong laughed. 'But it is so clear,' he said. 'Nanking. It shall be our garden, our heavenly kingdom. Trust me, loyal Kong Liu, we can do it.'

Kong gave a heavy sigh. 'Yes, Sire. But at what cost? The Imperials will annihilate our rearguard. And what of those who cannot travel?'

'Arm the old and the lame,' Hoong said. 'They will be our rearguard and we lose only those who would hamper us. We will be double blessed.'

'They will be wiped out,' Kong said, his voice rising.

'They will be martyred,' Hoong replied. 'They will die so the children of the Taiping Heavenly Kingdom may reach their heavenly home.' He brought his fist crashing down on the map table. 'And our heavenly home is *Nanking*.'

He turned away and waved his arm in dismissal. 'Make the arrangements,' he called then he strode from the chamber.

Kong sighed, put his hand to his chest and bowed. He swallowed his doubts and in his mind, prepared the order of march.

'She's small,' Yen Lin growled.

'She's a natural archer,' Jade replied. 'And she has heart.'

'How old are you, child?' Yen Lin asked, turning to Mei.

Mei tried to speak but a lump formed in her throat. She swallowed and tried again. 'I was fourteen in the New Year, Lady,' she croaked.

Yen Lin's eyebrows shot up. 'Fourteen, is it?' She rounded on Jade, her voice harsh. 'Truly, a veteran.'

Jade stood with her back straight and her shoulders square. 'Lady.' Her voice was strong and clear. 'You told me to gauge this woman's abilities. This I have done.'

Yen Lin's eyes narrowed.

'Woman?' she growled. 'What woman? Am I an *ahmah* who cares for brats?'

The skin above Jade's collar turned crimson.

'No. Lady,' she snapped.

'Do not forget who commands here, Jade,' Yen Lin growled. 'Not even my best archer is immune from discipline.'

She put her hands on her hips and looked from Jade to Mei.

'The only thing worse than a disorderly woman is two

disorderly women,' she muttered. 'And if I'm to have two disorderly women, I'll keep them where I can see them both.' Her eyes bored into Jade's. 'I give this one to you as a servant,' she said. 'Train her well. If she's still alive in a year or two, we'll see if she's an archer or not.'

'Yes, Lady,' Jade barked. 'Thank you.'

'I hope you thank me a year from now,' Yen Lin scoffed. She shook her head then strode from the barrack.

'Can I move yet?' Mei whispered from the corner of her mouth.

Jade exhaled in a loud hiss. 'Yes, you can move.'

'What does it mean?' Mei asked.

'It means we're both on trial,' Jade sighed.

'Am I an archer or not,' Mei pleaded.

'Oh yes, little sister,' Jade said. 'You're an archer alright.' She turned towards the door through which Yen Lin had just left. 'I just hope we can convince our commander. If I cannot...'

She shrugged and left the rest unsaid.

Rumours spread like summer locusts. Dispatches flew from one unit to another. Patrols rode out only to return with no news.

Mei watched Yen Lin lead the mounted archers out into the countryside. At dusk, they came home, dusty and hollow-eyed. Lather foamed at the horses' necks and flanks. Mei trotted alongside as they clattered through the streets. They drew up outside the Heavenly King's *yamen*. Yen Lin tossed her reins to Mei then ran up the steps leading to the *yamen's* entrance.

Jade gave the order to dismount and led the unit back to their stables. The women were round-shouldered and silent.

'What happened?' Mei whispered.

'We came across an Imperial column,' Jade answered. 'Their cavalry nearly got around us. We were lucky to make it back.

There are enemy positions to the west and south. We saw thousands of soldiers moving north.' She drew her thumb across her throat. 'If they establish a camp, they'll have us trapped.'

Mei lit the stable lanterns and took the saddle from Yen Lin's horse.

Jade nudged Mei and nodded to where their commander stood framed in the door.

'Pay attention,' Yen Lin called. 'Tomorrow night, we evacuate Yongan.'

A murmur spread amongst the women.

'Silence,' Yen Lin cried. 'Tonight, you will pack your gear. Final briefing is noon tomorrow. Questions?'

There was silence.

'Good. Get some rest.' She cast her eyes about the stable. 'Where's Mei?'

'Here, Madam.' Mei stepped forward.

'Come with me, child,' Yen Lin called. 'I need you to take a message to Captain Kong.' She walked into the dark and Mei scuttled after her.

An hour later, Mei was darting through Yongan's alleys. Tucked into her sleeve was a sealed scroll. She came to a storehouse wedged between the city wall and a row of tenements. The door stood open. Inside there was the glow of oil lamps. There was chatter and laughter.

From the shadows came a harsh voice. 'What do you want?'

A youth stepped into the light. He was in his middle teens and his hair hung in thick curls about his shoulders. A crimson scarf circled his brows. At first, Mei thought him handsome, then the lamplight caught his eyes. They were flat and empty.

'I said, what do you want?' he asked again.

'Stand aside,' Mei snapped. 'I have a dispatch for Captain Kong.'

'My name is Meng,' the youth said holding out his hand. 'I am his son. You can give it to me.'

'My orders are to hand it to Captain Kong and no one else,' Mei said, moving towards the open door.

Meng stepped into her path.

'Not so fast,' he said. 'Don't you remember me? I was at the village when Captain Kong found you.' He looked Mei up and down. 'You've grown,' he said and gave an approving nod.

Mei felt herself recoil from Meng's gaze. It was like an unwanted caress.

'Please,' she said. 'I must deliver my dispatch.' She gave an uncertain smile. 'I'll come back, I promise.' She made to step around Meng but again, he moved to block her way.

Meng's lips formed a smirk. 'Maybe you prefer women's company,' he said. 'I hear that's common among the archers.' He reached out to touch her but she brushed away his hand.

'You've become proud,' Meng snarled. He grabbed Mei's tunic and swung her hard against the wall, knocking the breath from her.

Mei hunched her shoulders and tried to twist free.

'Please,' she begged. 'I'll come back, I promise.'

Meng pressed his body against Mei's, crushing her against the wall. His breath was hot against her cheek. His mouth was wet against her neck. He slipped his hand under her tunic. She cried out as his fingernails dug into her breast.

He clamped his hand over her mouth and put his lips close to her ear.

'No one can hear you,' he whispered.

Mei bit down on his hand and tasted blood. Meng yelped. He stepped back and slapped her hard, making her ears sing.

'Pride is the deadliest sin,' Meng growled. 'The Reverend Father taught me there is only one cure.'

He grabbed Mei's wrist and twisted her arm behind her.

'Stay still,' he hissed. He fumbled at her britches and pushed them down over her hips. He pulled at his own britches and they dropped about his ankles.

Mei tried to cry out but could not catch her breath.

Meng pushed his knee between her thighs, forcing her legs apart. Then he gave a small, despairing cry and his grip loosened.

Mei gathered all her strength and pushed him away. She glanced down at his manhood. It hung flaccid between his legs.

Meng snatched up his britches. For a fleeting moment, his face had the look of a frightened child.

'Please don't tell,' he pleaded.

Then the frightened child was gone. His hand lashed out and grabbed Mei's throat. She clawed at his wrist but Meng squeezed tighter. Blood pounded in her temples, her legs became weak, white mist drifted before her eyes. Meng thrust her away and she sprawled across the flagstones. She rolled onto her side and drew her knees to her chest. She buried her face in her hands as Meng loomed above her.

'If you tell, I'll find you and kill you,' he snarled. He backed away and was gone.

Mei pulled her tunic tight about her. She could still feel Meng's hands on her body, still feel his mouth against her skin. She tried to stand but her legs would not carry her. She began to shiver. A sob wracked her body.

In time, her strength returned and she stood. The door to Kong's barracks stood open, the glow of lanterns invited her to enter.

Mei bit her lip and pressed her forehead against the wall. The stone was cool and its strength comforted her. She wiped her sleeve across her face and squared her shoulders. She pulled the dispatch from her sleeve and stepped though the open door.

# 7

TWO HOURS BEFORE midnight, Yongan's gates rumbled open and the Taipings filed through. There were soldiers, their wives, and their children. There were livestock and carts. The carts' wheels squealed under loads of weapons, grain, and gunpowder. Some had special guards: armoured men with weapons of steel. Yongan, once rich in silver, was rich no more.

The soldiers no longer wore uniforms scavenged from Imperial dead. Now, each wore unit colours: there was the jade-green of Captain Fu and Captain Kong's sky-blue. There was saffron, plum, indigo and many more. The column was a multicoloured snake with its head five miles from its tail.

Scouts ranged ahead whilst the infantry protected the families and the carts. Women suckled babies as they walked. Others bent double under bundles of household wares. Children made mewling complaints and soldiers cursed the crawling pace. Officers flanked the column, bullying stragglers into line.

The Taiping Heavenly King, Hoong Hsiu-chuan sat atop a cushioned palanquin carried by sixteen bearers. A parasol shielded him from light rain that fell throughout the night. Flanking him was a close escort of forty women mounted on horseback. They rode astride, like men. They wore yellow silk and slung across each of their backs was a Mongolian bow.

The rearguard commander was a young soldier named Chun

Wan-so. Weeks earlier, he had broken his leg in training and the bone was not fully set. For one so young, the command was large: two battalions, each a thousand strong. Under normal circumstances, the appointment would have been a huge boost to his status, but not today.

Chun Wan-so took a moment to check the lie of the ground and nodded his satisfaction.

'This will do,' he said to his companion, a grizzled old soldier who had once been woodsman. 'We have the high ground,' he continued, 'and there are steep slopes on each flank. Even with this force, we can give the army a good head start.'

'Do you really believe that?' his companion asked.

Chun cast his eyes over his force and his heart sank. They were battalions of the old and infirm. Some of his men held spears and there were a few swords. None wore armour.

'No, I don't,' he sighed. 'We're here because we'd slow the others.' He laid his hand on his companion's shoulder. 'You don't have to stay,' he said. 'Take the strongest and join the main force.'

'*Chehh*,' the old soldier scoffed. 'It takes young legs to chase an army in those hills.' His lips formed an ironic smile. 'And you'll need at least one man who can lift a sword. No, I think I'll stay.'

For a while, they gazed down at Yongan. The rain had eased and the fires they had set earlier gave an orange glow to the smoke and low cloud hovering over the city.

'Do you think they'll come soon?' Chun asked.

'I doubt it,' the older man answered. 'They can't push forward until they know the city is clear.' He did a mental calculation. 'We're safe for now. They'll hit us at dawn tomorrow, maybe a little later.'

Below them, a troop of Imperial infantry moved into view and formed a line across the road. Their officer raised a telescope and Chun suppressed an urge to wave. They're close enough to see our good position, he thought, but too far off to see our weakness.

The Imperial officer snapped shut his telescope then led his troops the way they had come.

'Off the road,' Chun ordered. 'First battalion left; second battalion right.'

Later he would set pickets but for now he would let them rest, God knows they needed it. He had until dawn tomorrow, then the Imperials would come to this hillside in force. Then, Chun Wan-so's regiment would fight.

And then, they would die.

The mountain range to the east of Yongan was a vast watershed. To the south, all rivers flowed to the southern seas, but beyond the high passes, the rivers ran north. At the highest point, the Taipings gave thanks for their deliverance, but while the priests invoked the Holy Spirit, many soldiers paid silent homage to *He Shan*, the River God.

Cloud covered the peaks and the Taipings wound through ravine paths slick with dew. Finally, they dropped down to the Kweilin Gorges where the Li River ran wide and slow between granite pinnacles.

The garrison at Kweilin hunkered down behind its walls as the Taipings stripped the wharfs of river craft. They embarked their non-combatants and loaded their stores.

Whilst the boats rode the Li's currents, Taiping soldiers marched along the riverbank, unburdened except for their weapons.

They came to the Shingan canal. There, to the chants of overseers, men sweated at ropes and hauled the boats twenty miles to the Shiang River. For a while, the Shiang was their pathway but at Suoyi Ford, Imperial militia stretched a boom across the river, forcing the Taipings to abandon their boats and march onto the Hunan plain. They overwhelmed the garrison at Taochow and from there, sent scouting parties south to the Kwangsi borders and east into Kwangtung.

At night, Taiping agents pasted big character posters on town walls. By day, recruiting parties unfurled banners and told stories of distant mountains and mystic rivers. They promised to restore the *Han* Chinese Ming dynasty and bring an end to the Manchu invader's tyranny. They told grand tales of their victories against the emperor's army. They spoke of the one true God who offered not only freedom but also everlasting life in a heavenly paradise.

The men and women of Hunan listened. They unbraided their queues and came to Taochow, first in their dozens, then in their hundreds and finally in their thousands.

Six weeks after seizing Taochow, Hoong Hsiu-chuan marched from the city at the head of fifty thousand soldiers. They marched back to the north and crossed the Shiang River. They seized towns and emptied treasuries and still, their numbers grew.

At Wuchang, on the banks of the Yangtze, victory came so fast, it caught the Taiping command unprepared. When Hoong Hsiu-chuan made his triumphant entry, cheering citizens lined the streets. Strings of firecrackers exploded in the city squares. Lion dancers pranced and twirled to the rhythm of drums and cymbals. In the armoury, gleaming weapons stood ready for inspection. In the stables, the horses were sleek and well fed. The quartermaster's shelves sagged under the weight of helmets and marching boots. There were comfortable barracks and regular meals.

And her treasury gave up more silver than any had ever seen.

The women's barrack at Wuchang was a bustle of noise and hurry.

# THE SCHOLAR'S BLADE

'Hurry,' Jade urged. 'We'll be late.'

'Wait,' Mei answered, packing away her bedmat. 'Where are we going?'

'Across the river,' Jade answered. 'There's a recruiting drive at Hongshan and we're part of it.'

Yen Lin stood in the doorway, her mouth a thin line.

'Your servant looks like an urchin,' she said. 'If she's to come along, get her properly dressed.'

'Yes Madam,' Jade answered. She rummaged in her pack and handed Mei a parcel of waxed hessian. 'Here, put this on,' she said.

Mei pulled away the bindings and her eyes widened.

'But...'

'Don't argue,' Jade snapped. She cast a sideways glance at Yen Lin. 'Hurry.'

Mei folded back the hessian wrappings, inside was a tunic and matching britches of yellow silk. She slipped out of her clothes and into the archer's uniform.

Jade looked her over.

'It's too big but it will have to do,' Jade sighed. She fastened a belt around Mei's tunic and pulled it tight. 'Pick yourself a bow,' she said. 'But don't use it for anything but show. It's bad luck to use another's bow.'

Mei hurried to obey, her eyes shone. She returned with a quiver of arrows and a full-sized bow.

'It's dirty,' Jade said. 'Rub it down with linseed.' She tugged at the string. 'It's heavier than you're used to. No matter, you won't need it.'

Yen Lin looked Mei up and down.

'That's better,' she said. 'But don't grow accustomed to the uniform.' She turned away from Mei and raised her voice so all could hear.

'You might think this is just a day out,' she said. 'But others will be watching; others who think women have no place in the army.' She paused to let her words strike home. 'Today I accept nothing less than soldierly behaviour,' she continued. 'Do you understand?'

'Yes, Madam,' the women called.

'Good,' Yen Lin said then she turned and strode from the barracks.

They pulled quilted jackets of pale green over their uniforms. Jade tossed a jacket to Mei but Mei's hands trembled so much, she fumbled the fastenings.

Jade bent over her, slapping away her hands. 'All this time as an archer, and I'm still dressing children,' she chided. 'Now, let me look at you.' She stepped back and smiled. 'Good,' she said. 'Now, let's see what the town of Hongshan has to offer.' She put her hand in the small of Mei's back and steered her to the door.

The mounted archers clattered through Wuchang's streets and into the open country. Behind Yen Lin, forty women rode in two files. At the rear, Jade and Mei rode side by side.

'A strong horse beneath you and brave comrades at your side,' Jade called to Mei. 'Could anyone want more?'

Mei fixed her eyes ahead and felt sure her heart would explode.

An uneven road led them through the open country and out towards South Lake. The road took them along the lakeshore where fishing nets hung to dry on wooden frames and ramshackle dwellings sat on spindly stilts in the inshore shallows. Close by the shore, fishermen stopped casting their nets to watch the women pass by.

Hongshan was just a country marketplace. It had a low wall and some houses but its main feature was a large square. On market days, people came from surrounding farms to buy and sell, to drink the local wine, and to catch up on the latest gossip.

But today the crowds had come just to see the longhaired soldiers who scorned the emperor's edicts and preached freedom. Dragontail banners lined the town square. There were firecrackers, cymbals and the thud of drums. The marketplace was a mass of people. They jostled around a platform where two soldiers gave a flowing display of swordsmanship.

The crowd fell quiet as the mounted archers trotted into the square. The old women shook their heads and clucked their disapproval. Young men gawked and jostled to get closer to the women soldiers.

Yen Lin raised her arm and the women reined to a halt. A man wearing sky-blue darted forward and held her bridle.

'Fetch your commander,' Yen Lin demanded as she dismounted.

Kong Liu stepped from the crowd and gave a mocking bow. 'I bid the gallant Yen Lin welcome,' he said in a warm baritone.

'Captain Kong honours me too much,' Yen Lin replied. She grinned and made a bow even more theatrical than Kong's.

Kong chuckled. 'You'll be surprised to learn your Captain Kong is now a colonel,' he announced. 'I have command of two thousand.'

'It's about time,' Yen Lin chuckled. She put her head close to Kong's. 'You're far too old to be a captain.'

'I'm too old to be a foot soldier,' Kong grumbled. He sought out Mei and waved to her as though she were a favourite niece.

Mei waved back but her smile faded as another figure stepped from the crowd.

Meng had grown taller and his shoulders had broadened. He had swapped his cotton tunic for black silk that shimmered as he moved. His trousers were black and tucked into Manchurian cavalry boots.

'Ah, Meng, my boy.' Kong put his arm across Meng's shoulder.

'Come and meet the only damned soldier who puts fear in this old fighter's heart.'

Meng put a hand to his chest and bowed. 'I am honoured, Lady,' he said. 'I hope to see your skills with the bow.'

Kong dismissed the comment with a snort.

'Skills, my boy? *Skills?* Only fighters have skills. Yen Lin's archers are here to look pretty and decorate our ruler's entourage.' His eyes sparkled. 'Call themselves archers? I'd match my newest recruit against any of these *girls.*'

Yen Lin's cheeks coloured.

'I think our brave colonel wants a contest,' she said. 'Maybe even a wager.'

Kong held up his hands as if in surrender. 'There are rules against gambling,' he said.

'Oh, modest wagers don't count,' Yen Lin mused. 'Five ounces of silver, no more. Unless you're afraid.'

'Afraid,' Kong growled. 'I wouldn't be afraid if it were fifty...'

'Then fifty it is,' Yen Lin snapped.

Kong paled. 'F-fifty?' he stammered.

'We can make it five hundred if you want,' Yen Lin said, arching an eyebrow.

Kong grinned and his eyes became sly.

'Five hundred?' he purred. 'Very well, I accept. Who is your champion?'

Jade threw her leg over her saddlebow and slid to the ground.

'What's this?' Kong demanded. 'The wager doesn't specify a woman, it specifies a *girl.*'

'You speak nonsense,' Yen Lin retorted. 'I have no girls.'

'I see a girl,' Kong said, nodding to Mei.

'She's a servant,' Yen Lin snorted. 'She is nothing. No more foolishness. Accept my champion or forfeit the wager.'

'Now we see the truth,' Kong said. He turned full circle and addressed the crowd. 'Would any man here wheedle out of a wager?'

'Take the challenge,' a voice called.

'Shoot or forfeit,' another shouted.

The crowd pressed closer. Yen Lin tried to speak but a chant of, '*Shoot, shoot, shoot, shoot,*' drowned her words. She turned on Kong and wagged her forefinger like a scolding *ahmah*.

Kong raised his arms. 'Silence,' he roared. 'Bring targets and clear a path.'

Soldiers pushed the crowd back, others brought two targets from behind the platform. They were wicker mannequins dressed in Imperial uniform. Fixed to their shoulders were bloody pigs' heads.

Kong grinned and rubbed his palms together.

'All is ready,' he said. 'Unless your champion isn't up to the job.'

'I accept the challenge,' Mei piped. The crowd roared its approval.

Kong smiled and walked around Mei like an inspecting officer.

'Brave girl,' he said. 'Braver than your commander, I think.'

Jade put her mouth close to Mei's ear. 'The bow's too heavy,' she whispered. 'Take mine.'

'No,' Mei said. 'It will bring you bad luck. You said so.'

Kong spoke to Yen Lin as though talking to a child. 'Don't look so miserable,' he said. 'Remember, I must use my newest recruit.' He paused then called, 'Soldier Besud.'

A man shouldered his way through the crowd and stood beside Kong. He had a flat face and small eyes. At his hip was a quiver of arrows. Slung across his back was a Mongolian bow.

'Besud was part of the Imperial garrison,' Kong said. 'Now he serves the Taiping cause.' He lowered his voice. 'Take care not to anger him, he's Mongolian.'

Yen Lin's eyes narrowed. 'You old bandit,' she growled. 'You've been planning this all morning.'

Kong grinned. 'Actually,' he said. 'I've been planning it all week. Do you have the silver with you?'

A soldier pinned heart-shaped markers on each target. He paced out the distance and used a stone to scrape a shooting line on the ground.

'Three arrows each at fifty paces,' Kong called. 'If it's a draw, we move back to sixty.'

Mei slipped her bow ring onto her thumb. She tested the bow's draw and her heart sank, it was more like iron than wood.

The crowd pressed forward.

'Who'll bet silver on the Mongolian,' someone called. There were shouts and the jangling of purses.

Besud leered at Mei and ran his tongue over his lips. He nocked an arrow. In an instant, the string sang and his arrow stood quivering in the centre of the heart-shaped marker. The Mongolian's face split in broken-toothed smile. He raised the bow and shot again. His second arrow stood quivering alongside the first. The third arrow flew from bow to target, striking above the other two shafts.

Besud scowled as the scorer bent over the marker. A hush fell over the marketplace. The scorer raised both arms, a hit.

Mei moved up to the line and pulled an arrow from her quiver. As she drew back the bowstring, her shoulders burned. She lowered the bow and took a deep breath. Again, she raised the bow, pulling hard on the string and pushing against the bow. At the moment of release, her arm trembled, shifting her aim. The arrow thudded home at the marker's edge.

The scorer inspected it and seconds later, raised both arms. A hit. The crowd's cheers filled the square.

Besud glowered those near him into silence.

Kong scowled. 'She must have nicked it,' he grumbled. 'Is this a trial of skill or a test of luck?'

Mei sensed movement and Jade's voice was soft in her ear. 'Don't let the bow steal your strength,' she whispered. 'At fifty paces it doesn't need the full draw.'

'Only shooters on the line,' Kong growled. 'Step away.'

Mei slotted her arrow onto the bowstring and drew it half way. She sighted and released. The arrow flew away.

The scorer went through the ritual of examining the target then declared a hit.

Mei shot her third arrow. The crowd roared their approval as the scorer confirmed a third hit.

Soldiers pushed back the crowd and the scorer scraped a new mark, sixty paces from the targets.

Mei shot first: three arrows, three hits.

Besud stepped up and equalled the score.

At seventy paces, Besud's first shot missed. His second and third cut the marker's edge.

Mei's first shot was low. A miss. She adjusted her aim and the second arrow cut the marker's bottom edge. Her shoulders were on fire. Her arms trembled. She nocked her third arrow and raised the bow. She released then shielded her eyes and squinted at the target. The arrow stood quivering at the marker's edge.

The scorer prodded at it and inspected it from different angles then he raised both arms, a hit. The score was level.

At eighty paces, the target marker was a white dot.

Besud grinned but as his arrow left the string, he growled his frustration. The scorer signalled a miss.

He shot again. Another miss.

On the third shot, he held his aim. A small vein throbbed at his temple but his arm was strong and steady. He released and the crowd fell silent. The scorer bent over the target then signalled a third miss.

Besud turned away, muttering.

'I declare a draw,' Kong called. 'All bets are off.'

'Easy, *Colonel*,' Yen Lin said, a light smile on her lips. 'My woman has yet to shoot.'

Kong gave a barking laugh. 'My man teethed on a bow,' he said. 'If he missed, the shot's impossible.'

'One shot,' Yen Lin said. 'Just one. If my woman misses, it's a draw. If she hits...' she shrugged and left the rest unsaid.

Kong scratched his chin. 'I don't know,' he said. He lowered his voice. 'Will you double the bet on this one arrow?'

'I haven't a pack big enough to carry so much silver,' Yen Lin scoffed. 'I'll do you a favour and keep it at five hundred. Are you ready, Mei?'

'Ready, Madam,' Mei called. The crowd was silent as she stepped up to the line.

Besud muttered dark chants. He twisted his fingers into the shape of horns and thrust his hand at Mei's face.

Mei nocked her arrow and stared at the distant target. This time, she must work the bow to its full power, nothing less would do. She pushed with all her strength against the stiffened grip. She drew back on the string. Her arm trembled. The arrowhead weaved from side to side.

'Relax, child,' Kong boomed. 'There's only five hundred ounces on this shot.'

'*Quiet!*' Yen Lin snapped.

Mei eased pressure off the string and lowered the bow. She took a moment to control her breathing. She focussed in on the target. The crowd, Yen Lin, the Mongolian, Kong Liu, they all became nothing. Her arm was steady, her breathing light. She clenched her teeth and brought the bow into the aim. She pulled

## THE SCHOLAR'S BLADE

back hard on the string. Her breath escaped in a hiss. Arrowhead and target became one. She released and the arrow floated to the target, flat and true. It thudded home.

The scorer held up both arms. A hit.

Joy flowed through Mei. She threw back her head and held her bow aloft. The women archers pressed around her, embracing her, pounding her back and her shoulders. Someone called her name. Mei's heart swelled. Tears stung her eyes. The women drew back and Mei looked into the face of her commander. She stood still and straight but could not control the smile fixed to her lips.

Yen Lin's face was unsmiling.

'You are young,' she said.

Mei struggled to catch her breath. 'I'll be fifteen in the New Year,' she answered.

Yen Lin shook her head. 'You're small.'

'I'll grow,' Mei said. There was an edge to her voice.

'And you are bold,' Yen Lin snapped.

Mei stared ahead and remained silent.

Yen Lin scowled. 'Too young, too small, and too bold,' she growled. She tugged at Mei's tunic. 'And look at this,' she grumbled. 'This uniform looks like a sack. I'll not have my archers dressed like yokels.'

'Madam?' Mei's voice was small.

Yen Lin smiled. The smile softened her face, giving her the look of a younger woman.

'It seems I have a new archer,' she said, putting her arm across Mei's shoulder. She spoke to Jade. 'I'm taking your servant,' she said. 'Make sure you teach the next one more humility.'

In a daze, Mei slung the bow across her shoulders and backhanded a tear from her cheek. Tonight she would lay her bed mat in the barracks of Yen Lin's mounted archers.

# 8

In 1853, the start of the Year of the Ox fell in February.

New Year's Day was a time for orange blossoms and firecrackers. For the old folk, there were warm dumplings and for the children, red packets stuffed with money. On the second day, people paid respects to their ancestors. On the third day, the Taiping army marched from Wuchang. They turned east in two giant columns that straddled the Yangtze. They advanced, ignoring Imperial strongholds and attacking the lesser towns, looting treasuries and drawing in more recruits.

Within the month, Taiping scouts gazed on the ancient walls of Nanking.

The army halted. Their camp stretched for miles along the Yangtze's banks. It bustled with soldiers, stablemasters, farriers, quartermasters, wagonmasters and armourers. Smiths set up clanking forges. Sparks flew from armourers' wheels. Fletchers turned arrows on pedal lathes. Commanders bellowed orders. Soldiers exercised.

And the general staff prepared orders of battle.

Yen Lin pulled herself into her saddle. Her orderly unfurled the yellow battle flag and the mounted archers trotted from the camp. For half a day they rode northeast. At first the road was easy. Later, it wound into hills and became treacherous with loose gravel. At each bend, the column halted and archers

## THE SCHOLAR'S BLADE

probed ahead, checking for ambush. Finally, they crested a hill and halted in a meadow bounded on three sides by forest pines. Below them, the Yangtze was a mile wide, a glittering serpent that slid through China's heartland. Between the archers and the river lay Nanking, cultural home of the *Han* Chinese.

Mei shielded her eyes against the sun and gazed upon the vista before her. The city was a place of boulevards and pagodas. There were palaces and grand *yamens*. There were gardens and lakes. The city walls stretched into the far distance.

In the city's eastern quarter, the Manchu citadel was a square of dark granite. At its centre stood a palace with crimson columns. Gleaming tiles of emerald green covered the roof and gilded devil hooks protected its eaves. A lump grew in Mei's chest. The palace had once been home to the Ming emperors but for more than two hundred years, Manchurian walls had held it captive.

Yen Lin snapped open a telescope and scanned the walls.

'Make a note, Mei. By my estimate the walls are at least twenty miles round.' She lowered the telescope and pointed to the northwest where a narrow section of wall jutted out towards the river.

'See that?' she said. 'It's like a little orphan just waiting to be gobbled up.'

She swung the telescope to the south wall.

'And there,' she added. 'By the bridge outside the south gate, the porcelain tower still stands.'

'I'll sketch a plan,' Mei said, pulling a scroll and a charcoal stick from her saddlebag.

Yen Lin took a sharp breath. '*Wait*,' she snapped. She stood in her saddle and twisted left and right, craning her neck.

'What is it?' Mei asked.

'*Hush!*' Yen Lin hissed. She pulled her bow from her shoulders and nocked an arrow.

The others sensed it too. The archers drew together and pulled arrows from their quivers.

Mei peered about her. All was still; all was quiet. There was no birdsong. No snuffling of little animals in the undergrowth.

Nothing.

'Move back to the road,' Yen Lin said, her voice tight. 'Slowly now.'

From their left came the blast of a horn and a troop of Imperial cavalry burst into the meadow.

Yen Lin paled. 'Back,' she cried. 'Back to the road.'

The archers turned about and spurred for the road. Ahead of them, a line of infantry ran from the trees, blocking the way.

'Enemy on two fronts,' Yen Lin cried.

The archers wheeled into two lines. One line faced the cavalry, the other line faced the infantry.

'*Shoot at will!*' Yen Lin shouted.

Bowstrings sang. Arrows hissed into both enemy lines.

Several Imperial cavalrymen threw up their arms and toppled back over their saddle cantles. A horse fell, legs thrashing. Another horse barrelled into the fallen beast and toppled forward, throwing its rider. More arrows flew into the cavalry line. Horses and men screamed. The charge fell apart as riders veered to the flanks and others milled about the centre.

'*Engage infantry!*' Yen Lin called.

The archers moved into a tight spearhead formation. A swarm of arrows droned into the infantry line.

Men cried out, staggered and fell.

'*Forward!*' Yen Lin shouted.

The archers gripped tight with their knees and advanced at a brisk trot. Someone called their battle shout. More took up the cry and the women's voices rose to a shriek. They stretched into a full charge and piled into the infantry line.

Mei bent over her saddlebow. She nocked and shot; nocked and shot again. Hands grabbed at her leg. A spear tip whispered past her cheek. She shot an arrow into an upturned face. Off to her right, a horse plunged and a woman screamed. A soldier clawed at Mei's bridle. She kicked the horse forward, barging the soldier aside.

Then she was through, lying flat against the horse's neck, slapping its rump with her bow. Yellow uniforms closed around her. Lather foamed at the horses' necks. Blood flowed from their nostrils. Still, they galloped on.

At length, Yen Lin raised her arm and the archers reined to a halt. The horses were wheezing. Sweat foamed at their necks and flanks.

Mei slung her bow across her shoulders and put her hands on her hips. She tipped back her head and sucked air deep into her lungs. Her heart pounded. Her eyes glistened. Never had she felt more alive.

'*Form column!*' Yen Lin called.

The women moved into position and Yen Lin trotted the column's length, noting gaps in the line and exchanging words with the archers. She halted beside Mei.

'You did well,' she said, reaching out and touching Mei's arm. 'Now we must report our sightings.'

Mei grinned, pleased by her commander's praise. 'We must wait a little,' she said. 'Jade's not here.' She looked back along the road. 'You know how she rides. She'll be here soon.' Mei looked to the other women but none would meet her eyes.

Yen Lin gripped Mei's hand.

'Today, we leave nine archers in the field,' she said. 'All were fine comrades, Jade is in gallant company.'

'No,' Mei said. She shook her head and her smile became a frown. 'Jade won't leave me.'

Yen Lin pulled her horse's head round and trotted to the front of the column.

'I'll wait,' Mei shouted. 'She'll catch up. You'll see.'

An archer reached for Mei's bridle but Mei jerked the horse's head away.

Another archer laid her hand on Mei's arm. 'It's the way of war,' she said. 'Once we were forty-one, now we are thirty-two,' she said. 'We must complete our mission. Jade's watching. We mustn't let her down.'

Mei turned her face away so no one would see her tears. This time, she did not resist as the archer took her reins and led her from the mountain.

All morning, the gunners sweated on the mountain road, prodding their artillery horses and lending their own weight to the gun carriages. There were ten guns. They were old pieces, their muzzles forged in the shape of dragons' jaws.

Ahead stretched a line of infantry. Behind them came more carts, creaking under the weight of powder, shot and water barrels.

'I've a silver coin says your gun explodes at the first shot,' the cart's driver called to his gun captain.

'And my silver coin says I'll spill your guts if you wish me any more bad luck,' the gunner snapped back.

The driver pulled a face. 'Just being sociable,' he said. He fell silent and slapped his cane against the artillery horse's rump.

A sweating soldier ran to them and leaned against the cart's wheel while he caught his breath. 'Can't you move any quicker?' he grumbled.

The gunner shrugged. 'This is a carthorse not a warhorse,' he snorted. 'You're welcome to lend your weight to the gun carriage.'

'Move as quickly as you can,' the soldier growled. He turned and strode away.

For the rest of the morning, the column wound into the hills until they came to a meadow bounded on three sides by pine trees. The infantry spread out and took up position near the tree line. The gunners wheeled the guns into line abreast while workers dug gun pits and built up earthworks. Quartermasters went from gun to gun, issuing powder and shot. The gunner and his driver stood side by side. Below them sprawled the city of Nanking.

'*Wah*,' the driver said. 'Is that not the most beautiful sight between heaven and earth?'

The gunner set his mouth in a grim frown. 'Between heaven and anywhere else,' he replied.

In silence, they drank in the vista of palaces, pagodas and gardens. The gunner spoke first. 'Yes,' he said. 'It is indeed beautiful. Now come and help, I've guns to sight.'

The sentries uncrossed their spears and allowed Kong Liu to enter the royal pavilion. Meng followed, clutching a bundle of maps. They found themselves in a silken reception chamber. The air was heavy with the scent of camphor and from somewhere, there drifted the tinkling music of a *qin*. The chamber was empty but for a campaign table.

'Will he make us wait?' Meng whispered.

As if to answer, the drapes fluttered and a woman stepped through. She cast down her eyes and held open the drape for Hoong Hsiu-chuan. Behind him was a man dressed in rags. He had wild hair and an unkempt beard. His eyes stared wide and he was chanting in some unknown tongue.

Meng stood slack-jawed. Kong grabbed his neck and forced down his head.

'Keep your eyes down until he speaks,' Kong hissed and for long minutes, they stood with their eyes on the floor.

'The Heavenly King welcomes his Loyal Colonel,' Hoong intoned at last. 'You may look on me whilst you report.'

Kong drew himself to his full height. 'The Imperial garrison numbers fifty thousand,' he said. 'But their troops are poorly trained and lack battle experience.'

He nodded to Meng who moved to the table and laid out the maps. Hoong stepped forward and bent over them. They showed Nanking's outer wall as a series of disconnected barriers.

'The outer defences are a joke.' Kong said. 'The inner wall looks more formidable, but it can't be defended. Not with fifty thousand troops, not with a hundred thousand.'

Hoong studied the map in silence. A lake protected the northern defences. To the south, the wall followed a manmade watercourse.

'There's twenty-five miles of wall,' Kong said, tracing his finger around the inner defences. 'And the Imperials must man every inch of it.' He flashed a grin. 'We, however, can concentrate our forces where we please.'

He ran his hand over the map. 'We have artillery in the hills and enough men to mount diversionary attacks.'

He jabbed his finger onto a western section where the wall jutted out like a spur towards the watercourse.

'But that's where we should launch our main thrust,' he said. 'It's the hardest to reinforce and it's close to the river. We can assemble our men upstream and surprise the defenders with a waterborne assault.' He rubbed his hands together. 'The ground's soft. I've already started mining the foundations. I'll have that wall down before we attack.'

'A fine plan,' Hoong said. He was silent for a moment then he looked Kong Liu in the face. 'Is it true the men call you General?'

he asked.

Kong reddened. 'It... it is true, Sire,' he stammered. 'They mean no harm. They...'

Hoong fluttered his sleeve. 'The men may have their general,' he said. 'I'll have my clerks draw up the appointment. You are dismissed while I consult my Celestial Father.'

Kong's mouth fell open. 'Sire,' he protested. 'The army is ready. We need your orders now.'

'Your new rank emboldens you, Kong Liu,' Hoong snapped. 'Remember, I am still your commander. You will wait outside while I commune with our Lord and protector.'

Kong Liu made to speak then thought better of it. He turned and with Meng scuttling behind, he strode from the reception chamber.

The sappers worked bare-chested and on their knees. Their sweat mingled with the grime already caked to their bodies. In the lamplight, their eyes showed white against dirt-blackened faces.

The shoring above their heads groaned and a trickle of soil spattered onto the tunnel floor.

The sappers froze, their eyes fixed on the roof.

'Hurry,' the gangmaster whispered. He pulled a cloth from his britches and mopped his face.

'Won't be long now,' called one of the sappers, a wiry ex-miner.

'*Hush!*' the gangmaster hissed. 'If these defenders were half decent soldiers, we'd all be dead by now.'

'At least we'd have a proper burial,' the sapper chortled.

'Where's the measuring twine?' the gangmaster whispered.

He ran his hands over the floor and grasped a thin strip of platted hemp. He gave it a tug and grunted with satisfaction as it tightened against the marker stake, back at the entrance. He pressed the twine against the tunnel face.

'That's it,' he whispered. 'One hundred paces.' He looked up at the roof. 'We're directly under the wall.'

The sappers lowered their tools and moved back from the face.

'Come,' the gangmaster said. 'We've done our bit. Let the explosives men see how they like crawling around down here.'

The sappers grinned at one another and made their way back to the entrance.

The parapet above Nanking's southern gate was thick with Imperial helmets. Spear tips glittered along the wall and catcalls split the air. From the battlements, a flight of arrows arced high and thumped into the ground fifty paces before the Taiping line.

'Our Imperial masters seem nervous,' Yen Lin commented.

'They should be,' Kong Liu grunted. He loosened his sword in his scabbard. 'How much longer?' he grumbled to no one in particular.

Meng rested his left hand on his sword grip. 'Relax, father,' he said. 'You'll unsettle the men.'

Kong turned his attention to the day's task. Ahead, a stone bridge led to Nanking's southern gate. He nodded to an elegant pagoda standing by the bridge. It rose to a height of nine segmented stories, towering above the city walls. Its beams were dark cedar and its facings were gleaming porcelain.

'It's been there four hundred years,' Kong said. 'Any half decent officer would have demolished it the moment he took command.'

'It's beautiful,' Yen Lin mused. 'Imperial love of beauty works in our favour. I have some clever eyes in that tower.'

'I hope she has her wits about her,' Kong growled.

'She had enough wit to take your silver,' Yen Lin chuckled. 'Watch the middle level for signal flags. Blue means enemy attacking from the east. White means defend the west.'

Kong looked about. 'Where's our main force?' he muttered.

'The generals don't consult me,' Yen Lin answered. 'But the wharves are jammed with soldiers.'

Kong smiled. 'So it's agreed,' he said. 'The main force goes in from the water.'

From the west, there was a rumble like rolling thunder. A cloud of smoke and dust rose and drifted towards the river.

'By all the Gods,' Yen Lin gasped. She pointed to the distant section of wall. Where there had once been stout masonry, there was a gap.

'It's down,' she cried. 'It's been mined.'

From the eastern hills, there was a bang followed by the howl of shot. Deep in the city, flame danced skyward.

Swarms of Taiping assault boats moved into the watercourse. Bare-chested men bent to the sweeps. The sweeps dipped and rose to rhythmic chants called from the helms. The boats raced in close to the city walls and grounded on the bank close to the breach.

'It's started,' Kong said. His voice was a harsh whisper.

'We'll cover your assault,' Yen Lin said. 'Any heads showing above those battlements will have arrows sticking in them.' She moved to join her archers.

'*Stand to!*' Kong bellowed. He cast his eyes over his regiment. Their uniforms were bright and crisp. Their weapons glinted in the sun. War banners floated above their heads. On each face was a tight smile. They were fighting dogs straining to be free.

Kong drew his sword. 'Are you ready, brothers?' he bellowed.

'*Ready!*' the regiment roared.

Kong pointed his sword towards the city gate. 'Then,

brothers,' he cried, 'come with me.'

Kong raised his sword and marched towards the wall. Behind him, there was a huge roar as his two thousand joined their voices to his. They hefted their weapons, they roared their battle cry.

And together, they charged Nanking's southern gate.

From the porcelain tower, Mei watched Kong's advance. She held two signal flags: one white, the other blue. She screwed shut her eyes. 'Blue is east; West is white. Blue is east; West is white.'

Ladders rattled against the buttress and sky-blue tunics swarmed up them.

Imperials stepped forward to meet the attackers. There was the drone of arrows. Defenders reeled back, pinned through the neck, chest and head.

Mei ran her eyes along the battlements. Smoke drifted between her and the wall.

'Blue is east,' she said again. *'Blue is east.'*

Kong Liu vaulted over the balustrade and spitted a defender on his blade. Other Taipings clambered over the wall and formed a fighting wedge. Smoke drifted in, blocking Kong's view along the parapet.

*'Meng,'* he bellowed.

'Father.'

'Take your men and secure the west flank.'

'Then what?' Meng asked.

'Damned if I know,' Kong snapped. 'Just do it.'

Something caught Kong's eye. From the pagoda there fluttered a blue flag.

'Blood and damnation,' he muttered. 'Enemy from the east,' he bellowed. 'Meng, cancel that order. To me brothers, *to me!'*

From out of the smoke, a column of Imperials advanced five

abreast. They held heavy-bladed infantry spears lowered to the attack position.

'Let's have them, brothers!' Kong roared. 'To me, *to me!*' He raised his sword and charged the Imperial line.

In Nanking's Manchu citadel, General Chinduku, the Imperial commander, closed his eyes and cursed the Gods. In every sector, commanders were demanding reinforcements.

At first, he had rushed reserves to the northeast only to divert them back to the southern defences. Now there were reports of assaults on the south and western walls.

Regimental runners lined up outside his door. Each clutched a strip of paper listing desperate requests from panicked commanders.

There was the moan of cannon shot. An explosion rattled the walls. Dust drifted from the rafters. Somewhere, a staff officer was ranting at a sentry. General Chinduku slumped across his maps and buried his head in his hands. He had built his garrison on a network of battle plans and defence drills. But now they meant nothing.

Now, everything had turned to manure.

In the southwest suburbs, the defenders melted away. Thousands of Taipings scoured parks and buildings, killing anyone in Imperial uniform. They searched the temples and outhouses. They broke into homes and dragged young men from their families. Some they stripped, searching for old battle scars. Others they just killed. As dusk fell, Taipings advancing from the west met their comrades moving up from the east.

On the south wall, Kong Liu massaged his sword arm and watched smoke drift above the rooftops. He turned to his companion.

'Your girls did well,' he said.

'I have no *girls,*' Yen Lin chided. Her lips curled in a wicked smile. 'As you should know.'

Kong chuckled. 'I'll give you that,' he said. 'Where's Mei? She did me fine service today.'

'She's with her comrades, she still mourns her friend,' Yen Lin answered. Concern furrowed her brow. 'You seem short of men. Did you take many casualties?'

'No,' Kong answered. He nodded towards the tower beyond the wall. 'Thanks to your *women* we beat off the counter attack. My men are with Meng. He's clearing the streets below us.'

Yen Lin's face darkened. 'I know you're fond of him,' she said. 'But...'

'Out with it,' Kong growled. 'Just remember, he took an arrow for me.'

'It's nothing,' Yen Lin said. She raised her eyes to Kong's. 'Forgive my foolishness. Let us enjoy our victory and give thanks for another day's life.'

'Let's not invite ill luck,' said Kong 'Tomorrow we assault the Manchu Citadel.'

'Yes,' said Yen Lin. 'I had almost forgotten. Tomorrow we face the citadel.'

Dawn rose over the Yangtze, and in the city, Taiping patrols stalked empty streets. On the southern wall, the men were hollow-eyed and silent. There was the rumble of ironbound wheels as horse-drawn cannon rolled through the south gate. Behind them came lines of soldiers, their faces grim, their spear tips bright.

'*Stand to!*' Kong bellowed.

The soldiers shuffled to their feet. Their uniforms were bloody and torn. Fatigue dulled their eyes but soon they would follow his banner and hurl themselves against the citadel. Kong felt a surge of brotherhood for these men.

Today, some would fall. But all would fight.

In the citadel war room, General Chinduku stood at a table piled with battle plans. Gathered round him were his field commanders.

'What is happening?' he barked.

The officers looked to one another, each wanting another to speak first.

'You,' the general said, pointing to a man at random. 'What's the state of your sector?'

The officer swallowed hard. 'Defences are... are strong and morale is high,' he stammered.

'And you?' Chinduku demanded of another.

'We will line the walls with rebel heads,' the officer snapped.

'Will you, indeed?' the general growled. He lowered his eyes and spoke gently. 'Are your families within the citadel?' he asked.

They all nodded.

'When...' The general paused and corrected himself. '*If* the Taipings break through, let every man return to his quarters.' He raised his hand, stilling their questions. 'We mustn't let our wives and children fall into enemy hands. It would be a dreadful disgrace.' He clenched his fists and stared at each man in turn. 'Do not let me down,' he said. 'Do your duty for the emperor, for me and for your families. Now, return to your posts and face what you must with courage.'

In silence, the officers filed from the war room. After they had gone, the general slumped into his chair. He growled under his breath. The growl rose to a roar. He hammered his fists against the table and with a sweep of his arm, brushed the battle plans onto the floor.

Over the years, the citizens of Nanking had built homes and warehouses alongside the citadel walls. Now the Taipings filled these homes and warehouses with gunpowder. They lit fuses and scuttled to safety.

When they came, the explosions jarred the bones and numbed the ears. Gouts of flame shot skywards. Smoke rolled along the lanes, stinging eyes and throats. Taiping soldiers crouched and shielded their heads as broken masonry clattered against nearby rooftops and cobblestones.

The artillery set to work. The citadel walls shuddered as barrage after barrage hammered into them. The western wall was first to break. The Taipings raised their battle flags, screamed their war cries and stormed the breach.

But no enemy rose to meet them. There was no clash of steel, no bang of musket. Instead, there was only the roaring crackle of many fires. Smoke poured from the citadel buildings and drifted across the compound.

Kong kicked at a discarded helmet and it clattered away from him.

'Where are they?' Meng asked.

Kong turned down the corners of his mouth and pointed to the blazing buildings. 'Can't you smell it?' he growled.

'I don't understand,' Meng said.

'Best an honourable death at their own hand than disgrace at ours,' Kong said.

'Is it over?' Meng asked.

'Some will be hiding,' Kong replied. 'We'll be winkling them out for days. But yes, it's over.'

Meng gazed about him. Through the smoke, the crimson pillars of the Ming Emperors' palace rose lofty and majestic.

'It's over,' Meng said, his voice hushed. He looked at Kong.

# THE SCHOLAR'S BLADE

'Now what do we do?'

Kong shrugged. 'We enjoy our victory,' he said. He pulled the scarf from his brows and pressed it over his mouth and nose.

But still, he could not block out the smell.

Seated on his gilded palanquin, Hoong Hsiu-chuan, King for ten thousand years and younger son of Almighty God, made triumphant procession into Nanking. He wore the yellow robes of Imperial authority and his headdress carried the emblem of a rampant dragon. Looking neither left nor right, he gazed into the far distance.

Ahead, marched an honour guard of five thousand. Behind him, rode thirty-two women archers, their yellow uniforms complemented by matching parasols. At the Heavenly King's right hand, the loyal general, Kong Liu kept his eyes on the crowd and his hand on his sword.

There were firecrackers and the reedy clarion of suonas. The clash of cymbals countered the *thrub* of dragon drums. As Hoong Hsiu-chuan passed, the people of Nanking prostrated themselves and knocked their foreheads against the ground.

On March 29th 1853, which was the forty-ninth day of the Year of the Ox, Hoong Hsiu-chuan proclaimed himself Heavenly King and first ruler of the Taiping dynasty.

He had founded his Heavenly Kingdom.

# EPISODE 2

## THE CHANGELING

# THE SCHOLAR'S BLADE

# 9

## NANKING, TAIPING CAPITAL
## SEVEN YEARS LATER, SPRING 1860

THE AUDIENCE chamber smelled of camphor and incense. It had a high ceiling supported by pillars of polished spruce. The floor was maple and gracing the walls were paintings of misted mountains, waterfalls, bamboo groves, and slim pagodas. Against the far wall, a gilded throne stood on a broad dais. The throne was empty, as it had been for the last two hours.

Waiting in the audience chamber was a collection of courtiers, attendants and princes.

*Princes!* General Kong Liu despaired of them. There was Abundance Prince and the self-styled Brave Prince. There were the Blessings Prince, Philosopher Prince, Scriptures Prince and many others. They stood in small knots, their heads together, voices hushed.

Kong did well to hide his irritation. Where were the warriors who should be the real princes? Dead or banished, replaced by these hangers-on who spent their days plotting small victories over one another. Kong gave his ruler credit for that, Hoong Hsiu-chuan used their petty rivalries to check their ambitions. But by all the gods, how the palace air had turned poisonous! He sighed and a voice of buttered honey chided him.

'Does our loyal general find the day tiresome?'

Kong regarded the man who stood next to him. He was

resplendent in court dress. His robe was scarlet and over it he wore a jacket of orange silk, embroidered with dragons and stars. He held the title Wise Prince.

Kong stifled an urge to turn his back on the man. Wise Prince? Prince of Bootlickers more like. Instead, he asked 'Will our heavenly ruler grace us any time today?'

'Calm yourself,' Wise Prince replied. 'Our lord's review of the testaments is at a crucial stage. Each day brings new evidence of his divinity.'

Not for the first time, Kong pondered the Taiping dilemma: was their ruler a messiah or a lunatic?

'It seems your wait is over,' Wise Prince said.

There was the thump of boots and two soldiers took position beside the throne. Their uniforms were a blend of purple and green. Their spear tips glittered.

Set back from the throne, a concealed door opened and Hoong Hsiu-chuan, celestial ruler of the Taiping empire entered the chamber. He walked with his eyes fixed above his line of sight. Behind him came a procession of crimson-robed mystics. They chanted in no known tongue, their hair wild, their eyes crazed.

'Hail, Heavenly King,' Wise Prince called. He fell to his knees and spread-eagled himself on the floor.

The man named Brave Prince knelt. Tears welled in his eyes. 'Glorify our lord!' he sobbed.

Around the chamber, the voices of princes, courtiers and lesser officials resonated off the ceiling, walls and floor. Each prince and courtier tried to outdo the others in praise. Their voices became louder and louder until they all blended into a deafening, formless babble.

Hoong Hsiu-chuan mounted the dais and glared them all into silence.

Kong dropped to one knee and lowered his eyes. He fumed

in silence as Hoong drew a scroll from his sleeve and studied it from under furrowed brows. At length, he tossed it aside and ran his hands over his thighs, smoothing out his robe.

'Shield Prince may stand,' he intoned.

The man named Shield Prince stood. His face paled and he cast his eyes around as though seeking an ally.

'Attend on me and take care,' Hoong snapped. 'Speak honestly. Do we march west to support our disciples in Anjing or do we move against the barbarian's eastern port?'

Shield Prince placed his hand on his chest and bowed. 'We should go west, Sire,' he said. 'If Anjing falls, the emperor will be at our gates within months.'

'His troops have been at these gates before,' Hoong Hsiu-chuan answered. He nodded towards Kong Liu. 'Our loyal general crushed their last siege.'

Kong Liu stood and looked Hoong in the face.

'I must agree with Shield Prince,' he said. 'I crushed only the Anhwei Army. The enemy at Anjing are special, they're Zeng Kuo-fan's boys.' He allowed himself a wry smile. 'They'll tear down these walls with their bare hands if old Zeng asks them to.'

'My lords, I expected better.' Hoong's voice became testy. 'In truth, the decision is made. We rule lands in east and southern China but without stable trade, we cannot consolidate. We have no ports worth speaking of and receive only a trickle of modern arms from barbarian smugglers. I command you to march east, to Shanghai.'

Kong's neck burned. 'But Sire, why was I not consulted?'

'Enough,' Hoong snapped. 'Who are you to question me?'

Kong bowed and bit his tongue.

Hoong fixed Kong with a flat glare.

'First, you will establish a forward base at Soochow,' he said. 'From there, it will be a simple matter to bring Shanghai's

Chinese quarter into my realm.'

Before Kong could speak, Hoong closed his eyes and showed his open palm.

'Do not interrupt,' he said. 'You claim to be a soldier, and soldiers do not debate, they obey.'

For a few heartbeats, the only sound was the rasping of Kong Liu's breath.

'Sire...' The word sprang from his lips like a rebuke. He paused and softened his tone. 'Sire, do you think the foreigners will line the roads and cheer as we march in?'

'The foreigners are weak and greedy,' Hoong replied. 'They want tea and silk; we want rifles and cannon. They are uncivilised but they are not stupid. They will not fight, they will trade.'

'They will fight,' Kong insisted. 'And when they do I will have no choice but to crush them.'

Hoong slapped his hand against his breast. 'How can they fight me?' He snorted. '*Me!*' They worship the one God who is my father.' His voice rose; his lips were white. 'They direct prayers to Jesus, my heavenly brother.' He pointed a quivering finger at Kong. 'You will not harm a single barbarian,' he commanded. You will attack only the Chinese quarter. You will leave the foreign settlements alone.'

Kong arched his eyebrows. 'But how can I wring concessions unless I attack them?' he pleaded.

Hong's voice shook. 'I need their weapons, not their blood, at least not until we are in Peking.'

He softened his voice. 'Kong Liu, you are my most loyal and noble general. When the foreigners see your cannon on the Chinese quarter's walls, they will sue for peace.'

Kong Liu sighed. 'So it is decided?'

'It is decided.' Hoong picked a scrap of lint from his robe. He took a moment to examine it then dropped it on the floor. 'You will assemble the army,' he continued. 'You will take Soochow then march on Shanghai.'

Kong Liu bowed and left his argument unspoken. Hoong Hsiu-chuan was no stranger to battle and on one point he was right, it was not a soldier's job to debate. But the foreigners were arrogant. There would be a fight, Kong was certain of it. And when the fight came, General Kong Liu would do his soldier's duty. He would crush the barbarians and drive them from the good earth of China.

In Nanking's central plaza, between the Ming emperor's palace and the walls of the Manchu citadel, five thousand soldiers knelt in prayer. Overlooking the plaza was a granite tower and from its galleries, silk-clad men and women looked down at the soldiers. The men boasted of old victories while the women hid their smiles behind silk fans and searched the ranks for the most handsome warriors.

'Amen.'

The preacher's voice carried across the plaza and with a rumble, the five thousand rose to their feet. They had been farmers, scholars, craftsmen and merchants. There were more than a few brigands among them too, but now they shared unquestioning devotion to one general. They were the Taiping elite. They were the personal brigade of General Kong Liu.

At the plaza's edge, Kong Liu sat astride a Han Hsiu warhorse. The horse shook its mane and pawed at the flagstones. Kong whispered into its ear and the beast calmed.

Kong had swapped his court attire for a campaign jacket of sky-blue and britches of raw black cotton. Pride swelled his heart as he ran his eyes over his brigade. All but a few were dressed in Kong's sky-blue. The officers wore silk; the junior ranks, cotton. The hair of new recruits brushed their collars while the veterans' hair hung loose about their shoulders. Above their heads fluttered an array of banners. Each bore the name of a unit commander: Wu, So, Yung and many more.

Some soldiers carried matchlocks, there was a spattering of muskets and even a few rifles, but most carried spears and broadswords. This was an army of steel.

Among the sky-blue was a knot of one hundred men, mounted on black geldings. Their tunics and britches were black. Fluttering above their heads was a dragon tail banner of black silk with the character 'Meng' picked out in gold thread. The geldings tossed their heads and chewed at their bits as though eager to be away.

Kong acknowledged Meng with a smile and beckoned him forward.

Meng's eyes gleamed; his teeth showed white.

'Our force is ready,' he said. 'We will crush all who stand before us.'

'Indeed, my boy,' Kong replied. He nodded towards the horsemen dressed in black. 'They look like they could bring us victory on their own,' he said.

'I recruited them from the *Nian* people,' Meng replied. 'They are the finest horsemen in all China and have no love for the emperor.'

Kong's brows furrowed. 'The *Nian* horsemen are all bandits,' he said, shaking his head. 'Can you trust them?'

'They are fierce fighters,' Meng said. 'And they are loyal to me. Give me your orders and they will obey.'

Kong seemed deep in thought. 'Our force is mighty,' he said. 'But it is a lumbering beast. I need eyes and ears to help see the way ahead.'

'My Black Dragons move quickly and strike hard,' Meng replied. 'Let us be your eyes and ears.'

Kong nodded. 'Do you have enough supplies for a few days in the field?'

'I do,' Meng answered. 'I can leave now.'

'Then do so, my boy. Sense out what lies ahead and report back only to me. Do you understand? Only to me.'

'I understand, Father.'

Kong reached out to touch Meng's arm. 'Be gentle with the people,' he said. 'We must have no enemies but the Imperials.' His voice hardened. 'Do you understand, Meng? None but the Imperials.'

A flash of annoyance darkened Meng's face. In an instant, it was gone.

'I promise,' he said then he wheeled away.

As Meng rejoined his men, Kong spurred his horse forward. A roar echoed from the ancient walls as he trotted into the plaza. A hush fell as he reined to a halt but Kong had prepared no speech. Instead, he drew his sword and raised it above his head. He stood in his stirrups and swept the blade in a slow arc until it pointed southeast. His voice broke as he shouted just one word.

'Shanghai!'

A cheer washed through the plaza. The soldiers banged their spear hafts on the courtyard paving. They beat the ground faster and faster until the drumming of their spears merged into a rolling thunder. At a signal from the guard commander, the drumming stopped and for a heartbeat there was crushing silence. Then each man raised his weapon to the sky and five thousand voices gave vent.

'SHANGHAI!'

At the rear, dragon drums started a throbbing cadence. Cymbal players took up the counter-rhythm. Dozens of bugle-like *suonas* blasted out a reedy clarion. Dragon-tail banners fluttered above the soldiers' heads. Massed spear tips shimmered in the sun. With a groan, the city gates swung open and strings of firecrackers exploded in a cacophony of celebration. A soldier began to sing. Others joined him. Soon, five thousand voices swelled and their song filled the boulevards and lanes.

They were the victorious warriors of *Taiping Tien Kwoh*. They were masters of a domain stretching from the Hunan Plain to the East China Sea. They had marched from Kwangsi to Nanking and scattered all before them. They had conquered great stretches of Anhwei, Hupei, Chekiang and Kiangsu provinces. They were invincible and they were marching east.

East to Shanghai.

Kong's five thousand was just a small part of the rebel host. Beyond the city's northern gate, a force of one hundred thousand stood ready. They marched east in a great snaking column. They skirted Tai Lake, whose mirror surface reflected green hills and an azure sky. They sang songs of their homelands, each regiment competing with others to sing the loudest. They marched through rice pastures more lush than even the Kwangtung veterans had seen.

Everywhere, the Imperials fell back. Every day, Meng's messengers carried reports of distant horsemen who galloped away as soon as the Black Dragon's gave chase.

The Taiping host marched on. They sang louder and their pace increased. They were the Taiping army and they were eager for victory.

Seven days after leaving Nanking, General Kong Liu rode unopposed into Soochow.

In Soochow's city records hall, Kong Liu tossed his helmet to an aide and cast his eyes about the chamber. The floor was a litter of scrolls and ledgers. A storage rack had toppled onto a work counter and lay at a perilous angle. Kong picked a random scroll from the floor then discarded it. He groaned and turned to the aide. 'I want these records catalogued and stored by week's end,' he ordered.

He walked to a counter and beckoned another aide who laid several maps before him. *Ah, maps,* Kong thought, a good one was worth an extra regiment.

The aide unfurled a map of Shanghai and Kong bent over it. It showed the city standing on the west bank of the Huangpu River. The Chinese quarter was a mile in diameter and looked like a flattened apricot. Thick walls surrounded it and strong towers protected its gates. The foreign settlements were larger but were home to just a few thousand Westerners. Would they defend the Chinese quarter?

According to Nanking's intelligence reports, the French were interested only in their mistresses, the British would bluster but do nothing and the Americans would put business before anything.

Kong growled under his breath. Damn the intelligence reports, his own spies learned more from reading Shanghai's broadsheets. They reported French troopships moored in the Huangpu, British soldiers billeted ashore and armed steamers patrolling the waterways around Shanghai. More troubling were the stories of American mercenaries courting the city merchants.

With a sweep of his forearm, Kong cleared the counter and unfurled a larger map. North of Shanghai, the Yangtze Delta formed a natural barrier. Sixty miles to the south, Hangchow Bay formed another. The two barriers were like the jaws of a nutcracker with Shanghai nestled between them.

Kong should have felt reassured but between the Yangtze and Hankow Bay lay sixty miles of marshy scrubland, crisscrossed by a spider's web of waterways, creeks and streams. With his army of one hundred thousand, Kong had to hold Soochow and secure that sixty-mile front.

Now his mighty force did not seem so formidable.

He turned his attention back to the map and considered where best to anchor his flanks. A Taiping garrison stationed where the Huangpu flowed into the Yangtze would choke the city's supply line. To the south, a decent sized force would deter an Imperial landing at Hangchow Bay.

With the flanks decided, Kong turned to the question of the centre. He needed a solid base from where to launch his attack. His fingers lingered over two dots, marking the towns of Sungkiang and Chingpu. They lay southwest of Shanghai and of the two, he preferred Sungkiang: it had a moat and sturdy walls. Navigable waterways connected it to the surrounding countryside.

*Yes!* That town was the key. Take Sungkiang and Shanghai was his.

Kong massaged his temples. Speed was everything. Tomorrow he would send columns north and south to secure his flanks.

'First the flanks, then the centre.' He chuckled, realising he had spoken aloud.

The flanks would be easy but Sungkiang was a fortress town and the surrounding landscape hid some nasty traps. The Huangpu ran just a few miles south of the town and the Imperials might outflank him. He needed clever eyes on the Huangpu riverbank to report any Imperial movements. But where on the riverbank?

He stabbed his finger down onto the map. *There.* Just a few miles south of Sungkiang, on the banks of the Huangpu was the village of Sishun. Kong smiled to himself. He had found the perfect place to station his clever eyes.

And he knew exactly who those clever eyes belonged to.

# 10

## SISHUN VILLAGE – SOUTHWEST OF SHANGHAI

MARK FALCHION called the study his *yamen*, a grand title given its size. It was not much bigger than a closet, but it had been hard convincing the doctor to surrender it. He wore a high-necked tunic of white cotton. His trousers were black and he wore velvet slippers. He winced as Tong Shu, the ward orderly, tugged back his hair and braided it into a queue.

'Who would believe it?' Tong Shu chattered. 'Second gardener and third housemaid.'

'Perhaps we'll have a third gardener,' Mark answered with a sly smile.

'Another housemaid more like,' Tong Shu grumbled. 'The signs are not auspicious for a boy.'

Tong Shu took Mark's hand and turned it palm up. He pursed his lips. 'Look at your hands,' he complained. 'Are those the hands of a scholar?'

Mark looked down at his hands, they were thick with calluses. The nails were cracked and grimy. He shrugged.

'The rains have been bad,' he said. 'We must all help in the fields.'

'The rains have been bad,' Tong Shu mimicked. 'Pang Yu has a broken arm, old Wong is too feeble.' He wagged a finger at Mark. 'There's always some excuse to dodge your studies,' he chided. 'A man can be an ox or a dragon but he cannot be both.'

## THE SCHOLAR'S BLADE

He gathered up his razor and scissors and turned to leave. At the door, he paused.

'Coolie or man of learning and culture,' he said. 'You must make the right choice.' He slipped through the door and his footsteps receded along the corridor.

Mark ran his hand over his brow. The skin was smooth where Tong Shu had shaved the front portion of his head. His queue hung thick and heavy down his back. He forced his eyes back to his desk and his heart sank. Spread out on the desk was a scroll of creamy silk. All day, Mark had stared at it and all day it had remained blank. He massaged his neck and slapped at a mosquito that sang past his ear.

Fluting birdsong distracted him. He gazed through the window into the garden where a pavilion with pillars of faded crimson stood beside an ornamental pond. He sighed and reached for a fine-haired brush. He dipped it into his ink tray and began to write a column of neat characters. He looked back into the garden and a smile cracked his lips as a crinkled face popped up above the windowsill. The lines in the face were deeper and the hair had turned to silver but the eyes still sparkled with mischief.

Mark clutched his chest in mock fear. 'May the gods save us from Brigand Chief Wu,' he cried. Then the smile fell from his face and he lowered his voice. 'My father will be angry if he finds you here.'

'Your father is visiting the farm of So Saang,' One-eared Wu replied. 'Foolish man skewered his own leg with a harvest sickle.' He peered over the top of Mark's desk. 'What are you writing?' He asked.

'It's my thesis on Confucian fidelity.' Mark tried to be enthusiastic but even to his own ears, the words sounded forced.

'Fascinating.' The old man pretended to yawn and patted his mouth with extended fingers. He leaned over the windowsill and lowered his voice. 'I've something far more interesting out here.'

Mark glanced at the study door. He grinned then slipped from his chair. He clambered onto the windowsill and lowered himself onto the grass. The sun was warm on his face. The perfume of peony and chrysanthemum surrounded him.

'Is it true?' One-eared Wu asked. The eye-crinkling smile had disappeared. 'Will your father send you away?'

Mark looked at the ground and shrugged. 'It had to come,' he confessed. 'I must journey to Soochow and study at the college of Master Wang Shi.'

The older man's eyes became sad. 'So, you will sit in a Soochow study and become a soft scholar,' he said. 'You've changed your ideas over the years.'

Mark fought a flash of resentment. 'With hard work and good fortune I can do well.' His voice became small. 'Or so my father says.'

One-eared Wu seemed ready to argue but instead, he pointed to a hessian bundle lying on the grass. 'We should train for one last time,' he said. He knelt and took two training *daos* from the bundle.

'Yes,' Mark said. 'One last time will be good.'

He stripped off his tunic and laid it aside. He arched his back and clenched his fists. He felt the muscles of his upper body tighten and bunch. He closed his eyes, tipped back his head and allowed the sun's warmth to wash over him.

*Mind; heart; centre,* he told himself. *Focus all into the* dao.

One eared Wu tossed one of the practice *daos* to Mark. Mark caught it by its grip and tried a slow cut.

'It's heavy,' he said. 'Even blunt, it can break a limb.'

One-eared Wu flashed a wolfish grin. 'Are you afraid of a frail old man?' he asked. He nodded towards the mission building

# THE SCHOLAR'S BLADE

'Look,' he chortled. 'People have come to see your humiliation.'

Mark turned to where Tong Shu stood among a group of patients, servants and ward orderlies who had come to watch. Tong Shu scowled and shook his head.

There was the light touch of steel on Mark's forearm.

'So easily distracted,' One-eared Wu said. 'An enemy with a combat *dao* would have taken that arm.'

Without warning, the old swordmaster darted forward. His sword swept towards Mark's shoulder.

Mark raised his *dao* to meet him but Wu dropped to one knee and hacked at Mark's thigh.

Mark jumped across Wu's blade and it swept beneath his feet. He hammered his own blade down at One-eared Wu's head.

Wu snapped his sword into an overhead block and braced his free hand against its trailing edge. The two blades rang together in a jarring clamour of steel.

Wu rolled away. In an instant, he was back on his feet, shaking feeling back into his left hand. He circled to Mark's right.

'Do you call that a blow?' he scoffed. 'You will be better as a soft scholar.'

Mark swung at One-eared Wu's hip. The old swordmaster blocked the cut and darted in with a thrust to Mark's chest. Mark knocked it aside.

One-eared Wu attacked again. The blades clashed and rang then clashed and rang again.

Mark advanced and retreated. He ducked, weaved, parried, thrust and cut. He sidestepped a thrust to his belly. His foot caught a tuft of grass. He stumbled. His guard dropped.

One-eared Wu moved in fast, his sword point thrusting towards Mark's breast.

Mark smiled and dropped to a half crouch. With all his strength, knocked Wu's blade up and to the side. He snapped his blade forward and pressed the point against One-eared Wu's windpipe.

'Better a soft scholar than a brigand who falls for an old trick,' he said.

One-eared Wu tossed his sword aside. He clasped his hands together at his chest and bowed. He turned away and retrieved his hessian bundle. He opened it to reveal his combat *dao*. The blade was polished and fresh-honed. The grip had a new covering of black leather.

'Is it the same one?' Mark asked, his eyes wide. 'It is. I know it is.'

'I can teach you no more,' One-eared Wu said. 'The sword is yours. Do not dishonour it and it will serve you well.'

Mark gasped. 'But... Master...'

One-eared Wu held up his hand. 'You are a passable swordsman.' His eyes twinkled. 'Give this old man the pleasure of placing his sword in deserving hands.'

Mark took the sword and held the sword at arm's length. The sun caught the steel, dazzling him. From its curved blade to its leather grip it was still the most beautiful object he had ever seen. He ran his hand along the flat of the blade and a sudden sense of loss was like a rock in his breast. There was no place for a broadsword, not even a fine *dao*, in the college of Master Wang Shi. Without a word, Mark offered the broadsword back to the old swordmaster.

One-eared Wu shook his head but Mark dropped to one knee and with both hands, proffered up the sword.

'I must put these things away,' Mark said, his voice hushed. 'My father says it is time I become a man. I have no choice. I must obey.'

One-eared Wu shook his head. 'Never have I seen such swordsmanship,' he said. 'You are no scholar to lock away in a fusty study.'

Mark looked into the face of his swordmaster.

'I am my father's son,' he said. 'I must obey. I must journey to Soochow.'

'The duty of obedience is strong in you,' One-eared Wu sighed. 'But what a shame.' He shook his grizzled head and his voice took on a bitter edge. 'No, not just a shame, it is a *waste*.'

One-eared Wu took the sword and wrapped it in its bindings. He turned and walked from the garden. And to Mark Falchion it seemed the hessian-wrapped bundle was the heaviest burden the old man had ever carried.

The next morning, Mark Falchion lingered by the kitchen door and enjoyed the smell of Moy Saam's plum sauce. On any other day, Moy Saam would be happy to see him but today, she was not at all happy. She stood with her fists planted on her hips, scowling down at a young woman.

The younger woman was slender and wore her hair cut short, like a farm boy. She had fine features but it was her eyes that struck Mark, they were large and doe-like.

For a moment, Mark could not move. He could only gaze at a young woman with a simple beauty unlike anything he had seen before.

'Who says we're short a scullery maid?' Moy Saam demanded.

The younger woman squared her shoulders. Her voice was strong and defiant. 'My auntie's third cousin knows a ward orderly,' she said. 'I was told to ask for Moy Saam. I was told she needs a scullery maid.'

Moy Saam narrowed her eyes. 'What is your name?' she demanded.

'I am Ping Song-mei,' the young woman answered. 'But everyone calls me Mei.'

'Show me your hands,' Moy Saam ordered.

The young woman called Mei held out her hands.

'Those are not a worker's hands,' Moy Saam snorted. 'Your auntie was mistaken, there's no job for you here.'

Mei sucked in her breath. 'But...'

'Are you deaf or stupid?' Moy Saam snapped. 'There is no work here, now go.' She turned away and continued to stir the plum sauce.

Mark stepped into the kitchen. The young woman turned to look at him then gasped and took a step back.

Mark smiled at her. 'I suppose I'm the first Westerner you've seen,' he said. He lowered his voice like a conspirator. 'But don't be afraid, I never eat young women.' He turned to Moy Saam. 'Is this the new scullery maid?' he asked.

'I've told her the job is filled,' Moy Saam clucked. 'She is just leaving.'

'Filled?' Mark asked. 'When did we fill it?'

'Questions, questions,' Moy Saam grumbled. 'Does the doctor ask me how to heal the sick?' Moy Saam wagged a finger at Mark. 'In here, I rule and I say the girl leaves.'

'But why?'

'I do not like her,' Moy Saam grumbled. 'Look at the way she stands. She is too proud. There is just one mistress here.'

Mei gave Mark a cool look then her eyes softened and when she spoke, her voice was pleading. 'Please, young sir, do not send me away,' she said. 'I've run away. I cannot go home.' Her voice quivered. 'I was *mi-jeh*. If I return, the whole family will beat me.'

'The girl is trouble,' Moy Saam clucked. 'You'll see, Master Mark. Employ her and it will be on your head.'

Mei touched Mark's forearm. '*Mar... Mar-oh-kah?*' She said, struggling with the unfamiliar word. '*Mark-ah? Mark?* Did I say it right?' She smiled up at Mark and let her touch linger.

Mark thrilled at her touch. He felt himself drawn into her doe-like eyes. His neck burned and for a moment he could find no words.

'Don't... don't be afraid,' he stammered. 'You can stay. Auntie Moy will explain your duties.'

Moy Saam shook her mixing spoon at Mark.

'She might get around you with her sad eyes and her pretty face,' she snapped. 'But it won't work with me.' She rounded on Mei. 'Next week, he journeys to Soochow,' she growled. 'Until then, you'll attend your duties. If not, I'll be the one doing the beating. Understand?'

Mei lowered her eyes. 'Yes First Auntie,' she said. 'I will attend my duties and not trouble you.'

Mark draped his arm across Moy Saam's shoulders. 'Thank you Auntie Moy,' he said. He ran his finger around the mixing bowl's rim. 'That's the best ever,' he declared, licking plum sauce from his finger.

'Out. *Out!*' Moy Saam clucked, elbowing him away. 'Don't get in my way.'

Mark flashed a smile at Mei and as he turned to leave, she smiled back at him.

Mark paused by the door. Something about the smile troubled him. It was neither a smile of thanks nor of friendship.

It seemed more a smile of triumph.

In the coming days, Mark found himself looking for excuses to visit the kitchen and his heart bounded whenever he saw Mei.

'Her days as a *mi-jeh* serve her well,' Moy Saam declared on one of Mark's visits. 'She works hard and she understands the workings of a kitchen. But...' She shrugged and left the rest unsaid.

'But?' Mark asked.

'She's a daydreamer,' Moy Saam answered. Always looking out of the window.' She drew closer to Mark and lowered her voice. 'Particularly when passing boats carry the emperor's soldiers.'

Mark felt a stab of jealousy. 'Maybe she is close to a soldier,' he muttered. 'Perhaps a brother or a friend.'

'Or a lover,' Moy Saam grumbled. She shook her head. 'There is something not right about this girl. She is not what she claims to be.'

'Maybe if I talked to her,' Mark suggested. His mood brightened at the thought.

Moy Saam frowned. 'She is pretty and you are a young man,' she said. 'Do not let her trick you into making promises. Now go.' She used both hands to shoo Mark away then turned back to her work.

Mark returned to his study. He surveyed the stacks of books and scrolls that were the sum of all his work. Everything he needed would be waiting for him at the college of Master Wang Shi but still, it seemed wrong to leave them all.

Afternoon became dusk and night fell. Mark left his study and walked down to the riverbank. The only sound was the lapping of water by the reeds and the metallic chirp of the cicadas. A full moon had turned the river into dark silver. There was a figure sat near the bank and as he drew closer, Mark recognised the form of the young woman, Mei.

'Is it alright if I join you?' he asked.

Mei smiled up at him and patted the ground beside her.

'I like it here,' she said. 'The night air is soft and warm.'

'Does Moy Saam treat you kindly?' Mark asked.

Mei shrugged. 'First Auntie is kind enough,' she said. She lowered her eyes. 'Kinder than those in my first household.'

Mark stretched out his legs and leaned back, taking his weight on his elbows.

'It must have been terrible,' he said. He turned to look at her. 'But don't be afraid, you're safe here. No one will beat you.'

'I should say sorry to you,' Mei said. 'On that first day, I flirted with you so you would help me get the scullery maid's post.'

Mark smiled. 'It was a day or two before I worked it out,' he said. 'But you needed the work and now I'm glad I helped.'

Mei cocked her head to the side. 'You're strange,' she said.

'So people say,' Mark chuckled.

Mei pointed at his face and made small circles with her fingertip. There was a trace of laughter in her voice.

'You are a foreign devil with a long nose, white hair and blue eyes,' she said. *'Blue!* You look like a demon. I should be terrified.' She hugged her knees and for a moment, seemed to be talking to herself. 'But you are kind. I see it in the way you talk to the people who come with their illnesses and injuries.' She paused for a moment then added, 'how is it that you speak Chinese so well?'

Mark shrugged. 'Sometimes I feel I am Chinese,' he said. 'Sometimes I feel Western.' His voice became wistful. 'Other times, I don't know what or who I am.'

Mei nodded and looked into the far distance.

'We are alike,' she said. 'I too do not know who I am.'

Mark moved closer to her and touched her hand. Mei stiffened and snatched her hand away. She pulled her tunic tight around her and buried her face in her arms.

'I... I'm sorry,' Mark stammered. 'I... ' his voice tailed off.

Mei turned her face to Mark. In her eyes, he saw a depth of pain.

'It is not your fault,' she said. 'In my last... my last *place*, there was a man. He was very young but he tried to take me by force. He... he hurt me.' Her voice was little more than a whisper.

'Maybe it was my fault. I don't know. All I know is that he made me feel unclean.'

Mark looked into eyes that had once been defiant but which now brimmed with tears. He wanted to take this beautiful, vulnerable woman in his arms and comfort her.

'Who did this thing? Where?' he asked.

'Do not ask,' Mei's voice was pleading. She reached out and pressed her fingertips against Mark's lips. 'I beg you, do not ask me questions.'

Mark took her hand and this time Mei did not pull away.

'Tomorrow I leave for Soochow,' he said. 'It is my father's wish, not mine.' Words began to tumble from him. 'I must... must say what I feel for you.'

'You must say nothing,' Mei said, her voice rising. 'You do not know me. You do not know who I am; what I am.'

'I will say what is in my heart,' Mark said. 'You cannot stop...'

Then Mei's arms were around his neck. Her lips were pressing hard against his, silencing him.

She drew back. 'You do not understand,' she said. 'This cannot be; this can never be.'

She stood and looked down at Mark. Her voice firmed. 'You must leave this place,' she said. 'You must all leave.'

'Leave?' Mark asked. 'Why should we leave?'

Mei's eyes flicked from the river to the clinic and back again. She was wringing her hands. Her voice fell to a near whisper. 'I cannot say,' she said. 'But you must go.' Then she backed away, turned and ran back to the clinic.

Mark made to follow her but the moment had passed. He could still feel the touch of her lips on his, still smell the scent of her hair. He stared out across the liquid silver of the river. Tomorrow he would leave for Soochow. His new life would begin and his old life would end.

# THE SCHOLAR'S BLADE

And then she would be lost forever.

Mei pressed her back against the scullery door. *Madness, madness, madness.* Duty; I must remember my duty. She shook her head, trying to banish all memory of the young man with pale hair and blue eyes.

The kitchen staff had retired for the night so Mei busied herself clearing away the last of the pots. She scrubbed down the work surfaces and scoured the kitchen floor until her knees were sore and her back ached. She sluiced the contents of her bucket down the drain then walked to the window.

Beyond the garden, moonlight made the river sparkle. For six days, she had watched boats plying the Huangpu. There were ferries under sweep and sail, cargo boats and even little sampans. There were British paddle steamers with tall stacks belching black smoke. Soldiers with scarlet tunics lined their decks.

And there were other boats: boats carrying Imperial soldiers. They rode low in the water, so overloaded that the river sloshed over the gunnels. They travelled in one direction only: downstream, away from Soochow. There were no banners, no raucous chat, no drums. Instead they travelled in silence. The soldiers had sat with their shoulders hunched, many with their eyes fixed astern as though watching for pursuers.

Her work done, Mei snuffed out the lanterns and pressed her ear against the door leading to the servants' quarters. Satisfied there was no movement, she slipped into the garden and walked down to the riverbank. She paused for a moment, making sure no one had seen her. Certain all was clear, she took a well-trodden path that led upstream.

Behind her, there was a footfall. It was so quiet she almost missed it. There was a heavier footfall. An arm snaked around her neck. A calloused hand clamped over her mouth. A knifepoint touched the soft skin below her jaw. A guttural voice was harsh in her ear.

'You are the woman, Ping Song-mei?'

Mei gave a sharp nod and the arm released her. She turned to face a man with a weathered face. He wore his hair in a topknot once favoured by the ancient warriors. His tunic and britches were black. He stepped back and eased his dagger into a sheath at his belt.

'I know you,' Mei said. 'You were with Kong Liu when he rescued me. You are the one they call Cho Lung, yes?'

'I am Cho Lung,' the man said. The moonlight caught his smile. 'I remember the day well. I've never seen Kong so roundly defeated.' The smile fell from his face. 'I'm here to receive your report,' he said. 'What Imperial troop movements have you seen?'

Mei told him of the Imperial troop carriers heading downstream.

'They have no spirit,' she said. 'They are afraid. Afraid and beaten.'

Cho gave a curt nod. 'Good,' he said. 'That's what we hear from the other outposts.'

'And there are British troop movements,' Mei added.

'British? Are they preparing defences?'

'I don't think so,' Mei answered. 'They patrol the waterways in their river craft but they make no attempt to land.'

Cho drew in a long breath. 'Your duty here is done,' he said. 'You must prepare to leave. Tomorrow, my commander will come to bring you out.'

'*Meng? Here?*' Mei gasped. She gripped Cho's arm. 'These people are decent,' she said. 'Meng must not harm them.'

'General Kong commands that the people must be treated with mercy,' Cho Lung said but he would not meet her eyes.

## THE SCHOLAR'S BLADE

Mei tightened her grip on Cho's arm.

'Meng? Merciful?' she snorted. 'You know him better. Meng must not come to the mission. I will slip away and meet you here.'

Cho shook away her hand. 'Captain Meng is our commander, not you,' he snapped. His voice softened. 'Do not worry. He is curious about the barbarians, nothing more. We come tomorrow. Be ready.' He turned away and melted into the dark.

Mei turned back towards the mission. *Meng*, here in Sishun. To warn the household would be treason but not to warn them... She put down her head and scurried back along the path.

Inside the scullery, she laid her sleeping mat in a corner and clambered onto it. She squeezed shut her eyes but visions of Meng, Mark Falchion, the doctor and the rest of them tumbled around inside her.

She pushed the thoughts away. Her duty was all that mattered. Why should she care about him? Why should she care about any of them? She rolled onto her side but sleep would not come. Tomorrow she would be gone and Mark Falchion would be forgotten.

But still, his face lingered with her.

It was nearly time.

Mark wore his scholar's gown over a tunic and trousers of soft cotton. He carried a staff as tall as himself. On his back was a pack containing a few belongings. Earlier, Moy Saam had bustled into his room, her eyes puffed and red. She had thrust a bundle of food into Mark's hands then scuttled away.

All day, the clinic workers had gone about their duties but there was none of their usual chatter or laughter. Mark had searched the mission for Mei. He had gone from room to room but there was no sign of her.

Now, on the jetty, Doctor James Falchion stood beside his son.

'I tell you, the girl's touched,' Doctor Falchion said. 'Moy Saam says she spends most of the working day gazing out of the window.'

'She's unhappy about something,' Mark Falchion said. 'I don't know what, but she thinks we're in some kind of danger.'

'Hush now, my son,' the doctor said. 'We've been here since before you were born. We're safe now and safe we will remain.'

'But father...'

'*Enough!*' the doctor snapped. He sighed and softened his voice. 'Let us part on good terms. Look, the boat is here.'

Near to the bank, a flat-bottomed riverboat manoeuvred against the Huangpu's current. A bat-wing sail, stiffened with horizontal battens, snapped against her mast. At the stern, two men worked her sweeps as the helmsman guided the boat closer inshore.

The riverboat nudged the jetty. A woman carrying a rattan cage full of chickens pushed past Mark and laid claim to a large area of deck. From the boat's fore-section, a group of thin-shouldered scholars gaped at Mark then fell into hushed chatter. They had smooth faces and wore well-cut gowns.

Mark bent his head. 'Father...' his voice was small.

James Falchion took Mark's shoulders in both hands. 'I know, my son. Doubts are normal.' He fixed Mark's eyes with his own. 'All will be well. Your mother was strong. She had fire in her, the same fire I see in you.' He chuckled. 'That bloody old bandit of yours could see it.'

Mark began to speak but the doctor waved his hand for silence.

'Put it behind you, my son,' he said. 'The time for playing with toy swords is over. Now you must become a man.'

Mark lowered his eyes and was silent.

'Do you have my letter to Master Wang Shi?' Doctor Falchion asked.

'I do, father.'

'Good, pay him close attention and learn well,' he said.

'I shall, Father,' Mark replied.

The two men faced each other in silence then James Falchion's grip on Mark's shoulders became firmer.

'Now, go to Soochow,' he said. There was a catch to his voice. 'When you return, you'll be a famous scholar. Here, take this.' He pressed a pouch into Mark's hand and Mark felt the hard edges of coins through the material.

'No Father...' Mark tried to return the pouch but James Falchion would not take it.

'Take it,' the doctor insisted. 'The first weeks in a new place are always hard.'

The two embraced and Mark stepped onto the boat. He cupped his right fist in his left hand and bowed.

The helmsman poled away from the landing and the sweepmen dug in with their oars.

Rapid footsteps sounded on the jetty and Mark looked up to see Mei standing at the jetty's edge. She clutched her hands to her breast and mouthed a few words but Mark could not make them out.

The boat edged forward, towards a bend where a willow overhung the bank.

Doctor Falchion backhanded something from his cheek and waved farewell. Mark Falchion stood at the stern and watched the only world he had ever known fall away behind him. The boat slipped past the willow then rounded the river bend.

And his old life was gone.

# 11

THE HELMSMAN ordered the sail hoisted and he manoeuvred close to the bank where the current was lighter. The sweepmen worked in perfect unison but even under wind and sweep, it was slow going against the current.

'How long to Soochow?' Mark asked.

'Upstream's always slow,' the helmsman said. He hawked and spat into the river. 'One day to the Grand Canal then it'll get easier.' The boat lurched and the helmsman leaned on his steering oar to compensate for the current. 'Two days,' he continued. 'No, better make it three. Three days to Soochow.

For the first time, Mark sensed a new life waiting for him. He gazed over the boat's stern and for a moment, it was as if the mission hospital had never been. He lay back, rested his head on his pack and let the sun warm his face. Ahead, lay what? Soochow was a city of culture, of grand buildings, broad parks. There would be men of learning, men with whom he could discuss the classics and the Confucian ideals.

He moved closer to the scholars.

'Good morning gentlemen,' he said. 'Do you journey to Soochow for study?'

The tallest of them gave Mark a cool glare.

'We shall address you when we have need of some menial service,' he said. The other scholars lifted their sleeves to their lips and tittered like flower girls.

# THE SCHOLAR'S BLADE

Mark stiffened and felt his grip on his staff tighten. A rebuke sprang to his lips, then he saw his callused hands and homespun gown. He bowed.

'I have intruded on your privacy,' he said. 'Forgive this unfortunate student.'

The tall scholar's cheeks reddened and he fluttered his sleeve as though dismissing a servant.

Mark returned to his place at the stern. His neck burned and his heart pounded. A small muscle in his cheek throbbed.

The helmsman put his head close to Mark's. 'The landowning classes do not change,' he whispered. 'But you showed them how a gentleman behaves. The tall one has lost much face.'

Mark's anger fell away and he was content to watch the countryside drift by.

Knee-deep in rice paddies, families toiled side by side. On a levee, a child armed only with a leafy switch, drove a huge water buffalo, its head swaying side to side like a stone pendulum. Mark waved to the child who abandoned his duties and skipped along the bank, smiling and waving.

*Soochow.* Mark thrilled at the word. The very name was magic. *Soochow.* A city of gardens, palaces and colleges. He smiled to himself. Some said the Soochow girls were the prettiest in China. Again, he checked his pack. The letter from his father to his old friend, Wang Shi, was safe amongst his belongings.

Evening fell and the boat drew into the riverbank. Mark curled up on the deck and listened to the chirping of the cicadas and the slosh of the river against the boat's hull. He lay awake and tried not to think of the scullery girl, but when he closed his eyes, she came to him. He swatted at a mosquito that sang around his ear. His eyes became heavy, his breathing slowed and he drifted into sleep.

In his dreams, he saw himself in the robe and cap of a senior scholar. He was at a desk covered with books and scrolls chronicling the works of Confucius and his disciples. The scrolls were everywhere. They jammed his shelves, they rested atop every piece of furniture, they were knee deep on the floor. It was vital he act on the right one, but he could not find it. He waded through a mass of paper. He examined scrolls at random but their contents were meaningless. They pressed in on him, burying him, choking him.

He woke and sat up gasping but there was only the chirping of cicadas and the slap of river against the hull. He lay back on the deck and closed his eyes but sleep would not come. His thoughts were a jumble of memories: his home, his father, the strange but beautiful scullery girl called Mei. And there was the pavilion garden where honed steel had moaned through the morning air and savage joy had filled a young man's heart.

It is over, he told himself. I am a man. He rolled onto his side and banished all thoughts of home, the woman and the sword.

Finally, he slept.

Morning broke to the sound of sweeps creaking in their oarlocks. The other passengers still slept. The sun was low and the air was cool. Mark rubbed the sleep from his eyes and rummaged his pack for a rice cake. Soon he would have to replenish his rations. He made a mental note to ask the helmsman to stop at one of the marketplaces found at the riverside landings.

Mark sat by the stern and let the sun warm his back. The boat was alone on the river but the solitude would not last. Soon there would be other sails to block the view and the shouts of boatmen jostling for the best line around the river bends.

'Don't see many foreigners on these boats,' the helmsman said. 'I would have expected someone like you to take the steamer.'

Mark answered with a smile and a shrug but the helmsman was in a mood to talk.

'You dress like a student,' he said. 'But you've the shoulders of a boatman. Have you worked the sweeps?'

'I've worked the fields...'

Ahead, a flurry of egrets erupted from reeds growing close to the riverbank. The helmsman stiffened. His face hardened. He lifted his steering oar clear of the water and the boat swung in the current.

From the reeds another boat appeared. Mark stood and watched it edge into the stream. There were three men on board. All were bare-chested. Their bodies were sun-darkened, their britches were torn and dark with grime. There was a flash of sun on steel. One held a sword.

The sweepmen's faces paled. They rested their oars and the boat began to drift in the current. The helmsman rounded on them.

'Pull!' he roared. 'Damn you, *pull!*'

The sweepmen exchanged looks then ran to the side, jumped into the river and swam for the shore. The helmsman cursed and leaned on the steering oar, guiding the boat to midstream.

'Take a sweep,' he snapped at Mark. He pointed with his chin to the other boat. 'They have the current. Quick, we must turn her.'

The other passengers woke. They rubbed their eyes and blinked in the morning light. They murmured and huddled together, confused by the shouts and suddenly pitching deck. The chicken vendor pointed at the other boat, put her hands to her head and began to wail. A scholar let out a girlish squeal.

'Quick, hide your valuables,' he cried.

'Best not,' the helmsman grunted. 'If they find nothing they'll slice you open to see what you've swallowed.' He pushed hard on his steering oar.

Mark grabbed a sweep and with all his strength, back-paddled. The boat's head came round. Her sail banged against the mast. The current caught the beam and they drifted sideways. The deck heaved, threatening to tip everyone into the river.

The second boat drew nearer. Now, Mark could see its crew clearly. One had a tattoo of a swooping eagle emblazoned across his chest. Another held a sword. The third had a livid scar running from eyebrow to chin.

The scar-faced man cupped his hands to his mouth. 'Take care, little ones,' he called. 'You might lose your valuables in the current.'

'Do something,' Mark yelled at the nearest scholar. 'Help with the sweeps. Do anything.' He kicked the young man in the backside but the scholar fell to his knees and began to sob.

Just yards separated the two boats.

'Keep her turning,' the helmsman rasped.

A grappling hook arced over the side and thumped onto the deck. The deck shuddered as the two boats ground together.

'These people aren't worth your blood,' the helmsman said. 'Save yourself.' He dived into the river and followed his sweepmen to the shore.

Locked together, both boats swung in the current. The scholars pressed their faces against the deck and covered their heads with their hands. The woman wailed louder, her chickens squawked and clacked their beaks.

The scar-faced man was first across. He pulled a knife from his belt and edged to Mark's left. The swordsman came next.

Mark pictured honed steel slicing through flesh and muscle. He spread his feet against the pitching deck. His stomach tightened. His heart pounded. His mouth was as dry as a clay oven. The deck tilted and his staff rolled to him. He scooped it up.

The swordsman grinned and beckoned Mark to come closer.

Mark rotated the staff, testing its balance. It cut the air with a soft moan. He checked himself. Old Wu's voice was soft in his ear.

*Never show your skill, focus the anger, focus the fear.*

The swordsman licked his lips. His sword point flicked from side to side. Remember old Wu's teachings, Mark told himself. The untrained always signal their attack.

The swordsman sucked in a breath. He lifted his blade.

Blood surged hard and fast through Mark's temples. His senses became needle focused. Years of practice snapped into place.

The swordsman snarled and leapt forward.

He's crude, thought Mark. Crude and *slow*.

Mark ducked under the blade and swung his staff against the swordsman's midriff. The swordsman grunted and doubled over. Mark brought staff down hard on the swordsman's skull. It connected with a *clack* and the swordsman sprawled forward, eyes glazed, mouth slack. The sword clattered to the deck.

Mark span to face Scar-face who crouched and held his dagger straight-armed before him.

Behind Mark, ropes groaned as the tattooed man lashed the two boats firm.

Mark risked a glance over his shoulder and scar-face took the chance to lunge. Mark caught the attack from the corner of his eye. He thrust hard with his staff and caught Scar-face square on the forehead. The impact jarred Marks's wrists but Scar-face let out a cry and fell back onto the deck.

From behind, a forearm snaked around Mark's throat and locked tight. Mark tried to shift his weight forward but a knee rammed into his back. He clawed for the man's head but could get no purchase. His knees buckled. White mist drifted before his eyes. His arms had no strength. A far-off pounding filled his ears. The staff slipped from his fingers. He extended his thumb and with the last of his strength, thrust back. His thumb connected with soft tissue and the tattooed man reeled away, cursing and nursing his eye.

Mark fell to his knees and retched onto the deck. The pounding noise seemed louder. It was like a hammer inside his head. He tried to stand but his legs would not support him.

The tattooed man nursed his eye and crept closer. The sun glinted off a curved blade. He dropped to a crouch. He smiled and rattled the knifepoint against the deck. His body swayed, first left then right. He lunged, sweeping the blade backhand towards Mark's throat.

Mark rolled his head and the blade *shushed* past him.

Unbalanced, the tattooed man staggered forward. Mark bunched his fist and rammed it into the tattooed man's groin. The man cried out. He toppled onto his side, clutching his groin. His mouth worked soundlessly.

Mark reached for his staff and used it as a crutch to push himself back to his feet. He shook his head to shake away a sense that his brain was full of cotton gauze.

The tattooed man was pushing himself up from the deck. His face was pale, his eyes were pained. He rose to his knees, scrabbling around for his knife.

Mark worked the staff in a short, fast arc. It struck the tattooed man behind the ear and he fell without a sound.

Mark looked up and saw a third boat closing on them. Black smoke billowed from a tall stack amidships. On either side of a broad hull, rotating paddles pounded the river into a creamy storm. A British ensign fluttered from her mizzen and gilt letters at the beakhead spelt out the word *Tarantula*.

# THE SCHOLAR'S BLADE

Men stood at the steamer's prow. They wore scarlet tunics and solar helmets that gleamed white. Each carried a long-barrelled rifle. The steamer scraped against the riverboat's hull and barefooted sailors jumped down from her deck.

'By Jove, you're an odd looking bird.'

Mark looked into the eyes of a slim young man of his own age. He wore a scarlet tunic and had an unkempt mop of ginger hair.

'I say, are you all right?' the young man asked.

Mark shook his head and it started to clear.

'Yes. Yes sir. I am, thank you,' he said. He steadied himself on his staff. 'I take it you are a British soldier.'

'Good God, no.' The young man seemed ready to choke at the suggestion. 'Jessop, Harry, Lieutenant, Royal Marines. And very glad to be at your service.'

Harry Jessop regarded Mark from under raised eyebrows. 'Indeed sir,' he said. 'You're a very odd bird. To where are you headed?'

'Soochow,' Mark answered.

'Soochow? Oh, I think not,' Jessop chortled. 'I think most definitely not. Soochow has fallen.'

'Fallen?'

'Yes sir, fallen,' Jessop said. 'Fallen to the blessed Taipings no less. Took the city on the second of June, they did. Emperor's bloody army gave up without a fight. At the first sight of the enemy, they hightailed it back to Shanghai, looting and pillaging all the way, damn 'em.'

Jessop slapped a smudge of dust from his sleeve. 'Chinese quarter's burstin' at the seams, don't y'know,' he continued. 'Farmers, soldiers, merchants. Never saw so many people begging around the settlements. The women are sellin' their children for God's sake.'

Mark struggled to take it in. 'The Taipings can't be in Soochow,' he gasped. 'I have important work there.'

'Not in Soochow you don't, old chum,' Jessop said. He put his hand on Mark's shoulder. 'I say, you don't look at all well. Shall I have the surgeon look you over?'

Mark pushed the hand away. 'No,' he snapped. 'I mean, no thank you, sir. Forgive my rough manners, you've been most kind.'

Sailors helped the scholars and the chicken seller onto *Tarantula's* deck. Two marines guarded the unconscious pirates.

Mark could only stare into the water. It could not be real. All his plans, all his father's wishes, all had come crashing down. He tried to think, but his head seemed full of cotton wadding. For centuries, Soochow had been a haven for learning and tradition, but now the Taipings were there. Master Wang and the other Confucian teachers would be in hiding, if they had survived at all.

'Can't hang around, old chum.' There was a splinter of urgency in Jessop's voice. 'We've had reports of Taiping scouts all round here. One of 'em even took a shot at us this morning.' He took Mark's arm and guided him towards the steamer.

Another Marine stepped forward. He had florid cheeks and mutton-chop whiskers. White chevrons decorated his sleeves.

'What shall we do with these sleeping beauties, *sah*?' he barked.

'Chuck 'em in the cable locker, Sar'nt Verrals,' Jessop snapped. 'We'll hand them to the authorities in Shanghai.'

'Cable locker it is, *sah*.' Sergeant Verrals pointed at four marines who were leaning over the steamer's railing. 'Right, you lot,' he bellowed. 'Get yourselves down 'ere and 'elp these Oriental gentlemen to their stateroom. Lively now.'

Mark knelt beside the swordsman. A broad strap secured a

leather scabbard to his back. The scabbard was scuffed and dirty but the leather was good quality.

Mark retrieved the sword from the deck. It was a broad-bladed *dao*. The hilt guard was a disc of filigreed brass. The grip was rosewood and the interlocking signs of *Yin* and *Yang* decorated the pommel. The *Yin* aspect was pure jet; the *Yang* was creamy ivory. The blade was slim where it joined the hilt but broadened at the centre before tapering to a vicious point. He tested the edge, it was like one of his father's scalpels.

He swung the sword in a slow arc. The blade was heavy but it had the balance of a goldsmith's scale. He rotated his wrist and the impetus from the first cut carried through into a second.

It essays all by itself, Mark thought, all it needs is guidance.

He executed two flashing sweeps, alternating from one side of his body to the next. He suppressed a surge of joy and brought the blade to rest.

From *Tarantula's* prow, two marines watched the impromptu display of swordsmanship and swapped admiring nods.

Mark turned to Jessop and handed the sword to him.

'Mister Jessop,' he said. 'Please take this as a souvenir of today's action.'

Then he strode to the steamer's companionway and clambered up to the deck.

Mark sat at *Tarantula's* prow and let the thump of her paddles dull his feelings. He pictured the look of crumpled disappointment he would see on his father's face. There was nothing he could have done, he told himself. For a moment, a sense of relief washed through him then there was a flash of guilt. How could he have forgotten the virtues of duty and obedience?

A mile from the clinic, he stood and shielded his eyes against the noon sun. Ahead, a smudge of grey-brown hovered close to the river. The tang of burnt wood drifted in the air.

'Burning off the spring growth, I expect.' Jessop's tone was light but Mark could not shake off a tingle of alarm.

Closer to home, the smell became more pungent. From *Tarantula's* prow, Mark watched the cloud grow larger. His mood darkened and he willed the steamer to move faster. The steamer neared the final river bend where the willow dipped its branches into the water. Now, smoke filled the sky. It drifted across the river and clung to the water's surface. It stung the eyes and throat.

Mark's knuckles were white on the railing as *Tarantula* rounded the final bend. A cry leapt from his throat. The clinic walls, once lime-washed to a gleaming white were now scorched black. Smoke streamed from the windows. With a groaning rumble, the roof crashed in on itself, shooting sparks and flame skyward.

There was a shout of, '*Stand to!*'

Boots thudded against the deck as marines ran to the side railing. They pulled cartridges from their belt pouches. Ramrods clattered in rifle barrels.

'*Bayonets!*'

Oiled steel slid from scabbards.

Beyond the smoke and flames, something moved. It looked like a dark, snake-like beast, shimmering through the fire-haze. The beast took form and became a column of horsemen. There were black tunics and glittering spear tips.

Mark turned to Jessop. 'Order your men ashore, Lieutenant,' he shouted. He pointed to the horsemen. 'Hurry, they're getting away.' He ran to the gangway. 'What's wrong, Mister Jessop. *Quickly*. Get your men ashore.'

Harry Jessop put a hand on Mark's arm. 'Be calm, Mister Falchion,' he said. 'There's too many. We must get back to

## THE SCHOLAR'S BLADE

Shanghai and report.'

Mark shook away Jessop's hand. 'Report?' he snapped. His eyes were wild. '*Report?* Damn your report, my father's in there.' Realisation struck him. 'My God, so's Mei.'

'Easy, Lad.' Sergeant Verrals stepped closer to Mark. 'Won't help if we're all dead, will it now?'

Mark clambered onto *Tarantula's* railing but strong hands dragged him back.

'What the 'ell...!' Sergeant Verrals exclaimed.

All eyes turned to the shore. A rider had detached himself from the others. He wore a black tunic and there was a crimson scarf tied around his brows. His hair hung about his shoulders in thick curls. He rode close to the jetty and reined to a halt. The horse pranced as though eager for action. The rider sawed at the reins then stood in the stirrups and shouted to the men lined along *Tarantula's* railings.

'What's he saying, Mister Falchion?' Jessop asked.

'He's wants you to send me to him so he can strangle me with my lackey's queue.'

A marine raised his rifle. 'Reckon I could knock the bugger off 'is 'orse, no bother,' he growled.

'Stand fast, private Leary,' Jessop ordered. 'We're not here to start a war with the bloody Taipings.'

The mounted Taiping made a show of spitting on the ground. He wheeled his horse away and kicked its flanks. The animal shot forward and horse and rider disappeared into the smoke.

Private Leary gave a sniff and lowered his rifle. 'Could have dropped 'im,' he grumbled. 'Could have dropped 'im clean.'

'Buggers're movin' off, *sah*,' Sergeant Verrals called. 'Do you want a shore party?'

'No Sar'nt,' Jessop sighed. 'My compliments to the skipper, ask him to make all haste for Shanghai.'

'I'll thank you to put me ashore, Lieutenant,' Mark's voice was cracked ice. 'There are people who need help.'

Jessop remained silent.

Mark waved his arm towards the flames. 'Good God, Lieutenant. Those people are innocents. There are women and children there.'

Jessop grasped the railing and let out a weary sigh.

'Sarn't Verrals,' he said. 'Get a man in the tops to look out for any movement beyond the mission buildings.'

Verrals came to attention. '*Sah*,' he snapped.

'Then take half the side party and move onto the jetty. And for God's sake, tell them to keep their bloody eyes peeled.'

Verrals grinned and threw out his chest. 'Yes, *Sah*,' he bellowed. 'You 'eard the officer. Hop to it lads, sharp now.'

Mark leapt ashore as the steamer crunched against the jetty. He ignored Jessop's calls and ran to the mission. Heat seared his skin; smoke stung his eyes. He ran from one end of the blazing building to the other. He called his father's name. He shouted out to Mei but there was only the roar and crackle of the flames.

There was movement in the shrubbery.

'Who's there?' Mark demanded. 'Come out. Come out now.'

It was Tong Shu, the ward orderly. He emerged from the shrubbery and spread his arms, encompassing the devastation. Tears cut lines through soot caked to his cheeks. His mouth worked silently and when the words came, they were a whispered croak.

'Look, Master Mark,' he said. 'Look what they have done. Why would they do such a thing? Why?'

Mark laid his arm across Tong Shu's shoulders. 'Where is everyone?' he asked.

Tong Shu buried his face in both hands. His shoulders shuddered.

## THE SCHOLAR'S BLADE

Mark forced down the panic that ballooned inside him. He spoke softly. 'Uncle,' he said. 'Where's my father?'

Tong Shu shook his head. 'They beat him and they took him away.'

Mark's voice was small. 'And Mei? Did they hurt her?'

Tong Shu turned away. Sobs wracked his body.

Mark's mouth dried. His father, taken. Where? Why? And where was Mei?

As the marines formed a skirmish line beyond the burning clinic, Jessop strode towards Mark, his sword drawn.

'Mister Falchion, a moment, sir,' he called. He drew close to Mark and lowered his voice. 'There's an old Chinese lying in a pavilion behind the main house. He's badly injured, I fear. He keeps saying, "Talk. Doctor," over and over. He may have some information for us.'

Jessop and Mark picked their way through glowing embers and scorched debris. A sudden flare forced them to drop to a crouch and shield their faces. They came to the pavilion garden. The pavilion's pillars were fire-blackened. Shattered masonry littered the lawn. Inside the pavilion and flanked by two marines, One-eared Wu lay propped against a wall. His face was grey, blood soaked his tunic. As Mark came close to him, the old man tried to sit up.

'Stay there, Master Wu,' Mark said. He dropped to one knee and with his finger and thumb, lifted the hem of the old man's tunic. He winced. The last time he had seen such an injury, a wild boar had gored a farmer. The man had died within the hour.

'I'll get something to make you comfortable then we'll sew up this little gash,' Mark said. He started to rise but One-eared Wu clawed at his arm.

'Too late.' The old man tried to smile but a heaving cough left him gasping. A trickle of blood ran from the corner of his mouth.

'I tried to stop them, Mark, but the tall one, the leader, he cut me down like a blade of barley.'

'Who did this, Master?'

'Devils.' The old man wheezed and more blood oozed from his mouth. 'Devils dressed as Taipings. Black robes; black hearts.'

'Where's my father? Where's Mei?' Mark fought to keep the panic from his voice.

'The girl has heart,' One-eared Wu answered. 'She refused to leave your father.' He screwed shut his eyes and bit his lip. 'They thought he was a priest. They had him on his knees with his neck stretched for the blade.' He smiled through his pain. 'And what a blade, it was a prince's blade.'

'Where, old teacher? Where did they take him?'

'Who knows?' The old man sighed and seemed about to drift into sleep. He sucked in a slow breath then continued. 'They thought he was a priest. I told them he was a doctor so they took him. They took him and the girl went too. It's my fault.'

Mark patted the old man's hand. 'Don't speak so,' he said. 'You saved his life.'

'I know those eyes, young Mark,' One-eared Wu wheezed. 'Don't be foolish. You must leave, leave now.'

'I cannot, I must bring him home. I must rebuild this place.'

'And when you face the Taipings, then what?' The old man's voice became a croak. 'Will you smile and bow? Because if you do not, they will kill you.' He gripped Mark's arm. 'What would your father say? What would *he* tell you to do?'

One-eared Wu's eyes glittered. 'Promise me, promise you will leave now.'

He arched his back and bared his teeth. His grip slackened and his eyes closed. His breath rattled and he lay still.

Mark patted the old man's arm. 'Very well, teacher, I will leave,' he said.

## THE SCHOLAR'S BLADE

Grief and rage tumbled around inside him. The muscles around his throat tightened.

'But I will return, old friend,' he whispered. 'I will search for them and when I find them, I will remember you.'

# 12

FROM THE GUTTED clinic at Sishun, the Black Dragons rode north.

Tied to his saddle was Doctor James Falchion. Twine secured his wrists and he had long since lost feeling in his hands. There was a bruise under his eye and blood matted his hair. Thirst burned his throat. He lolled sideways and winced as pain tugged at his ribs.

Behind Doctor Falchion trotted a packhorse laden with his instruments and medicines. Behind the packhorse, rode Mei. She was unbound and rode with her back straight and her head high. It puzzled Falchion how a simple scullery girl could carry herself like the soldiers who had captured them.

Falchion's mount stumbled, throwing him forward. He cried out and his guard shot him a warning glare.

What manner of men were these? Falchion asked himself. They moved with calm efficiency. Their leader was a man with dark and hollow eyes that seemed bottomless and without pity. 'Meng,' his soldiers had called him.

Memories came back to him in searing flashbacks. He had tried to stop them carrying away his medicines and a soldier had cuffed him to his knees. Hard hands had pinned his arms and forced down his head. There was the testing caress of a blade on his neck. He remembered his breathing, fast and shallow. He had screwed shut his eyes and recited the Our Father.

Then, a familiar voice spoke. 'Don't kill him. He's a doctor.

## THE SCHOLAR'S BLADE

He can treat sword cuts and the gut rot.'

The old bandit was there, a broadsword in his fist and defiance burning his eyes. His voice had been clear and deep. 'You have your supplies, now leave.'

Without a word, Meng had knocked the broadsword aside and slashed his own blade across the old man's belly.

Falchion had bellowed his rage and struggled to release himself. As he tried to writhe free, pain had flashed through his skull and catapulted him into darkness.

Now, the column picked its way through swampy flatlands. At dusk, Meng called a halt and they made camp on the slopes of a low, scrub-covered hill. A soldier dragged Falchion from his saddle, propped him against a tree and tied his ankle to an iron pin, which he hammered into the ground.

Falchion eased his back against the tree trunk. His lips were cracked and his tongue felt twice its normal size. His head throbbed and there was no feeling in his hands. By morning, he thought, there will be gangrene in those hands. It would have been kinder to take his head.

A shadow fell across Falchion and he looked up into the face of the Taiping commander, Meng.

'What do you mean to do with me?' he asked.

'I mean to see if you are useful,' Meng replied.

Falchion gawked at him. Meng had spoken in flawless English.

A smile played on Meng's lips. 'You seem surprised,' he said. He squatted on his haunches so his eyes were level with the doctor's. His lips twisted in scorn. 'Surprised that some of us have had a fine *Christian* education.'

He stood and smoothed down the front of his tunic. He glared down at the doctor. 'You had best pray to your Christian God that you are indeed, useful.' He beckoned to another soldier then turned and stalked away.

The second Taiping moved closer. He had a weathered face and dressed his hair in a topknot. He dropped to one knee and tested Falchion's bindings.

'If Captain Meng decides you're useless, he'll gut you just for the sport of it,' he said. 'Better to cut your throat now and get it over with.' He pulled a slim dagger from his belt.

Doctor Falchion screwed shut his eyes and waited for the stab of pain. Instead, there was a tug at his bindings and they fell away. His hands began to tingle. The tingle became burning agony. He massaged his wrists and gritted his teeth, he would not let this Taiping enjoy his suffering.

'You're a tough old weasel,' the soldier chuckled. He shoved a water bottle into Falchion's hands.

Falchion sputtered as the water stuck in his throat and stung the back of his nose.

'Slowly, drink slowly,' the soldier cautioned.

Falchion forced himself to sip the water and felt some strength seep back into his limbs.

The soldier cut a wad of dried beef and offered it skewered on his knifepoint. Falchion took it then paused.

'Are you an officer?' Falchion asked.

The soldier threw back his head and laughed.

'Me? Cho Lung? An officer?' he scoffed. 'No, I'm no officer. But do you see those men?' He used his dagger to point to the other soldiers. 'They are my comrades and my brothers but they do as I tell them.' He slowly shook his head. 'If they do not, they will feel my anger and believe me, they do not want that.'

He scratched his chin with his knifepoint then settled himself cross-legged beside Falchion. 'I hear foreign doctors are all drunk from breakfast to bedtime,' he said. 'But if we must have you tagging along, you're no good half starved and with your hands rotted off.'

Falchion slipped the wad of beef into his mouth and began to chew. It tasted like salty leather. He watched the sun's disc drop towards distant hills and the clouds turn from white to orange. The sun dipped below the horizon and night fell like a dropped blanket. Falchion cast down his eyes and spoke in a whisper.

'Have they...' he struggled over the words, dreading the answer. 'Have they... touched the girl?'

Cho Lung scowled. 'Are we Imperials?' he snorted. 'Our general would have the head of any man who used a woman that way.' He gave a low growl. 'Aye, and the balls of any top soldier who stood back and let it happen.'

'So why take her? Why not let her go?'

'It's not for me to say,' Cho answered. 'But I'll tell you this, the girl's got heart.'

He stood and brushed grass from his britches. 'She's safe enough. And for now, so are you.' He bent over Falchion and pointed at the doctor's face. 'But heed this,' he growled. 'If you stop being useful, neither I nor your God Himself can save you.' He stepped away and walked into the night.

Doctor James Falchion settled himself back against the tree. The cicadas started their chirping chorus. Men moved around the camp, chatting and rattling cooking pots. Horses stamped and snorted. He listened to the camp's noises and wondered how he might reach his instruments. A scalpel was as good as a dagger on a dark night. He sighed and shook his head. He could no more cut a man's throat than he could abandon Mei to these soldiers. The man called Cho had a gruff decency, but what of the others?

He put the question aside, he was a doctor and if need be, he would suture their wounds and ease their pains. But he was old and could not ride like these Taipings. He might even slow them down.

And if that happened, Doctor James Falchion would die.

*Tarantula* thumped her way past the eastern wall of Shanghai's Chinese quarter. It was a fortress wall; a wall of dark granite that sat heavily on the embankment. Showing above its parapet was a jumble of watchtowers and rooftops.

Further along the Huangpu's Shanghai embankment, fortress walls gave way to Western trading houses with wide verandas and Doric pillars.

On the water, little *sampans* bustled about tall clipper ships. There were riverboats driven by sail and sweep. Smoke poured from the stacks of steamers. Under bat-wing sails, an ocean-going junk plodded the fairway, heading north to the Yangtze and from there to the open sea.

'Soon be landed old fellow.'

Mark had not heard Jessop come up behind him.

'Whose is the wonderful *yamen*?' Mark asked, pointing to where a Chinese-style building dominated the waterfront. It had pagoda-like sections rising to a height of four storeys.

'British Customs and Excise,' Jessop said. A shadow crossed his face. 'Thieving buggers to a man.' He pointed to a handsome, redbrick building next to the Customs House. 'And that's the Shanghai Traders' Club,' he added. 'You'll need mighty good connections to get in there.'

Mark was not listening. 'I've heard you can drive bullocks twelve abreast along Shanghai's streets,' he said.

'Can't say I've tried,' Jessop replied. He grinned. 'I suppose you could manage that along some of the streets.' He lowered his voice to a conspiratorial whisper. 'But only if you really want to.' He placed his hands on the railing. 'What are your plans?' he asked.

Mark lowered his eyes. 'My plans are in ruins,' he said. 'I'll seek employment, then...' His voice tailed into silence.

'Do you have money?'

'Some.' Mark tapped the pouch hidden in the folds of his gown. 'Enough to tide me over.'

'Excellent.' Jessop slapped Mark's shoulder. 'I recommend the Sea Horse Hotel on the Yang King Pang Canal. Clean, well-run and only sixty dollars a month. All meals a dollar. Top notch value.'

Mark swallowed hard. Sixty dollars was a fortune.

'I'll report your father's abduction to the consulate, but...' Jessop shrugged. He reached into his tunic and took out a small card. 'Here, take this,' he said.

Mark took the card and read it twice. It bore Jessop's name and rank and gave his address as care of the British Consulate. Mark thought it a strange gift and his cheeks burned when he realised he had nothing to give in return.

Jessop chuckled at Mark's discomfort. 'If I can be of any small service, you'll find me at the Hotel de l'Europe most afternoons.' He raised a finger as if remembering something. 'Oh, and maybe I can introduce you to someone who could use your...' he paused, struggling to find the right words. '...Your more *unusual* talents.'

There was a shout from the bow. Chains rattled through the port and the anchor splashed into the water. The deck came alive with sailors. A petty officer stalked amongst them, his eyes everywhere.

'We've anchored off the Jardine and Matheson pontoon,' Jessop said. 'I'll call a *sampan* to drop you there.'

Sergeant Verrals clumped to a halt beside Jessop, threw him a salute and whispered into his ear. Jessop gave a nod and backed away from Mark.

'Duty, I'm afraid, old chap.' He raised his hand in farewell.

'Don't forget, Hotel de l'Europe any time after midday.' He turned and strode across the deck. Sergeant Verrals gave a little skip to match Jessop's step and marched after him.

Mark leaned against the railing and pictured his father standing on the Sishun jetty. He remembered Mei's touch on his arm and the touch of her lips against his. There was the raw memory of death in the garden pavilion.

Then he drank in the crowded anchorages and the shoreline with its gleaming trading houses. The city was all he knew it would be. It was a city of dreams.

It was Shanghai.

'Hey, Mister!' The voice belonged to the sampan boy who had rowed Mark to the pontoon. The boy's foot rested on Mark's pack and he held out his hand, palm open. 'Now give money,' he said in squeaky English.

Mark tossed him a copper coin. The boy frowned and his voice became resentful. 'Give more money. Give now.'

Mark fished out another coin and threw it to the boy. The boy muttered under his breath and hefted Mark's pack onto the pontoon. Mark stepped off the *sampan* and the boy sculled back into the stream.

The pontoon bobbed in the swell. Mark shouldered his pack, gripped tight to his staff and stepped ashore. Mooring lines groaned as cargo lighters scraped against the river wall. Ropes squealed through pulleys. Coolies bounced along gangplanks, backs bent under hessian sacks. Overseers called out the timing as men hauled on lines attached to cargo nets. Mark ducked as a net laden with barrels swung past his head. He left the cargo basin and walked onto the waterfront boulevard called the Shanghai Bund.

He turned full circle, never had he seen so many people.

## THE SCHOLAR'S BLADE

They dashed about, heads down. A man barged Mark aside and moved on without a word. A leper clutched at Mark's leg. A sidewalk cook stirred bean curd into a sizzling wok. In the carriageway, draught horses and bare-chested coolies hauled carts laden down with cargo. There were rickshaws bearing silk-clad Chinese and olive-skinned Parsees. Sedan chairs swayed between the shoulders of sweating bearers. The rumble of wheels, the calls of rickshaw boys and the shouts of street traders tumbled together in ear-battering confusion. The city bristled with noise and urgency. So much bustle, such wonderful buildings, such roads.

And such prices!

Through his gown, Mark touched the pouch his father had given him. First, he must find somewhere to stay then he would get a hot meal inside him. According to Jessop, the Sea Horse Hotel was a half mile to the south. Tomorrow, Mark decided, he would start at the Bund's southern end and work his way north. He was sure to find a business house to employ him. Tomorrow, things would look better.

The sun was high and despite a breeze off the river, the cotton tunic under Mark's gown clung to his back, damp and itchy. He adjusted his pack and set off along the Bund. His steps were light and he found himself humming a half-forgotten tune. It is easy to feel good on such a day, he thought. The Shanghai Bund must be the widest, longest, most wonderful road in the entire world.

Memories of a fire-blacked ruin prickled his conscience. He pushed the memories away. He needed time to think, time to plan. But try as he might, Mark could not escape the arithmetic. He could not pay a month's rent at the Sea Horse nor any other hotel.

'Excuse me sir.'

The voice seemed far off, an irritating distraction.

'I say, excuse me.'

Mark glanced round to see a European following him along the kerb.

'Yes sir, you sir.'

The man wore a brown suit with a broad yellow check. The jacket was too tight and the trousers stopped short of his ankles. He had a pomaded moustache and slick hair parted down the centre. His lips were fleshy with a hint of petulance. He carried a mahogany cane, which he waved to emphasise his words.

'Hold up old chap.'

He drew level with Mark, and mopped his face with a red handkerchief.

'Damned climate,' he wheezed. 'Fit only for Chinkies and other heathens.'

He looked Mark over and for a moment, was silent. He gave a small cough and stuck out his hand.

'Buttersmith, Roger Buttersmith.' He inclined his head. 'May I assume you have been, *er*, upcountry?'

'If my appearance bothers you, I'll bid you good day.' Mark ignored the handshake and stalked off, unsure why he had taken such dislike to the man.

Buttersmith scuttled after him. 'Please... please wait.'

Mark stopped and Buttersmith caught up, panting and mopping his face.

'Your appearance is, *um*, a little remarkable.' He held up a hand. 'But don't take on. I mean no offence, none at all.'

'Perhaps you can tell me how I might help you,' Mark asked, his voice tight.

'Ah, help indeed. You and I can help each other, can we not?' Buttersmith grinned and gave a flamboyant wink.

Mark shook his head. 'I don't follow,' he said.

'Accommodation, sir,' Buttersmith continued, as though

talking to a child. 'Do you have somewhere to stay?'

Mark sighed and his shoulders sagged.

'I see, your face says it all.' Buttersmith put his head close to Mark's. 'The *prices*. The town's simply full o' robbers.'

Mark shook his head then turned and continued to walk south.

Buttersmith followed, chatting like an old friend.

'I'm looking for new lodgings myself,' he chirped. 'My thieving landlord's charging seventy a month and not even a decent meal thrown in.'

He smiled and waved to the occupants of a carriage that rattled by.

'Got myself a crack at Dent and Beale's staff Mess,' he continued. 'It's supposed to be for Dent's juniors but they've some spare rooms.' He looked around as though checking for eavesdroppers. 'Fifty a month *and* full board. Fancy, just fifty. Right next to the Customs House too.'

'Fine,' Mark said from between clenched teeth. 'Excellent. Fifty a month. Take it and good luck.'

Buttersmith tagged along like an unwanted puppy. 'Can't, old fellow.' His voice became sly. 'Not unless I find someone to share, that is.'

Mark stopped and looked Buttersmith in the face.

A light smile played on Buttersmith's lips. 'What do you say old fellow? Fifty a month, all found.'

Mark paused, weighing the possibilities. 'Dent and Beale?' he asked, more to gain time than information. 'How far is it?'

Buttersmith swivelled on his heels and pointed his cane at a building set back from the road. 'Why, I do believe it's right here.'

The building was two stories high. A deep veranda ran the full length of its upper floor. Mark could see young men lounging in its shade. Fixed to the gate, a brass plate read:

## Dent, Beale and Company Junior Mess

'The young gentlemen are very well connected.' Buttersmith's voice was like soft oil. 'A man's nothing without connections. You'll secure a good position within days or my name's not Roger Buttersmith.'

Mark reached for the gate but there was a tug on his arm.

'Not so fast old fellow. How can I say this? I fear Dent and Beale have, *em*... a rather conservative dress code.'

Mark hesitated, feeling out of place.

'But not to worry,' Buttersmith continued. 'I'm well acquainted with the master of the house and I'll be glad to make arrangements for us both.'

Relief washed through Mark. His lips cracked in a smile. He had found lodgings and soon he would make useful contacts. Truly, Shanghai was a wondrous place.

Buttersmith rubbed his thumb and his forefinger together. 'I'm afraid, sir, I must make the arrangements in advance.'

'Of course, Mister Buttersmith, of course.' Mark reached into his gown, pulled out his pouch and counted coins into Buttersmith's hand. 'Fifty you said. Here, it's all I have.' A rush of doubt nagged at his confidence. 'You won't be long will you?'

'Not at all my friend. Back in a jiffy.'

Buttersmith jingled the coins, pushed open the gate and took the steps leading to the front door two at a time. He grinned at Mark and disappeared into the lobby's gloom.

Mark waited by the gate and watched the people pass by. The Chinese, serene in their silks. The Europeans, red faced in their jackets and wing collars. Out on the river, ships flying the ensigns of France, America, Holland and Britain vied with steamers, sail-driven lorchas and Chinese junks. Mark wondered how they did not pile into one another. If China is the centre of the world, he thought, Shanghai must be the centre of China.

A European emerged from the house and stared at Mark from beneath eyebrows so arched, they almost touched his hairline. He strode off, muttering to himself.

Twice Mark pushed open the gate but each time he decided to give Buttersmith a few minutes more. After what seemed hours, Mark forced himself to walk the length of the path. The door loomed above him. He raised his hand but his knuckles made barely a sound against the heavy wood. He turned a brass handle and the door swung open.

He stood framed in the doorway and let his eyes grow accustomed to the gloom. The lobby had a high ceiling and polished floorboards. Compared to the street, it was quiet and cool. Standing just inside the door was a man who wore a dark, high-necked tunic fastened with brass buttons. He had muttonchop whiskers and a bulbous nose. His face flushed as he spied Mark.

'Whot 'ave we 'ere?' he demanded. He grabbed Mark's arm and pulled him to the door. 'No argument now, Sunshine. Orf you go or I'll give your jacksie a kicking you'll not forget in a hurry.'

He bundled Mark onto the porch and slapped his hands together like someone who has finished a dusty chore. He screwed up his eyes and squinted at Mark.

'Gawd luv us.' he said. Are you a white man, a Chinaman or bleedin' what?'

'If you'll let me explain, sir,' Mark pleaded as he smoothed out the creases in his sleeve. 'My new acquaintance, Mister Buttersmith, is arranging our lodgings. Now please take me to the master of the house...'

'Oh my Lord, it speaks like a proper person it does. Don't

know nuffin' about no lodgings,' the man sniffed. He tugged his jacket straight. 'But what a day it's been. Some young Johnny barged in an hour ago. In through the front and out the back as fast as you like.' He planted his fists on his hips and scowled at Mark. 'Now I'm guessing you're not one of Dent and Beale's young gentlemen, so be orf with you.'

The door slammed with a cavernous bang. Panic burned Mark's neck. He ran to the lane leading to the back of the house but found it empty. He ran back to the Bund. He looked to the north and to the south. A pit opened in his stomach as his eyes searched the footpath and carriageway.

But the people of Shanghai just went about their business and passed him by.

By the time Mark found his way back to the Jardine and Matheson pontoon, the sun was an orange ball peeking between the trading houses. It cast long shadows across the Bund and turned the Huangpu into liquid copper. The coolies had stopped their labours. Crates and piles of netting littered the quayside boardwalk. The river slapped against the pontoon, which creaked in the swell.

Mark rifled his pack and found the last of Moy Saam's dumplings. He sat and rested his back against a crate. There was a rustling behind him and a voice drifted from the shadows.

'Greetings, little brother.'

Mark peered into the dark and made out a figure silhouetted against the river. The figure was naked from the waist up. Stringy muscle covered his arms and shoulders.

'Will you not share what's in your pack?' The voice was at once cajoling and menacing.

Mark rose to a half-crouch and reached for his staff.

'Come any nearer and I'll crack your skull,' he growled.

## THE SCHOLAR'S BLADE

'Crack skulls, little brother? What? All of them?'

A rumbling noise surrounded Mark. It was a noise a waking army might make. From behind every crate, every coil of rope, each pile of canvas and wooden chest, more figures emerged. Their numbers grew until Mark could no longer count them. They stood shoulder to shoulder and edged closer. Mark lunged with his staff but still they advanced. He reached for his pack but it was beyond his grasp.

'Stay, little brother,' the voice crooned. 'Stay if you think it worthwhile.'

Mark backed away, all hope of recovering his pack gone. His heart raced. He risked a look over his shoulder. The way back to the Bund was clear. For a moment he paused, then he turned and ran.

He ran with his soul full of fear. He ran as though all *Yan Luo's* demons were after him. Behind him, something clattered against the road. He realised he had thrown away his staff. Watchmen raised their lanterns. Drunken soldiers cheered his passing. Mark Falchion ran until his breath came in heavy sobs and his heart was set to burst. He ran until the strength drained from his legs. Then he fell to his knees and the bile rose in his throat. A shudder ran through him and he vomited at the roadside.

Eventually, his heart stopped pounding, his breathing eased and his strength returned. But he did not stand.

Instead, he buried his face in his hands and began to weep.

# 13

From its marble-floored lobby, through to the wood-panelled China Coast Bar, to the elegantly relaxed Tai Pan restaurant, to the opulence of the Library Lounge, to its superbly stocked wine cellar, right down to its green baize billiards tables, the Shanghai Traders' Club was the very model of a London gentleman's retreat.

Paintings of English foxhunting scenes graced the walls. Silent stewards in starched jackets padded the corridors. In the Library Lounge there were overstuffed armchairs. Newspaper racks bore copies of the *North-China Herald* and there were even back copies of *Punch* magazine. There was the smell of camphor oil, cigar smoke and fine brandy. The club was a place where men of consequence could either take time to relax or to meet like-minded men to shape the future of great trading houses.

But there were times when like-minded men met to decide far weightier matters.

General Sir John Michel sank into his armchair and enjoyed the breeze from an array of ceiling *punkahs*. The only sound was hushed conversation, the wafting of the *punkahs* and the rustle of newspapers.

Michel crossed his legs and plucked at the sabre-edged crease running down the front of his trousers. As a young subaltern, soldiering had been simple: follow the colours, obey orders and trust higher command to know right from wrong. He smiled to himself. Now, as he prepared to take command of Her Britannic

Majesty's army in China, soldiering looked very different. He swirled brandy around his snifter and raised it in salute to his companion.

Michel felt a surge of brotherly affection for the naval officer sitting opposite him. Compared to the dapper Sir John, Admiral Sir James Hope looked uneasy amongst the club's furnishings. He was heavyset with broad shoulders and a belligerent brow.

The two men looked very different but they had much in common. Michel was a soldier's soldier. He liked nothing more than to discuss soldiering with his junior officers. His openness with the enlisted men shocked even his own staff officers. For his part, Admiral Hope had the granite exterior typical of his generation. Between decks, his men dubbed him 'Fighting Jimmie.' His duties kept him chained to the shore, but his men knew him as a master of the sailing art.

Behind Michel, a steward coughed and leaned forward, offering a tray upon which lay an embossed card. Michel removed the card and made a show of reading it although he knew perfectly well to whom it belonged.

'Thank you Barnet,' he said. 'Please show the gentleman in.'

As the steward withdrew, Michel fixed Hope with a cautionary look.

'Now James, don't go scaring the boy off, he said.' He peered around the wing of his armchair and, satisfied no one could hear, he continued speaking. 'Our Mister Alabaster might be new to the Consular Corps but he knows the Taiping situation better than anyone.'

Hope gave a non-committal grunt and frowned into his port glass.

'Gentlemen, Mister Chaloner Alabaster.' The steward had returned. Behind him hovered a young man. The steward bowed then seemed to fade into the wood panelling.

Chaloner Alabaster had a smooth forehead and bloodless lips. He had thinning hair and wispy mutton-chop whiskers.

Sir John grinned. 'Michel,' he announced, reaching over and grasping Alabaster's hand.

The young man's eyes popped. 'Honoured Mister... I mean, General... *er*, Sir...'

'Yes, yes, and all the rest.' Michel waved a dismissive hand. 'And this scallywag sailor is Admiral Sir James Hope.'

'Delighted, sir,' Hope grunted, looking far from delighted.

Michel waved Chaloner Alabaster to an empty armchair and the younger man perched on its edge like a schoolboy taking tea with his housemaster.

'Brandy Mister Alabaster?' Michel asked.

'What?' Chaloner Alabaster's eyebrows shot up. 'Ah... yes. I mean, yes *sir*. Brandy would be most agreeable.'

'Agreeable is it?' Hope muttered.

'To business, gentlemen.' Michel brought his hands together in a light clap. 'This damned rebellion is getting too close for comfort. The city's jammed with refugees, food prices are out of control and medical services are on the verge of collapse. The Taipings are secure in Soochow and according to reliable intelligence they mean to come further east.'

Hope squinted at Michel. 'And? Come along John, out with it.'

Michel shrugged. 'I'm just a simple soldier, James, but I'll lay a pound to a pinch of snuff they mean to have Shanghai.'

Hope snorted and shifted in his seat, spilling port down the front of his jacket. He pulled a huge handkerchief from his pocket and dabbed at his lapels.

'Damn. What? Shanghai? They wouldn't dare.'

'No? Think of it, man. I've only a regiment of foot and you've what? A few marines?'

'But... but...' Hope spluttered. 'The Crown... it would never forgive the insult. One shot and the Taipings'll bring the might of empire on their furry little heads.'

'Will they?' Michel's voice was harsh. He turned to Chaloner Alabaster and his voice became soothing. 'Well, Mister Alabaster, you know the Foreign Office mind. Can we expect help from London?'

Chaloner Alabaster ran a finger round the inside of his collar. 'I, *er*... believe...'

'Come on my boy, you tell him.' Hope's voice had the tone of a crusty uncle.

Alabaster' eyes darted from Hope to Michel and back again.

'Well, actually...' He took a deep breath. 'Her Majesty's Government thinks it vital we remain neutral in the Chinese civil war.' He drained his brandy snifter in one swallow.

Hope cocked his head as if he had misheard. 'What? Neutral? Bloody *neutral?*'

Alabaster blanched and his neck seemed to withdraw into his shoulders. His voice became small. 'It's the *status quo* sir. It's the...'

Hope's face turned scarlet. 'You'll be less keen on the *status quo* with your bollocks dangling from a Taiping spear tip,' he growled. 'Bloody neutral indeed.'

Michel held up is hand. 'Steady, James, steady. He's right.'

Hope bristled. His cheeks reddened.

'Hear me out, James,' Michel coaxed. 'The Taipings don't need the foreign settlements. They'll hoist their guns onto the walls of the Chinese quarter and dictate any terms they want.' He sipped his brandy and frowned. 'Do you see the French or the bloody Americans rushing in troops?' He held up a finger, cutting off Hope before he could speak. 'That lot will watch us fall and scoop up some juicy trade deals when we do.'

He turned to Chaloner Alabaster. 'I understand you've been following the Taiping situation, Mister Alabaster. What can you tell us?' he asked.

'The Taipings are overextended, sir,' Chaloner Alabaster said, growing in confidence. 'They hold vast areas of hinterland but have no ports of note. Their weapons belong in museums, they lack military structure as we know it and their enemies press them on all flanks. Their only foreign trade is through smugglers who bleed them dry. They're desperate, I believe they'll attack.'

'It pains me to think of the untapped trade bottled up in the Taiping lands,' Michel said. 'But make no mistake, James, their ruler's a madman. He claims God-given sovereignty over the whole world. If he takes Peking, God knows where we'll be.'

Hope sighed. 'We can't just let them walk in, John. We'll lose everything. Fifteen years up the spout. Fifteen years, wasted.'

Michel lowered his voice, forcing the others to lean closer.

'I fear it's more serious than it sounds,' he said. 'As we speak, I'm putting together an expeditionary force in Hong Kong. I've orders to march on Peking and make the blessed emperor honour the treaties we dragged out of him in 'forty-two. Now there's the situation with the blasted Taipings. If we're not careful, we'll end up fighting 'em both. How's that for neutrality?'

Alabaster gave a small cough. 'The... er... French will think we're using the situation to bring China under the British Empire. So will the Prussians and the Americans. Under all circumstances, gentlemen, we must avoid war with the great powers.'

'War?' Hope threw Chaloner Alabaster a sceptical look. 'I doubt it'll come to war.'

Michel chuckled. 'You know the Frogs, James, they distrust us on principal. The Americans would kick our backsides just for hell of it. And as for the Prussians, well, the less said.'

Hope squinted at Michel as though he were peering through a blizzard. 'You're at it again you old bugger. Come on, let's see your damned cards.'

Michel rolled his brandy around his glass.

'Some Chinese business types have put together a force of irregulars,' he continued. 'I've heard they're mighty impressed by its commander.' He tapped the side of his nose. 'Best keep it under your hats, eh.'

Hope bunched his fists. 'I hope you're not talking about the Yankee crimper who's been poaching my gunners? Lost three this week, two the week before. He'll decorate a navy yardarm if I lay hands on him.'

Michel grinned. 'Take care, James. His Excellency the American consul might voice an objection.'

Chaloner Alabaster gave a thin smile and pulled a sheet of paper from his jacket.

'My report, sir.' He handed the paper to Michel. 'The fellow goes by the name of Frederick Ward. He comes from a good family but he's something of an outcast. He's been a sailing officer, he's mined gold in California and was some kind of constable in Texas. He even served with the French army in the Crimea.' He raised an eyebrow. 'Seems the French let him go after an unruly incident with a colonel.'

Hope sniffed. 'What's that? God save us from a Yankee freebooter with Frog connections.' He gave a half-laugh. 'Texas Constable indeed. A mercenary's a damned mercenary.' He shook his head. 'Let's have the American consul cancel his passport and ship him home?'

'Slow down James.' Michel placed a hand on the Admiral's sleeve. 'I'm afraid I've not been completely open with you.'

Hope rolled his eyes. 'Now there's news,' he said.

'I've had my eye on this chap Ward, he's a most unusual

fellow. With a little help, this particular mercenary might solve the Taiping situation for us.'

Hope grunted his disapproval. '*Hrrmph*. He's got the world's best gunners, what more could he want?'

'He could do with a liaison officer. Don't want him cozying up to the French do we?' Michel let the question hang, a knowing smile on his lips.

Hope frowned. 'Can't say I like the idea but I suppose you're right, damn you.' He hunkered down in his chair. 'Can't spare a sailing officer, it'll have to be a marine,' he said. 'I've one young fellow, bit of a puppy but a bright chap. Goes by the name of Jacobs. No, Jessop, Harry Jessop. Family's as rich as Crœsus. Keeps an apartment at the Hotel de l'Europe.' He fluttered his hand in resignation. 'He's attached to *Tarantula* but they'll have to do without him. I'll have him report to you first thing tomorrow.'

The soldier and the sailor smiled and sank back into their armchairs. Sir John Michel let the punkahs' breeze cool his face. China, he thought, beautiful and dangerous, like an ambitious harlot. His days of following the colours were long gone, now he had to ape the politicians he despised. But if helping one mercenary saved British trading rights and spared the lives of his soldiers, then he had done a good day's work.

He gazed at the ceiling. Dear oh dear, he thought, General Sir John Michel in cahoots with an American mercenary.

Whatever next?

The man had the bushiest side-whiskers Mark Falchion had ever seen. Resplendent in a purple coat, he stood at the top of broad stairs leading to the Hotel de l'Europe's grand frontage. Gleaming buttons and gold braid covered his chest. He wore a top hat and knee high boots. He placed his fists on his hips and glowered down at Mark.

Mark examined his own clothes: streaks of tar from the wharf and filth from the gutter smeared his gown. His hands were black with grime. He pictured his face, no doubt just as grubby. Hunger nagged at his guts and his head swam.

He had Harry Jessop's calling card in his hand. Any time after noon, the young officer had said. Mark looked at the doorman and his heart sank. A card signed by the emperor himself won't get me through that door, he thought.

A boy wearing knee-britches scuttled from the hotel lobby and whispered to the doorman. The doorman nodded and strutted down the steps. He put a whistle to his lips and blew a loud blast. A pair of sedan chair bearers waiting in the shade of a nearby tree, hoisted their chair and jogged towards the hotel.

A Westerner wearing a crumpled suit of white linen emerged from the doorway. His paunch hung over his waistband and there were damp patches under his arms. He stared at Mark, gave a sniff then puffed his way down the steps. He pressed a coin into the doorman's hand and crammed himself into the sedan chair.

With the doorman's back turned, Mark ran up the steps and paused before the hotel's revolving door. He reached for the door but it swung away from him. He let out a yelp as the following section banged against his elbow.

'*Oi*, what are you bleedin' up to?' The doorman raised his hand and strode up the steps.

Mark dived into the revolving door and pushed. He gasped as the following door leaf bore down on him, threatening to knock him down. He pushed faster and the door catapulted him into a cool lobby. He staggered forward, fighting for balance.

The lobby floor was polished granite. Against the walls, tall plants stood in porcelain pots. The ceiling soared two stories high and from it swung an array of cooling *punkahs*. A staircase cut a graceful arc from the lobby to a first-floor gallery. Mark drank it all in, his eyes wide.

Against the lobby's far wall, there was a reception counter, behind which stood a clerk. He had glossy hair and a thin nose on which was perched a set of *pince-nez* spectacles.

Mark fixed a smile of sham confidence to his lips and walked to the counter. The clerk gaped at Mark and glanced about, looking everywhere but at Mark. Mark planted himself before the counter but the clerk put down his head and busied himself with some papers.

A knot formed in Mark's stomach, he struggled to keep his voice calm. 'Please inform Lieutenant Jessop that Mister Mark Falchion is here,' he said.

The clerk pretended not to hear.

Behind Mark, booted feet hurried across the lobby. Mark rapped his knuckles against the counter. His voice took on an edge. 'I have had a trying day, sir. Please do me the kindness of telling Lieutenant Jessop I'm here.'

A hand gripped Mark's arm. 'Now my lad, let's be 'aving you,' the doorman growled. 'Nice and easy. No trouble now,'

'Let go, sir.' Mark snapped. 'I have an appointment with one of your guests.' He spread his feet and refused to move.

'You've an appointment sure enough,' the doorman said. 'And it's with the street outside. Best not keep it waiting, eh?'

Mark reached across his body, took an overhand grip on the doorman's wrist and pushed hard against the joint. The doorman let out a yelp as he found himself forced up onto his toes.

Mark spoke through clenched teeth. 'There's a distinct lack of hospitality in this city, sir. Now, please announce me to Lieutenant Jessop.'

'I'll 'ave you,' the doorman snarled. He balled his fist but

Mark put more pressure on the wrist joint. The doorman cried out and screwed shut his eyes.

'Goodness me, Mister Falchion, it seems you're always in some scrape or other.' There was no mistaking Harry Jessop's voice. 'Now, be a good chap and release our Mister Cludge.'

Mark released the doorman and he stepped back, clutching his wrist to his chest.

'Bastard,' he hissed. 'I'll 'ave you, sure as anything.'

'It's all right, Cludge,' Jessop said. 'He's with me.'

'If'n you say so, Mister Jessop, sir.' The doorman glared at Mark and still nursing his wrist, stalked back to the door.

Jessop looked Mark over and gave a low whistle. 'My God, I shan't ask how you've been enjoying city life.' He turned to the reception counter. 'Timmins,' he called.

The clerk drew himself upright and snapped his lapels straight. 'Ah, Lieutenant Jessop,' he fawned, 'how may I serve you today, sir?'

'To start with, Timmins, let me introduce Mister Falchion.' Jessop paused, as if expecting a response. 'Mister *Mark* Falchion...'

Timmins' expression remained blank.

'Of the Suffolk Falchions, man. You do know the *Suffolk* Falchions, do you not?'

Mark opened his mouth but Jessop kicked his ankle.

'Why, *er*... of course,' Timmins stammered. 'I, *um*... who has not heard of the *Suffolk* Falchions?'

'Who indeed, Timmins?'

Jessop thumped Mark on the back. 'Looks like you could manage a bite to eat. Irish stew I think, with extra dumplings. Did you get that, Timmins?'

'Yes sir, Mister Jessop.'

'And have a bath drawn for Mister Falchion, if you please.'

Timmins bobbed his head. 'Certainly sir. Will you require

room service for the food?'

'Indeed I will, Timmins, indeed I will. And as pronto as you can, please.'

Jessop took Mark's elbow and steered him to the staircase.

'Perfect timing old chap, he said.' He glanced over his shoulder and spoke in a whisper. 'Couldn't have worked better if we'd planned it.'

They climbed the staircase, walked along the gallery and turned into a corridor. Fresh cut flowers scented the air. Thick-piled carpet muffled their footsteps. At the end of the corridor was a door bearing a brass plate etched with the words, *Elgin Suite*.

Jessop winked. 'I think you'll find today's meeting beneficial,' he declared. 'Yes indeed, most beneficial.'

The door opened onto a large drawing room. There were leather armchairs and mahogany side tables. Pictures of craggy mountains and seascapes hung at the walls. In the middle of the room was a table with a baize top. French windows opened onto a deep veranda.

Standing by the French windows was a man with skin the colour of roast coffee. A heavy jaw gave him the look of a street brawler. He wore a tunic of forest green and dark blue britches tucked into calf-high boots. The butt of a revolver poked from the flap of a cross-draw holster hanging from his belt. He was taller than Mark and a little older. He stepped towards them.

'Good afternoon Vincente.' Jessop pronounced the name, *Vincent-ay*. He smiled and shook the man's hand as though he were an old friend.

'Hello Harry.' Vincente's voice was a mixture of gravel and molasses. It carried a trace of Spain.

'Are the others here?' Jessop asked.

'Not yet.' Vincente pulled a watch from his pocket. 'They'll be

## THE SCHOLAR'S BLADE

an hour at least.'

Jessop touched Mark's arm. 'Mark, let me introduce Mister Vincente Macanaya.' His eyes sparkled. 'He's a black-hearted Manilaman from the Philippine Islands. But he's passable company.'

'I am honoured, Mister Macanaya.' Mark clasped his hands together at his chest and bowed.

'May *Santo Nino* save us from formal Englishmen,' the Filipino chuckled. 'From the Bund to Bamboo Town they just call me Vincente.'

There was a knock and a steward wheeled in a trolley bearing a dome-like cloche. With a flourish, he whipped away the cloche to reveal a tureen brimming with a delicious-smelling stew. He spread a linen cloth over the table, laid a single place then withdrew.

Mark tried not to eat like a savage but the stew was the most wonderful meal he had ever eaten. Finished, he pushed himself back from the table.

There was another knock and the same steward announced Mark's bath. He bowed Mark from the *Elgin Suite* and led him along the corridor to a room where porcelain tiles reflected soft amber light from wall-mounted oil lamps. Duckboards covered the floor and a steaming tub dominated the room. The steward handed Mark a towel and indicated he should undress.

As Mark lowered himself into the water, the steward gathered up his clothes and left.

Minutes later, another steward entered carrying a tray on which there was a razor, a foaming shaving mug and a bottle of bay leaf lotion. As the bath soothed away Mark's tensions, the steward soaped his chin and scraped the razor over his jaw. He slapped stinging lotion onto Mark's face then dressed his hair and reset his queue.

Mark must have drifted into sleep because he woke to find the water had cooled. On a stool next to him lay his clothes, sponged, flat-ironed and folded.

As he walked the corridor back to the *Elgin Suite*, a sense of unreality folded around Mark. It was as if the last few days were not real at all, it was as if they were just a collection of borrowed memories.

He let himself back into the suit and found three others had joined Vincente and Jessop. One was a middle-aged Chinese. He had a melon-shaped head topped with a velvet cap. He wore a pair of spectacles that magnified his eyes, giving him a look of permanent surprise. A gown of dark silk stretched tight over an ample paunch.

The others were Westerners. One was short and slim. His back was straight and his shoulders were square. Sabre sharp creases ran the length of his trousers. Despite his slight stature, he carried himself like a man more used to giving orders than taking them.

The third newcomer was younger. He had an unkempt mop of black hair and a heavy moustache. His eyes were like polished bullets. A slim goatee emphasised a square chin. The five men stood huddled over a map, its edges weighed down by a pistol and a half-empty brandy bottle.

Vincente looked up. 'Gentlemen,' he announced. 'Mark Falchion has returned.'

The older Westerner slipped the pistol into his jacket and the map rolled shut with a snap. Vincente stood at Mark's side and extended his arm. 'Mark, let me present Sir John...'

'Enough, young Vincente,' the older man snapped. 'I'm not here, remember?'

Vincente flashed him a white-toothed smile. 'Then who shall we say drank all the brandy, sir?'

The older man let out a throaty laugh. 'You're a scoundrel Vincente,' he chortled. 'If you were under my command I don't know if I'd promote you or have you flogged.'

Vincente indicated the younger Westerner. 'And this, Mark, is Colonel Frederick Ward.'

Ward gripped Mark's hand. 'Delighted, Mister Falchion.' He spoke with the flat vowels of a Salem New Englander. 'Harry Jessop tells me you're a fair hand with a quarter staff.'

Mark's cheeks reddened. He hoped no one would ask what had become of his staff.

The older man spoke. 'It's time I took my leave, Gentlemen.' He turned to Jessop. 'Come, Harry, see me down to the lobby, then the rest of the day's your own.'

'I have a small gift for Mister Falchion, Sir John.' Jessop's eyes sparkled. 'May I join you in a moment?'

'Very well, my boy, but don't keep me waiting.'

Sir John Michel moved to the door but at the threshold, held back. He fixed Ward with an earnest stare. 'Now hear this Mister Ward, we're much in agreement, but I'll not have you crimping any more of the Royal Navy's gunners.'

Ward inclined his head. 'The admiral's gunners are safe from me, sir,' he said.

Michel gave a curt nod and turned away and the door clicked shut behind him.

Ward winked at Vincente. 'Except for those lookin' for a career change, eh Vincente?'

'Good job I didn't hear that,' Jessop said.

Jessop and Vincente swapped knowing smiles then Jessop turned and walked to a mahogany door that opened onto another room.

Mark stayed silent, feeling like a new student on the first day of school.

A few seconds later, Jessop reappeared. He carried a slim package wrapped in brown paper. He handed it to Mark.

'Open it, Mister Falchion,' he said. 'I think you'll find it to your liking.'

Mark tore at the paper and uncovered a sword pommel bearing the interlocking symbols of *Yin* and *Yang*. The *Yin* aspect was pure jet; the *Yang* was creamy ivory. Mark ripped away the rest of the paper to reveal a rosewood grip and a leather scabbard. No longer was the scabbard dull and scuffed. It held a lustrous gleam and smelled of beeswax. Mark eased the blade half way from the scabbard. The hilt-guard shone like minted gold, the steel glistened under a sheen of armourer's oil.

'Sergeant Verrals had the orderly give it a scrub.' Jessop was bouncing up and down like a happy schoolboy.

Ward nodded to the sword. 'I hear, Mister Falchion, you're also a fair hand with one of those.'

Mark fought an urge to exercise the sword right there in the drawing room. He pushed it back into its scabbard and it glided home with a satisfying *shhlikk*.

'I can't, Harry...'

Mark tore his eyes from the sword but Harry Jessop had gone, leaving him alone with Ward, Vincente and the middle-aged Chinese.

Without thinking, Mark slipped the scabbard's carrying strap over his shoulder and settled the sword against his back. He reached up and touched the rosewood grip. It was just where he knew it would be. A flash of completeness surged through him. It was as if the sword had always been there: part of his everyday dress; part of *him*.

'Young Jessop speaks well of you Mister Falchion. Is it true you're fluent in Chinese?' Ward asked.

Mark nodded. 'My spoken Chinese is passable sir, and I write the language quite well.'

'Capital.' Ward clapped his hands. 'What do you say to twenty dollars a month, all found?'

Mark thought he had misheard. 'Twenty? All found?' A grin split his face. 'That... that would be wonderful, sir.'

'Hold up, youngster.' Ward raised a cautionary hand. 'Don't you want to know how you'll earn your twenty?'

Mark's smile crumbled. 'Nothing illegal I hope.'

Vincente threw back his head and bellowed with laughter.

Ward chuckled. 'Illegal, my boy? *Illegal?*' Oh my, you can bet someone will think so.' He put his arm across Mark's shoulders. 'I forget my manners, may I call you Mark? Let me introduce our main backer, Mister Yang Fang of the Takei Bank. Mister Yang, meet Mark Falchion.'

Mark clasped his hands before his chest and switched to formal Chinese. 'Sir, I am honoured. Please tell me how I may serve you.'

Yang spoke to Ward in sibilant English. 'His Chinese is indeed passable. In fact, it is most passable.'

'So, is he up to it?'

Yang bowed. 'I defer to your greater knowledge of such matters, Colonel Ward.'

'Sure, and you'll let me take the rap if it goes wrong.'

Yang smiled and shrugged.

'Mister Falchion... Mark... you seem mystified,' Ward said. He guided Mark to the table, unfurled the map and weighed it down with an ashtray. He clamped a cigar between his teeth and pungent smoke filled the room.

'Kiangsu province,' he continued. 'Here, Shanghai: beautiful, rich, corrupt.' He jabbed his finger on a point near the city. 'And here, Taipings.' He repeated the gesture several times. With each finger jab, he became more agitated. 'Taipings here, here and here. And what do you think is here?' He raised an eyebrow. 'You've got it. More *goddamned* Taipings.'

Mark frowned. How had the Taipings taken so much so quickly?

Yang Fang gave a discreet cough. 'Ah... please excuse my presumption,' he said. 'You see, Mister Falchion, the Taipings are in Kiangsu with just one aim, to seize Shanghai's Chinese quarter.' His eyes became sad. 'We businessmen have begged the foreign powers for help but they say the Chinese quarter is the emperor's problem.'

'Civil war,' Ward said. 'Taipings against Imperials, been at it for years. Take your pick: the Imperials are ossified and corrupt; the Taipings have murdered and robbed their way across China. God knows how many they've killed.' He blew smoke at the ceiling. 'The British insist they're neutral,' he continued. 'But they forget, this is China.'

Ward moved to the French windows and stared out onto the Bund.

'Right now, British troops are preparing to march on Peking,' he said. 'They mean to force the emperor to relax controls on the opium trade.' He turned to face Mark and his voice dripped scorn. 'Now, there's a gallant cause for you.' His face became troubled. 'The foreign powers think they can play politics with the rebels,' he continued. 'But when the Taipings are in the Chinese quarter, they'll stack the deck and call the deal.'

'Luckily, there's us,' Vincente chipped in. 'And we don't care about treaties and such.' He stretched out in an armchair and threw his leg over the chair arm. He drew on his cigar and a haze of blue smoke drifted about his head. 'All we care about is our twenty a month.' He blew on the cigar tip, making it flare. 'Didn't you say, "paid in advance," Colonel?'

Mark stiffened. It all came together like a cudgel blow: guns, maps and talk of payment. How could he have been so stupid? When they came, his words seemed inadequate.

'You're...you're *mercenaries*.'

'That's right,' Vincente replied. 'Me, the colonel and a couple-of hundred boys out in the Guanfulin swamps. All mercenaries. But the fight's noble enough, if that's what's troubling you.'

Mark lifted the sword from his shoulders and dropped it onto the sofa.

'I'll have no dealings with mercenaries,' he croaked. 'You're no better than brigands.'

Ward gave a wry smile that did not reach his eyes. 'What do you think, Vincente?' he said. 'Seems Harry Jessop was wrong about this one. There's no fire in him.'

He glared at Mark and his voice hardened. 'Can't you see? Must I explain? The British, the French, the Americans, you, me, Vincente, we have a common cause.'

Mark snapped back his answer. 'I've nothing in common with the likes of you.'

'Really,' Ward countered. 'Are you sure?'

Mark shook his head. 'You... you've no idea,' he replied. 'You know nothing of promises I've made. You don't understand my... my duty.'

Ward's eyes glittered. 'You're right,' he growled. 'I've a lot to learn, but I know the Taipings. They don't build, they destroy.' He fixed Mark with a steady gaze. 'They destroyed your home, they abducted your father and they killed your friend.' Red spots coloured his cheeks. 'You talk of duty. So tell me, what is your duty? To set yourself up in a rooming house and clerk for the rest of your life?'

Mark hunted for an answer but could find none.

Ward pointed to somewhere beyond the French windows. 'There's a hundred thousand Taipings out there and who will stand against them?' He paused as though waiting for an answer. When none came, he bunched his fists and continued. 'The British? The French? The Americans? Maybe, but I'll lay odds they won't.' He inclined his head towards Yang, the banker. 'But thanks to Mister Yang and his backers, there's me, there's Vincente and, if you can pull your head out of your ass, there's you.'

Ward's eyes burned. His lips were thin and white. 'And with or without you, Mister Falchion, we are going to keep the goddamned Taipings out of Shanghai.'

He took a long pull on his cigar and his brows furrowed. 'Are you getting any of this?' he snapped.

Mark was silent. The words were like a slap. He pictured his father standing on the jetty at Sishun, a hand raised in farewell. He saw the gutted ruins of his home and the agony in the eyes of One-eared Wu. And where was Mei?

The only sound was the *tock...tock...tock...* of a wall clock.

Mark lifted the sword from the sofa.

Vincente smiled and blew a smoke ring.

'He gets it alright, Colonel,' he said. 'I hope he doesn't mind waiting for his twenty dollars.'

# 14

TOP SOLDIER Cho Lung rolled his eyes, was he was the only man who understood the importance of orders? The Black Dragons had been in camp for just two days and without orders, the men had become fractious. One soldier had even challenged Cho's authority, forcing Cho to beat him insensible.

But now, there were orders.

The dispatch rider had thudded in from the west. The rider's clothes and boots were mud spattered. Lather covered the horse's neck and flanks. Without slackening speed, the rider made straight for the tent where Meng's banner fluttered. As he vaulted from his saddle, Meng's guards had crossed their spears, barring his way. Then Meng had ducked out from under his tent flap and ushered the dispatch rider inside.

Cho sighed. *Officers,* they thought sentries were blind, deaf and illiterate. Within the hour, Cho knew every detail of the dispatch. Meng's Black Dragons were to break camp and head west to link up with a large Taiping column. Together, the whole force would advance on the town of Sungkiang, some thirty miles southwest of Shanghai. They would destroy the town garrison and secure the surrounding area.

Then there would be garrison duties. Cho frowned. He hated garrison duties. The men would become idle and there would be more heads to bang together.

It was not all bad news, there would be proper barracks and

plenty of work to keep quarrelsome soldiers busy. Yes, Cho told himself, garrison duties were never easy but those worries would have to keep. First, there was some soldiering to do.

The Black Dragons kicked dirt over their campfires, packed their gear and rode west, back to their lines. After two hours, they turned south. With the sun at its noon high, they crested a low hill and looked down on a plain bordered by two creeks.

On the water, boats jockeyed for the best sections of riverbank. Ashore, Taiping soldiers sweated under the burden of supplies and weapons. Some wore sky-blue, others units wore orange, jade-green, purple or crimson. Five regiments, thought Meng, a full army corps of thirteen thousand soldiers.

Meng scanned the mass of men and stores until he spotted a sky-blue banner. He whooped and kicked his gelding in the ribs. The beast tossed its head and skidded down the embankment. At the bottom of the slope, it found its feet and thudded across the turf.

As horse and rider drew close to the banner, six officers straightened from a campaign table. Meng wrenched at the reins and the gelding slid to a stop. Clods of earth spattered the officers' robes. Five drew back from the campaign table, shielding their faces. The sixth stood fast. He wore a simple tunic of sky-blue and around his brow was a scarf of pure white. His hair was steel grey and a silver beard brushed his chest. On his lips was a smile of welcome.

Meng unhooked his feet from the stirrups and vaulted from the saddle. He dropped to one knee and pushed his right fist against the palm of his left hand. He threw back his head and looked into the older man's eyes.

'General Kong. Father!' he cried. 'I await your orders.'

Kong placed his hands on Meng's shoulders. 'Stand my son,' he said. 'How went your mission? Do you have my agent safe?'

Meng stood and tugged his tunic straight.

'Yes, Father,' he replied. 'She is with the troop. She reports no military traffic moving upriver to meet you.' He flashed a white-toothed grin. 'The Imperials quake in their holes, the foreigners dither in their counting houses and our enemies await you with terror.'

'Then we must not disappoint them.' Kong put his arm across Meng's shoulder and lowered his voice. 'Did you meet any opposition?' he asked.

Meng shrugged. 'A little, when we extracted our agent.' His lips twisted in a smirk. 'We were not too severe in our punishment.'

Kong nodded. 'Good,' he said. 'Loyalty is best won, not forced.' He swept his arm in a wide arc. 'What do you think? Is this not a grand force?'

'It is, Father.'

'Indeed, and this is just a small part of our strength,' Kong said. He put his head close to Meng's and lowered his voice. 'In truth, it's not grand enough.' He bent over a map spread on the table. 'Our commander wants me to take two towns, here and here.' He pointed at two dots on the map.

Meng noted their names, Chingpu and Sungkiang.

'And I must secure the whole damned centre.' Kong grumbled. He scowled and shook his head. 'We shall be spread thin. We can't afford casualties.' He gave Meng a light punch on the chest. 'There must be none of your heroic charges, my boy. Every man lost makes the burden on the rest all the heavier.'

Meng leaned closer to the map and frowned. It looked impossible: the towns were fifteen miles apart and the intervening countryside was scrubby flatland with a mix of marsh and meandering creeks. Small groups could pick their way along the few tracks but larger units would have to stay close to the waterways.

'The enemy is weak and disorganised,' Meng said. 'We will prevail.'

'I knew you'd say that.' Kong's mood brightened. 'For the time being, I'm lending you and your Black Dragons to Colonel Fu.'

Colonel Fu was a man of middle years. His hair was silver-flecked and he wore a tunic of Jade Green.

But it was not Fu who drew Meng's attention. Behind the colonel stood a soldier, also dressed in jade green. He was tall and the bulge of heavy muscle showed beneath his tunic. He had a thick jaw and narrow eyes that seemed to take in all around him. His weapon was a *guandao*. Like a spear, it had a long shaft but where a spear had a steel point, the *guandao* carried an oversized sword blade. The blade looked like an oriental scimitar but on its trailing edge there was a notch coupled with a backward facing hook. The hook could either snare an enemy's weapon or rip out a man's guts. It was a devastating weapon that took a strong man to wield. The muscular soldier carried it with the ease brought only by a lifetime's training.

Meng turned his attention back to Colonel Fu. He executed a cursory bow and spoke through clenched teeth. 'Colonel Fu's gallantry is legend,' he said. The man is a clod, he thought.

'As is the courage of Captain Meng,' Colonel Fu replied. His voice oozed scorn.

Kong beamed at them both. 'So now we are all friends. Comrades and friends. There is no stronger bond between men.'

Meng and Fu regarded each other through hooded eyes.

'We must move today,' Kong declared. 'Sungkiang's military commander will fight like a tiger but the town magistrate has a high regard for life, especially his own.' He brought his hands together with a slap. 'So, we'll give them an escape path and with luck, take the town without loss. If we succeed, the Imperial camps will be awash with tales of our invincibility.'

Kong nodded to an aide who gathered up the maps. 'We've been over the plan,' he said. 'Are there questions? No? Excellent. Today we march; tomorrow we rest in Sungkiang.'

The officers gave grim smiles, bowed and dispersed back to their units.

Meng took Cho Lung aside. He spoke softly. 'Who is the soldier with Colonel Fu?' he asked.

Cho pulled a face. 'He's the colonel's bodyguard,' he grumbled. 'His name is Shan. The man's a fearsome fighter but he's a snake.'

'I always need fearsome fighters,' Meng said. 'Have someone speak to him quietly.'

Cho scowled and shook his head. 'He will poison our unit,' he said. 'Best leave him where he is.'

Meng's eyes glittered. 'You will do as I instruct,' he hissed. 'I might have a task for the soldier called Shan.' He flashed a wolfish smile. 'It is a task that will suit him very well.'

Meng stepped back and became the affable commander. 'But that must wait,' he said. 'For now we have our orders: Today we march; tomorrow we rest in Sungkiang.'

Colonel Kwan Yin-lung of the Imperial Blue Standard Army banged his fist against the parapet above Sungkiang's western gate and stared into the face of the dithering mandarin who was the town magistrate.

'Sire, we must fight,' he snarled.

The magistrate had narrow shoulders and a thin face. His cheeks were hollow, his eyes were dull and rheumy. Each night the sentries reported the smell of opium drifting from his quarters.

The magistrate wrung his hands. 'We have not prepared,' he bleated. '*You* have not prepared. The defences are in disrepair, there are too few cannon, we haven't enough soldiers and there's hardly a musket between them.'

Colonel Kwan clamped his jaw tight. The magistrate spoke true but where was the money for repairs, men and weapons? He pictured the plush furnishings in the magistrate's *yamen* and the silk gowns gracing his mistress.

The magistrate began to pace the battlements, muttering to himself. The colonel followed in silence. The defences needed work but the walls were solid enough. What troubled the colonel most was the awful mathematics of battle. He had five thousand soldiers to man four miles of walls. If the enemy focussed their attack on just a few sections of wall... he squeezed shut his eyes, banishing the thought.

'Excellency,' the colonel called to the magistrate's back, 'if we are to honour our Imperial oath, we must fight.'

'Fight... fight *that*?' The magistrate flapped his sleeve at the ground before the western wall and not for the first time that day, the colonel shuddered.

Spanning the wall's length was the enemy. The sun glittered off thousands of spear points. Fluttering above them were hundreds of banners. Along their ranks, fireworks crackled and flared. At the rear, *sounas* blared their reedy clarion. In the open space between the moat and the Taiping front line, young men strutted and showed off their sword handling. Their blades flashed and span. One young man tossed his sword high above him then snatched it from the air before it hit the ground.

The colonel almost laughed, the magistrate would shit in his britches if he knew about the rest of the Taiping force. Section commanders reported thousands more Taipings massed at the northern and southern walls. According to Colonel Kwan's best guess, a full army corps of battle-hardened enemy stood ready to storm Sungkiang.

'We will retreat, it is my final word,' the magistrate said with a sniff.

'What shall I tell my commander, Excellency?' Colonel Kwan was on the verge of begging. 'Shall we say we gave up without a fight?'

'We... No, *you* will tell him I had no choice. The enemy force is too great. Our... our defences are inadequate. I am not the soldier here. *You* will write the report.'

'I will be disgraced, Sire. My family will lose all face.'

The magistrate shut his eyes and showed the colonel the palm of his hand.

'You should have thought of family honour when you were letting the walls crumble into the moat. You are a soldier and you will find the words. Now, have my belongings packed. I will leave nothing.'

The magistrate turned and scurried from the battlements.

The colonel sighed. The Taipings did not lay sieges, they were forever in a hurry and cared nothing for casualties. They would attack and it would be soon. The situation was hopeless. The whining mandarin was right, and that made the colonel's misery all the worse.

Even as he argued to stay, the colonel knew escape was possible. The Taipings were hard against the walls to the north, west and south but by some miracle, their force at the eastern wall numbered only dozens.

Soon the enemy commander would see his mistake and rush troops to fill the gap. But it would take time and time was a soldier's best friend. Colonel Kwan had time to organise an evacuation, not much time, but some. He would order the Sungkiang garrison to slink away without firing a shot or wetting a blade. With his usual skill, the magistrate would avoid responsibility and Colonel Kwan's name would join a list of Imperial officers who chose to run rather than fight.

The weight of failure crushed down on the colonel. He was a veteran of battles against the *Nian* and the Taiping rebels. He had won victories and suffered defeats but never had he fled without a fight.

The colonel looked out over the battlements but compared to his impending shame, the enemy's strength meant nothing. He had but one choice. He would ensure the escape of the magistrate, his women and his baggage. Next, he would see his troops away in good order. But he would write no report. Today one blade would not go unwetted. As the last of his soldiers marched through the eastern gate, Colonel Kwan Yin-lung of the Imperial Blue Standard Army would retire to his quarters.

There, he would take the only honourable course.

In the late afternoon, General Kong Liu's thirteen thousand entered Sungkiang. Kong sat astride his Han Hsiu warhorse and wore his finest robe. Meng rode on Kong's right. Relegated to the general's left, Colonel Fu rode in silence. Soldiers lined their way. There were firecrackers, drums and the blare of *suonas*.

Meng clenched his fist as pain bit into his hand.

'How were you injured?' Kong asked.

Meng turned away and muttered something that Kong did not hear.

A sly smile crept across Kong's lips. 'Speak up my boy,' he said.

'I was examining a captured spear,' Meng said. He hunkered down in his saddle and stared straight ahead.

Kong slapped his thigh and laughed out loud. 'Wounded by an enemy spear,' he chortled. 'The ballad weavers will sing of your heroism.'

'I'll order my unit doctor to heal it,' Meng sniffed.

Kong leaned closer to Meng. 'I don't know why you bothered with a barbarian doctor,' he said. 'I don't trust Westerners. Our agent had best stay close to him.'

Meng shrugged. 'I could drop him into the moat,' he said.

'Don't take our Heavenly King's orders lightly,' Kong cautioned. 'If you kill a Westerner, make sure to cover your tracks.'

They passed through the outer gate into a courtyard then through an inner gate that led to the town proper. The streets and lanes were empty. A lone dog barked then skulked away. An upper storey window shutter slammed. Kong scanned the lanes, doorways, rooftops and shuttered windows.

'Where are the townsfolk?' He asked.

'Hiding,' Meng said. 'They are goats. They fear anything new.'

'I hope there's no problem with them,' Kong said. 'We'll have enough trouble with the enemy.'

'Crucify a few,' Meng said. 'Then we'll have no trouble.'

Kong turned to Colonel Fu. 'Any sign of the gallant defenders?' he chuckled.

'We found the garrison commander in his quarters,' Fu answered. 'Dead by his own hand.'

Kong nodded. 'Got his men to safety then took the path of a true soldier,' he said. 'We must give him a proper burial. Arrange an honour guard.'

They rode into the central plaza and the soldiers fanned out to form a three-sided box before the town *yamen*. Kong and his officers dismounted.

'Where's the damned preacher?' Kong thundered.

'Excellency.' A man wearing a robe of white silk stepped

forward.

'Well?' Kong snapped. 'Get on with it.'

The priest raised his arms. There was a rumble as the soldiers dropped to one knee.

'In the name of the Father, the Holy Spirit and of God's two sons, we give thanks for our victory,' the priest chanted. 'We thank thee...'

'That will do,' Kong said. 'The Lord and I appreciate your brevity.' He looked around. 'Where's Colonel Fu?'

'Excellency?' Fu answered.

Install your regiment in the barracks and prepare guard rosters. Tomorrow, the rest of our force will march to secure the centre ground.' He gave an apologetic shrug. 'I will leave you your regiment,' he said. 'The others must come with me.'

Fu gasped. 'But sir, I have only...'

'Two thousand soldiers,' Kong said. 'Two thousand, six hundred if you count the officers and top soldiers.' He put his head close to Fu's. 'I know it's not enough,' he said. 'But I can't spare more.'

'A thousand more, Sire,' Fu pleaded. 'Five hundred.'

'You have Meng and his Black Dragons,' Kong said. 'They've taken a lot of casualties but I swear, each man fights like ten.'

Fu's voice was heavy with sarcasm. 'You honour me, sir.'

Kong grinned and clasped the colonel's shoulder.

'Take heart,' he said. 'I couldn't leave the garrison in safer hands. Fu and Meng, there's no finer team.'

Fu and Meng glowered at one another.

'With the centre secured, this garrison will be our base for the march on Shanghai,' Kong said. 'Then you will have so many soldiers, you won't know where to put them all.'

'I will keep the garrison safe, sir,' Fu said.

'I know you will, old friend,' Kong chortled. 'And to make

doubly sure, I'll tell my agent to keep close watch on Meng's barbarian. I don't trust foreigners.'

Colonel Fu surveyed his apartment. He nodded his approval. It was a simple affair: just a narrow bed and a desk with a straight-backed chair. Folding doors opened onto a veranda with views across the rooftops to Sungkiang's eastern gate. A tapestry depicting a rampant dragon against a background of imperial yellow, separated the apartment from an antechamber where Fu's aide would spend much of his days fending off unwelcome petitions from the town's self-appointed leading citizens.

Fu walked to the desk, which was already covered in administrative papers and scrolls. He sat and found the chair as uncomfortable as it looked. He sighed as he shuffled through the stores inventories, manpower status reports, duty rosters, sickness lists and all the day-to-day tedium that kept an army working.

'Dispatch,' he called, then remembered his aide was inspecting the garrison supplies. He nodded to himself. It was good he was alone because waiting in the antechamber was General Kong's agent. Fu suppressed a surge of distaste. Real soldiers took the enemy head on, they did not skulk in shadows. But without spies, Fu was blind, not only to the enemy outside the walls but far more pressing, to the enemy within.

He paused for a moment then called, 'You may enter.'

There was a tread outside his door. The tapestry moved aside and the agent entered the apartment. She wore loose-fitting trousers and a cotton tunic several sizes too big for her. She had fine cheekbones and her lips were full. Her most striking features were her eyes, they were large and soft. She moved to Fu's desk, bowed then spoke in a clear voice.

'Excellency, how may I serve you?' She straightened her

shoulders and looked Fu square in the face.

Fu frowned. The agent's self-assurance bordered on insolence. He glowered at her but the woman did not flinch. Fu gave a short cough and shifted in his chair.

'What is your name, child?' he asked although he knew everything worth knowing about the woman.

'I am adopted daughter of His Worship Ping Sang,' she said. 'My given names are Song-mei but everyone calls me Mei.'

Fu stroked his beard. 'Adopted, you say. A *mi-jeh*. I've not heard of your father but I'm sure he was a fine man.' There was a brief silence then he cleared his throat. 'So child, tell me about Meng's barbarian.'

'I have nothing to report, Excellency,' Mei answered. 'Except he does not belong to Captain Meng. Indeed, he follows no council but his own. He is a worthy doctor and cares nothing for politics.'

'*Shehh*, he deceives you,' Fu growled. 'You can't trust foreigners.'

'I believe we can trust this one.' Mei's tone was steady.

'We shall see,' Fu said. He flapped his sleeve towards the door and bent over his desk.

Mei did not move.

Fu looked up. 'Well?' he snapped.

'Excellency,' Mei clasped her hands before her chest and bowed. 'My orders were to observe any military craft traversing the Huangpu. That duty is over and my comrades are in the field. They need me.'

'Do not worry about your comrades,' Fu snorted. 'Lady Yen has all the mounted archers she needs.' He bent back to his papers. 'Your doctor's a foreigner,' he snapped. 'You can't trust them. Watch him, watch him close.'

'Very well, Excellency,' Mei sighed. She bowed once more

then slipped through the door and was gone.

Fu decided he did not like this young woman. Had she never learned to lower her eyes when addressing a man? He was tempted to call her back but what would he say? The heavenly ruler had decreed that women held up half of heaven. Fu banished her from his thoughts.

There were matters more pressing than barbarian doctors and uncourtly women.

'It will not do, Mister Cho,' Doctor James Falchion groaned. 'A stable's no fit place for a surgery.'

Cho Lung arched his eyebrows. 'Who are you to complain?' he growled.

'Listen to the doctor,' Mei snapped. She wiped her hand along the stall rail and held it up for Cho to see. 'Look,' she said. 'Filth. How do we heal the sick and injured in here?'

'You dare question me?' Cho barked.

Mei thrust out her chin. 'Why not? An ignorant soldier thinks he can question an educated doctor.' Her voice was shrill. 'Does this stinkhole of a town not have a Christian mission or an apothecary?' she demanded.

Cho opened his mouth to speak but Doctor Falchion interrupted him.

'Of course, the old apothecary,' Falchion said. He grinned like one who suddenly remembers where he put a lost treasure. 'I was there during my last visit. It's near the magistrate's *yamen*. Quick, Mei, gather our equipment. Mister Cho, I'll need men to carry everything.'

'But... my orders...' Cho sputtered but Mei and the doctor had busied themselves collecting the medical stores.

Doctor Falchion regarded Cho from beneath arched eyebrows. 'Why the delay?' he said. 'If we hurry we can be there before dusk.'

'But...' Cho Lung gave a weary sigh and strode to the stable door. '*Trooper*,' he bellowed. 'Yes, you. Get off your arse and fetch two comrades.'

To himself he muttered, 'There's baggage to shift.'

Night had fallen by the time Mei, Cho Lung and the doctor had unpacked the last of the instruments. Falchion placed his hands in the small of his back and stretched.

He remembered watching the old herbalist weighing out his potions on a traditional *chang*. Now the herbalist had fled and the herb boxes stood empty.

'Such treasures, all gone,' Falchion sighed. 'We Westerners have so much to learn.'

'Doctor.' There was laughter in Mei's voice. 'Why do you not eat?' She wagged her finger as though chastising a child. She took Falchion's arm and pointed to a table where she had placed a bowl of steamed vegetables. 'You are an old man,' she said. 'You need your strength.'

'Who are you calling old? Disrespectful child. If I was your father I would...'

'You would be old enough to be my respected grandfather. Now eat.'

Falchion scowled. 'Respect?' he huffed. 'When was the last time you showed a man respect?'

Mei put a finger to her chin. 'Hmmm, let me think,' she mused. 'It's been so long since I met one who didn't act like a baby.'

She pulled a chair away from the table and bustled the doctor into it.

'And why aren't you married?' Falchion demanded.

Mei's eyes sparkled. 'Because I'm too busy looking after a

cantankerous old man,' she chuckled. She placed her fists on her hips and scowled in mock anger. 'It's late,' she said. 'Now eat your supper.'

There was a crash and the door banged open. Mei gave a small cry as two black-uniformed soldiers ducked under the lintel.

Falchion rose from his chair. 'What is the meaning...?'

Cho Lung shot the doctor a warning look.

The spearmen stiffened to attention as another figure ducked through the door.

'Captain Meng.' Falchion bit back the bitterness in his words. He bowed and softened his voice. 'You are welcome here.'

Meng ignored Falchion. He bunched his fists and moved towards Mei. Mei snatched a scalpel from the bench and held it stiff-armed before her.

Falchion stepped between them.

'Mei is here by General Kong's order,' he said. 'I don't know why, but I thank him for it. Now, Captain, tell me how may we serve you?'

Meng glared across Falchion's shoulder and into Mei's face.

'If I raise a finger, you both die,' he snarled. 'Tell me why I should not do that.'

Mei's eyes burned, her lips were white. 'Because it will give Colonel Fu his excuse to take the head of every cockroach in a black uniform,' she said.

James Falchion turned to Mei. 'And you will be dead, and I will be dead,' he snapped. He held out his hand and his voice became gentle. 'Give it to me, child. Please, for both our sakes.'

Mei's hand trembled. She lowered her eyes and the scalpel clattered onto the bench.

Meng's cheeks blazed. 'You think to control men with your harlot's smile.' He curled his lip. 'Do you think I desire you? Know this: you are nothing; your life is *nothing*.' He made to push the doctor aside but Falchion stood his ground.

Meng's eyes swivelled to Falchion.

'And you? If you want to live, you'd better earn your rice.' He thrust out his hand. A strip of cotton bound tight around the hand was stiff with crusted blood.

'It is a small thing,' Meng snapped. 'A scratch.'

'Let me see,' Falchion said. 'Come, sit by my bench. Mei, bring the light.'

Meng laid his arm on the bench, palm upward. He winced as Falchion peeled away the makeshift bandage.

'It's a nasty cut,' Falchion said. 'Any delay and you might lose that hand.'

'Then fix it,' Meng commanded.

Falchion turned to Mei. 'Bring my scalpel,' he ordered. 'I'll need swabs, sutures, dressings and lots of carbolic.' To Meng he added, 'Hold on to something, Captain, this is going to hurt.'

# 15

MARK FALCHION stood in silence: back straight, feet apart, arms folded across his chest. The *dao's* grip showed above his right shoulder. His expression was calm but he was in awe of the banker, Yang Fang's study. The floorboards were lustrous black. The walls were stark white and adorned with scrolls of creamy silk. Each bore a single Chinese character written with sweeping brush strokes: 'duty,' 'diligence,' and 'fidelity.' In a corner, a peach-blossom filled the air with perfume. Yang himself sat at a desk of dark lacquer inlaid with mother of pearl images of mountains and mythical creatures. On the wall facing him, incense smouldered at a shrine to the God of Fortune.

Despite the surroundings, Banker Yang was not in a good mood.

'Fifty more rifles?' he gasped. 'In all my years at the Takei Bank, I have never seen the like.' He squinted at the requisition and ran a finger down the list of supplies. 'And why so many cartridges?'

Ward leaned back in his chair. 'I guess this is a bad time to talk about uniforms,' he said.

Yang's eyes widened, his spectacles magnifying his discomfort.

'*Uniforms?*' He shook his head. 'You coddle the men, Colonel, really you do. Your officers are as rich as princes and you pay the enlisted men eight dollars and fifty cents. Each man. *Every month.*

And now I must clothe them. Who ever heard of such a thing?'

Yang Fang sighed and dipped a fine-haired brush into his ink tray. He signed the requisition and stamped his personal seal below the signature. He handed the requisition to Ward. 'Take this to Fogg and Company,' he sighed. 'They will see to it.'

Ward slipped the paper into his jacket. He rose but Yang motioned him back to his chair. 'Please stay,' he said. 'There is someone you must meet.'

Yang clapped his hands and a face peeked around the doorjamb.

'Ting, show in our visitor,' Yang ordered. 'And bring our finest tea,' he added.

Ting nodded and scuttled away. He returned a few minutes later and bowed a tall Chinese into the room.

The newcomer had regal cheekbones and a hawk-like nose. His lips were thin and he had a wispy moustache. He wore a high-necked jacket of dark blue over a gown of white cotton. The jacket was open at the breast, revealing a square of embroidered silk. Embossed on the square was the image of a lion, picked out with golden thread. His cap was velvet and three peacock feathers hung from a crimson button perched at its crown.

Mark gasped, the embroidered square, the button and peacock feathers identified the newcomer as a military officer of the highest rank.

Yang stood. He cupped his right fist in his left hand and bowed. The military mandarin returned the gesture, taking care not to bow quite so low.

Yang remained standing whilst the stranger sat without a glance at anyone.

An Imperial officer entered and took position by the mandarin's right shoulder. He was of Mark's age and had a face of carved stone. He stood over six feet tall. He had a thick neck and his tunic stretched tight across heavy muscle. The embroidered square on his chest showed a white horse. His cap's crown was scarlet and decorated with a pair of mink tails. His left hand rested on the hilt of a heavy cavalry sword. He glowered at Mark and for a moment, the two faced each other like fighting dogs.

Mark broke away from the challenge and bowed to the military mandarin. He spoke in formal Chinese. 'Excellency, you honour us with your presence.'

The stranger half-closed his eyes and replied in English. 'You are impertinent, young man.'

'Excuse my young colleague,' Yang Fang wheedled. 'He means well but he has country manners.' He shot Mark a hard look then turned to Ward. 'Colonel, this is General... I mean... Mister... *um*... Hung?' He spoke the name as if it were a question.

Ward reached out his hand but Hung steepled his fingers and gazed at the ceiling.

'Mister Hung has certain... *er*... intelligences,' Yang said and gave a self-conscious laugh.

Ting returned carrying a tray bearing a patterned teapot and three cups. He served tea to Hung, Yang and Ward then backed away.

The door clicked shut and Ward turned to the banker. 'Intelligences, Mister Yang?'

Yang made to speak but Hung raised his hand, silencing him. The mandarin's voice was a blend of scorn and honey. 'I believe, Colonel Ward, you will soon undertake an adventure into the village of Chiating.'

Yang took a sharp breath and lowered his eyes.

Ward stiffened. 'It's news to me, sir.'

Hung's lips formed a thin smile. '*Ah*... news to you perhaps, but not to me. Your backers will insist on it. They want to see some success for their money.'

Ward fixed Hung with a solemn look. 'Suits me fine, sir. But what's at Chiating?'

'Some dusty Taipings, no more,' Hung replied. 'Certainly no honour; no credit.' He puckered his lips and sipped from his cup. He savoured the tea and nodded his approval. When he spoke, his voice was crisp. 'You have a camp at Guanfulin do you not?'

'I do,' Ward answered.

A shadow flickered across Hung's face. 'It is a mosquito-infested, stink hole is it not?'

Ward nodded.

Hung's voice became hard, the silk no longer masking the steel. 'You have demanded a more secure base, a base with proper fortifications.' His lip curled. 'You *demand* a garrison town. Like Sungkiang perhaps?'

'You are correct, sir. Its location makes it vital to the defence of Shanghai.'

Hung relaxed and the velvet returned to his voice. 'But there is a problem,' he said. 'Our Kiangsu viceroy could never pass command of Sungkiang from a Chinese officer to some, *ah*... foreign mercenary. It would be a dreadful loss of face.'

The skin above Ward's collar was scarlet. 'So we rot in Guanfulin,' he growled.

'It is indeed a conundrum, Colonel Ward,' Hung mused. 'How best to nurture our considerable investment without ruffling the pride of our commanders.'

Ward and Hung watched one another, each waiting for the other to say something. Hung was first to speak.

'But fortune smiles on us, Colonel. Reliable *ah*... intelligences suggest the Taipings have recently resolved this conundrum.' He stroked his moustache. 'You shall have your fortified garrison soon enough, but only if you are bold enough to take it.' He paused for a moment then continued. 'What do you know of triads, Colonel?'

'Do you mean Heaven and Earth societies?' The words sprang from Mark's lips before he realised he had spoken. 'Forgive me, sir,' he mumbled. 'I spoke out of turn.'

Hung swivelled his eyes onto Mark. His voice shook with restrained fury. 'You grace them with too fine a title, young man,' he said. He turned back to Ward. 'Well, Colonel? We were speaking of *triads*.'

Ward gave a non-committal shrug.

Hung let out a long sigh. 'I thought not,' he said. 'Westerners think triads are just grubby criminals who prey on other Chinese.' His voice became sharp. 'These triads say they are patriots who will overthrow our Manchurian emperor and recover the lost honour of the *Han* Chinese.' He frowned and shook his head, 'But make no mistake, they are without honour. They run guns to the Taipings and sell information to us. They charge tolls to use public roads but rob any merchant who travels on them. They even squeeze money from the Western business *Hongs* to avoid labour troubles.'

'Most informative sir,' Ward commented. 'But what's this to do with us?'

Hung groaned like a teacher with a dullard pupil. 'Triads are like flies in a street market,' he said. 'They infest everything. They are the trader who supplies our food, they are the clerk who keeps our records, they are the coolie who takes away our night soil.' He shook his head. 'You ask, what is this to you? You have clerks, laundry men, cooks and coolies.' Hung emphasised each point by thudding his fist against his knee.

Ward coughed and shifted in his chair. 'Are you saying we have no secrets?'

Hung swirled his tea around his cup and watched the patterns formed by the leaves. 'I expect not,' he replied. 'But the situation is more dangerous than you suppose.' He looked into Ward's face. 'What are a few secrets when the triads can make your life impossible? Lost supplies, broken equipment, mysterious sickness. All this can cripple an army, let alone a small force such as yours.'

Ward chewed his lip. 'So what's to be done?'

Hung tipped back his head and regarded the ceiling.

Banker Yang leaned forward. 'You must do as we do,' he said. 'You must pay them off.'

'Pay?' Ward snapped back. '*Pay?* I'll not...'

Hung silenced him with a raised hand. 'You seem shocked, Colonel,' he said. 'But I strongly suggest that before you go charging into battle, you *ah...* make certain accommodations. A soldier must protect his rear.'

'My budget is for men and weapons sir,' Ward said.

Yang Fang answered with a sly smile. 'Any half-witted clerk can skim a few coins from his budget to pay for... what shall we say? Incidentals?'

'Or maybe some luxuries, right?' Ward smiled but there was no humour in it.

The mandarin ignored the exchange. To Ward he said, 'There is in Shanghai's Chinese quarter, one named Gon Liao. You will send someone to deal with him. My department will advance ten thousand ounces of silver but we cannot be associated with any negotiations.'

Ward made rapid calculations and raised an eyebrow. 'That's quite a sum,' he said. 'Fifteen thousand American dollars by my reckoning.'

'It is closer to sixteen thousand dollars,' Hung replied. 'Mister Yang will hold the bullion here.'

The banker sighed and gave a slow nod.

'Excellent,' Hung purred. 'Now, all we lack is someone

trustworthy to deliver our terms.'

Mark cupped his right fist in his left hand and bowed. The words tumbled from him. 'This person begs to serve his emperor, sir.'

'Haul in your t'gallants, young Mark,' Ward growled. 'I expect we've not heard it all.' He fixed Hung with a hard stare. 'Well, sir, what exactly does this job entail?'

'Your young colleague offers to serve the country of his birth,' Hung said. He eased himself back in his chair. 'He has some small grasp of our language and I believe him to be impudent enough.' Hung turned to Mark. 'That was well-spoken, young man but do you think yourself able?'

Mark bowed. 'Please give me your instructions, sir.'

Hung gave Mark a cool look. 'The mission, young man, entails going to a certain house in the Chinese quarter, seeking out Gon Liao and advising him of our most generous offer. He will not refuse, triads place money above all things.'

A thrill surged through Mark but before he could answer, Ward interrupted. 'What's the catch, Mister Hung?' he asked.

Hung's voice dripped surprise. 'Catch? There is no catch. But to aid this operation, I will attach one of my *ah*... officers to your staff.'

Ward shook his head. 'I choose my own officers, thank you, sir.'

'Then you will choose this one.' Hung nodded to the Imperial officer standing beside him. 'Lieutenant Tang is an officer of the Peking Banner Cavalry, our most elite unit. He comes from fine Manchurian stock. His family has lived in Peking for two hundred years but to the *Han* Chinese, he is no more than a foreign invader.'

Hung turned to Yang. 'I have instructed Lieutenant Tang where he may find Gon Liao, he will prove most useful in this regard.'

He beckoned to the lieutenant, who leaned forward and put his head close to Hung's. Hung spoke to him in whispered Chinese.

The lieutenant snapped back to attention and barked a reply. '*Shue!*'

'*Hau!* A volunteer,' Hung cried. 'Lieutenant Tang will find Gon Liao's nest and I have given him special orders that will ensure the mission's success.' He stood and smoothed down the front of his gown. 'Do not worry about your base, Colonel Ward,' he said. 'Soon, you will have Sungkiang.'

He turned and with Yang Fang bowing to his back, he swept through the door.

Lieutenant Tang stood with his shoulders square and his eyes fixed on a point just above his line of sight. The knuckles gripping his sword hilt were white.

Ward rolled his eyes and spoke to the ceiling. 'What the hell am I to do with this damned cigar-store Indian?'

Yang blinked behind his spectacles and shrugged.

Ward walked around the lieutenant as though he were inspecting an honour guard.

'Well, gentlemen,' he declared, 'it seems we have a new staff officer.' He lit a cigar and pungent smoke filled the room. Lieutenant Tang wrinkled his nose. Yang scowled and wafted the smoke towards the window.

Ward clamped the cigar between his teeth and hooked his thumbs into his waistband.

'He sure is a big fellow,' he said. 'And he looks fierce enough.' He frowned then gave a nod of approval. 'Well, Mister Tang, I guess we should welcome you aboard.'

At the sound of his name, Lieutenant Tang stiffened and filled his lungs. '*Woh bu hui shuo ying yu,*' he bellowed.

## THE SCHOLAR'S BLADE

Yang groaned and cradled his head in his hands.
Ward turned to Mark, his eyebrows raised.
Laughter bubbled in Mark's throat. 'Colonel,' he said, 'the lieutenant says he doesn't speak English.'

The sun was low as Mark Falchion and Lieutenant Tang headed out of the foreign settlements. Mark had added a cotton hood to his scholar's gown and now it covered his head like a monk's cowl. He tugged the cowl forward so his face was hidden in its shadow.

Lieutenant Tang wore a worker's tunic and baggy trousers.

Neither carried a weapon and Mark missed the *dao* tugging at his shoulders.

'I still can't do this vermin's sign.' Lieutenant Tang spoke with the soft consonants of Peking. He extended the fingers of his right hand then tried to tuck the little finger back into his palm. 'It's impossible,' he hissed.

'Watch,' said Mark. He made a fist, lodged the tip of his fourth finger into the heel of his palm, raised his thumb then extended the remaining three fingers. He held his hand before Tang's face. 'There, I identify myself as a faithful messenger of the triad brotherhood.'

Tang tried again but still could not master it.

Mark rolled his eyes. 'When we get there, just look threatening and leave the rest to me,' he said.

'I'd like to know where a simple village boy learnt such things.' Tang lingered on the word, 'simple.'

Ahead, the wall of Shanghai's Chinese quarter rose above the moat. The stone was grey and streaked black with mildew. A bridge led to the city's northern gate. Beneath it, the moat was thick with reeds. The smell of sewage drifted from the water and the carcass of a pig floated close to the bridge stanchions. At the far end of the bridge, a gatehouse guarded the entrance to the city. Ironbound gates stood open but beyond them, there was only shadow. It was a dismal place and as they drew close to it, Mark's neck hairs prickled.

On the bridge, silk clad merchants mingled with half-naked coolies. There was no laughter, no chatter. Mark put a warning hand on Tang's arm. Standing in the gatehouse shadows were two soldiers. They wore caps with upturned brims. In the gloom, their tunics were a splash of red and white. In the centre of each man's chest was a patch bearing the word 'Brave.' Each carried a heavy-bladed spear.

'Quick, do you have any coins?' Mark's voice was an urgent whisper.

Tang curled his hands into fists. 'I'll break their skulls if they're squeezing bribes from civilians,' he growled.

'Stay calm,' Mark cautioned. 'Remember why we're here.'

Near the gate, the bridge narrowed, forcing the crowd to press in on itself. The guards pulled a man from the crowd. One snapped a question at him and without waiting for an answer, cuffed him across the head. There was little force in the blow but even from ten paces, Mark felt the man's humiliation.

Mark's breath came fast and heavy. His heart banged against his breastbone. He bowed his shoulders and changed his gait to a shuffling half-trot, head down, eyes on the ground. They passed through the gate. The guards were behind them.

'Stop!'

Mark's heart bounded. To their left and right, there was only dark stone. The way out lay through a second gate at the other side of the courtyard. There, two more soldiers chatted and leaned on their spears.

'Stop,' the guard called again. 'Stop or I'll have the turnip you call a head.'

Tang turned to face the guards. 'You should keep a civil tongue,' he barked. He planted his fists on his hips and spread his feet wide.

'My, we have a brazen one,' the first guard said. His companion smiled and levelled his spear.

'Why can't you do as I say?' Mark hissed. He lowered his eyes and moved between Tang and the guards. He clasped his hands together at his chest. 'Sir, forgive my servant,' he wheedled. 'He's a stout fellow but his wits are slow.'

The guards looked Mark over. 'Elegant words for one so poorly dressed,' said one. 'I think we should take you to our commander. He'll know what to do.'

Mark bowed. 'Please do not inconvenience your senior officer.' He held out a silver coin. 'Perhaps, your worship, a small gift will compensate for my servant's disrespect.'

The guard smirked and slipped the coin into his tunic. 'Move on, turnip,' he said and waved Mark through.

They crossed the courtyard and passed through the second gate. A rat scurried away as they stepped into the alley beyond.

'Are you mad?' Mark said in a tight whisper. 'You nearly got us arrested.'

'If you'd acted like a man, they would not have troubled you,' Tang retorted. 'Why, oh why did my commander burden me with a foreigner?' He shoved Mark between the shoulders. 'Now move,' he snapped. 'I think you haven't the stomach for this.'

Mark staggered forward. A flash of anger burned through him. His breath became fast and shallow. He bunched his fists.

Tang pushed him again.

Mark turned and threw a snaking punch at Tang's jaw. Pain stabbed through his fist as the blow connected. He cursed and tried to shake away the hurt.

Tang reeled back. He gaped at Mark then gave a hard laugh.

He dropped to a half crouch and balled his fists. His eyes glittered. He took a step forward.

'What if he doesn't accept?' Mark asked, nursing his hand.

'What?' Tang squinted at Mark as though he had misheard.

'Gon Liao. What if he doesn't accept?'

'You strike me. *Me?* And now you talk of Gon Liao.' Tang hunched his shoulders and raised his fists. 'Do not worry about the mission,' he growled. 'I will break your back and continue alone.' He put down his head and charged.

Mark sidestepped, made a half turn and swept his thigh against Lieutenant Tang's legs. Tang's feet left the ground and he went down hard.

Mark looked left and right. Had anyone heard? He bent over Tang. 'Are you hurt?' he whispered.

Tang pushed himself to his knees and shook his head like a waking bear. A growl rumbled from his lips. He sprang from the ground and lunged.

My God, he's fast, thought Mark. Almost too late, he stepped aside. Tang reeled past and slammed into the tenement wall. His legs shook and he slid down the stonework. Mark stood over him and held out his hand. Tang knocked it aside.

'Take it,' Mark snapped. 'We have important business.'

Tang grabbed at a ledge and dragged himself up. There was blood on his forehead. He seemed to stagger then his fist lashed forward.

The blow slammed against Mark's head. Lights flashed behind his eyes and the alley's cobbles came up to meet him. Pain ripped though his body as a kick connected with his ribs. He rolled to the side and another kick floated past his head.

Tang teetered on one leg then toppled onto his back.

Mark pushed himself to his knees. His legs had no strength. He scrabbled at the wall but Tang was already up, teeth bared,

# THE SCHOLAR'S BLADE

fists clenching and unclenching.

'Halt!'

At the end of the alley, a lantern silhouetted two soldiers. Spear tips gleamed in the half-light.

'I said, *halt!*' The soldiers advanced, spears level.

Tang turned to meet them.

'*Leave them!*' Mark shouted. He grabbed Tang's sleeve and pulled him away. He tightened his grip and dragged the lieutenant after him. Half-running, half-stumbling, they rounded a corner where darkness swallowed them. They paused, panting in the shadows. The soldiers' footsteps slowed then stopped.

'They'll not risk an ambush down here,' Tang wheezed. He grabbed the front of Mark's gown and drew back his fist. Then he lowered his hand and pushed Mark away. 'Gon Liao is close,' he said. He turned and stalked away into the dark.

Together they moved deeper into the city. The lanes and alleys were ink black except for splinters of light from ill-shuttered windows.

'What if he refuses?' Mark asked.

Tang hunched his shoulders and hurried on. Mark grabbed his arm and pulled him to a halt.

Tang turned, his eyes burning into Mark's. 'You are a mosquito,' he snarled. 'You annoy me.'

'I must know,' Mark persisted. 'We must decide what to do.'

'If he refuses,' Tang growled, 'I will follow my orders and I will kill him.' He held his fists before Mark's face and made wringing motions as though strangling a chicken.

'You're insane,' Mark hissed. 'Gon Liao's servants will cut you down the moment you lay hands on him.'

'Then I must be quick.' Tang jabbed his forefinger against Mark's chest. 'And they will not cut *me* down, they will cut *us* down. So when you make your offer, you'd best be persuasive.'

Tang strode on and Mark followed. The moon peeked above the tenements and silver light filled the alley. Two men stepped from the shadows and blocked their way. They wore black tunics and britches. Strips of black linen circled their brows. The taller of them put his hand on Tang's chest. Tang stiffened but did not resist. The other reached for Mark's cowl.

'Why hide your face, little brother?' he said. 'There should be no strangers here.'

Mark placed his right hand over his heart and made the messenger sign. The man's eyes widened. He stepped back, bowed and swung his arm to indicate a wrought iron grill that secured a doorway.

'Keung,' he called. 'Open the gate. Quickly, there's a dispatch.'

The grill squealed open and Mark and Tang stepped through into a narrow corridor. The air was hot and heavy. The dark smell of opium mingled with the fusty stench of mildew. Another man emerged from the shadows. He pointed to where a pool of yellow light lit a stairwell.

Mark walked head down, face buried in the shadows of his cowl. Behind him, Tang's footsteps thumped against the rough stone floor. On the landing above them, two men flanked an ironbound door. They stood with their feet apart, shoulders square and their arms folded. Neither of them questioned Mark when he reached the landing. The messenger sign was the only pass he needed.

The landing door swung open and the light from a hundred lanterns dazzled Mark. A cacophony of noise battered his ears. Men thronged at tables where unsmiling table-captains threw dice, turned playing cards, counted *fan-tan* beads, and rattled *paai-gau* tiles. Players shouted, and waved wads of banknotes. Joy and despair gave vent together. A man dressed in fine silk spat on the floor and pointed an accusing finger at the *daai-saai* table-captain. Two men moved in behind him and he was gone. Other players jostled to claim his place.

Mark moved deeper into the gaming hall. At one wall, incense burned at a shrine to *Guan Yue*, protector of the oppressed. At another wall there hung a drape bearing the likeness of a phoenix flanked by winged dragons.

In the midst of the clamour stood a serene man dressed in a brocade gown of scarlet and green. He had a wispy beard and skin like old parchment. His eyes were quick and bright. In the fashion of Ming dynasty nobility, he wore golden sheaths over his fingernails. He regarded Mark with a blend of curiosity and amusement. He stroked his beard and his eyes twinkled.

Mark bowed and made the messenger sign.

The old man inclined his head and made the sign of the Hill Chief, the highest triad ranking. He turned and walked to the drape. Two men closed in on Mark, two more flanked Tang, another pulled aside the drape to reveal a crimson door, bound with polished brass. The door opened and the older man stepped through. The men flanking Mark each extended an arm, indicating that Mark and Tang should follow. The door closed behind them, shutting out the din of the gaming hall.

They were in a windowless chamber. Tasselled lanterns provided soft light and carpet muffled their footsteps. Embroidered drapes covered the walls. One bore the same phoenix and dragon motif Mark had seen in the gaming hall. Two high-backed chairs stood side-by-side facing a dais on which stood a third, elevated chair. Behind the third chair there was a screen of dark lacquer, decorated with depictions of pagodas, mountain streams, and humming birds. From behind the screen there drifted the tinkling notes of a *zeng*.

'You have come to talk with one named Gon Liao,' the older man said in a musical voice He pulled his robe tight around him and sat on his elevated chair. He smiled and inclined his head. 'This Gon Liao bids you welcome.' He indicated the chairs before the dais. Mark and Tang both sat.

Gon Liao clapped his hands and the *zeng* fell silent. A young woman stepped from behind the screen. She had blue-black hair piled high and fastened with a jade comb. Her neck was slender and her skin was fair. She wore a gown of filmy silk. For an instant, a lantern held her in silhouette, showing the swell of her breasts and the curve of her hips. The woman stepped through a bead curtain and returned carrying a tray bearing a glazed teapot and three cups of wafer thin porcelain.

Gon Liao shrugged an apology. 'I fear there is only jasmine tea,' he said. 'I live but a simple life.'

The woman knelt before Mark and poured tea into a cup. She cradled the cup in both hands and offered it up to him. For a moment, her eyes held Mark's, bold and inviting. She smiled and leaned closer. A thrill jolted Mark as her breast caressed his knee.

Gon Liao chuckled. 'Even under your cowl, I sense your youthful ardour, Mister Falchion.'

The woman gave a small laugh then stood and glided towards Lieutenant Tang, who grunted and waved her away.

'And you, Lieutenant Tang of the Peking Banner Cavalry,' Gon Liao continued. 'My sworn enemy, I think.'

Tang's eyes narrowed. He tensed and leaned forward.

Gon Liao smiled like a favourite uncle. 'Do not think to attack me, Lieutenant,' he said. 'There is a crossbow aimed at your heart and violent death is a bad start to negotiations. Do you not agree, Mister Falchion?'

Mark ran his eyes over the drapes. There was no sign of concealed openings but Gon Liao's easy confidence convinced him they were there. One-eared Wu had told him of such things: mechanical crossbows pre-targeted on key points throughout the room. Just a small movement from Gon Liao could be the signal. Then there would be the *tunk* of crossbows and a steel-tipped bolt would bite into Mark's chest. He tried to rock his chair but found it bolted to the floor. He dried his palms on his gown and pulled the cowl from his head.

'Ah, so much better.' Gon Liao sipped his tea. 'You have both entered my *Hung Mon* under false pretences,' he said. 'There are many Imperial officers in my pay but, to my regret, none so worthy as the gallant lieutenant.' He wagged his finger. 'And we have never invited foreigners into our brotherhood. I am duty bound to kill you both, quite horribly I fear.'

Tang's nostrils flared. His breathing was fast and heavy.

'Stay calm Lieutenant,' Mark said. 'Remember our mission.'

'Ah yes,' Gon Liao said. 'The reason for your presence.' He raised a finger like a host who has forgotten the wine. 'It has come to these ears that in the Takei Bank there are ten thousand silver ounces destined for the coffers of this old man.' He smoothed down the front of his gown. 'Now, I wonder how I must earn such an excellent sum.'

He's treating it as a game, thought Mark. Then he looked into Gon Liao's eyes and remembered the hidden crossbows. He cleared his throat. 'You must do nothing,' he said.

Gon Liao gave an eye-crinkling smile. 'A most agreeable arrangement,' he chuckled. 'But what kind of nothing must I do?'

Mark kept his voice steady. 'You must do nothing to impede any expedition mounted from Shanghai against the Taipings.'

Gon Liao nodded more in understanding than agreement. 'This is a big nothing,' he answered. 'In fact it is a huge nothing. The Taipings and we triads both wish to replace the Manchu usurpers with the true sons of China.' He looked at Tang. 'I do not mean to offend our honoured visitor, but the Taipings are our allies in this. Why should I make an arrangement with you?'

Mark spoke without thinking. 'I... if we... if you support the Taipings, you exchange one tyrant for another. They are everyone's enemies...' His voice tailed off.

'Do you think to convince me with that?' Gon Liao said. He gave a silky laugh. 'You are most callow, Mister Falchion. Please, Lieutenant Tang, enlighten this young man.'

Tang spoke to Mark as if to a child. 'Visit any Taiping city and take a stroll along the walls,' he said. 'You will find them decorated with the heads of gamblers, brothel keepers and opium smokers.'

'The lieutenant speaks true,' Gon Liao said. He smiled, but this time his eyes did not sparkle. 'Is that not a sorry waste of commerce?' He leaned forward. 'I would have given the promise you seek without ten thousand ounces of silver,' he said. He slapped the arm of his chair and the mischief returned. 'But now it is a matter of face and my face demands twenty thousand.'

'Twelve,' Mark snapped back. Banker Yang would cluck like an old hen but he was safe in his counting house and Mark Falchion was here.

'Fifteen,' Gon Liao retorted.

Mark opened his mouth but Gon Liao raised a cautionary finger. 'Take care my young friend, a skilled player knows when to walk away from the game.'

A silence lingered between them then Gon Liao laughed. 'Excellent,' he said. 'We are agreed.' He stood and motioned for Mark and Tang to do likewise. Mark stood, stepped back from chair and allowed himself a smile.

Tang lounged back and picked at his teeth with a fingernail.

Gon Liao inclined his head. 'I see the lieutenant's courage equals his pride,' he said. He turned to Mark. 'And you also, Mister Falchion, you are indeed your father's son.'

It was as if a fist had gripped Mark's heart. 'You know of my father?' he croaked.

'I do. Presently, he tends wounded Taipings in the town of Sungkiang. Much to everyone's regret he is not very busy.' Gon Liao's voice became sharp with sarcasm. 'The all-conquering Imperials abandoned the town without a fight.'

Scarlet spots burned Tang's cheeks.

'Your father lives,' Gon Liao said. He gave a knowing smile. 'I hear his assistant is a beauty.'

Mark took in a sharp breath. Questions sprang to his lips but Gon Liao held up his hand.

'Take care, my young brother,' Gon Liao said. 'Nothing is as it seems and sometimes, people are not what they pretend to be.' He lowered his voice, his eyes gleamed. 'Life can be tenuous,' he continued. 'Their captor is a Taiping named Meng and where normal men have a soul, this Meng has a dark and withered thing.'

Memories of the wrecked pavilion and of One-eared Wu flashed into Mark's head. His voice was hard and flat. 'Does this Meng wear black silk and carry a fine sword?' he asked.

Gon Liao nodded. 'Now I read your heart,' he said. 'But do you have the skill to face this Meng? Do you have the courage?' He shook his head. 'Have no faith in your mercenary comrades, they will do only what serves their interests.' Gon Liao fixed Mark with a steady gaze. 'You must think before you act. If I were a gambler I would not lay one bronze coin on your chances.'

Then he was the cheerful host again. He clapped his hands and a retainer stepped forward. 'This man will escort you to the northern gate,' he said. 'The city guard will not trouble you.'

Mark turned to go but Gon Liao called him back.

'Mister Falchion, I have a small gift for you.'

He reached into his gown and drew out a thin chain from which hung a small pendant. At its centre was a blue gem. In the lantern light, the gem gleamed and Mark felt himself mesmerised by it. He reached out to it but Gon Liao grabbed his wrist. Mark tried to snatch back his hand but the old man's grip was like a manacle. Mark winced as Gon Liao twisted his wrist, forcing him to open his hand, palm up. Gon Liao smiled like a village sage but in his eyes there was only cold dispassion. He held the pendant close to Mark's face.

'Look,' he commanded. 'It is the purest sapphire, it is like a tiny blue lantern, I think.' His voice was silky. 'It is like the blue lantern we hang to mourn our loved ones when they pass to the afterlife.'

Mark tried to look away but Gon Liao's eyes held him like a moth on a pin.

'Or maybe the blue lantern portends only symbolic death. Symbolic death before starting a new life,' he continued. 'Did your old swordmaster tell you of our ceremonies? Did he explain how we hang the blue lantern to welcome novitiates into our brotherhood?'

Gon Liao dropped the chain and pendant into Mark's hand then released his grip. The spell broke, leaving Mark gasping.

'Wear this stone close to your heart,' Gon Liao urged. 'Never discard it for soon you will have need of it.' He smiled. 'I see my words puzzle you but do not worry, when the time comes you will understand.'

Mark slipped the pendant over his head and it felt cool against his skin. Behind him, the door opened. The gaming hall din hammered into the chamber but Mark did not hear it. His heart veered from joy to dread and back again. His father. Mei. Both alive. Alive behind the walls of Sungkiang. His jaw tightened. He had the name of the man who had sacked the mission hospital and cut down One-eared Wu. The same man who held Mei and his father.

# THE SCHOLAR'S BLADE

*'Meng!'*

As Mark spoke the name, something stirred inside him. Something ugly, like a worm in a plum. He shook his head. Destiny, once so clear now tossed him about like a leaf in a gale. The world was upside down leaving Mark Falchion with just two choices. If Ward and his two hundred wanted Sungkiang, he would fight beside them.

But if Ward did not move on Sungkiang, then Mark Falchion would fight there alone.

# 16

Top soldier Cho Lung hated Sungkiang. He hated the soot-stained buildings, he hated the mosquitoes that swarmed around the moat, he hated how the swampy heat made everything smell of mildew. And as anyone who mentioned it soon learned, Cho Lung especially hated garrison duty. In garrison, soldiers became bored and a bored soldier was a soldier looking for trouble.

Cho took a moment to survey the defences and did not like what he saw. The walls were stout but unlike other fortress towns, the parapet had no defensive crenellations. His soldiers would have to lean over the balustrade to repel attackers and that made them easy targets for enemy musket fire and arrowshot.

The town gates were a better prospect, they were ironbound teak. The main, outer gate led into a courtyard surrounded on all four sides by sheer walls of granite. There, any attackers would find their way forward barred by another gate every bit as daunting as the first. The only way for them to escape the courtyard was either back across the moat or forward through that inner gate. All the time, they would be under musket fire, arrow fall and hurled spears.

The gates held another surprise for attackers. The outer gate was vulnerable to artillery but not so the inner. This inner gate did not align with outer gate, it was off to one side. To anyone outside the walls, the inner gate was invisible and as a result, impervious to artillery.

Cho nodded his approval. Yes, he thought, this courtyard is the perfect killing sac.

He leaned out over the balustrade and looked down at the moat. Once there had been a bridge but now, only charred stanchions showed above the water's surface. Now, the only entry into Sungkiang was through a gate on the other side of town. Cho scowled. One way in meant one way out. If the enemy breached the western defences, the Black Dragon's would be trapped here, on the eastern wall. There would be no escape, at least not unless they learned to walk on water.

*Water.* Why did the word trouble him so? Of course, the watergate. Half submerged in the moat close by the Black Dragons' position, was a moss-covered archway. Local farmers had once carried produce to a small jetty inside the walls but now, a massive grill of wrought iron blocked the way in. No one had used it for years. The lifting mechanism was a mass of rust and the ropes had long since rotted away.

The grill did not stand square and there was a gap between it and the stonework. This did not worry Cho overmuch, there was not enough space for a man, let alone an armed man, to squeeze through. Still, the thought of leaving any gate unwatched niggled like an unscratchable itch.

Cho sighed, he was an old soldier and he would handle things. The other top soldiers called him an old woman but he knew there would be a battle. The Imperials had gifted the town to the Taipings but they would be back. Later would be better than sooner. The men needed to rest and to practice their weapon skills.

Yes, Cho hated garrison duties but for now at least, there was work to keep quarrelsome soldiers busy. The Black Dragons had to haul six howitzers onto the wall guarding the eastern gate. There, a finicky artillery officer fussed them into position.

The work was going well but still, Cho was unhappy. Colonel Fu had assigned his bodyguard, the tall and muscular Shan, to oversee everything. Now, Shan stood on the parapet with his feet spread and his heavy bladed *guandao* in his fist.

One of Cho's men lost his footing and the rope slipped from his hand. Others took up the strain but could not control the gun. It swung around and teetered on the ramp's edge.

Shan lay down his *guandoa* and ran to the gun. He stripped off his tunic and braced his back against the gun carriage. He flexed his shoulders, drew in a deep breath and gripped tight to the carriage's underside. He began to lift. The muscles of his chest and shoulders bunched. Sinews stood out on his neck and torso. His lips curled back from his teeth. His face became crimson.

'PULL!' he bellowed.

All along the battlements, soldiers turned to watch.

'I said PULL!'

Cho watched, half hoping the gun would topple into the courtyard and carry Shan with it.

Then it moved. At first, Cho thought it just a trick of the light. But no, only the gods knew how, but the gun had moved.

'PULL, you goat turds!' Shan roared.

The ropes groaned. The blocks squealed. Shan let out a heaven wrenching bellow and the gun was sitting safe and square on the ramp.

As the gun began its slow progress back up the ramp, the soldier who had lost his footing scurried forward. His face split in a grin as he handed Shan his tunic. He clasped his hands together at his chest and bowed from the waist.

Shan slipped back into his tunic. His face was expressionless stone. Without a word, he bunched his fist and slammed it hard against the soldier's temple. There was a sound like a slaughterman's hammer striking bone. The soldier went down and lay still. Shan stood over him, raised his foot and stamped down hard on the man's chest.

The soldier's body twitched. Blood gushed from his mouth.

'STAND BACK!' Cho bellowed. 'LEAVE THAT MAN!'

Shan raised his eyes to meet Cho's. He hawked up a gob of spittle and spat it on the unconscious soldier. With his eyes still locked on Cho's, he aimed a sidekick at the soldier's head. The soldier's head bounced against the ramp's stone flags. Shan smiled up at Cho then turned and walked back up the ramp.

Cho fumed in silence. Meng wanted Shan in the Black Dragons and what Meng wanted Meng got. The giant Taiping would be a problem but Cho knew how to handle problems. He would deal with Shan even if it took a half-troop of Black Dragons or a dagger in the dark.

But that was for another time. General Kong had left only one regiment to guard Sungkiang's four miles of walls. One regiment - just two and a half thousand men. Twice as many would be too few. Good food, comfortable barracks, and even the troublesome Shan would have to wait

Because first there would be one more battle to fight.

The steamer's bow carried the name *Dancer*. She smelled of new paint and years of regular scrubbing had left her teak decks almost pure white. Canvas awnings stretched fore and aft from her wheelhouse.

At the stern, a group of Filipino troopers threw dice and chattered in their laughter-filled language. The skipper was an animated Italian called Captain Antonio. He had a bulbous nose and the thickest eyebrows Mark Falchion had ever seen. From under his cap, a fringe of dark hair stuck out like half-packed jute.

Mooring lines secured *Dancer* to a pontoon close to where

Soochow Creek flowed into the Huangpu River. In the midstream fairway, ships lay with flaccid sails hanging from static yards. Ashore, the buildings shimmered in the noon haze.

There was not a whisper of breeze and Mark envied the sailors their loose shirts. The tunic of his new uniform was forest green. The britches were dark blue and tucked into calf-high boots. The *dao* hung heavy across his shoulder. He pushed a finger into his collar and pulled the material away from his throat. Standing by the wheelhouse, Lieutenant Tang was in full uniform.

'Doesn't this heat bother you?' Mark's tone was resentful.

'It would if I wore western uniform,' Tang answered.

Sweating coolies bounced up the springy gangplank, each bent almost double under the weight of a slim crate. Stencilled in bold letters on each one were the words, 'Christian Sharps Company - Connecticut.'

'Steady with those boxes,' Vincente bawled.

Standing beside Mark, a sour-faced customs official frowned at his copy of *Dancer's* manifest. 'And those would be?' he asked.

Mark ran a finger down the manifest. 'Farm equipment,' he said. 'Item twelve.'

'Since when has Christian Sharps Corporation made farm equipment?' the customs officer snorted.

Vincente was all cheer. 'Why would peace loving folk like us want anything to do with Mister Sharps' rifles?' he quipped. 'Farm equipment,' he said and jabbed his finger onto the customs officer's manifest. 'It says so right there. Superintendent Crooker's already cleared it.'

The customs officer sniffed and made a large tick on the manifest. He pointed to a stack of smaller boxes sat on the foredeck. 'And those?'

'That's the skipper's snuff.' Vincente said with a cherubic smile.

'Snuff.' The customs officer's voice was flat and sceptical. 'Correct.'

'Twelve hundred pounds...' He paused and regarded Vincente from under knotted brows '... of snuff.'

'The finest quality,' Vincente replied, earnest and wide-eyed.

The customs officer scowled and handed Mark a sheet of paper. 'Sign here to declare you're carrying no contraband. Contraband includes...'

'Yes, yes. We know the list,' Vincente took the sheet, licked the tip of his pencil and signed with a flourish.

The customs man muttered under his breath and slipped the manifest into his pocket. He gave a loud sniff and strode down the gangplank.

Vincente's face split in an eye-crinkling grin. 'I guess Captain Crooker didn't cut him in,' he whispered.

A sailor guarding the crates on the foredeck stuffed his pipe with tobacco and scraped a match against one of them. The smile dropped from Vincente's lips. *'Douse that flame,'* he roared.

The sailor blinked back his surprise, blew out the match and backed away.

Vincente winked at Mark. 'Tricky cargo, snuff.'

Harry Jessop joined them at the gangway. He wore a linen shirt and pale-brown trousers tucked into polished riding boots. With his thumb and forefinger, he held his shirt away from his chest.

'My God,' he sighed, 'it's cooler in the boiler room.' He shielded his eyes and scanned the pontoon. 'Customs gone?'

Mark tugged at his tunic. 'How come you don't have one of these?' he grumbled.

'Only got one jacket old fellow, but it's scarlet and Sir John won't let me wear it. Just an observer, see? I'll have to suffer in silence.'

Jessop nodded towards Tang. 'Everyone's talking about the marvellous job you and the Chinese fellow did. Seems like you hit it off pretty well.'

Mark massaged his ribs. 'You might say so,' he muttered.

Jessop's face became serious. 'Are you all right, old chap? You've not been yourself since you got back from the Chinese Quarter.'

'I'm well enough,' Mark answered with forced cheer. 'But I've a lot on my mind.'

Captain Antonio stuck his head through the wheelhouse window. He gave an exaggerated shrug and held out his hands in a pleading gesture. 'Hey, gentlemans, we go now, *si*?' He ducked back into the wheelhouse and blew *Dancer's* whistle.

The gangplank rattled onto the deck and smoke streamed from *Dancer's* stack. At the bow and stern, sailors threw the mooring lines to workers on the pontoon. *Dancer* drifted from the pontoon. Her paddles began to turn and the deck vibrated.

As the steamer eased forward, a breeze came over her bow, ruffling the awning. Mark unbuttoned his tunic and enjoyed cool air against his skin. He touched Gon Liao's pendant and puzzled over his words, *'You will soon have need of it.'*

The paddles churned the water into foaming chocolate. Dancer steered into Soochow Creek and headed west. The fine business houses fell behind and stone river-frontage gave way to reed-covered embankments. At the bow, a sailor swung a weighted line into the water then reeled it back in, counting knots tied every six feet.

'Two an' arf,' he called.

Vincente eyed the riverbank. *'Stand to,'* he called.

The Filipinos abandoned their dice. One disappeared through a deck hatch and minutes later, he was passing newly unpacked carbines up to the others. The troopers levered open the breeches, checked the sights then spaced themselves along each beam.

'Trooper Dante,' Vincente called.

A Filipino stepped forward. Vincente took the trooper's carbine. 'Ever seen one of these, Harry?' he asked, handing the carbine to Jessop.

Jessop turned it over in his hands. The barrel was less than three feet long and there was a hinge where the trigger guard connected to the forestock.

'Yankee sporting gun, isn't it? Looks businesslike but I doubt it's a match for an Enfield. A Royal Marine can get in three, maybe four shots a minute with an Enfield.' He handed the carbine back to Vincente.

Vincente smiled. 'What do you reckon, Trooper Dante? Can you manage four shots a minute?'

Dante stifled a snigger. 'I can try, Vincente.'

Vincente unsnapped a pouch hanging from Dante's belt. He pulled out a waxpaper cartridge and handed it to Mark. 'Know anything about guns?' he asked.

Mark cradled the cartridge in his hand. It was a half-inch wide cylinder of waxed paper with a lead ball at one end. It was heavier than it looked.

Vincente took back the cartridge and tossed it to Trooper Dante then spoke to Jessop.

'With an Enfield, your marine takes his cartridge, bites through the paper casing, pours the powder into the barrel, rams home the ball and fits a percussion cap. If the ball hasn't jammed in the rifling, he's ready to shoot.' Vincente's lips formed a sly smile. 'Four shots a minute, Harry? With an expert rifleman firing volleys, maybe. But Royal Marine or not, no one betters three aimed shots a minute, not with an Enfield.'

Jessop shrugged. 'Very well, for the sake of argument, three. Either way you'll not find anyone faster than a marine.'

Vincente worked a lever behind the carbine's hinged triggerguard and the breech slid open. He pushed the cartridge into the chamber and his eyes sparkled. 'Watch, Harry, and be amazed.'

Jessop frowned and moved closer.

Vincente levered shut the breech and pulled back the hammer. He fitted a percussion cap, took aim at the riverbank and squeezed the trigger. The stock slammed into his shoulder and a jet of spray exploded amongst the reeds. He lowered the carbine and gave a satisfied nod.

'Sharps breechloader,' he said. 'It'll bring down an American buffalo at five hundred yards; drop a man at a thousand.'

He threw the weapon to Dante who caught it with both hands. The trooper dropped to one knee and pulled another cartridge from his ammunition pouch.

Vincente raised an eyebrow, his voice was teasing. 'Got a second hand on that fancy watch of yours, Harry?'

A smile spread across Jessop's face and he pulled a watch from his pocket. 'Three shots a minute, Vincente,' he chuckled. 'He'll manage no more than three. I'll put money on it.'

Vincente grinned. 'Five dollars?'

Jessop nodded. 'Five it is,' he chuckled.

'Then count him in, Harry,' Vincente said. 'Count him in.' He winked at Dante.

Jessop held his watch at eye level. 'Ready? And three... two... one... *go!*'

Dante levered open the breech and thumbed in a cartridge. He fitted a percussion cap and took aim. The carbine banged Smoke drifted sternwards.

'One,' Jessop chirped.

Dante already had another cartridge in the breech. The Sharps banged again.

'Two.' Jessop tapped the watch face and held it against his ear.

The Sharps banged once more.

'Twenty seconds.' Jessop's eyes widened. 'Three shots in twenty seconds. I've not seen...'

The Sharps banged again. Trooper Dante moved like a machine: unhurried, precise, practised.

'Thirty seconds.' Jessop squinted at the watch. Dante had fired five shots.

Smoke curled between the deck and awning. Still, Dante loaded and fired then loaded and fired again.

'Sixty seconds.' Jessop slumped back against the wheelhouse. 'Nine shots. *Nine* in one minute.' He reached into his pocket and fished out a five-dollar bill.

Vincente shook his head. 'Silver only, please Harry. And I made it ten but let's not quibble. I've a man at Guanfulin who's managed twelve.' He patted Dante's shoulder and the trooper returned to his place at the railing.

Harry Jessop scratched his head and gave a rueful smile.

'Well, bugger me,' he said.

For three hours, *Dancer* thumped upstream. At some point, Captain Antonio left Soochow Creek and the steamer meandered along narrow waterways. Sometimes, children ran along beside them skipping and waving. A water buffalo turned its head to watch them.

Mark laid the *dao* across his knees and sat with his back to a crate. The thud of the paddles and the vibrating deck lulled him. His head lolled, his eyelids fluttered and he drifted into a contented sleep. He woke with a start as *Dancer* scraped against a jetty and her gangplank trundled along the deck. Troopers stacked crates on the wharf where a sullen quartermaster checked them off against his list.

'Harry, stay here with me,' Vincente called. 'Mark and Lieutenant Tang, get yourselves ashore and introduce yourselves to the mess steward. He's a thief but he'll fix you up with quarters and vittles.'

Mark and Tang negotiated the gangplank and stepped onto the jetty. The air was still and clouds of insects swarmed around their heads.

Tang shielded his eyes against the evening sun and turned a full circle. 'Where are the horses?' he demanded. 'Are we peasants who fight on foot?'

Just beyond the landing, a small stockade stood at the centre of a clearing. A body of men marched from the stockade and halted before the gates. All were Westerners and wore tunics of forest green. Some carried muzzle-loading rifles but most had Sharps breechloaders. Their tunics were unbuttoned and their drill was awkward. A sergeant shouted an order and the men executed a ragged left face. One staggered and dropped his rifle. The others burst into laughter.

'He's drunk,' Tang exclaimed. 'They're all drunk.'

Nearby, a team of men drilled with a field gun. The gunners had weathered faces and sported tar-stiffened pigtails.

Beyond the stockade were lines of tents. Close to each entrance flap, three rifles stood upright, their barrels interlocked. One tent was larger than the others and by its entrance a lopsided sign read, 'Officers Mess.'

Mark and Tang made their way past the stockade and ducked through the mess tent's flap. Inside, oil lamps sputtered and cast an orange glow. A dining table dominated the mess and in one corner was a makeshift bar. Stood at the bar were men wearing an odd assortment of clothing. One wore a short hunting jacket, another, a banker's frock coat. There were military tunics of scarlet and some of brown.

One officer was taller than the others. He was long-limbed and wore his hair cropped to golden stubble. He had a chiselled jaw and fleshy lips. A puckered scar showed against one cheek. He wore white britches and a blue tunic devoid of military insignia. Hanging at his side was a curved sabre.

One by one, the officers fell silent and turned their eyes on the newcomers. Mark took a deep breath.

'Gentlemen, can someone direct me to the mess steward?' he asked.

The man in the blue tunic smiled at the others. He stepped away from the bar and stifled a belch. His eyes were bloodshot and rheumy.

'*Hauptman* Gunter Schneider, late of the Prush...Prussian Household Lancers.' His voice was like iron scraping through gravel. 'I am at your service, *Mein Herr*.' He gave a curt bow. 'So, now you must tell me what you are,' he said. 'Maybe you are Chinese.' His eyes narrowed. 'Or perhaps you are an *Englischer* schoolboy playing a game of dress-up.'

'What is he saying?' Tang hissed.

Mark's reply was a half-whisper. 'He's drunk. Pay him no attention.'

Schneider arched an eyebrow. 'So, the Chinese-English boy speaks.'

For a moment, Mark was silent then he lowered his eyes. 'Forgive my manners,' he said. 'My comrade speaks no English.'

Schneider gave a harsh laugh. '*Ja*, it is good to mind your manners, boy.' He lowered his voice. 'For if you do not, we will test our swords.'

The men at the bar grinned and nudged one another. 'Come on Gunter, old chap,' someone called. 'Show him what we think of his kind.'

Schneider spread his arms as if in welcome. 'But I also forget my manners,' he declared. 'Let me bid you welcome to our humble officer's mess.' Disappointment clouded his face. 'Sadly, your servant must wait outside.'

Schneider addressed the men at the bar. 'Am I not right gentlemen? No Manilamen and...' He put his face close to Tang's. 'Definitely no Chinese.'

Tang half drew his sword. 'I will take his head if he continues to defile me with his breath.'

Mark laid his hand on Tang's forearm and the lieutenant eased the blade back into his scabbard.

'*Ach*, the Chinkie also has a voice.' Schneider looked Tang over like a sideshow attraction. 'But does it speak a civilised tongue?'

Mark stepped between them. 'Sir, we have just arrived from Shanghai.' He fought to keep his voice calm. 'Please tell me where I might find the mess steward. Then we will trouble you no further.'

Schneider's voice became a purr. 'You do not enjoy my company?'

Mark clasped his hands before his chest and bowed. 'Pray, do not think that, sir. My companion and I are tired...'

'So, my conversation fatigues you?'

Mark fell silent.

'This is a matter of *Ehrensache*, boy, of honour. Understand?'

Mark stared into Schneider's' face. For a heartbeat, the two men held each other's gaze then Mark let out a slow breath. 'There are Taipings to fight, sir. We should save our energies for them.'

Schneider's voice rose to a shout. 'You dare tell me my duty. *Mein Gott*, we will have this out now.' He peeled off his jacket and tossed it to another officer.

The officer patted Schneider's shoulder. 'You show him, Gunter. Don't need his sort here.'

'What are you waiting for, boy?' Schneider snarled. 'Outside. Now.' He drew his sabre and cut the air.

Mark reached for the *dao* then checked himself. He heard his own voice, hard and scornful. 'Sir, I believe the drink has the better of you.'

'*Ah-ha*, at last we see the truth of your insolence. You will join me outside or I will cut you down in here.'

'Steady on, old fellow,' another officer crowed. 'Remember Colonel Ward's orders, no duelling, especially not in the bloody mess.' He laughed, showing yellow teeth. 'I said, "No duelling in the mess," what?'

'I've ten dollars says the boy doesn't last thirty seconds.' The voice belonged to a florid Dutchman.

'Make it twenty and you're on,' another called. The noise at the bar rose to a clamour as the Dutchman took down bets in a small book.

Schneider elbowed past Mark and ducked through the tent flap. Mark made to follow but Tang pulled at his arm. 'What's happening?' he demanded.

Mark's voice was a growl. 'The Prussian says I've insulted him. He insists we fight. I'm going to teach him some swordsmanship.'

Tang's grip was insistent. 'Now is not the time,' he growled. 'See how steadily he walks. The pig is not as drunk as he acts.'

Mark shook off Tang's hand and ducked through the flap. Outside, the air was still. The only sound was the metallic chirp of insects. Schneider exercised his sabre with whispering cuts to the left and right. The evening sun glittered off its cutting edge.

The officers stumbled from the mess and formed a circle around the two swordsmen.

Mark slipped the *dao* over his head and handed it to Tang. He stripped off his uniform tunic and flexed his shoulders.

'My God, he's a strong-looking boy,' someone said. 'He might last a full minute.'

From the lines of tents men came running, looping their braces over their shoulders. Others struggled with their boots, hopping towards the circle, demanding to know if they had missed anything.

Tang offered Mark the *dao* hilt first and the blade scraped against the scabbard's brass lip. Mark watched the sunset play on the steel. He wanted to exercise the *dao*, wanted to hear it sigh through the air, wanted to feel its perfect balance. One-eared Wu's teachings whispered to him:

'Hide your training; hide your skill.'

Schneider puffed out his chest and placed his left fist on his hip. He swept his blade down in an arcing salute.

As he watched the Prussian's blade, Mark's stomach tightened, his heart pounded, his mouth dried.

The Prussian smiled. He spread his arms and bowed to the growing crowd of officers and soldiers.

The man is confident, Mark thought. No, he decided, the man is simply arrogant. Cold anger swelled inside him. More of One-eared Wu's words came back to him:

'Focus the fear; focus the anger; mind and body becomes one with the dao.'

Mark dropped to a half-crouch and took the *dao* in a two-handed grip. Inside him, fear and anger merged into something cold and pitiless. His heart stilled. A calmness descended on him. The shouts and laughter of the crowd faded into nothingness. Now, there was only Mark Falchion, the *dao* broadsword and the Prussian officer.

Schneider grinned and beckoned Mark forward. In that instant, the smile fell from his lips. He cried, '*et la*,' and lunged.

Mark spun the *dao*. Steel rang against steel, knocking the sabre aside.

Schneider stepped back. *'Sehr gut, Liebling,'* he chuckled. 'Very good. Now we must begin the lesson in earnest, *ja?'* His eyes glittered. He moved to Mark's left. The point of his sabre traced slow circles.

Mark's eyes followed him, watching for a move that would signal an attack.

The sabre point dropped. Schneider's breath hissed from between clenched teeth. He lunged.

Mark swung the *dao* to block the thrust. Almost too late, he saw the thrust change to a scything cut. He swept the *dao* in quarter-circle, hammering the sabre aside, exposing Schneider's body. He sliced up and to the right, slitting the Prussian's shirtfront from hip to shoulder.

Schneider gaped at his ruined shirt. He ran his fingertips across his chest. The skin was unbroken.

Mark's voice was a low growl. 'Has the lesson started yet?'

'By Jove, what control,' a voice called from the crowd of onlookers. 'I think you've met your match, Gunter old fellow. Anyone fancy five dollars on the young 'un?'

Schneider let out a roar and charged, hacking left, right, and overhead.

Mark backed away, spinning the *dao* to block each cut. Each parry jarred his wrists and shoulders. Mark feinted left then moved right and lunged, aiming for Schneider's belly.

Schneider knocked the *dao* away and thrust at Mark's chest.

Mark sidestepped and the sabre sighed past him. Schneider backed away. His lips were white, his breath was ragged. He used his sleeve to wipe sweat from his eyes.

He's tiring, Mark thought.

Schneider lunged again but the thrust lacked power. Mark

danced to the side. Schneider stumbled past him and Mark hammered the *dao's* pommel against the Prussian's shoulder.

Schneider's face twisted in pain. He cried out and his sword arm sagged. He made to raise his sabre but Mark used the *dao's* weight to beat it down.

Schneider fell to one knee, clutching his shoulder. 'I will gut you...' He fell silent as the *dao's* cutting edge touched his throat. He stared up at Mark, his eyes wide, his lips bloodless. He let go of the sabre and showed Mark his open palms. His face was pale. He shook his head and made a small mewling noise.

Blood pounded in Mark's temples. Something dark uncoiled inside him. He stared down at Schneider. The Prussian's neck was pale and soft. Mark drew in a slow breath. He raised the *dao*.

'BELAY THAT!'

Striding towards them were Ward and Vincente.

'Stand down Mister Falchion,' Ward snapped.

Mark ignored him. He stood over the Prussian, the *dao* ready to strike.

'I said STAND DOWN!' Ward bellowed. 'Stand down or I swear to God, I'll have you flogged.'

Inside Mark, the dark thing shrank away. The tension left his muscles. He tapped the *dao* against Schneider's shoulder and backed away.

Schneider struggled to his feet and recovered his sabre. His lips formed a snarl. He let out an animal cry and raised his sword.

There was the distinctive triple *click* of a Colt revolver being cocked.

'Easy, Mister Schneider, easy now.' The voice was Vincente's. He held his revolver, aimed firm and steady at Schneider's head.

Schneider lowered his sabre. He smiled and gave an exaggerated shrug. 'We are just exercising our skills, *Oberst* Ward, no more.'

## THE SCHOLAR'S BLADE

He turned his back to Ward and put his head close to Mark's. His voice was a rasping whisper, 'Next time I will spit you like a suckling pig.'

He turned back to Ward. 'Just exercise, *Herr Oberst*. No more than that.' He aimed a casual cut at a tuft of grass and sauntered back to the mess tent.

Ward rounded on Mark. 'What the hell was that about?' he demanded.

Mark lowered his eyes. He spoke in a small voice. 'It was as Mister Schneider said, sir. Just a simple test of skill.'

Ward gave a doubtful sniff.

Vincente slid his Colt back into its holster and snapped shut the flap. He nodded towards the *dao*. 'I guess that's not just for decoration,' he chuckled. To Ward, he said, 'Leave this with me, Colonel. I'll talk to them.'

Ward glowered at Mark then turned and stamped away.

Vincente laid his hand on Mark's shoulder. 'There's more to you than we thought,' he said. 'You've laid down a marker. After today, no one here will trouble you.' He raised a cautionary finger. 'But watch out for Schneider, the man's a snake. You made him look weak and stupid. From now on, watch your back and stay out of dark alleys.' He draped his arm across Mark's shoulders. 'Now, let's find that mess steward and get you two settled.

# 17

NEW ORDERS confirmed the rumours: there would be action. The camp at Guanfulin became a sweating, cursing, snarl of chaos. Leather lunged sergeants chivvied men into platoons and companies. Then stood them down. Then formed them up again. Where there had once been calm, now there was turmoil.

'Where's the ammunition?'

'Where are the field guns?'

'Where's bloody B Company?'

A jury-rigged derrick collapsed, dumping artillery shot onto the jetty. Troopers chased a dozen balls that rumbled across the jetty's timbers and splashed into the shallows.

Captain Antonio cackled like a lunatic and blew *Dancer's* whistle until Vincente threatened to heave him into the river.

Mark Falchion's head throbbed. What did he feel? Fear? Excitement? Maybe it was it both. Perhaps it was neither. *Sungkiang*. His father was at Sungkiang. So was Mei. Had they hurt her? Had they...? He screwed shut his eyes, soon there would be answers.

By the jetty, two troopers were throwing dice. 'Four and above means yer'll live, Bluey,' said one. He blew into his fist and rolled the dice. It came up two. 'Never mind, mate. We'll throw 'er again, all right?'

Mark watched in silence. Should he ask the soldier to toss the dice for him? He cursed himself for a fool and climbed the gangplank to *Dancer's* deck.

Ward and Vincente were huddled over a map spread on the forward hatch. Ward was red-faced. He was talking rapidly and jabbing his finger down onto the map. Vincente pinched the bridge of his nose and shook his head. At Mark's approach, Ward stood.

'Ah, Mark, there you are.' He draped his arm across Mark's shoulder and guided him to the railing. 'I won't have it,' he chided. 'I've told Schneider and I'm telling you, next man to raise a sword against his comrade gets a public bambooing, understand?'

Before Mark could answer, Ward pounded his shoulder. 'Capital,' he roared. 'Now, come and tell me what you think.'

Vincente's mouth was a thin line. 'Colonel, I ask with the deepest respect, have you taken leave of your senses?'

'But it's so simple,' Ward replied. 'I always keep my plans simple.' His eyes gleamed.

A thread of alarm tugged at Mark. Was the gleam a spark of genius or a flash of insanity? In a heartbeat, it was gone.

'We'll find their weakness and lever it open,' Ward chortled. 'What a prize, man! Think about it.'

Vincente pursed his lips. 'Sir, where are the reconnaissance reports? Where is the intelligence review, the battle plan, the logistics order, the placement of reserves? Is the ground suitable for moving artillery? I beg you to reconsider. Failing to plan...'

'... Is planning to fail.' Ward sighed. 'Yes, yes. I know. But the laurel is too great. Sometimes we must seize the chance. Hit them now, they won't expect it.' He slapped his cane against his thigh. '*Damn*, I wish I'd learned of it sooner. I must have Sungkiang.'

He waved his hand across the map. 'Look where it's placed. Waterways leading west, east, north and south. If they hold Sungkiang, the Taipings can bring in supplies from Soochow and move their troops anywhere within the Shanghai environs. If we hold Sungkiang, they're snookered. They can't supply and they can't advance. It's the goddamned key to everything.'

Schneider banged to attention beside them. '*Herr Oberst*, my men are ready to board.' His voice was thick and as he spoke, he swayed from side to side.

Ward stood close to the Prussian. His voice was a dangerous whisper. '*Dammit*, Schneider, you'd better not be drunk, not now.'

'A tot, *Mein Oberst*, no more.'

Ward clenched his fists. 'And the men? My God, I'll not have you scupper me.'

'The men are fighting fit, sir, I swear it.'

Schneider clicked his heels and executed an unsteady about face. He shot Mark a venomous stare then stumbled down the gangplank.

Mark moved to the railing and Harry Jessop joined him.

'I wish the colonel would rethink this... this *adventure*,' Jessop sighed.

He nodded towards Schneider's men who were drinking from their canteens and laughing like young blades at a country dance. 'I'd lay a month's pay there's more than water in those canteens,' he added.

A rifle banged and a bullet splintered the woodwork above the wheelhouse door.

There was a burst of laughter from the men waiting to board. One had fallen onto his backside and was staring at his rifle. Blue-grey smoke curled from its barrel.

Schneider pulled the man to his feet then bunched his fist and clubbed him back down to the ground.

'*Mister Schneider*,' Ward bawled. 'That man is dismissed without pay. From here on in, I will hold you personally responsible for any more indiscipline.'

Vincente gave the order to embark and Schneider's troopers stumbled up the gangplank, mumbling like sullen schoolboys.

Captain Antonio stepped from the wheelhouse and ran his eyes along *Dancer's* beam. 'Cast off for'ard,' he called. 'Cast off aft.'

The gangplank trundled onto the deck. Mooring ropes thumped onto the jetty and *Dancer's* crew poled her away from the riverbank. The deck vibrated as the starboard paddle dug into the water. *Dancer's* prow came around and the steamer edged towards midstream. Captain Antonio reached for the whistle cord but Vincente shot him a warning scowl. The little Italian shrugged and pushed the ship's telegraph to 'Half Ahead Both.' The telegraph jangled and both paddles started to smack the water.

As the sun set to starboard, *Dancer* clawed her way from the Guanfulin landing. Mark's heart was a pendulum swinging between excitement and dread. He held tight to the railing and watched the jetty fall behind. At last, they were heading south.

South to Sungkiang.

Meng should have been happy. General Kong had agreed he could make up the Black Dragon's losses from Fu's regiment. Meng did not know which pleased him most: being back to full strength or watching Fu's rage as Meng cherry-picked his best men.

The first of them had been Fu's personal bodyguard, the man called Shan. The quartermaster had trouble finding a tunic to fit him but now, dressed in black, he stood beside Meng. He held his *guandao* gripped firm in his right fist; his strong features were as impassive as ever.

Indeed, Meng should have been happy but still, doubt

gnawed at his guts. The general had gone, leaving just over two-and-a-half thousand men to defend four miles of walls. Meng frowned. It was not enough, not nearly enough.

He flexed his hand and felt the sutures tug at the wound. It will mend, he thought, already the swelling was down. The barbarian doctor knew his trade well.

Meng rested his hand on a howitzer. The guns were good enough at lobbing shells over walls and into enemy towns but in defence they were next to useless. At short range, their barrels could not depress enough to fire on attackers close to the walls. Colonel Fu should have insisted on proper field pieces but, to be fair, the walls had no embrasures and without embrasures, field guns would have been no use either.

Meng sighed: too few men, bad fortifications and the wrong cannon. What a way to defend a town.

He looked along the wall. From the gate tower, the wall stretched a half mile in each direction. Spaced every one hundred paces were braziers stacked with kiln-dried wood. If this is a joke, Meng thought, it's a cruel one. The braziers were placed to illuminate night-time attackers, but in the dark they did a better job of illuminating the defenders.

He felt a presence behind him, it was Cho Lung.

'Will, they come?' Meng asked.

'*Ha*,' Cho barked. 'Don't ask will they come, ask when?'

Meng banged his fist against the howitzer. 'Then I hope it's soon,' he said. 'This constant stand-to will take the edge off the men.'

'They'll be ready,' Cho growled.

Meng moved to the parapet and savoured the evening air. 'What do you think of our doctor?' he asked.

The question took Cho by surprise. 'He's decent enough for a barbarian,' he muttered.

# THE SCHOLAR'S BLADE

Meng frowned. 'What about the *woman?*' He spat the last word.

Cho gave a noncommittal shrug. 'Soochow girls are prettier,' he said. 'But pretty or plain, girls are just girls.' He peered over the balustrade and nodded towards the moat. 'If this one bothers you so much, there's room for her down there.'

In silence, the two men watched the distant tree line. 'Are they out there now?' Meng asked, more of himself than of anyone else.

'The enemy is everywhere,' Cho answered. 'No matter how many times we are victorious, there are still more battles to win.' His lips twisted in a wry smile. 'I'm turning into an old woman,' he said. 'It's not my duty to ponder the reasons for war.'

'No,' Meng answered. 'It's your... it's *our* duty to kill Imperials and their lackeys.' He flashed Cho a smile. 'And for that,' he added, 'we need a hundred stout men of *Han* and a leathery old top soldier to bully every scrap of courage from them.'

A mile from Sungkiang, Captain Antonio set the engine room telegraph to, 'All Stop!' and nudged *Dancer* against the riverbank. Crewmen jumped ashore and hammered iron mooring spikes into the turf. In the marshy ground, the pins could not take *Dancer's* weight and the steamer threatened to drift back into the stream.

'Haul on those lines,' Captain Antonio bellowed. 'Keep her close to the shore.'

More sailors leapt ashore. They grabbed onto the lines and hauled *Dancer* back to the riverbank.

'The ground's too soft to move the artillery,' Vincente groaned.

'Then we'll leave it here,' Ward snapped. He clasped his hands behind his back and paced the deck. 'Too slow,' he groaned. 'We're moving too darned slow.'

He's right, Mark thought, time's leeching away. It was after midnight and half their equipment was still aboard *Dancer*. To make things worse, the earlier clouds had cleared and now a full moon lit the riverbank like a giant lantern. It was bright enough to read the stencils painted on the ammunition boxes. Mark offered a silent prayer for the night air to coax a mist from the surrounding marshes.

Vincente put his hand on Ward's shoulder. 'It's not too late to turn back,' he said. 'Give me two more weeks. *Santa Nino*, I can have everything ready in *one* week.'

Ward sucked on his teeth. 'I can't, Vincente. We've come too far, I can't go back with nothing.' He squared his shoulders and his voice became crisp. 'Gather the officers for final briefing. Snappy now, please.'

Vincente shook his head then stepped down the gangplank and called Ward's officers together for their final orders.

The night air cooled. A mist rose from the marshlands and the moon slid behind a grey veil.

From a nearby bamboo grove, a group of men watched as the troopers faded into the mist. The watching men were unwashed and their queues were unkempt. All but one had swords hanging from their belts. One had an arrow nocked to a bow.

Their leader was a big man with muscle bunched at his chest and shoulders. He had a flat face and the trailing ends of his moustache hung below his jaw line. He held a double-headed war axe, pillaged years earlier from a caravan far to the west. The blades were bright steel, inlaid with brass. Tonight, he had smeared them with mud so as not to catch the moonlight.

A man stumbled and swore. The whole group dropped to a half crouch.

'Quiet, fool,' the leader growled.

Each man held his breath, listening for a challenge but there was only silence.

'Stay close,' the leader whispered. 'There's going to be a fight and where there's a fight there's good pickings.'

He signalled the others to move forward. In silence, they followed the troopers into the mist.

Ward's troopers became plodding spectres. Their sergeants ran up and down the lines, keeping the squads together. Then, up ahead, something tall and solid blocked their way. Its summit was lost in the fog. To the left and right it stretched into the night.

Ward raised his arm and a whispered order to halt travelled down the column.

Mark and Harry Jessop moved up and stood beside Ward. Together, they squinted into the gloom.

'What is it?' Mark croaked.

'Don't know,' Ward whispered. 'If it's a ridge, it's not marked on the map. *Dammit*, more delay.' He touched Harry Jessop's arm. 'Bring up the column and form two lines facing the front,' he whispered. 'Vincente to command the left; Schneider the right. And for God's sake, keep them quiet.'

Jessop gave a sharp nod and disappeared. Minutes later, the muffled clank of equipment and the rustle of grass signalled the column fanning out on either flank.

A Filipino trooper emerged from the dark. '*Señor* Vincente's compliments sir,' he whispered. 'Left flank is secure.'

'Someone should go forward and take a look,' Mark suggested.

'My very thoughts,' Ward answered. 'Do the honours please, Mister Falchion,' he said. 'Be back here within five minutes.'

Mark dropped to a half-crouch and moved forward. He glanced behind him but already, the troop was just a formless shadow. He took another few steps and the mist closed around him. His mouth was ash dry. His breath came in short gasps.

A foraging animal rustled in the grass and he thought his heart would stop.

Then from the right flank, a voice called, 'Take care lad, them Taipings love pretty boys.'

Mark froze. Were the Taipings close? Had they heard?

Ahead, the ridge rose sheer and smooth. Mark dropped onto his belly and lay still. He squeezed shut his eyes and promised that if he lived to see morning, he would soldier no more.

From somewhere ahead, voices drifted through the mist, muffled and teasing.

Mark held his breath. There were figures moving along the ridge's peak. He crawled forward. His hand splashed into still water and a cloud of mosquitoes buzzed around his head. He squinted into the dark. Now, across a stretch of water, he could see dressed stone. The obstruction was not a natural ridge at all, he was under the shadow of Sungkiang's western wall.

In minutes, he would be scrambling up a ladder, drawing his sword, fighting Taiping defenders.

Or he would be dead.

He turned and started to crawl back to the troop's protection. He could just make out Harry Jessop's shape. Then, from the mercenary's right flank there was a burst of laughter.

And from Sungkiang's wall, came a shouted challenge.

'HALT!'

The guard wore Colonel Fu's jade-green. He leaned over the parapet and peered into the night.

His officer ran to the wall. 'What is it?' he demanded.

'Out there... something.' The soldier pointed into the dark, half wishing he had kept quiet.

The officer laid his hand on the soldier's arm. 'Easy boy,' he said. His voice was soothing. 'Tell me what you heard.'

The soldier's cheeks burned. 'It... it sounded like laughter...' His voice tailed off.

'Laughter?' The officer choked on the word. 'Could it have been a night bird?'

'Maybe. I don't know... No, it was laughter, I'm sure.'

The officer paced a few feet along the walkway. He turned to the soldier. 'You'd better be right,' he said.

'I'm certain,' the soldier replied.

The officer chewed his lip, his breath escaped in a hiss.

'Very well,' he snapped. 'Light the brazier then give the artillerymen a kick.' The officer cupped his hands to his mouth. '*Muskets!*' he shouted. 'To me. *Now!*'

Men came forward and rested muskets against the parapet. The officer checked the angle of fire then stepped back.

'*Fire!*' he shouted.

Muskets banged and spat flame.

More musket-men ran from the shadows.

Striding behind them was Colonel Fu. 'Explain yourself,' he barked.

On the tower there was the *thump* of a howitzer and the walkway shuddered under their feet.

'Who ordered a barrage?' Colonel Fu roared. 'Who?'

The officer stiffened and looked straight ahead. 'There are infiltrators beyond the wall, sir,' he said. 'They were... laughing.' He spoke the last word in a small voice.

'Laughing? *Laughing?*' Colonel Fu dragged a startled soldier back from the parapet. 'Cease fire,' he bellowed. '*Cease fire!*'

Another howitzer thumped, drowning the colonel's fury.

Harry Jessop dropped to a crouch as musket balls *zhipped* overhead. He moved to his right and stumbled over a trooper lying in the grass. He grabbed the man and hauled him up. The trooper reeked of brandy.

'Pass the word and do it quietly,' Jessop snapped. 'Do not return fire. I say again, *do not return fire.*'

The trooper gave a lopsided grin and stifled a belch. 'Under... Understood, sir,' he said. He turned away, cupped his hands to his mouth and yelled. 'Hold your fire, boys. Don't shoot at the bastards.'

Jessop pushed the man down into the turf, silencing him. My God, he thought, the next volley will be among us. A hard knot filled his chest. The battle not yet started was already lost.

'Steady boys.' Jessop's voice was a harsh stage-whisper. 'On your feet, quiet now. Move back to the tree line.'

On both flanks, troopers levelled their carbines and backed away. Jessop glanced back at Sungkiang and held his breath. The firing had stopped.

Then from his right came a shout, 'Shaggin' Chinks. Have some of this, you yellow bastards.' There was a bang and a stab of orange flame.

A rifle ball thudded into the brazier, showering Colonel Fu with embers. He gaped at the brazier and his eyes showed large. Then years of experience snapped into place.

'You,' he pointed to a soldier, 'douse the brazier. And you. Yes, you. Send out runners. Get more muskets. *Now!*'

He rounded on the officer.

'Take charge of the artillery. Load with grenade shells and traverse each gun after every shot. I want the area swept clear.'

He clapped his hands. '*Spear men*, pay attention. Don't watch me, don't watch your comrades, watch your front. *Your front!* Prepare for ladders.'

From further down the balustrade, there was a *thump* of a howitzer and a fuse traced a sparkling arc through the sky. The shell exploded one hundred paces out.

In the darkness beyond the moat, someone screamed.

Harry Jessop spread his arms like a farm boy gathering chickens. 'Move back, boys. Easy now.'

There was the crackle of musketry. Muzzle flashes flickered along the parapet. Musket balls pummelled the ground and *zhipped* around Jessop's head. A trooper cried out. Another fell without a sound.

A shell moaned high above them, its fuse sparkling. The ground bucked. A skull-splitting *crack* filled Jessop's world. Nearby there was the slap of metal on flesh and someone screamed.

'Sar'nt Patterson,' Jessop bawled. 'Put a volley onto the parapet then pull back twenty yards. Now, damn you, *move!*'

'Yes sir,' the sergeant called back. 'Right lads, form line. *Form bleedin' line!*'

Cartridges rattled into breeches.

'Aim at the muzzle flashes,' Patterson called. 'Wait for it... *wait.*'

A line of flashes rippled along the battlements.

'*Fire,*' Sergeant Patterson roared. The troopers fired a ragged volley.

'Back, boys, *move!*' Jessop shouted. 'Get a bloody grip, Sar'nt Patterson.'

The line moved back. Flashes stabbed from the battlements and musket balls threw up clods of turf where the troop had been.

'Well done, lads,' Jessop called. 'Move back. Easy now.'

Harry Jessop clutched onto his plan like drowning man clinging to a log.

Where's Mark? he thought. And where the hell's Schneider?

Later there would be a butcher's bill to tally.

And later, by God, there would be accounts to settle.

Mark began the slow crawl back towards the mercenary lines. Behind him, the clatter of musketry goaded him on, ahead, the thud of lead on turf held him back. A blast of air swatted his face. A ball *whacked* the ground beside him. He made ready to sprint.

From the mist Harry Jessop's voice called, 'Move back, boys. Easy now.'

'My God,' Mark whispered. 'Harry, don't leave me.'

The troopers faded into the dark. The mist swallowed them.

'Damn you Harry Jessop,' Mark screamed. 'Don't leave me.'

Mark pressed his face into the turf as musket balls hammered the ground ahead, cutting him off from the retreating troopers.

Later, all was quiet but still, Colonel Fu was unhappy. 'I don't like it,' he grumbled. He turned and stumped away along the parapet walkway.

The guard commander kept pace with him, trying not to trip over the litter of equipment strewn along the battlements. 'We're doing our best, Excellency,' he wheedled, 'but in the mist and the dark...' He shrugged and fell silent.

'I know, I know.' Colonel Fu shook his head. 'But for the last hour, there's been nothing. If they're still there, they should be attacking or shooting or... or something. Any word from the other sectors?'

'None, Excellency.'

Colonel Fu slapped his hand against the parapet. 'Who were they?'

The guard commander had no answer.

The colonel massaged his temples. 'Imperials don't skulk around in the dark.' He gave a humourless laugh. 'If the officers lose sight of their men, they're off to the nearest wine store.' He shook his head. 'Best save the powder. Tell the gunners to stand down and send half the muskets back to their units.'

The guard commander bowed. 'Certainly, Excellency.'

Colonel Fu stared into the night. 'When's dawn?' he asked.

The guard commander looked up at the sky. In the southwest, the moon was a watery glow behind a veil of mist. 'An hour, sir, maybe less.'

Colonel Fu nodded. 'At first light I want a hundred spears out there. Send a message to Meng, tell him I want prisoners.'

'Immediately, Excellency.'

'And one more thing,' Colonel Fu held up a finger as though he had just remembered something. 'Light a brazier in the courtyard. If we find anyone, we'll tickle some information from them.'

The colonel returned to the parapet. Who was out there? He swore under his breath then put the question behind him.

He would know soon enough.

Mark Falchion rose to his feet. How long since the last howitzer had fired? An hour? Longer?

Soon it would be light. The mist was lifting and the first streaks of dawn hung in the sky. He should have moved sooner but memories of shrapnel and musket fire had kept him hugging the ground.

He tried to remember where the tree line was. A small voice told him to run, to put distance between himself and the wall. He forced himself to move slowly. On the battlements they would be listening. He glanced over his shoulder. The parapet stood out clear against a sky brightening from the east.

A slaughterhouse stench hung in the air. Mark trod on something soft. A hand grasped his ankle. A voice croaked,

'Water for *Jesu's* sake, water.'

Mark knelt beside the wounded trooper. 'Shut up. *Shut up*,' he hissed.

He unhooked his canteen and held it to the trooper's lips, anything to keep him quiet. The trooper gripped Mark's hand and gulped the water. He choked and a cough racked his body. The cough became a gurgling sigh and the trooper lay still. Mark backed away and tossed the canteen aside.

A glow lit the eastern sky and the dawn spread like an unfurling carpet. Now Mark could make out the tree line, two hundred yards ahead, maybe a little more. He began to walk. His shadow stretched ahead, long and stark. He lengthened his stride and started to jog.

Behind him, there was a binding groan. He looked back and watched the town gates swing open. A horse pranced onto the bridge. Its rider was tall and wore a tunic of shimmering black. More hooves drubbed on the bridge as other riders emerged from the gatehouse. The dawn sun winked on bright spears.

Mark's stomach tightened.

*Horsemen!*

His thoughts flipped from one hopeless choice to the other: hide in the shrinking shadows or run for the trees.

The riders fanned out in a semicircle. At their centre rode a standard-bearer. He carried a black banner adorned with a golden character, 'Meng.'

The lead rider stood in his stirrups and scanned the open ground. He called out and swung the tip of his sword towards Mark. He slapped his horse's rump with the flat of his blade and the beast bounded forward. Two other riders spurred alongside him. The horses shook their heads and kicked up clods of earth, making heavy work of the soft ground.

Too late, Mark turned and ran. He stumbled then recovered

his stride and broke into a flat sprint. The ground sucked at his boots. The *dao* dragged against his shoulders. The trees were one hundred yards away. Behind him, the thud of hooves drew closer. Mark felt Taiping spear points bearing down on a spot between his shoulders.

Just fifty yards more and he would be in the trees.

To Mark's right, a horseman galloped past. The horse's nostrils flared, its eyes showed large and white. The rider wore black, his hair streamed behind him. He held the reins with one hand and in the other, he held a spear.

The Taiping whooped and wheeled to a stop between Mark and the trees. Behind Mark, two more horsemen slowed from a canter to a walk. Mark stopped running. He threw back his head and sucked air deep into his lungs. His legs trembled, his head swam.

'Do we take this one or skewer him, Captain?' the Taiping shouted to the horsemen behind Mark.

'Fu wants prisoners but I say skewer him,' a voice answered.

Mark turned. There were two of them, one wore a tunic and britches of black cotton. The other was tall and his clothes shimmered like black silver.

'Wait,' the tall man purred. Maybe I was too hasty.' A smile touched his lips. 'Give him a count of five. An ounce of silver says he doesn't make it to the trees.'

'He can run, this one, Captain Meng,' the first Taiping answered. 'The bet's yours.'

'*Meng!*'

Mark whispered the name and inside him, something ugly stirred.

The tall Taiping laid his sword across his saddlebow. One-eared Wu had been right, it was a prince's blade. Memories of wood smoke stung Mark's eyes. He saw the agony of his dying swordmaster. His heart began to thud slow and heavy. He reached over his shoulder and the *dao's* blade scraped against the rim of his scabbard.

'Ah, the quarry has claws.' Meng's voice was mocking.

Mark crouched and held his sword in a two-handed grip. He pivoted like a woodsman surrounded by wolves.

'If you want sport, come closer,' he said.

The first Taiping's eyes widened. '*Wah*, the barbarian speaks. It can talk.' He grinned and couched his spear. 'It can talk, but can it run?' He kicked his horse and it lurched forward.

Mark watched as though in a dream. Horse and rider seemed to move through clear syrup. They're so *slow*, he thought. He watched each ripple of muscle under the horse's coat, each flicker of the Taiping's eyes.

Wait, *wait*.

The Taiping lowered his spear point and threw his weight forward.

*Now!*

Mark twisted aside and the spear whispered by his chest. He swung the *dao* like an axe. He felt it bite through flesh and scrape against bone. Hot blood soaked his face. The Taiping screamed and slumped against his saddle. The spear slipped from his fingers. The horse galloped on.

Mark span to face the other Taipings. He stabbed his sword into the turf and scooped up the dropped spear. He windmilled it, testing its balance.

'Move left,' Meng ordered his companion. 'Get behind him.'

The soldier seemed not to hear. His face was pale, his jaw was slack. His eyes narrowed. He couched his spear.

'I said get behind him,' Meng barked but the man kicked his horse forward.

Mark gripped the recovered spear in both hands and ran to

meet the charge. Somewhere a voice screamed, '*Shaaa: kill.*' The voice was his.

The soldier screamed his answer, '*Shaaaa.*'

Mark ducked under the soldier's spear then thrust upwards, under the soldier's ribcage. The clash lifted Mark clear of the ground. It shattered the spear and ripped it from his hands. The horse reared, hooves lashing. The soldier toppled over its rump, slammed into the turf and lay still. The splintered spear showed white against his black tunic.

Mark's head buzzed. His arms felt wrenched from their sockets. Five paces away, the *dao* stood with its point buried in the ground. He tried to stand but his legs gave way.

Meng raised his sword and nudged his horse forward.

There was a sound like tearing silk and something streaked from the tree line.

The horse screamed and skittered sideways. Meng sawed at the reins, fighting to stay in the saddle. The goose-feather flights of an arrow stuck, quivering in the horse's shoulder.

Meng ducked as another arrow skimmed past his head. He mouthed an obscenity then he pulled the gelding's head round and kicked it into a lopsided canter.

At the tree line, the underbrush rustled and six men emerged. They were unwashed and their queues were unkempt. One carried a bow with a nocked arrow. He was short in stature. Sinewy muscle covered his shoulders and upper arms.

One stood apart from the others. He was taller than Mark. His skin was the colour of mahogany and the tips of his moustache trailed below his jaw line. He wore a sleeveless jerkin. Muscle bunched at his shoulders and chest. He held a double-headed war axe.

Hard hands pinned Mark's arms. Someone rifled his pockets. The archer retrieved the *dao* and capered about, brandishing it in a pantomime of swordsmanship.

The leader jerked his thumb at the retreating rider. 'Don't dawdle, brothers, he'll be back with his comrades.'

Mark tried to twist away but could not free himself.

'I thank you for my life,' he said. 'Now, I command you to release me.'

The tall man let out a rolling laugh. 'You are a strange one,' he chuckled. 'Are you barbarian or Chinese? Perhaps you are one pretending to be the other.'

'I am Falchion,' Mark declared. 'I am sent by the emperor to evict the Taipings from Sungkiang.' He paused to let his words strike home. 'If harm comes to me, the emperor himself will demand your head.'

The tall man flashed a white-toothed grin. 'The emperor's man, eh?' He spread his arms and made a mocking bow. 'Well Sire, my name is Lo Haak, lord of these roads and forests.' His eyes glittered. 'And your emperor is welcome to any part of me he's man enough to take.'

The others laughed but there was no humour in it. Despite the growing warmth, a chill ran through Mark.

Lo Haak grabbed Mark's queue and wrenched it back. He pressed the axe's cutting edge, cool and sharp against the soft skin of Mark's neck. 'My head prefers to stay where it is,' he growled. 'Will your emperor be content if I send him yours instead?'

# 18

THE FILIPINOS guarding *Dancer's* side railings were fewer in number. Along the deck, other troopers sat in silence, shoulders hunched, heads bowed. An injured trooper moaned as he nursed his wound. Another who had suffered not a scratch, stared into the far distance and recited a child's poem over and over.

Sergeant Patterson had set up an aid station at the prow. He worked stripped to the waist, his arms bloodied to the elbows. Two troopers pinned a third to the deck and forced a strip of leather between his teeth.

Ward stood silent at the stern and watched the sun reflect gold from the river. He had a cigar clamped between his teeth but it had long since burnt out.

Vincente frowned. 'The colonel's taking it hard,' he said.

Harry Jessop's face was grey, his voice was heavy. 'What's the bill?'

Vincente leaned against the railing. 'My unit has a man wounded and one confirmed dead,' he sighed. 'I have four missing, including Trooper Dante.' For a moment, he was silent. 'You'll remember him, Harry. He was a good hand with a Sharps.' He nodded to the other troopers. 'All told, I reckon a third are missing.'

'Damn Schneider's men for drunken fools,' Jessop growled, 'I'll lay a month's pay most are half way back to Shanghai. And where's Schneider?' His lip curled as he spoke the Prussian's name.

Vincente shrugged. 'He's not on board. I've listed him missing.'

'If he's alive, I hope the Taipings are having an entertaining time with him,' Jessop muttered. He pinched the bridge of his nose. 'What a fiasco.'

'We've lost some good officers,' Vincente said. 'Young Falchion went forward to reconnoitre and never came back. I think we can assume the worst.'

Jessop brushed a lock of hair from his brow.

'The Chinese lieutenant's not on board either,' he said. He rested his forearms on the rail and looked out over the water. 'He made it back to the tree line but no one's seen him since. He wouldn't run. He was a surly bugger but he was steady. The final shell must have done for him.'

Vincente's eyes were glassy. 'Good men; men we can't afford to lose.' He squared his shoulders. 'We'll go back.' His defiance was loud and angry. 'There's weakness there. They had to bring up support...'

'If your backers pull their funds, you'll go nowhere.' Jessop's voice was matter-of-fact.

Vincente clenched his fists. 'They can't disband us,' he growled. 'We can beat the Taipings, I know we can.'

Jessop gave a wan smile that did not reach his eyes.

'When the Shanghai bankers came in, they had no idea of the cost,' he said. 'Well, they've a bloody good idea now. Pay, gear, weapons, food, it costs plenty.' He massaged the back if his neck. 'Do you know what they'll do? They'll figure the cost of replacing men, arms and equipment. Next, they'll figure the cost of dealing with the bloody Taipings. Then they'll go the cheapest route. They can't see beyond their balance sheets.' His voice was heavy with resentment. 'The foreign powers will squabble like children and it will all end in tears.' He looked at Vincente with sad eyes. 'If your backers pull out, Shanghai's sunk.'

As the sun rose higher, Jessop and Vincente moved forward to catch the breeze.

At the bow, the leadsman called the depth.

And a brooding Ward sucked on his dead cigar.

The bandit chief, Lo Haak, slid his axe back into his belt. He yanked hard on Mark's queue and kicked him behind the knees, forcing him to the ground. Two others pulled back Mark's arms and looped his elbows around a bamboo pole. They bound his wrists to his waist then hauled him up. The bamboo dug into Mark's back and the bindings chaffed his wrists. Someone slipped a halter over his head and tightened it around his neck. The sinewy archer gave the rope a tug and Mark staggered forward.

The archer's name was Mouse. He had a bouncing gait and as he walked, he sang a tuneless song. 'Tell me, barbarian,' he asked. 'Where did you learn to speak and how did you come by such a fine sword?'

Mark did not answer.

The small bandit shrugged. 'Please yourself, but a little conversation makes a long journey easier.'

Lo Haak led them along a forest path. After a while, they emerged into the open and made their way along narrow levees running between rice paddies. A water buffalo raised its head to watch them pass. Women shooed their children to the safety of small houses. They left the farms behind and passed through villages where doors and windows slammed shut at their approach. They walked with the sun beating down on their heads. Whenever Mark slowed, Mouse tugged at the halter, forcing him to stumble along as best he could.

As evening fell, they came to a deserted farmhouse. They passed under a crumbling arch and into a courtyard where weeds grew in cracks between the flagstones. Patches of lime-washed rendering had peeled from the walls to reveal the sand-like bricks beneath. The house had once been grand but a wall had collapsed and the roof had fallen in. Broken rafters leaned at crazy angles against the eaves.

Mark fell to his knees. Thirst burned his throat. His back and neck ached where the bamboo had forced back his shoulders. His feet throbbed in the heavy boots.

Mouse sat next to him and drank deep from a water bottle. 'Forgive me, young lord,' he said. 'You must think I've the manners of a swineherd.' He pushed the bottle to Mark's lips. 'Here, drink your fill.'

Mark strained forward but Mouse pulled the bottle away and Mark fell sideways onto his shoulder. Mouse chuckled. 'When my master cuts your throat, may I keep your sword?'

A shadow fell over them and Mark looked up to see the bandit chief, Lo Haak, standing over them, feet apart, hands braced on his hips.

'*Enough!*' Lo Haak barked. 'If he's to fetch a decent price, we'd best keep him in good condition. Loosen his bindings.'

Mouse sprang to his feet and glared at Lo Haak. 'Loosen them?' The sinewy bandit's lips twisted in a humourless smile. '*Shehh!* Each day you are more like an old woman.'

Lo Haak bunched his fists. 'Take care, little Mouse,' he growled. 'My blade is sharp and your throat is as soft as any. Now, do as I command.'

Mouse put his face close to Lo Haak's. 'Is a blade faster than an arrow?' he hissed.

Lo Haak's fist snapped forward and connected with a hard *thwack*.

Mouse reeled away but managed to stay on his feet. He backhanded a smear of blood from his mouth. His breath came fast and shallow. His eyes burned.

'This time I obey,' he said. 'But the time will come...' He scowled then squatted beside Mark and slid the bamboo pole from his arms.

The effect was immediate: the pain in Mark's back and shoulders eased. He rolled his head, loosening knots in the muscles of his neck.

'And the wrists,' Lo Haak commanded. 'Tie his ankles to a fallen beam.'

Mouse slipped a knife blade under the cords securing Mark's wrists to his waist.

'You are safe, Barbarian,' he whispered. 'And so is your steel... for now.'

He pulled off Mark's boots and looped a cord around his ankles. He drew it tight and grinned as Mark winced. He tied the other end of the cord to a fallen beam then thrust the water bottle into Mark's hands.

Mark took a long pull from the bottle. The water stuck in his throat, stinging his nose and making him cough.

'Brother Chu, Brother Sang,' Lo Haak called. 'Find a good spot outside to stand guard.'

Two bandits hefted their weapons and slipped through the door.

Lo Haak eased himself down beside Mark and settled his back against the wall. He pulled a strip of dried beef from his belt pouch and handed it to Mark.

'Here, eat,' he grunted.

Mark gripped the beef between his teeth and pulled hard with both hands. It tasted of salt and felt as hard as green pine. He tore off a chunk and chewed in silence.

'I saw you with the Taipings,' Lo Haak said. 'You handle your weapons well.' He nodded grudging appreciation. 'You had a Chinese swordmaster, I can tell.'

'I did,' Mark answered. 'A one-eared bandit called Wu.'

Lo Haak shook his head. 'Wu? Never heard of him.' For a moment, silence settled between them. Lo Haak shifted position and spoke as though making casual conversation. 'What will your comrades pay for your safe return?' he asked.

Mark almost laughed at the thought of Banker Yang paying money for his freedom. Instead, he shrugged and continued to chew in silence.

Lo Haak's voice hardened. 'Do not play games, little brother. We didn't save you for the sport of it.'

'Why should I be worth anything?' Mark answered.

Lo Haak shrugged. 'You're a foreigner,' he said. 'Foreigners look after each other.' He took the dried beef from Mark and cut himself a slice.

'And if no one wishes to look after me?' Mark tried to sound relaxed but there was a catch in his voice.

'Your throat is soft and the river is deep.' Lo Haak put the jerky in his mouth and began to chew.

'Would you kill a brother?' Mark asked.

Lo Haak threw back his head and laughed. 'I never knew my father,' he chortled. 'But if he spawned any brother of mine, I'll wager he looks nothing like you.'

Mark placed his hand above his heart. He lodged the tip of his fourth finger into the heel of his palm, raised his thumb then extended the remaining three fingers.

'Here is my sign, he said. 'It is the sign of the dispatch carrier.'

Lo Haak's face darkened. 'What is this?' he bellowed. 'You dare ape the sacred ritual of *Hung Mon*?' He wrapped Mark's queue around his fist and pulled hard, forcing back Mark's head.

# THE SCHOLAR'S BLADE

He slid a dagger from his belt and pressed it against Mark's cheek.

'Speak the thirty-six oaths,' he snarled. 'Speak them now, or I'll have the skin off your face slice by slice.'

Mark spoke through clenched teeth. 'Any child can recite by rote,' he gasped. He grabbed the front of his tunic and ripped it open, scattering buttons across the floor. 'Look,' he said, 'do you recognise this stone?'

Lo Haak hooked the pendant with his dagger. 'Where did you get this?' he demanded. 'From which of my true brothers did you steal it?'

'It was given freely in Shanghai, from the hand of Gon Liao.'

Lo Haak's lip curled. '*Ha!* Gon Liao has underlings to deal with coolies and foreigners.'

Mark looked into Lo Haak's face. He made a fist then extended the thumb and fourth finger.

'And this is the sign of the hill chief,' he said. 'It is the sign of the supreme head of Shanghai's triads. It was Gon Liao's sign to me when I revealed myself to him.'

Lo Haak's mouth worked. He lunged with the dagger but checked himself. He chewed his lip, his voice was hushed. 'Is it true? Have you hung the blue lantern? Have you passed through the door?'

'I have,' Mark lied.

Lo Haak slumped against the wall and let the dagger drop to his side.

'If you lie...' His eyes bored into Mark's. 'I am not convinced, foreigner, but for now I have no choice but to treat you as a brother.' He beckoned to Mouse. 'Cut him loose, Mouse,' he ordered.

Mouse slunk forward. He scowled as he cut the cord securing Mark to the fallen beam. He turned away but Lo Haak growled another command. 'The sword, Mouse. Give him back his steel.'

Mouse flashed Lo Haak a pleading look but Lo Haak jerked his head to where Mark's sword lay beside Mouse's bow. Mouse retrieved the sword and thrust it into Mark's hand. He spoke loud enough for Lo Haak to hear. 'Remember, barbarian, you promised the sword to me.'

'Forget the sword, Mouse,' Lo Haak sighed. 'Go collect kindling for a fire.'

Mouse muttered under his breath and went outside.

'He wants my sword,' Mark said.

'He wants more than your sword,' Lo Haak grumbled. 'But what he wants will end badly for him.'

Mark drew the *dao* a few inches from its scabbard and let the setting sun play on the steel.

Lo Haak gave a throaty chuckle. 'A good blade is better than a good woman,' he said. 'It does as its master bids and is not as sharp as a woman's tongue.' He cut himself another strip of beef jerky and handed the rest to Mark. He paused then tossed Mark his dagger. Mark caught it by the grip and sliced himself a strip of the dried beef.

'You are a skilled swordsman,' Lo Haak said and now he was not smiling. 'But don't forget, you'll never have the speed of Mouse's arrows.'

'Am I brother or not?' there was an edge to Mark's voice.

'For now, brother, for now. But if you betray us, Mouse will have your sword and your master will have your head in a sack.'

'There's no profit in that,' Mark replied with a shrug.

Lo Haak gave a scornful laugh. 'It seems there's no profit in you at all.'

There was silence as they chewed on the beef and watched a darkening sky through the shattered roof.

'Do you know the area around Sungkiang?' Mark asked.

# THE SCHOLAR'S BLADE

'Of course I do. What foolishness is this?'

'I don't ask if you know the pathways and villages, I ask if you really *know* it.' Mark's voice became harsh and probing.

'You insolent whelp,' Lo Haak snapped. 'I've been dodging the village watch and most of my own clansmen since you were weaned.' He gave a scornful snort. 'Do not ask if I know the land.'

'Would you serve a foreigner?'

'Damn you, I serve no man.'

'Would you serve a foreigner for silver?' Mark persisted.

Lo Haak arched an eyebrow. 'Silver, you say. And where would you get silver?'

Mark lowered his voice. 'I have none,' he said. 'I speak for my colonel, my master.'

'Your master was a fool to take drunken barbarians across the marsh approaches.' Lo Haak's voice was heavy with contempt. 'Did you see us? Did you hear us? *Ha!* We smelled your boat even before we heard it.' He snatched the dagger from Mark's hand. 'We watched you abandon your big guns,' he continued. 'If the Taipings were not also fools, you'd be dangling over an open fire. You'd be telling them all you know, aye, and a few things you don't.'

'You'd have done it differently, I suppose.'

'My mother's old auntie would have done it differently,' Lo Haak retorted. 'Why come over the marshy ground when to the east the ground is firm enough for cannon? Why come so close to the town in a clanking, smoking beast of a riverboat? Local boatmen charge just a few copper coins...' he knotted his brows. 'You mentioned silver?'

'Get to Guanfulin.' Mark looked around, checking for eavesdroppers. His voice became a whisper. 'Talk to my colonel,' he continued. 'Tell him of the firm ground and the boatmen. Prove these things to his scouts and there will be more silver than you can carry.'

'Damn your impudence.' Lo Haak's eyes flashed. 'Do not give me orders.'

'Fine.' Mark shrugged and leaned his back against the wall. 'There's more to life than silver.'

For a while, Lo Haak was silent. 'And you?' he asked. 'While I am at Guanfulin, where will you be?'

Mark stretched out his legs and folded his hands behind his head. 'I do not wish to go anywhere. I still have business in Sungkiang.'

'How do I know this is not a trap to snare me?' Lo Haak gave Mark a haughty look. 'My capture commands a high price.'

Mark waved his hand in dismissal. 'Send an underling.'

'Send one of my men?' Lo Haak snorted. 'To transport silver? You're more addled than your master.'

Mark drew close to Lo Haak. 'Then you must go yourself. Say Falchion has sent you. Tell Colonel Ward I will join him after I have brought my father from Sungkiang.'

'Your father? If this is some trickery...'

It was Mark's turn to laugh. 'If this is trickery, you can have my head. But only after the Taipings have finished with it.'

Lo Haak traced a circle in the dirt with his dagger. 'Indeed, you are cracked but I believe lunacy's common amongst barbarians.' His lips curled in a sardonic smile. 'It seems we are agreed.' He shook his head. '*Aiiyah*. I must trust a barbarian as a brother. The world is mad indeed.'

Mark leaned back and closed his eyes. He had gained himself a little time but still there were many questions. Was Ward alive? Had any of them survived? Would they attack again or would Mark go alone into Sungkiang?

Mark's tunic hung open and the evening air was cool against his chest. Mouse returned and made a pile of twigs and dried grass. Soon, smoke curled from a small fire. Somewhere, a night bird called and the cicadas began their chirping chorus. Men found small spaces and settled down for the night. Mark's arms felt heavy. His eyelids drooped. All the pain, fear and despair of the last twenty-four hours drained from him.

   He slept.

# 19

AT THE TREE LINE, beyond the walls of Sungkiang, Lieutenant Tang opened his eyes. Pain nagged inside his skull. The metallic taste of blood filled his mouth. He tried to stand but his legs gave way and he fell to his knees. Where was he?

In flashes it came back to him: musket balls spattering around them, the smack of lead on flesh, screams of wounded men. By some miracle, they had retreated in good order. Step by humiliating step: retreat, halt, fire a volley; retreat, halt, fire a volley. Somehow, they had made it back to this tree line.

Then what? A scorching flash, a jarring *crack*, then nothing.

Nearby, there were shouts and the clash of steel. Tang squinted into the clearing but his eyes would not focus. He shook his head and his vision began to clear. He made out the shapes of two mounted Taipings. One was slumped against his saddlebow. His horse circled with no living hand to direct it. The second was riding for safety.

There was another man; a man on foot. He wore a green tunic and his hair was the colour of gold. Was it...? *Yes!* It was Falchion.

Other men stepped from the tree line. They were not Taipings. They were unwashed and unshaved. Their clothes were thick with grime and their hair was dishevelled. One held a double-headed war axe to Falchion's neck. Tang grabbed for his sword hilt but his scabbard was empty. Nausea swept through him and again, his vision blurred. When it cleared, Falchion and the

## THE SCHOLAR'S BLADE

others were gone.

Tang struggled to his feet. His tunic hung from him in shreds so he ripped it away. He touched a bruise below his heart and cried out as pain flashed through him. For a moment, he swayed on legs as weak as saplings. Nearby, something gleamed in the grass. It was his sword. He retrieved it and slid it back into its scabbard.

He ran through his choices. A sensible man would make a wide circle through the forest, show his sword to some terrified boatman and take the waterways back to Guanfulin. But what awaited him there? A rabble of beaten mercenaries, no doubt already drunk. To the south lay the Huangpu and from there, Shanghai was only two days' journey.

Tang considered his likely reception in Shanghai. He pictured himself, bloody and bare-chested, reporting his failure to the haughty mandarin named Hung. It mattered nothing that the failure was not his, he had been part of it and that was enough to guarantee him life in some shabby outpost far to the west.

Would the mercenary colonel stand as his witness? Probably. Would Hung pay heed to a failed mercenary? Unlikely. If Tang were to save his career, he needed a witness who understood Chinese ways; someone who knew the full truth of the matter.

Tang staggered to where he thought the bandits had disappeared into the forest. Trust a barbarian to let common bandits take him prisoner, he thought. Falchion is indeed a fool.

'But I must act the bigger fool and follow,' he said aloud. He cursed under his breath then moved into the forest and let the shadows swallow him.

There was a trodden path and it seemed logical he should stick to it. Soon, the forest thinned and opened into a clearing. There were rice paddies and a few low dwellings. As he drew near, women ushered their children inside and slammed shut the doors.

Tang's head swam and the pain in his ribs nagged at him. Again the strength left his legs and he dropped to one knee. He felt a presence beside him and looked up into the face of an old woman. Her voice was thick with the local accent and at first, he could not make out her words. She thrust an earthen flask at him.

'You are hurt. Here, drink. Drink.'

Tang snatched the flask. He drank heavily and felt strength seep back into his legs. He stood and nodded his thanks to the old woman. He turned to go but the old woman held onto his arm. She pointed to Tang's body which showed a livid bruise larger than an open hand.

'You are hurt,' she said again. 'Come. I have *jiang huang* and *yu jin*. Come.'

Tang allowed himself to be pulled towards a nearby house. It had mildewed walls and a sagging roof. Wooden shutters blocked the windows and as he ducked under the lintel, he took a moment to let his eyes adjust to the gloom.

The dwelling had just one room, a hessian curtain divided off the sleeping area. Shelves, cluttered with pots of various sizes covered the walls. There was the musty smell of dried herbs that hung from a bamboo pole placed next to an open hearth. Against one wall stood a rough hewn table and two chairs.

The woman pointed to one of the chairs and Tang sank down onto it. She moved about the room, all the time chattering under her breath. She took two pots from a shelf and drew out equal measures of dark leaves. She put them into a stone pestle, spat on them and ground the mixture with an ebony mortar. After grinding the mixture into a paste, she scraped it onto a strip of coarse cloth. She signalled Tang to raise his arms. Tang winced as she drew the cloth tight around his body and tied it off.

'There,' she said. 'Do no heavy work for a week.'

'It burns,' Tang grumbled.

'Good,' the old woman said. 'That means it's working.'

She moved to a chest half hidden in the shadows and pulled out a tunic of dark cotton. For a moment, she clutched it to her bosom then thrust it at Tang.

'There is a chill in the evening,' she said. 'Take this. It is not like the fine garments you are used to, but it will keep you warm.'

Tang took the tunic and slipped it on. It fastened at the neck and was a good fit. 'It belonged to a big man,' he said.

The woman smiled and stared into the distance. 'Yes,' she said, smiling. 'He was my man but the fever took him.' She cocked her head to one side and her voice became brisk. 'You are a soldier, I think.'

Tang said nothing.

'I have no love of soldiers,' the woman continued, 'Particularly Manchu soldiers but I have less love for the one they call Lo Haak.' She lowered her voice. 'I am old,' she said. 'I see things others do not. I look at you and see a man who is searching for someone.' Her lips formed a half smile. 'Perhaps you are looking for a Westerner. A Westerner who has been captured by the bandit named Lo Haak.'

Tang's eyes narrowed. 'You have seen them?'

'They passed this way,' the woman answered. 'Follow the path leading west. There is an old house that Lo Haak sometimes uses.' The lines on her brow grew deeper. 'It was once a grand place but the earth spirits do not favour it.' She shook her head. 'Go,' she said, flapping her hand towards the door. 'Go and find your Westerner but take care, Manchu soldier, Lo Haak and his underlings will take great joy in killing you.'

Tang put his hand to his heart and bowed. He ducked back under the lintel and followed the path that led west.

In the late afternoon, he sighted the farmhouse. He crouched down in wheatgrass that grew thick and wild on either side of the path. A thin mist lingered close to ground near the house and he wrinkled his nose against a foetid smell. Despite the afternoon heat, a chill shuddered through him. The woman had spoken true, this was not a good place.

The house had once been grand but now the roof had fallen in and patches of rendering had peeled from the outer walls, revealing crumbling brick. There was an archway leading to an inner courtyard but it looked ready to collapse in a strong wind. As he watched, a line of smoke began to drift through the broken roof.

The sun was low in the western sky. An hour to sunset, maybe a little more. Tang loosened his sword in its scabbard then hunkered down in the wheatgrass. He was not aware of having slept but when he opened his eyes, night had fallen. He cursed himself. Had they moved on? Had they posted sentries?

He scooped up a handful of earth and smeared it across his cheeks and brow. He stood and moved towards the house. He moved slowly, testing each step, fearful a loose pebble or dry twig might betray him. He passed beneath the archway and flattened himself against the wall, watching listening. He closed his eyes as pain nagged at his ribs. He waited for it to ease, then edged along the wall to where a shutter dangled from a rusted hinge. He held his breath as a sudden breeze made the shutter groan.

Inside, there were muffled voices. Tang peered around the window frame. The light of a campfire flickered off the walls and picked out one... two... three figures. Off to one side there squatted a fourth man who was easily the size of Tang. He held a dagger and was in whispered conversation with someone. In the campfire's light, Tang could make out the sheen of pale skin and golden hair.

He cast his eyes around the ruined space but shadows hid the nooks and corners. Were others hiding there? Probably. How many? What weapons? He hissed his frustration. He could do nothing until dawn revealed the answers.

Behind him, something scuffed against the courtyard paving. He snatched at his sword hilt but the sting of a knifepoint against the angle of his jaw stilled him.

'Be calm, my friend.' a mocking voice whispered. 'That is a mighty sword, but are you fast enough?'

Hard hands gripped Tang's arms. The touch of steel became more insistent, guiding him towards the farmhouse door. A fist hammered between his shoulder blades, slamming him against the door. It crashed open and splintered against the wall. All eyes turned towards them. For an instant there was silence.

The muscular man sitting with Mark Falchion rose to a half crouch. His lips formed a silent snarl. He held his dagger straight armed before him.

Tang's pulse pounded hard and fast between his temples. He bunched his fists. The battle fury rose in his breast.

And in his heart, there burned pure murder.

# 20

MOUSE HAD an arrow nocked. He raised the bow and drew back the string.

'Mouse, no,' Mark implored. 'He's my comrade.'

Mouse's eyes fell on Mark's *dao*. His lips formed a wicked grin. The arrowhead swung towards Mark.

Lo Haak was on his feet. His eyes narrow; teeth bared. His arm snapped forward in a powerful, underarm throw. There was the shimmer of steel and the wet smack of steel on flesh. The bowstring sang and the arrow thudded into a fallen beam. Mouse's eyes widened and his mouth worked. He clawed at a dagger embedded to the hilt below his breastbone. He fell to his knees and toppled forward. His body jerked then lay still.

Lo Haak walked to Mouse and with the toe of his boot, rolled him onto his back. Mouse lay on the floor, his eyes staring at a dark sky.

'Stupid, stupid, stupid,' Lo Haak muttered. He pulled the dagger free and wiped it on the dead bandit's britches.

'He desired your sword,' he said to Mark. 'But more than that, he wanted to be master here.' His voice became hushed. 'His next arrow would have been for me.' He pointed a finger at Mark's face. 'Mouse was stupid but know this, little brother, today I killed a fine archer. He will be hard to replace.'

He barked a command and two bandits carried Mouse's body into the night.

Tang's voice cut through the silence. 'I arrest you in the emperor's name,' he boomed. 'Tremble and obey.'

Lo Haak strode to Tang. 'And in the name of Lo Haak, you can tremble and kiss my backside,' he snarled.

Tang made to free himself but the two guards held him firm. His words dripped scorn. 'I did not expect one so brave to need so many guard dogs.'

'I'm alive and will remain so,' Lo Haak snorted. 'Can you say the same?'

Tang glared into Lo Haak's face. Lo Haak glared silently back.

Mark stepped between them. 'Tang, for God's sake,' he pleaded, 'there are too many.' He turned to Lo Haak. 'Brother Lo, this man has more courage than grace but he is my comrade. If you fight him, you must fight us both.'

Lo Haak paused then took a half pace back. He nodded to his followers, it was no more than a twitch but they lowered their weapons.

Lo Haak rounded on Mark. 'I spare this fool not for you,' he growled, 'but for your master's silver. You'd best pray he's willing to part with it.'

Mark guided Tang to a section of wall. The lieutenant groaned and slumped to the floor. Mark handed him a water bottle. 'You're wounded,' he said.

'It's nothing,' Tang gasped. 'Why did you not let me take them?'

'*You*? Take *them*?' Mark almost laughed.

'You stopped me from performing my sworn duty. You will have much to explain when we reach Shanghai.' Tang slumped onto the floor and screwed shut his eyes. At length, his breathing became deep and regular.

Mark let him sleep. Tang was brash and arrogant, but he had tracked Mark from the killing ground at Sungkiang to this place. The others had left him to die. Tomorrow, Mark decided, he would search the banks of a nearby creek. He was sure to find some comfrey to take away the bruising and maybe willow bark to ease Tang's pain. Mark allowed himself a smile. Boiled into broth, the mixture would taste like goat turds but it would get the lieutenant back on his feet.

Mark lay on the floor and closed his eyes. Fatigue washed over him. Within seconds, he slipped into a dreamless void.

In the pale dawn, Lo Haak shouldered his pack and tucked his war axe into his belt. 'I go alone,' he growled. 'Then, barbarian, if you have betrayed us, only one is lost.'

He jerked his thumb towards Tang who lay resting near the embers of last night's fire. The lieutenant's face was pale. Each breath was hollow and a rasping.

'I'll tell your master of the Manchu's manners,' Lo Haak chuckled. 'By that token, he'll know I took you alive.'

Hearing his name, Tang opened his eyes and tried to lever himself upright. His face twisted and he fell back fighting for breath.

Lo Haak frowned. 'He's not long for this life by the look of him.' For a moment, his eyes were sad. 'It's a pity, he has backbone.'

He called his men forward and raised his voice. 'Obey Brother Chu as you would obey me,' he commanded. 'I shall return before seven days are up.'

The man named Chu grasped Lo Haak's hand.

Lo Haak nodded towards Mark and Tang. 'Treat these two as brothers,' he ordered. The two men embraced and the bandit chief put his mouth close to Chu's ear. 'And if I do not return within seven days, kill them both.'

Then he turned and strode from the courtyard.

## THE SCHOLAR'S BLADE

Tang moaned. All night he had twisted and writhed. Sweat had covered his body and he had called out a name: perhaps a blood relative or comrade Mark thought.

He examined Tang's ribs. The bruising had grown darker. Mark had seen it before. A darkening bruise, clammy skin, laboured breathing. It meant only one thing, internal bleeding.

There was a nudge to Mark's back and he turned to see Chu standing behind him. The bandit thrust a grubby pouch into Mark's hand. Mark loosened its drawstring and sniffed the contents. They were musty with age but there was the hint of capsicum and the tang of ginger or perhaps turmeric.

'Boil half in water,' Chu ordered. 'When it goes like old porridge, bind it tight to his wounds. Brew the rest into a tea and make him drink it. There's more if you need.'

An older bandit named Sage Wen sidled up to Mark and gave him a toothless grin.

'It worked when the village guard beat Beggar Ching half senseless,' he said.

'We used it on Black-eyed Jun when he fell from a whorehouse window in Soochow,' a pickpocket named Three-hands Sang said. He gave a long sigh. 'He died the next day.' A lewd smile cracked his face. 'But that doesn't count because the whores had already half killed him.' He rolled his eyes in mock ecstasy and the others burst into ribald laughter.

As Mark boiled the contents of Chu's pouch, fumes rose from the cooking pot and the bandits retreated outside, making a show of holding their noses.

With the brew reduced to sludge, Mark scraped it onto a broad leaf and bound it tight to Tang's body. He added more water to the brew and brought it back to the boil. When it was the colour of weak tea, he ladled some into a bowl and held it to

Tang's lips. Most of the brew spilled down Tang's chest but after several attempts, he swallowed some.

The next morning, the lieutenant's skin remained deathly pale but his breathing was steady. When Mark removed the poultice, the edges of the bruise had turned from dark purple to blue.

As Mark prepared a fresh brew, Tang covered his nose with both hands.

'What is that stench?' he demanded.

'Breakfast.' Mark gave him a wicked smile.

'You cannot beat me in combat so you poison me,' Tang groaned.

Mark ladled the brew into a bowl and held it to Tang's lips. This time he took it all.

'Now rest,' Mark ordered. 'You must regain your strength.'

He lay the bowl aside and dabbed Tang's lips with a strip of cotton. Rest easy, Lieutenant, he thought, because soon we must leave this place. And when the time comes, we'll need all your strength and all your courage.

Strength crept back into Tang's body fibre by aching fibre. Each day the bruise on his chest grew smaller. Purple gave way to blue, then brown, then pale yellow. At first Tang could only prop himself on his elbows. Then he could sit upright and feed himself. On the third day, he stood on trembling legs. On the fourth day, with Mark supporting him, he walked to the door.

Later, Mark peeled the dressing from Tang's body. Skin once blue-black was now the colour of dirty parchment. There was movement beside them and Mark turned to see Chu peering at Tang's injury.

'It's healed well,' the bandit said. He cocked his head and frowned. 'Does it still hurt?' He prodded Tang hard in the ribs.

Tang roared and clawed at Chu's neck.

'The cure's healed his guts but it's done nothing for his

humour,' Chu grumbled. He shrugged and walked away.

Tang's breathing eased. 'I am like an old man,' he grumbled. 'A barbarian keeps me alive and the scum of the swamps insult me.'

Mark sat on the floor and drew his knees up to his chin.

'Fate is strange,' he said. 'I doubt they'd have spared us even if banker Yang had paid a ransom.'

Tang gave a sulky grunt but Mark ignored him.

'The man that Lo Haak killed,' he continued, 'the one they called Mouse, he saved my life at Sungkiang. And these men you call scum helped me knit your insides together.'

The room fell silent except for the pot bubbling over the fire.

After a while, Mark stood, and walked into the sunshine.

On the sixth day, Mark's sword disappeared. Before lying down for the night, he had propped the *dao* in a corner beside his sleeping place but he woke to find it gone. He searched the farmhouse, feeling sure Sage Wen or Three-hands Sang had moved it as a prank.

At first his search was methodical but the more he looked, the more desperate he became. He moved into the courtyard where he found Three-hands Sang.

'Where's my steel?' he demanded.

The pickpocket just smiled and shrugged.

Mark grabbed his jerkin and was about to knock him down when a soft voice stopped him.

'Hold, Brother Mark. I have your steel.' The voice belonged to Chu.

Mark released Three-hands Sang. He dropped to the ground and sat there, scowling.

Mark rounded on Chu.

'Then, brother, you'd best return it.'

Chu reached out for Mark's shoulder but Mark swatted his hand aside.

Chu stepped back and bunched his fists.

'Easy, Brother Mark.' Chu's voice was calm but his eyes flashed a warning. 'No one has stolen your sword. We are brothers here...' He held up a hand, stilling Mark's question. 'We are brothers but your position is unclear.' His eyes narrowed. 'By now, we should have heard from Brother Lo Haak.'

'Do you call me traitor?' Mark's voice had an edge.

'I discount nothing,' Chu answered. 'Maybe tomorrow will bring news of your good faith. If not...' He shrugged and left the rest unsaid.

'And if I choose to leave now?' Mark snapped. 'Will you stop me?'

Chu was unmoved. 'If I must,' he said. 'But even if you manage to leave, your blue eyes and golden hair will mark you well. If you walk out of here, you'd best keep walking until you reach your homeland.'

Mark made to brush past Chu but the bandit placed a hand on Mark's chest. His voice was harsh. 'It would be better if you went into the house,' he said.

Mark spoke through clenched teeth. 'Let me past.'

Chu's hand against Mark's chest was light but insistent.

Mark aimed a straight-armed punch at Chu's face.

Chu swayed to the side and the punch snapped past his ear. He spread his feet and raised his fists in a loose guard. Then his eyes grew large and he flashed Mark a look of searing contempt.

'So, *brother*,' he sneered. 'It seems Lo Haak was right to doubt you.'

From behind Mark, there came an oiled click. He turned. Framed in the courtyard entrance were four men. They wore uniforms of forest green. All four had skin the colour of roast coffee and each had a carbine pressed against his shoulder.

Another man came through the gate. The newcomer had an unruly mop of ginger hair and on his face was a wide grin. He snapped an order and the Filipino troopers lowered their carbines.

'By Jove, Mark, we'd given up hope.' Harry Jessop strode forward, his hand outstretched.

Mark ignored the proffered hand.

The smile dropped from Jessop's face. 'Are you all right? You're not wounded are you?' He reached out to touch Mark's arm but Mark stepped away from him.

'You left me, Harry.' Mark's voice was cold and hard.

Jessop looked at Mark, his eyes uncomprehending. 'Mark... I...'

'You left me to die, Harry.'

Jessop spread his arms. 'Mark, we were under fire. My men... my command...'

Mark's hands were trembling. He was back before the walls of Sungkiang with musket balls hammering the ground around him and Jessop's troopers fading into the mist.

He was about to speak but rolling laughter silenced him. A grin split Chu's face and all four bandits rushed forward.

'Peace, my children,' Lo Haak called. 'Gather round, for I bring news and I bring gifts.'

Lo Haak shrugged off his pack and from it, pulled two burlap pouches that jingled when he shook them. The men pressed close to him, chattering and grinning. Lo Haak upended the pouches and silver coins spilled out in a glittering stream. They bounced and rolled on the ground as the men laughed and chased after them.

Drawn by the commotion, Lieutenant Tang had come to the doorway. His face was pale and he held tight to the doorframe.

'I thought you'd be dead,' Lo Haak chortled.
'You don't deserve such good fortune,' Tang answered.
'Do you have news of Ward?' Mark asked.
'I was two days in a cell before I saw your master.' Lo Haak answered. He spat on the ground. 'His doltish officers thought I was after their chickens.' He jerked his head towards the troopers. 'My escort,' he growled. 'An escort! For *me. Ha!* Your master is indeed a fool.'
Tang blinked back his surprise. 'Ward's still at Guanfulin?'
'He is.' Lo Haak said. 'But we shall talk of him later. Now, I have gifts.'
He rummaged in his pack. 'For the gallant ox, I bring...' he gave Tang an apologetic shrug, '... only the acclaim of his comrades,' he chuckled. 'I doubt they were so full of praise when they thought you alive?'
Tang stalked back into the house, sulking.
'For me, a spyglass.' With a flourish, Lo Haak pulled a battered telescope from his pack. He snapped it open and sighted on a tree, one hundred yards beyond the gate. He beckoned to Sage Wen. 'Come and look.' His voice was mysterious and coaxing. 'It's a wondrous thing.'
Sage Wen did not move.
'*Shehhh!*' Lo Haak chided. 'Don't be a woman.'
With Lo Haak holding the telescope steady, Sage Wen moved closer but at the last moment, pulled back.
'It's a trick meant to blind me,' he said, his tone accusing.
The others laughed and urged him on. The old bandit threw Lo Haak a doubting look then settled his eye against the eyepiece.
'*Wah,*' he gasped and stepped back. He stared at the distant tree then fixed his eye back to the eyepiece. 'How can it be?' he demanded.
Lo Haak's laughter rolled around the courtyard. 'Do not be

afraid, it's a simple toy that makes distant things seem closer.' He tucked the telescope into his belt and touched a forefinger to his lips. The men crept closer. Lo Haak reached into his pack and lowered his voice.

'Now, little ones,' he teased, 'for someone who is more Chinese than barbarian, I bring this.'

From his pack, Lo Haak pulled a bundle of black leather and tossed it to Mark.

Mark caught it and turned it over in his hands.

'What is it?' he demanded. 'Quick, tell me.'

'Not so fast,' Lo Haak said. 'On the road, I obtained more than trinkets. Do you want to hear my news?' He flashed a smile. 'I hear the keeper of Sungkiang's apothecary fled the town before the Taipings arrived.' He cast his eyes about and the bandits encouraged him with grins and expectant nods.

'So?' Mark snapped back.

Lo Haak shrugged. 'Maybe it's not important,' he said. 'But rumour has it the apothecary shop is now occupied by an old barbarian with wondrous healing skills.'

Mark gripped Lo Haak's arm. 'What have you heard?' he croaked. 'Is there word of a woman?'

'Ah, now I have your interest,' Lo Haak answered. 'Indeed this doctor does have an assistant. They say she's a beauty but far too proud for the likes of us.'

'Are they... are they safe?' Mark asked.

'They are safe,' Lo Haak answered. 'But for how long? According to my fellow travellers, a Taiping lord desires the woman,' he added. 'They say that power and desire are a deadly mix although I hear some women cannot resist them.' He landed Mark a light punch on the arm. 'Now,' he boomed, 'open your gift.'

Mark took a slow breath. His father and Mei were alive. For

now he could hope for no more. He tugged at the twine but Lo Haak's news clouded his mind and numbed his fingers.

'*Shehhh*,' Lo Haak growled. 'You're useless.' He slipped his dagger under the twine and it fell away, revealing a leather jerkin. It had no sleeves and a single thong fastened it at the waist.

Mark pulled off his tunic and slipped into the jerkin. The leather was soft and pliant. He tied the thong and the jerkin strained against the muscles of his chest and shoulders. Gon Liao's pendant hung exposed against his chest. He worked his arms in wide circles, without sleeve to restrict them, they felt light and free.

'It fits you well,' Lo Haak said. 'On my journey I met an ill-tempered fool who gave it up with only a little argument.' He reached into his pack and pulled out two more leather strips. Each was as long as a man's forearm and decorated with brass studs. Leather laces criss-crossed seams running their full length.

'Arm vambraces,' Lo Haak said. 'They will support your sword arm and the studs can deflect a light blade.'

Mark slipped his arm into one of the vambraces but struggled to tie it.

'Watch,' Lo Haak commanded. He held the laces in one hand. 'You must learn to do this yourself.' He twisted the laces together, gripped one end with his teeth and pulled it tight. 'It takes practice,' he said. 'Now you try.'

Mark slipped his arm into the other vambrace but still struggled to fasten it.

'He'd not be so clumsy with a flower girl's bodice,' called Sage Wen.

Mark twisted the lace and the vambrace tightened around his forearm. He pulled it taut with his teeth then grinned and raised a clenched fist in triumph. The watching bandits rewarded him with a ripple of applause.

## THE SCHOLAR'S BLADE

Mark extended his arms to their full length. Studded leather encased his forearms from wrist to elbow. He flexed his fingers and bunched them into fists. The muscle of his forearms strained against the leather.

Lo Haak walked around Mark and nodded approval. 'Now we see you in the proper garb of a *Han* fighter,' he said. He tugged at the jerkin's shoulder and brushed away a speck of dust. 'There might be some blood at the neck but it won't show.'

Jessop's voice cut across Lo Haak's. 'Mark, we must talk. I bring orders from Ward.'

Mark shot him a withering look. 'Orders, Harry?' he said. 'Why should I be interested in orders?'

'The unit's not a lady's circle,' Jessop barked. 'You have a job to do.'

Mark spoke as if to a servant. 'Tell Ward I have business in Sungkiang,' he snapped. 'He'll understand.'

'I wouldn't be too sure.' Jessop snorted. 'You and Tang are ordered back to Guanfulin. I'll march you at gunpoint if I must.'

Lo Haak and Chu moved to Mark's side.

'What does the barbarian want?' Lo Haak growled.

'He says I must go with him. If I refuse, he'll force me.'

Lo Haak's hand was heavy on Mark's shoulder. 'Say the word and we'll cut them down.'

'No,' Mark cautioned. 'I don't want the riflemen hurt.' To Jessop he said, 'You'd do well to reconsider, Harry. Tang isn't fit to travel and if you use force on me, all I've gained here will be lost.' He emphasised his point by nodding at Lo Haak. 'Tell Ward I'm going into Sungkiang, I'll give him a full report when I'm out.'

Jessop softened his tone. 'Mark, don't do this. In a few days...'

Mark held up his hand, silencing Jessop. 'Say nothing, Harry. If the Taipings catch me they'll make me talk, there's nothing surer.'

For a moment, silence hung between them, then Jessop lowered his eyes. 'Very well, Mark,' there was resignation in his voice. 'You leave me no choice. I'll tell Ward you're organising local irregulars. I owe you that.'

'You owe me a lot more, Harry.' Mark's voice dripped bitterness.

Jessop turned and without looking back, he strode from the courtyard. The troopers backed away then turned and followed him.

As he watched them leave, Mark spoke in a voice too quiet for the others to hear.

'Why did you leave me, Harry? Why did you leave me to die?'

Chu emerged from the farmhouse, cradling the *dao* in both hands. He thrust the weapon into Mark's hands then bowed and punched his right fist against the flattened palm of his left hand.

Mark slipped the dao's carrying strap over his shoulder and rejoiced as its familiar weight settled against his back. He passed his eyes over the men around him. They were unwashed and ignorant but they stood with their backs straight and their shoulders square. They knew no master and they had told no lies. In their company, Mark found a sense of belonging unlike any other. It was not the warm embrace of family, neither was it the rowdy comradeship of soldiers. It was a sense of connection; a sense of brotherhood.

There was a smile on Lo Haak's lips. 'You should try your sword,' he said. 'The vambraces might feel awkward at first but they will lend strength to your arms.'

Mark flexed his arms and sucked in a slow breath. The leather jerkin was soft against his skin. The vambraces hugged his forearms. He reached over his shoulder and grasped the *dao's* hilt. It was just where he knew it would be.

He slid the dao from its scabbard and held it in a single-handed grip. He swung it in a slow arc to his right and it parted the air with a gentle sigh. He let the momentum from the cut drive the *dao* into scything sweep to the left. The sun sparkled off the steel as it spun faster and faster, each movement flowing like liquid silver into the next.

Sweat formed on Mark's brow. A joyous rage grew in his breast. The *dao* was part of him; it *was* him. He changed grip from his right hand to his left then back again, the move so seamless that none of the watchers noticed it.

His body swayed as he worked the blade left and right: cut, block, cut, parry, thrust and cut again. He dropped to one knee and brought the sword to rest. His chest heaved, his eyes gleamed.

Lo Haak took Mark's arm and guided him to his feet.

'As a young boy, I listened to tales of men with hearts of Hubei steel,' he said. 'Tales of men who would die before breaking the warrior code.' He shook his head. 'In Peking, a Manchu sits on the dragon throne. In Nanking, the rebels kneel to the barbarian God.'

To Mark it seemed that tears were welling in the bandit's eyes. When he continued, there was a catch in Lo Haak's voice.

'Now a barbarian brings back the days of Chinese legend.' His grip on Mark's shoulder tightened. 'Indeed, the world is mad,' he said. 'And this base born brigand thanks the gods for it.'

# EPISODE 3

## THE FORTRESS

# 21

Meng rested his hands on the balustrade and looked down into the courtyard where a dozen prisoners squatted on their haunches. He frowned. The barbarian swordsman would have been the prize catch but he had escaped, leaving Meng two men short.

Rounding up the others had been easy. Some had suffered wounds and the rest had hidden amongst the dead, too scared to run. Now they squatted in the courtyard, pale and wide-eyed.

Surrounding them, hard-faced guards stood with their weapons ready. In the courtyard's centre, smoke curled from a brazier filled with glowing coals. Straddling it was a tripod of rough staves and from the tripod's apex, a block dangled from a hemp rope.

The man named Shan stood motionless beside the brazier. His upper body was naked. Sweat gleamed on the muscles of his chest and shoulders. A light smile played on his lips.

One prisoner stood apart from the others. He had fair hair and wore a mud-spattered tunic of dark blue. When captured he was carrying a sword, marking him as an officer. His lips were pale; his face ashen.

'Do you think he is afraid?' Meng asked, pointing to the officer.

'If he isn't, he should be,' Cho Lung replied.

Meng nodded. Yes, he thought, the fair-haired officer is afraid and a frightened officer is a useful officer. Meng weighed the benefits of sparing him, but there was no rush. The longer the delay, the greater the terror and the greater the terror, the more useful the barbarian officer would be.

Across the courtyard, Colonel Fu stood at the opposite balustrade. Despite his coterie of aides, he looked very alone. He raised a hand and guards hauled a prisoner to his feet. The prisoner made small whining noises and tried to shrug off their grip. His legs gave way and he slumped to his knees. He stared, wide-eyed at the colonel.

'Your honour,' he pleaded. 'I'm a good Christian boy, I'm like you.'

Cho leaned over the parapet, straining for a better view. 'You know the barbarian tongue, Excellency. What's he saying?'

'He's calling Colonel Fu a Chinese monkey in a green dress,' Meng replied.

'*Wah*, he's got guts.' Cho gave a respectful nod.

'We'll see,' Meng mused.

The guards tried to pull the prisoner back to his feet but his legs would not carry him. He hung between them like a drunk as they dragged him to the brazier. The flagstones tore at his britches and scuffed his boots. The guards pinned him to the ground whilst Shan tied the rope around his ankles. As Shan pulled the knot tight, he grinned and ruffled the prisoner's hair as if he was a favoured nephew.

Cho's lip curled. 'The pig's enjoying it,' he spat.

'Yes, he is,' Meng replied. 'I knew I'd made a good choice.'

'Oh God, sir,' the prisoner sobbed, 'I've told you everything. *Pleeease*.'

One of Fu's aides stepped up to the balustrade. He had narrow shoulders and wore a robe of jade-green silk. The colonel whispered into his ear and the aide leaned over the parapet.

'Do not persist in your lies,' the aide called in English. 'My colonel must know how many were in your force last night.' His voice was reedy, like a girl's.

The prisoner tried to wriggle back on his elbows. His face was the colour of bleached parchment.

'As God is my judge, your honour, there were only two hundred.' Tears welled in his eyes. 'I swear on our Holy Saviour. Oh God Almighty, on my mother's grave, *I swear.*'

'Two hundred against our thousands? You lie,' the aide shrilled back. He whispered to Colonel Fu then stepped away.

Meng watched Colonel Fu. The garrison commander's face was like stone. He had not expected the interrogation to go this far. Now the prisoners would suffer and for what? For nothing. To Meng, the truth was there, naked and clear but the colonel was too stupid to see it. The prisoners were not proper soldiers, just mercenaries and like any mercenary, they would sell all they knew for a handful of silver. They would certainly never brave the fire. The explanation was obvious: the prisoner's story was bizarre, it was ridiculous, it was unbelievable. But it was true.

Meng supposed he should share his insight with the colonel but he wanted to see how the prisoners handled themselves. How soldiers faced death said a lot about their commander and Meng wanted to know what kind of commander led so few against so many.

Across the courtyard, Colonel Fu gave a sharp nod and the rope squealed through its block. The prisoner whimpered as first his feet then his shoulders left the ground. He shouted a stream of wheedling oaths that became a drawn out wail. Then, even before the smell of burnt hair and scorched flesh drifted up to where Meng stood, the prisoner's screams echoed from the courtyard.

# THE SCHOLAR'S BLADE

In the office of Yang Fang, senior partner of Shanghai's Takei Bank, the windows stood open but there was no relief from the midday heat. Ward's collar chaffed his neck. His shirt was damp and clung to his back.

The military mandarin named Hung, steepled his fingers. 'It will not do, Colonel Ward,' he said. 'It will not do at all.'

'The fault is mine alone, sir.' Ward tapped the breast pocket of his jacket. 'My letter of resignation is here.'

Yang Fang sat behind his lacquered desk. His eyes darted between Ward and Hung. 'I think... *er*, under the circumstances... *um*, Colonel, it is best for all...' He pulled a handkerchief from his sleeve and mopped his brow. 'It is so very close today, Excellency, I mean *Mister* Hung.'

Hung raised a finger and Yang fell silent.

'Mister Yang means to say you have caused much difficulty, Colonel,' he said. 'And it is ah for you to *ah*... resolve that difficulty. Am I right, Mister Yang?'

'What? *Um*... yes, of course, Excell... I mean Mister Hung,' Yang mumbled.

Hung's eyes bored into Ward's. 'Your financial backers, Colonel, are wary of committing more funds. What say you?'

'I say again, gentlemen, the fault is mine,' Ward answered. 'I let the prize cloud my judgement.' He gave a small cough and shifted in his chair. 'My worst regret is leaving so many good fellows at Sungkiang.'

Hung nodded. 'You do well to accept responsibility,' he said. He graced Ward with a tight smile. 'But I must sound harsh. Your men let you down. Some were even drunk.'

Ward frowned. 'Good or bad, they were in my charge. However, there is some consolation. I've received news that two of my best officers survived and are currently gathering intelligence at Sungkiang.'

'You will not be surprised that I have received the same news,' Hung purred. 'Lieutenant Tang is indeed a most enterprising officer and I rather took to the impudent foreigner who is so adept at our language.'

He leaned forward and his voice became brisk. 'But now, Colonel Ward, we must move on. The emperor decrees that Shanghai's Chinese quarter must not fall to the Taipings. He cannot have the foreigners trading modern weapons for Taiping tea and silk. He would sooner evict all foreigners from the city.'

'That's a mite harsh,' Ward replied. 'But I'm with you in principle. So long as the Taipings threaten Shanghai, we must be ready to take them on.' He paused, expecting Hung to comment. When the mandarin stayed silent, he continued. 'I have discharged most of those involved in the assault on Sungkiang. Paid 'em off and let 'em go. A few performed well and they are the core of my new officer cadre.'

Hung and Yang glanced at one another then nodded for Ward to continue.

'I have appointed Vincente Macanaya my chief aide,' Ward announced. 'We are recruiting an interim force among the city's Filipino population.'

Hung took a sharp breath. 'Filipinos, Colonel Ward? He said. 'I have heard nothing good about *Filipinos*.'

'They are fierce fighters, sir,' Ward said. 'Mister Macanaya swears he will curb their indiscipline.' He held up a hand to fend off any argument. 'And when Vincente makes a promise, sir, he darn well keeps it.'

Hung looked at the ceiling. 'Very well, Colonel,' he sighed. 'We shall take your word for it. How soon can you put this *interim* force in the field?'

'A month to recruit the right men,' Ward answered. 'Another to train them,' he said. 'Two months in all. No longer, I promise.'

# THE SCHOLAR'S BLADE

'Really? Two months?' Hung stroked his moustache and gave a soft laugh. 'I believe, Colonel, you had best think again.'

'Sir?'

Hung sighed. 'For all we know, Colonel Ward, the Taipings might be marching on Shanghai as we speak.' His eyes burned. 'They are vipers with a nest just thirty miles from this very room.' His breathing became harsh. 'From Sungkiang they can marshal and supply their troops in the field. But that will not happen. It will not happen because you will take Sungkiang from them. Then, not only will the Taipings have lost a vital base, they will have to watch their rear if they attack us. Do you not agree?'

Ward was silent. Hung's military insight was faultless.

The tall mandarin leaned back and relaxed. 'To support you in this venture, I will move nine thousand Imperial troops to within an hour's march of Sungkiang.'

Ward exhaled a slow breath.

'You are silent, Colonel. Should I assume the prospect of joining hands with the emperor's troops does not fill you with pride?'

'You... you do me too much honour, sir.' Ward paused, searching for the right words. 'After the battle, the town will need a sizeable garrison. We... we must ensure the emperor's soldiers do not suffer too many casualties during the assault.'

'It is true they have not enjoyed much success in this campaign,' Hung admitted. 'Perhaps you want to keep them from under your feet.'

Ward inclined his head. 'You see clear through me, sir,' he answered.

Hung leaned forward and fixed Ward with a steady gaze, 'You also have not enjoyed much success,' he snapped. 'From their encampment, my nine thousand are well placed to either support your endeavour or to march into Shanghai and evict every foreign trader, clerk, barroom host, manual worker or indeed, any man, woman or child with a white face. On the sixteenth of this month, I will decide which of these actions I will take.'

Ward gave a low whistle. 'The sixteenth? But that's just over two weeks.'

Hung shrugged. 'You and I both understand soldiers, Colonel Ward. If I keep them bottled up beyond the sixteenth, they will likely become, *ah*... fractious.'

Ward scratched his chin and did some rapid calculations: recruitment, kitting-out, drill and weapon training.

'It's too soon,' he said. 'We're short of small arms and we've no cannon at all.'

'I have obtained for you, ten field guns,' Hung said. 'Two twelve-pounders and eight six-pounders. I hope British guns are adequate to the task.'

'They're first-rate guns but when do I train the gunners?'

'Your gunners are the envy of the world, Colonel,' Hung said. 'I believe Admiral Hope of the most excellent Royal Navy would like to have them back.'

Ward could not help but smile. 'No argument there, sir. Fightin' Jimmie sure would love to get his hands on 'em.'

'So, it is agreed?'

'I'll do my best, Mister Hung.'

'You will do more than your best, Colonel,' Hung snapped. 'On the sixteenth of July, your force will storm Sungkiang.' He fixed Ward with a hard stare, 'A large force of Imperial troops will stand by. I will decide on their *appropriate* deployment when I receive news of your attack.' He rose and smoothed the creases from his gown. He gave Yang a short nod then swept from the room.

## THE SCHOLAR'S BLADE

There was silence broken only by the call of street vendors drifting in from the open windows.

'Well, you heard the man, Mister Yang.' Ward said at last.

'Indeed I did Colonel. It seems you have an irksome task on your hands.'

Ward pulled a sheet of paper from his jacket and dropped it onto Yang's desk.

'Along with my resignation, sir, I took the liberty of preparing a list of essentials,' he said. If you'll countersign it I'll drop it off at Fogg's.'

'Indeed, a most irksome task,' Yang chortled. He hooked his spectacles over his ears and unfolded the paper. His lips moved as he read. He looked up, blinking at Ward.

'Good... good gracious,' he gasped. 'Why so many rifles?'

Ward's lips curved in a cherubic smile. 'I guess this is a bad time to ask about the mess silver,' he said.

The Sungkiang stables smelled of dung and wet hay. A smoking oil lamp did little to disperse the gloom. Two men leaned over the gate of a stall where a black gelding shook its mane and stamped a hoof against the earthen floor.

'It's still early,' said the man who was the stablemaster. 'But there's no fever and he's a strong beast.

'Show me,' Meng snapped.

The stablemaster nodded and opened the gate. The gelding tossed its head and showed the whites of its eyes. The stablemaster made soothing noises and laid a gentle hand on the gelding's muzzle, calming it. He took the lantern from its bracket and pointed to a patch of shaved skin on the gelding's shoulder.

The arrow wound showed as puckered flesh held tight by thick sutures. The gelding snorted and the skin around its wound quivered.

'Easy my beauty,' the stablemaster whispered. He stroked the gelding's neck. 'Give him a month or so, Captain,' he said, pride swelling his voice. 'If there's no fever, he'll be ready for active duty.'

Meng bent his head and examined the wound. 'Will he still be the swiftest?' he asked.

The stablemaster shrugged. 'Maybe not the swiftest,' he said. 'But he'll be fast enough and his courage is undiminished.'

'Not the swiftest, you say?' Meng persisted.

A shadow crossed the stablemaster's face.

Meng scowled and drew himself to his full height. 'Destroy him,' he snapped.

The stablemaster's eyes widened. He shook his head and spread his arms. 'But... but sir. Such a fine...' he stammered.

Meng's eyes bored into the stablemaster's, silencing him.

'I said, destroy him,' he hissed. He turned and strode from the stable.

The stablemaster sighed and stroked the gelding's muzzle. The gelding snickered and worked its lips against the stablemaster's hand. The stablemaster slipped a halter round the gelding's neck then pulled a broad-bladed knife from his belt.

With a heavy heart, he led the gelding from the stall.

Three hundred yards from Sungkiang's east wall, Mark Falchion and Lieutenant Tang crouched in the tree line's underscrub. Mark shuddered as memories became suddenly real. The rotten-egg smell of burnt gunpowder and blood, the *snap* of musket balls close to his head, the sting of soil spattering against his face, the terror of finding himself alone.

'Are you ill?' Tang asked.

'Of course not,' Mark answered.

'You shivered. I thought you had a chill.'

# THE SCHOLAR'S BLADE

In silence, they scanned the open ground between the tree line and the town wall.

Tang scratched at an insect bite on his cheek. 'Am I a lizard who hides in the grass?' he muttered.

'*Hush!*' Mark hissed. 'Do you want your head decorating that wall?'

'They'll need good ears to hear me from there,' Tang scoffed.

Mark palmed sweat from his eyes and snapped Lo Haak's telescope open. He propped it against a tussock of grass and looked into the eyepiece. The gate arch sprang at him. The teakwood gate was grey and cracked with age. Rust-streaked bands of iron ran in horizontal slats from one side to the other. Mark tried to remember his childhood visits to the town. Was there a courtyard beyond the gate?

He shifted his view. Once, there had been a bridge over the moat, but now only shattered stumps peeked above the moat's surface.

On the far side of the moat, and flanking the gate, a stone promontory formed a platform that jutted into the moat. Above it, the town wall loomed tall and solid, its stones dark with summer mould.

Mark trained the glass on the gate tower and watched a sentry walk along the wall. His uniform was black and he carried a spear. He paused to exchange words with another sentry.

'What do you think?' Mark asked, handing the glass to Tang.

Tang raised the telescope. 'Teak gates. Not good, teak gets harder with age.'

A breeze ruffled the undergrowth and Tang had to brush aside a clump of grass.

'Did you see the guards?' he continued. 'They don't take their eyes off the open ground, even when they're talking to their comrades.' He lowered the glass and nodded with grim approval. 'They're veterans.' He handed the telescope back to Mark.

Mark panned across the wall until the glass fell on an arched opening half-submerged in the moat. A rusted portcullis blocked the archway. It stood at an odd angle, like a sash window with broken runners.

'What do you see?' Tang demanded. He tugged at the telescope and Mark surrendered it.

'See that watergate?' Mark asked. 'Does it give you any ideas?'

Tang squinted through the eyepiece. 'It's not lying square,' he mused. 'It must be lodged against something, fallen masonry perhaps.' He threw Mark a sceptical look. 'You're surely not thinking of putting troops through there.'

Mark was silent.

'You waste your time,' Tang said with scornful finality. 'If the commander's any good he'll have a sentry down there. You'll get one, maybe two men inside before he raises the alarm.'

'How about one man?' Mark mused.

Tang frowned. 'If the sentry's asleep and if our man's lucky.' He shook his head. 'Why do we even discuss it? One man can do nothing.'

The ground beneath them trembled as a column of mounted Taipings rounded the northern buttress. Mark and Tang pressed their faces into the turf as the troop cantered onto the open ground then changed formation to line abreast.

Mark raised his eyes and watched the nearest horseman pass just fifty feet away. The thud of hooves faded and a skein of dust drifted over their hiding place.

'Lo Haak spoke the truth,' he said. 'The ground's firm enough for horses.'

'Horsemen aren't artillery,' Tang answered. 'But yes, the ground seems firm.'

# THE SCHOLAR'S BLADE

Mark snapped shut the telescope 'That's what we came to find out,' he said.

And the watergate is just a bonus, he thought.

He gave Tang a nudge and together they crawled back among the trees.

Vincente Macanaya stood by the jetty at Guanfulin and listened to the cicadas chirping their evening song. Water slapped at *Dancer's* hull. Her mooring ropes creaked as the current tugged at them.

Behind Vincente, a footfall told him that Ward had joined him. Together, they stepped onto the jetty.

A sentry rose from *Dancer's* deck and levelled his carbine.

'*Halt!* Stand and report.'

'Easy, Trooper,' Vincente answered. 'It's just two old comrades looking to have a private chat.'

'Advance and be recognised.' There was a *click* as the sentry palmed back the carbine's hammer.

Ward and Vincente raised their hands. 'I hope you've remembered the damned password, Vincente,' Ward sighed.

The sentry was a native of the Philippines and had the casual toughness common in men found around Asia's wharfs. As Ward and Vincente stepped closer, he snapped to attention.

'*Señor* Ward, Mister Macanaya... sir. I...'

'*Santa Nino*, stand easy Trooper. And my name is Vincente, Vin-cent-ay.' Vincente spoke as though addressing a child. 'Only people who owe me money call me "sir." You're alert, well done.'

'Yes sir.' The sentry grinned and puffed out his chest.

Ward flipped open his cigar case and offered it to Vincente. A match flared and both men drew on their cigars until the tips glowed red.

'How many have you recruited so far?' Ward asked.

'I've enough to start training,' Vincente answered. 'We should be up to full strength in a day or two.'

'What do the scouting parties report?' A sly smile played on Ward's lips.

'Firm ground to the east of Sungkiang,' Vincente replied.

'And?'

'Very well,' Vincente grumbled. 'It seems firm enough to support the six-pounders, maybe even the twelves.'

'So our colourful friend was telling the truth.' Ward tipped back his head and blew a stream of smoke.

'I still think we should have checked his story before paying him,' Vincente said, trying not to sound too sullen. 'We know Falchion and the lieutenant were alive when Harry Jessop saw them but can we be sure they're still safe?'

'They're alive.' Ward said. 'I'm sure of it.' He gave a soft chuckle. 'What did that damned bandit call the lieutenant?' He cocked his head. 'An ill-tempered Manchu with the grace of an ox and...?'

Vincente smiled as he finished the line, '... and the manners of a Manchu tax collector. Alright, we can assume they're alive. I hope Tang keeps quiet long enough to stay that way.'

Ward pressed his palms together as if in prayer. 'May the Lord help him keep his opinions to himself,' he chuckled.

They looked into the shadows of the far bank where the trees were a black mass swaying against the evening sky. Ward and Vincente smoked their cigars and listened to the slap of river against jetty.

Ward broke the silence. 'Can they carry it off?'

'I'd feel better if it was my men out there,' Vincente replied.

'I know, old friend,' Ward said, his voice was soothing. 'To my mind there's nothing you and your men can't do, but Falchion and Tang have tapped into the local talent. They're right where we need them.'

Vincente let out a sigh. 'If you say so, Colonel.' He stared into the dark. 'But I won't trust any... any... *tríada*.' He spat the last word.

Ward blew out a stream of blue-grey smoke. 'Lo Haak's a bandit and a triad,' he said. 'But I'll take my allies where I find them.'

Vincente held his peace. When Ward decided to trust someone, it was an end to the matter. With a start he realised Ward had spoken.

'Sorry Colonel,' he said, 'I was lost in thought.'

'I said, do you think we can transport everything upriver, by sampan and at night?'

Vincente thought for a while. 'Six men to a boat,' he mused. 'Ten at a push. I figure thirty boats for the troops. As for the guns...' he gave a non-committal shrug.

Ward scuffed at a loose splinter with his boot. 'The six-pounders aren't a problem, they weigh what, seven hundred pounds?'

Vincente shook his head. 'We'll not open Sungkiang's gates with six-pounders,' he said. 'And the twelves each weigh more than a ton.'

'There's just two big guns,' Ward answered. He began to pace the jetty. 'We'll rig boats together and plank them over to make gun platforms. I know we can do it.' He clamped the cigar between his teeth. 'I bet we can transport guns, ammo and, Goddamit, the gunners with just fourteen, no, better make it sixteen sampans. Add thirty for the troopers and four more in reserve.'

He paced faster, leaving a trail of cigar smoke. He spoke more to himself than to Vincente, the words tumbling from his mouth. 'Thirty-four boats for men and supplies, sixteen for the guns.

Fifty, we can manage fifty sampans, surely.'

'At night,' Vincente cautioned.

'Yes, yes.' Ward waved his hand, scattering glowing cigar ash. 'Practice, Vincente. The key is practice.'

'I'll draw up an exercise schedule, Colonel.'

'Excellent. Good man. Night exercises. Capital idea.'

'Can we trust Lo Haak to scout the ground and recruit the boatmen?'

'Don't forget Falchion and Tang, they'll be there too.'

Vincente smiled, the old Ward was back.

'What if the *tríada* sells out?' he asked. 'The transfer point will be perfect for an ambush.'

Ward's eyes gleamed in the glow of his cigar. 'You sound like those lounge bar experts in Shanghai, Vincente,' he retorted. 'But we're not like them. There's nothing we can't handle.' He patted Vincente's shoulder. 'Arrange the training, old man. By the sixteenth, we'll be in Sungkiang.'

'Or in hell.' There was an edge to Vincente's voice.

Ward gave a harsh laugh. 'Indeed, or in hell, my friend.' He turned and stumped back along the jetty. 'Or in hell, my friend. Or in hell,' he called over his shoulder.

Then he disappeared into the night.

The plan had Ward stamped all over it, thought Vincente. It was brash and it was outrageous. It might even work, but if Lo Haak sold out to the Taipings, Ward would have another fiasco on his hands.

Vincente took one last draw of the cheroot and flicked it away. It cut a glowing arc through the dark and hissed as it found the water. He shook his head and muttered under his breath.

'Now, where in *Santa Nino*'s name do I find fifty sampans?'

# 22

THE WOMAN stood barefoot at the sampan's stern. She had a seamed face and there were streaks of silver in her hair. Cradled in a sling on her back, a spike-haired baby slept. She flashed a gold-plated smile and threw Mark Falchion a mooring line. Mark pulled the sampan close to the riverbank and secured the line to a tree.

'Do you know the way, Auntie?' Mark asked.

The woman pointed upriver. '*Hor hor. Sungkiang,*' she cackled.

Lo Haak gave a throaty chuckle. 'No one knows these waterways better,' he said. 'She'll take you all the way to Shanghai if you want.'

Tang's voice was hard with accusation. 'We are ordered to stay here and wait for the main force,' he said. 'How does Ward execute deserters?'

Mark rounded on him. 'He asks stupid questions until the deserter strangles himself from frustration.'

Tang would not be silent. 'This is foolishness,' he snorted. 'You risk everything for the sake of a woman and an old man.'

'To whom does a son owe the highest duty?' Mark demanded. 'Commander or father?'

'*Philosophy!*' Tang spat. 'Are you scholar or soldier? A true man of *Han* understands discipline.'

'Then I am proud to be barbarian,' Mark retorted.

'Children, children.' Lo Haak spread his arms in a gesture of embrace. 'You must not part like this.'

Mark sighed and the anger left him. 'You're right, I'm a little jumpy,' he said. 'Don't concern yourself, Lieutenant, I'll be back with my father and Mei before dawn.'

He stepped aboard the sampan and slipped a coin into the woman's hand. He settled himself in the prow but had to steady himself as the boat rocked and water sloshed over the gunwale.

The woman scowled as Tang settled himself opposite Mark.

'There are cutthroats everywhere,' Tang said, thrusting his chin to where Lo Haak stood. 'I'll escort you to Sungkiang, no further.' He hunched his shoulders and stared at the water.

Lo Haak unfastened the line and tossed it to the woman. She used her oar to pole the sampan away from the riverbank then fitted it into the stern lock and used a fishtail action to scull into midstream.

Mark and Tang sat in silence as the sun dipped below distant hills, turning the water into melted copper. The moon rose and the copper became silver. The night deepened and a silky mist rose from the water's surface. The only sounds were the *chirruping* chorus of frogs, the creak of the oar and water chuckling down the sampan's sides. Mark lost track of the time and may have slept. The woman's voice stirred him.

'*Wei, Sungkiang,*' she called, pointing into the mist.

'*Silence!*' Mark hissed. 'There might be outposts.'

'*Hor, hor,*' the woman said again, this time louder. '*Sungkiang.*'

She turned the sampan off the main creek and into a side channel. Reeds swung inboard and Mark swept them aside with his arm.

'*Sungkiang,*' the woman whispered.

Ahead, the town wall showed blacker than the backdrop of the night sky. Mark wrinkled his nose against a stench of sewage and foetid water. He nodded farewell to Tang and slipped over

## THE SCHOLAR'S BLADE

the side.

'*Wait.*' Tang leaned from the sampan's prow, threatening to pitch it over. 'Stop this madness,' he whispered. 'You don't even know where your father is held.'

'Lo Haak says he's at the old apothecary, I'll start there. Now go.' Mark made shooing motions with both hands. '*Go.*'

He turned away and the mist swallowed the sampan.

The water was waist deep and blood-warm. Ooze sucked at Mark's boots. Tendrils of mist drifted about him. He pushed aside a clump of reeds. His heart bounded as a water bird lunged at him and *cawled* an alarm. A drawstring tightened around his stomach as nearby reeds shook and something ruffled the water's surface.

The moon peeked through the clouds and Mark made out the silhouette of a head sat on a pair of bulging shoulders.

'Tang,' he whispered, 'what are you doing?'

'Earlier I questioned your sense of duty,' Tang whispered back. 'I... I spoke in haste.'

There was an awkward silence then Mark grasped Tang's shoulder and nodded his thanks.

Together, they half-walked, half-swam to where the shadow cast by Sungkiang's wall blanketed the moat. Without warning, the creek bed fell away and Mark pitched forward. He scrambled to find footing but there was no bottom and his boots dragged him down. He fought his way to the surface and thrashed through the water, careless of any noise.

Then he touched slime-covered stone and hooked his fingers into a crack where the mortar had crumbled away. For a while, he clung to the stonework, watching, listening. All was silent. Not a ripple disturbed the water's surface.

'*Tang,*' he whispered but there was no answer. 'Lieutenant, are you there?' Again, no reply.

Indecision gnawed at Mark. Should he wait? Should he go on? Was anyone on the battlements? Had they heard? Were they watching?

He rested a moment then started to pull himself hand over hand along the wall. There seemed no end to it. He tried to picture the moat and the watergate. Had he gone the wrong way? Did he have the strength to go on? Did he have the courage?

There was a buttress. He made his way around it and touched rough metal. It was a thick lattice of pitted iron. For a moment he exulted in having found the watergate but knowing what lay ahead made him pause. Tang's right, he thought, this is madness.

For a moment, he considered his choices then he reached down and grabbed onto a submerged section of ironwork. He gulped three deep breaths, screwed shut his eyes and dragged himself down.

As the moat closed over him, water plants slid against his face. He pulled himself deeper and pain stabbed at his ears. The moat seemed bottomless. Something slithered between his fingers. He lashed out and without thinking, released a gout of air.

Soon he must breathe.

His knee sank into mud. He felt along the bottom of the grill, searching for a gap. There was none. He pulled himself across the grill's face, all the time feeling for a space. His head banged against stone that rose sheer and vertical. He had explored the grill's full span and found no way through.

Air, he needed air.

His hand brushed against a block of broken masonry lodged at the foot of the buttress. He probed further and there, between the iron lattice and the mud, was a gap. It was small, smaller than Mark had expected. He turned on his back, grabbed the bottom of the grill and pulled himself into the space. Mud slid over his neck and flowed into his jerkin. Iron raked his chest. His throat tightened. The tightness spread to his lungs.

Air, they demanded air.

His arms burned as inch by muscle wrenching inch he dragged himself through. There was a pull on his scabbard. Something had snagged the *dao's* hilt. He pulled hard against the grill but he was stuck fast. He wriggled his shoulders and hips but could not move forward. His heart hammered at his breastbone.

*Think!*

He pulled himself back towards the moat and felt the scabbard strap loosen. He reached over his shoulder and grabbed the *dao's* hilt. The sword slid halfway from the scabbard but again it snagged. He pulled harder and the *dao* jerked free. He swung it around and with one hand, held it tight against his chest.

With his free hand, he started to pull himself back through the gap. Iron scraped against his chest and belly. Then he was clear. He kicked for the surface, his throat and lungs on fire. He burst through the surface and sucked in a great gulp of air. His muscles felt like old rope. He looped his arm through the grill and slid the *dao* back into its scabbard.

The darkness was complete. Somewhere there was the hollow slap of water on stone that told Mark he was in some kind of chamber. He rested a moment then swam towards the sound. His hand connected with a stone shelf just inches above the water's surface. He put his hands on the landing and levered himself up. His strength failed and he splashed back into the water. On the second try, he pushed harder against the stone and threw his weight forward. He flopped onto the landing, rolled onto his back and lay there gasping.

Nearby, there was the clink of flint on metal and a lantern sputtered into life. It threw yellow light across the landing and lit the shape of a man. In the soft light, his eyes were like empty sockets. His lips curled in a cruel smile. A spear point glittered.

'I thought I knew all the rats in this hole.' The sentry's voice echoed from a ceiling lost in shadow. 'But what honoured guest comes here now?' He touched the spear point to Mark's neck. His voice was heavy with mock concern. 'Sadly, I'm not permitted to leave my post,' he said. 'I have no choice; I must kill you now.'

The spear point broke the skin below Mark's ear and a trickle of blood ran down his neck. Mark tried to push himself up but it was if a great weight straddled his chest. The sentry laughed and pressed down harder.

A rumble echoed in the chamber. A wave lapped over the landing's edge, wetting the sentry's boot.

The sentry backed away and held the lantern at arm's length. He dropped to one knee and lowered his head until his face was just inches from the water. He flinched as a bubble broke the surface close to his nose.

A shape exploded from the water, drenching the landing. It had bared teeth and flared nostrils. A Manchurian oath echoed from the walls and the shape took form. Lieutenant Tang threw himself forward and wrapped his arms around the sentry's legs.

The sentry let out a shrill cry and toppled over backwards. His spear clattered against the landing. The lantern rolled away, throwing tumbling shadows. He tried to claw his way backwards, scrabbling for his lost spear.

Tang braced himself against the landing and flung himself back, pulling the sentry with him. For a moment, the sentry's face showed white on the water's surface. He let out a sob as a forearm snaked around his neck. He slid beneath the water and there was silence.

Mark peered into the dark but could see nothing. There was only the sound of water lapping against stone. Then Tang's head broke the surface. His mouth gaped; his breath came in hard sobs. He reached for the landing and rested there with his head cradled on his forearms. He put his palms flat against the landing, levered himself from the water and collapsed onto his stomach. He rolled onto his back and lay with his chest heaving.

Mark retrieved the lantern and it revealed a flight of steps carved into the chamber wall.

'We must go,' he wheezed. 'When it's time for the guard to change, his relief will sound the alarm.'

Tang scrambled to his feet. His voice trembled with the effort of speaking. 'So, we head for the old apothecary's shop.' He pointed to the steps. 'You know this town; you must lead the way.'

Mark slumped against the wall. 'Give me a moment,' he said.

Tang slapped at the wall and fumed in silence.

Mark drew himself to his full height and sucked in a breath. 'Yes, I'm certain my father's there,' he said. Then he shrugged. 'Unfortunately, I've no idea where it is.'

Gunter Schneider was having a bad day. He knew he should not complain, after all, he was lucky to be alive. Thank God for Meng. As the captured troopers had been roasted over the brazier, Meng alone had seen they were telling the truth. But *Gott im Himmel*, it had been close.

Schneider smiled, he had the measure of Meng. Meng wore Taiping garb, but his was a private war. Schneider had no idea what drove him, but he meant to find out. Such knowledge was sure to bring some advantage for Gunter Schneider.

After telling Meng all he knew, Schneider had expected a post in Soochow or maybe even Nanking, training the Taipings in musketry and infantry strategy. Instead, he was stuck in this shithole called Sungkiang with no proper duties and, even worse, with precious little in the way of fun.

He licked his lips, it had been more than a week since his

last drink and he was not enjoying his newfound abstinence. He ducked into a doorway as the night watch emerged from an alley ahead of him. The watch crunched past, their faces indistinct in the light of a lantern carried by the lead man.

Schneider took a moment to check the lane before continuing on his way. There was plenty of time but expectation hurried his pace.

He cursed under his breath. He knew he was close to Sungkiang's central square but he must have taken a wrong turn. These damned alleys all looked the same. He took a moment to regain his bearings and he recognised a house with a broken roof. He smiled, the apothecary's shop was not far.

The Taipings had closed the town brothel so what was a man to do? Rumour had it the old doctor had an assistant who was fresh and fiery. Schneider quickened his steps. He missed his brandy but in the makeshift surgery was something he missed far more.

They would have to die, of course. First, he would spit the old man on his sabre. Messy but silent. Then he would spend time enjoying the girl before silencing her too. He chuckled and rubbed his hands together. He had to be careful, the Taipings were maiden aunts in their prudery. Death was a daily routine, but they could not abide rape.

Schneider was not worried, he was an old hand at this. First some medicinal brandy, then a little sugar. He rounded a corner and found himself at the town square. In the dark, he could make out the shape of the courthouse.

Soon, he would be there soon.

'What do you mean, you don't know where it is?' Tang's voice was a strangled whisper.

Mark shrugged. 'I've some idea,' he said, 'but it's been years

## THE SCHOLAR'S BLADE

since I was here.'

Tang's breath exploded in an angry hiss.

'I can find it if we get to the town square,' Mark offered. He moved towards the stairs but as he climbed, his legs trembled and he had to steady himself against the wall. At the top of the stairs, a door opened onto an enclosed yard. Light showed through a warped shutter and Mark could make out the mouth of a narrow lane.

'If we head west we're bound to find the square. The apothecary's shop is just behind the courthouse,' he said.

'You think,' Tang grumbled.

'No, I'm sure,' Mark lied.

He listened for movement then with Tang following, he crossed the yard and slipped into the lane's shadows. Above them, the sky showed as a band of stars wedged between rows of dark rooftops. The lane twisted left, then right then forked and twisted left again. They reached an intersection and Mark paused.

'You're lost, aren't you?' Tang accused.

Mark slumped against a wall and looked around for a landmark. 'It can't be far.' His voice betrayed his uncertainty.

'Listen,' Tang snapped.

They pressed themselves against the wall. Close by, there was the *crunch, crunch, crunch* of booted soldiers.

'It's the town watch,' Mark whispered. 'We must move.'

At the end of the alley, a lantern showed as the watch rounded a corner and made straight for them.

'Be still,' Tang hissed. 'If we run, they'll raise the alarm.'

'We must...'

'Be silent.' Tang placed two fingers against Mark's lips. 'Follow me in everything. Do you understand? *In everything.*'

The lantern came closer.

Tang stepped into the guards' path. 'Hold, bothers,' he called. Mark tugged at the lieutenant's arm but Tang elbowed him away. '*In everything,*' he whispered.

The soldiers halted in front of Tang. The lantern glinted off spear tips. The soldiers' faces were drawn and hard.

'Who breaks curfew?' the commander called. 'Don't you know the garrison's on alert?'

'Forgive me, elder brother,' Tang pleaded. 'We arrived from the country this afternoon and are unaccustomed to these lanes.'

The commander wrinkled his nose and took a step back. 'I can't deny your country fragrance,' he said. The others laughed. 'Soldier Tam,' the commander ordered. 'Bring the lantern. Let's see what we have here.'

The lead man held the lantern close to Tang's face. His eyes widened. 'They're armed,' he gasped.

The others crowded forward, forcing Mark and Tang back against the wall.

Tang spread his arms, hands open. 'Brothers, we mean no harm. We are fresh from the road. There are brigands out there.'

'Your companion looks strange,' the commander said, pulling the lantern closer.

'My companion is...' Tang cupped a hand to the side of his mouth and lowered his voice '... an albino.'

The soldiers murmured amongst themselves. Several shuffled back.

'Do not be afraid, brothers,' Tang declared. 'He is a kindly soul. No matter what the stories say. Don't let his pale hair and pink eyes trouble you.'

'He has *pink* eyes?' The commander peered closer.

'Leave them,' a soldier wheedled, 'I know of such men, they bring nothing but ill luck. It's time we were off duty. Come, there's no danger from these simpletons.'

The others muttered agreement but the commander was not satisfied.

'Where do you lodge?' he demanded.

'With old Chan, elder brother,' Tang answered, plucking a name from the air. 'He lives close to the apothecary's but as you can see, we've lost our way.'

The commander jerked his thumb towards the end of the alley. 'Keep going ahead,' he snapped. 'Turn right at the end of this lane and go straight on to the town square. The apothecary's behind the courthouse. Now be off. And don't let me catch you out of curfew again.'

Tang bobbed his head. 'Thank you, elder brother,' he said. He grabbed Mark by the scruff of his jerkin and pushed him in the direction shown by the watch commander. The guard reformed and crunched away.

'You're insane,' Mark hissed.

'You speak true,' Tang snapped back. 'Insane to follow you.' He pushed Mark ahead of him and in silence, they stumbled on.

The courthouse had heavy ironbound doors. Tasselled lanterns of waxed paper hung from its lintel. The lanterns were unlit and the courthouse doors were locked.

Gunter Schneider shrank into the shadows as footsteps thudded across the square. He touched his sword hilt. Who else could be out after curfew? There were two of them and they hurried past Schneider's hiding place without a sideways glance. One was tall and muscular. The other had a broadsword strapped to his back. He was smaller than his companion but he moved with lithe self-assurance. Schneider tried to identify them by their dress but it was too dark.

Taking care to stay in the shadows, the two strangers skirted the courthouse then turned off the square. They headed in the direction of the apothecary shop so Schneider tagged on behind them. They stopped at the apothecary's door. There was a muffled knock. They knocked again. The rap of their knuckles was soft and urgent.

They are nervous, thought Schneider. They should not be out of doors. So, what business did curfew breakers have with our good doctor?

For the moment, Schneider put thoughts of the girl behind him and from the shadows, he watched.

Mei wiped a smear of blood from the workbench and massaged the back of her neck, freeing knots of tension in her shoulders. It had been a hard day.

First there was Yap the town brewer. The Taipings had banned his wine and he took a terrible risk with each batch he cooked up. He suffered from jaundice and double vision. Doctor Falchion had given him something to ease his liver pain but could do little else. Yap was drinking himself to death.

The day's last patient was a Taiping soldier with a wicked gash to the thigh. It had taken more than an hour to clean and suture the wound but Mei was sure the doctor had saved the young man's leg, maybe even his life. She shook her head: men with spears; boys with spears more like. It had been a stupid training accident but the soldier's comrade had wept with relief when Doctor Falchion had tied off the last stitch.

'You did well, Mei,' Doctor Falchion said. 'You have a gift for healing.'

Mei turned away so the doctor would not see how the compliment pleased her.

As she busied herself clearing away instruments and soiled dressings, Mei watched the doctor from the corner of her eye. His son, Mark, was the first Westerner she had ever seen. At first, his blue eyes and golden hair had startled her. But then came the memory of his smile and the touch of his lips on hers. She shook her head, banishing the thought.

Doctor Falchion pinched the bridge of his nose. There were dark lines under his eyes and a grey tinge to his cheeks.

'You have had a hard day,' Mei clucked. 'You need rest.' She bustled him to his sleeping chamber and for once, he did not resist.

The sleeping chamber had no windows and it smelled of dust. Its only furniture was a cot and a rickety table. A smoking oil lamp provided some light. The doctor dropped onto the cot and bent to remove his shoes. There was a knock at the surgery door and Falchion made to stand.

Mei waved him back onto the bed. 'Stay there,' she ordered, wagging her finger like a bad-tempered auntie. 'I will send them away.'

'No.' Falchion pushed himself to his feet. 'It might be serious.'

Mei pursed her lips and stood with her hands on her hips, blocking his way. 'Get back to your bed.' She pointed an imperious finger at the cot. 'If it is serious I will fetch you.'

'No you bloody won't,' Falchion muttered.

Mei walked to the door, determined to give the caller the edge of her tongue.

'The doctor is sleeping,' she called. 'Come back tomorrow.'

The caller knocked again. This time there was something urgent, almost desperate about the knock.

'Who's there?' Mei demanded. She placed her ear against the door but there was only silence. She sighed and shot the bolts. She cracked open the door and light flooded into the lane.

*Mein Gott,* Schneider almost said the words aloud. He moved further into the shadows and his scabbard clinked against a wall.

The men swung round to face him, knees bent, hands reaching for their swords.

Schneider pressed himself hard against the wall. The moment the door opened, he had seen their faces. It *is* them, he told himself. How could it be? The *Englisch-Chinesisch* boy and the Manchu officer, here in Sungkiang.

Schneider held his breath. He could feel their eyes probing the shadows. Then they backed through the door. It *snicked* shut and darkness returned to the alley.

Schneider wanted to clap his hands with glee, the medicinal brandy could wait and so could the woman. The English boy, the Manchu and the doctor were his. He would find a way to keep the woman for himself but the men would talk, oh my, how they would talk.

Tomorrow the Taipings would take them to the eastern courtyard where they would burn, slice and tear every last scrap of information from them.

And Gunter Schneider wanted very much to be there when they did.

# 23

MARK FALCHION was about to knock again when there was the scrape of bolts on the other side of the door. Light appeared at the doorjamb and revealed part of a woman's face.

'I must see the doctor,' he whispered. The door opened wider and a rush of joy swelled Mark's heart.

'Mei!'

Mei gave a small gasp. 'How...?' Her lips trembled into a nervous smile.

From the shadows, there came the clink of metal on stone.

Mark pivoted on the balls of his feet and reached for the *dao*. Tang dropped to a crouch. Mark's eyes searched the shadows, his senses bowstring tight. Nothing moved. There was only blackness and silence.

'Did you hear it?' Tang whispered.

'I'm not sure,' Mark answered. 'What was it?'

'I don't know,' Tang answered. 'Maybe nothing.' He sounded unconvinced. 'We were lucky once, the watch mustn't catch us here.'

They backed through the door and shut it behind them. Mei rammed home the bolts.

'How... how can this be?' Mei asked, her eyes wide, her face pale.

Mark touched his forefinger to his lips and put his ear to the door.

Mei shook her head. Her eyes flicked from the *dao* broadsword, to the brass-studded vambraces and to the leather jerkin that emphasised the muscle of Mark's chest and shoulders.

'You... you are much changed,' she said. She reached out and ran her fingertips along Mark's arm.

At her touch, Mark's heart leapt. 'Lady... I...' His tongue felt stuck to the roof of his mouth.

'You were supposed to be in Soochow,' Mei said. 'I thought...' She shook her head like a child trying to understand a grownup's story.

'There's no time,' Mark said. He laid his hand on hers and she did not pull away from his touch. 'Much has happened, and...' He looked down at the floor then into her face. '...and I have much to say to you.'

Mei's lips parted. She took a small step closer. They stood just inches apart.

'And I also,' she said in a husky whisper. 'There is much I want to say...'

'Mark?'

Mark turned to see his father framed in the doorway. Doctor James Falchion moved like a man woken from a deep sleep. For a moment, the two Westerners were silent then James Falchion grasped Mark by both shoulders. His voice trembled.

'Mark... my boy. Is it really you?'

'It is, father.'

The older man threw his arms about the younger and they embraced. The doctor patted Mark's shoulder and stepped back. His eyes were red and his cheeks were wet. He gave a self-conscious cough.

'The dust... it gets in my eyes...' He looked his son up and down. 'Mark, what is this? What have you done?'

Mark's voice was small. 'What can I say, father?' He could not meet the doctor's gaze. 'Events have taken me down a different path. Have I failed you?'

The doctor grasped his son's hand in both of his. 'Don't take on, my boy. You caught me by surprise, that's all. I never thought to see you as anything but a revered scholar.'

Mark squared his shoulders. 'The scholar's gown was your plan, father, never mine. It... it was not to be.' His words seemed inadequate.

The doctor sighed. 'You are a good man,' he said. 'Too good to remain a soldier.' He gave a gentle laugh. 'If soldier you are, you look like a brigand.'

Mark smiled. 'Enough, father,' he said. 'There's no time, we must go.'

'Go?' The doctor spread his arms, encompassing the surgery. 'I cannot go. I'm needed here.'

'You must, Father, you and I must leave here.' Mark grasped his father's shoulders. 'There will be a battle. I must get you to safety.'

'A battle? Here? But what of the townsfolk?'

Mark rolled his eyes. 'There's no time,' he said. 'I can't help the townsfolk. Soon there will be a battle. We must leave.'

The doctor frowned. 'If there's to be a battle, I must stay,' he declared. 'In war, the innocents suffer more than anyone.'

Mark turned to Mei and their eyes locked. 'Lady, if you hold any sway with this foolish old man, I beg you, tell him to come with me.'

'Pay no attention, Mei.' Doctor Falchion said. He looked at Mark. 'Soldier or not, you cannot know the happiness it gives me to see you.' He shook his head. 'But I won't abandon these people. You'll get past the guards easier without me. Now, be gone.' He folded his arms. 'I'm bull-headed and cantankerous but I have my duty.' His tone softened. 'And I think, my son, so have you.'

Tang was keeping station by the door. 'The old man is stubborn,' he snapped. 'But he's right, we must go.'

'Father,' Mark pleaded.

The doctor folded his arms and looked up at the ceiling.

Mei tightened her grip on Mark's arm.

'You and your companion are in great danger,' she said. 'I will care for the doctor until we...' She lowered her eyes then she drew in a sharp breath and squared her shoulders. Her voice became brisk. 'Go. Go now. The Taipings will not harm him. This is my promise to you.'

Mark took Mei's hand and their fingers intertwined. For an instant, there were no Taipings, no Ward, no Shanghai, just Mark Falchion and this Chinese woman with gentle hands and soft eyes.

Tang's voice broke the moment. 'Come,' he urged. He grasped Mark's arm and pulled him towards the door.

Mei held onto Mark's hand. Only when they were at arm's length did she release him. She moved to the door and drew back the bolts.

'You must go,' she said. Her voice caught in a half sob. She would not meet Mark's eyes as she pushed him towards the alley.

'Hurry,' Tang barked. 'I think I can find our way back to the watergate.' He dragged Mark into the alley then stopped.

'Something's not right,' he hissed.

Mark sensed it too. He shrugged off Tang's grip and dropped to a crouch. His eyes and ears probed the night. He reached for the *dao*.

A voice called from the shadows.

'*Stand!*'

Lanterns flickered into life. Spear tips glistened. The elongated shadows of a dozen Taipings stretched across the alley.

Adrenaline flashed through Mark. The *dao* materialised in his hand.

'I said, *stand!*' a voice commanded. 'Put up your swords.'

The Taipings levelled their spears. Their eyes glittered. Mark felt their tight resolve. This time we are cornered, he thought. This time, we are finished.

'Easy, *Liebling*, easy.' Schneider sauntered into the light. 'Soldier Tong,' he called. 'Please tell the men not to charge just yet.'

An unseen soldier translated Schneider's words.

The Prussian made a mocking bow. 'It is, what you say, a small world, *ja?*'

Mark gawked at the Prussian.

'*Schneider!*' he spat. 'I see you've kept yourself safe.'

Schneider grinned. 'Better safe than the alternative,' he chuckled. 'Unlike me, I think you prefer a glorious death.' A slow smile crept over his lips. 'Go ahead my pretty *Englisch-Chinesisch* boy. You may have your glory and I will have the woman.' He winked. 'I will make her squeal with pleasure.'

Tang's sword was in his hand.

'On my signal,' he growled. 'Take the traitor first.'

'Wait,' Mark whispered.

'*Shaaaa*,' Tang roared. He raised his sword and charged. There was the *Tak* of a spear haft against bone and Tang's body smacked against the flagstones.

Soldiers grasped Mark's arms. A spear point scraped against his throat. Someone snatched away his sword. Rough hands pinned his arms.

'*Ach*, you disappoint me,' Schneider chided. He snapped his fingers and soldiers pulled Mei and the doctor from the surgery. 'Release the girl,' he called. 'I shall question her later.' He put his lips close to Mark's ear. 'Later and in much depth.' He licked his lips and stepped back.

Mark strained against the hands pinning his arms. 'If you touch her...'

Schneider's lips curled back from his teeth. 'Do not worry, *Liebling*, after I have taken her, I shall tell you every wonderful detail.'

Soldiers prodded the doctor towards Mark. Others slipped halters over their necks and tied their hands. A handcart rattled along the lane and soldiers heaved Tang into it.

A spear haft dug into Mark's back then Taipings and prisoners shuffled into the dark.

Mei rammed home the bolts and snatched a surgical knife from the bench. The touch of the steel comforted her. She moved around the surgery, extinguishing the lamps. She squeezed shut her eyes and bunched her fists.

*Think!* she commanded herself.

She moved back to the door and pressed her ear against it. The alley seemed silent but indecision taunted her. Stay or go? Schneider might be skulking in the dark, waiting for her. But how safe was she in the apothecary? He will be back, Mei decided. Maybe in days, maybe in minutes. In Sungkiang, there was only one man who could protect her. But how to get to him?

She groped for the bolts. They scraped open and she winced, certain the Prussian must have heard. She opened the door a crack. Outside, the dark was total. She sucked in a breath and holding the knife stiff-armed before her, she stepped into the alley. She flattened herself against the wall and looked left and right, watching, listening, smelling.

Then she put down her head and ran.

Lieutenant Tang swung his head like a stunned bull. Dried

blood covered his face. He tried to move but iron manacles held his wrists to the wall.

'Tang, can you hear me?' Mark whispered but the lieutenant managed only a moan.

They were in a narrow pit cut into the courtyard by the eastern gatehouse. The pre-dawn sky was grey. Watery light seeped down through the bars of an iron grill, just inches above their heads. Straw covered the floor, it was damp and smelled of horse urine. Footsteps moved around the courtyard. Mark strained against his chains.

'Save your strength, my boy,' the doctor chided. 'You did your best.' He wrinkled his nose against the straw's smell. 'This will be most unpleasant when the sun's up,' he said.

'What are you babbling in your barbarous tongue?' Tang's voice was slurred. He winced. '*Waah*, what did they hit me with?' He opened his mouth and worked his lower jaw in circles.

There was a smell of burning coals.

'Someone's making breakfast,' Mark said.

'You don't know much about Taipings,' Tang snorted.

A Taiping soldier appeared at the pit's rim. He squatted on his haunches and looked down at the prisoners. With the light behind him, he looked like an ordinary guard but then Mark noticed how his tunic shimmered in the dawn light.

'Why did you come to this place?' the Taiping asked in flowing English.

Doctor Falchion's voice cracked as he spoke. 'Mark, this is our host, Captain Meng.' He worked saliva onto his tongue and nodded towards Mark. 'Captain Meng, this impossible young man is Mark Clegge. Mister Clegge is a passing acquaintance of mine.'

Meng spoke like a concerned friend. 'Ah, doctor, I shall not ask how you slept.'

He moved to where he could better see the three of them.

'Mister Clegge and I have already met,' he said. 'You and he bear a remarkable resemblance. Might his name also be Falchion?'

Doctor Falchion lowered his eyes and did not answer.

Meng gave an icy smile and fixed his eyes on Mark. 'Mister Falchion,' he purred. 'Or may I call you Mark? No? Of course not, it would be far too presumptuous. So tell me, why are you here?'

'Because your guards put me in here,' Mark snapped back.

Meng's teeth flashed white. 'I will ask you again, why are you and your kind here, in China?'

Mark stared at the wall.

'I will tell you why,' Meng spat. 'To defile us with your priests, to enslave us with your opium and to hire out your unwashed soldiers to the tyrants who oppress us.'

He waved his arm and two guards appeared at the pit's edge. They hauled open the grill and one jumped down to unfasten the manacles. A ladder scraped against the pit wall and they used their spears to prod Mark, Tang and Doctor Falchion up into the courtyard.

Mark massaged his wrists and turned a full circle. Fifty or more black-uniforms lined the courtyard. Dozens more crowded the gate tower.

Mark cast his eyes around, searching for some weakness. There were two gates: the first led to the world outside, the other, an inner gate, led into the town. Seen through Lo Haak's telescope the outer gate had looked formidable but seeing it now, Mark got a sense of its menace. Armies have broken themselves on this gate, he thought.

The gate placement was unusual. They stood at right angles to one another. Attackers who breached the first gate had to turn through ninety degrees to assault the second. Artillery outside the walls could not come to bear on the inner gate. Even if they breached the outer gate, attackers would find themselves trapped. The courtyard was a perfect killing zone.

Mark's eyes moved to where smoke curled from an iron brazier. Straddling the brazier was a tripod of wooden staves and from it hung a rope and a wooden block. Beside it, stripped to the waist stood a muscular Taiping. Sweat gleamed on the muscle of his upper body. A light smile played on his lips.

Meng cocked his head and looked at Mark as though he were some kind of oddity.

'Your dress is unusual for a Westerner,' he said. 'You speak our language and Schneider tells me you have some pretension with weapons.'

He snapped his fingers and a soldier scuttled forward with Mark's sword. Meng slid it from its scabbard and gave an appreciative nod.

'An excellent weapon,' he declared. The air sighed over the blade as he executed a sideways cut. 'But I prefer something with more finesse.'

He returned the *dao* to its scabbard and tossed it back to the soldier. He reached for the goldthread grip of his own sword and eased it from its scabbard. The light played on the golden dragon running the blade's length. Meng touched the point to Mark's chest.

'I had hoped your father's charming assistant would be here to see this,' he said. 'I believe you and she are close.'

Denial sprang to Mark's lips but Meng held up his hand and chuckled.

'It does you no credit to deny the obvious,' he said. His eyes narrowed. 'Tell me, does she come to you at night?'

He flicked his wrist and his blade swept close to Mark's cheek.

'Does she climb into your bed?'

Mark flinched as the point shimmered past his throat.

'Does she press her body to yours?'

Meng's breath was harsh; his lips were bloodless. His voice became a guttural snarl. 'Does she make soft noises when you take her?'

He raised the blade and sliced down, hard and fast. As the blade arced towards his upturned brows, Mark screwed shut his eyes and waited for the steel to bite into his brain.

The blade stopped, quivering an inch from his forehead. Meng gave a humourless laugh and slipped the sword back into its sheath.

'Swordsmanship is a matter of control,' he said. He moved closer to Mark and their faces almost touched. 'And today, Mister Falchion, you will learn much about control.'

Meng looked hard into Mark's face. Mark wanted to shrink back from those eyes. They reached into him and sucked out his courage.

Meng stepped away and slipped back into the role of concerned host.

'Schneider tells me you were in the assault on our western wall.' He spoke as though making light conversation. 'I want you to tell me the current strength of your force, the state of your weapons and the strategy and timing for your next attempt on this garrison.'

'Ward is disgraced.' The lie fell easily from Mark's lips. 'The Shanghai traders are in panic. Give them time, they'll sue for peace.'

Meng nodded and smiled like someone enjoying a private joke.

'Yes, of course, you are unwilling to divulge such vital intelligence,' he said. 'I would have been disappointed had it been any other way.'

He nodded to the man at the brazier then turned back to Mark 'It does not matter,' he said. 'My man, Shan, will prove far more persuasive.'

The muscular Taiping named Shan, smiled and lowered the rope until it trailed on the courtyard flagstones.

As the brazier's true purpose hit Mark, the metallic taste of fear filled his mouth. He knew nothing of Ward's plans, but that would only prolong his agony. Death would be a release but when would it come? In minutes or in hours? He clamped his jaw tight and squared his shoulders.

'You are defiant, Mister Falchion.' Meng inclined his head in sham respect. 'My compliments, you are better prepared than the other barbarians who died here.'

He stepped aside, clearing the way to the brazier. 'But remember what I said, this lesson is not about courage, it is about control. So tell me how you will control yourself when I put your father to the fire?'

'You... You can't,' Mark gasped. 'He knows nothing.'

Meng shrugged. 'I know,' he said, 'but casualties of war are so often the innocents.' He snapped his fingers and pointed to Doctor Falchion.

Two guards stepped forward. One pinned the doctor's arms, the other tied his wrists.

The doctor's face paled. His lips moved but he made no sound.

Mark drove a straight-armed punch at the nearest guard. It connected with a hard *swack*. The guard grunted and staggered back.

The other guard jabbed his spear haft into Mark's midriff. Mark gasped and toppled to the flagstones. A boot slammed into his face. Lights flashed behind his eyes and he tasted blood. He tried to stand but the guard put a boot on his neck and pushed him down.

Meng squatted beside him. 'You are a good soldier,' he whispered. 'I think your father will know much pain before you turn traitor.'

The second guard dragged the doctor to the brazier, forced him to his knees and then onto his back.

'Mark... Captain Meng,' Doctor Falchion pleaded. 'My God... My God!'

The Taiping, Shan, grinned and mocked the doctor with soothing noises as he secured the rope around his ankles.

'He must suffer, at least a little,' Meng mused. 'In fact, they must both suffer: your father and your comrade. If they do not, how can I know you are telling the truth?'

Shan flexed his shoulders and leaned back on the rope. It squealed through its block, tightened and lifted the doctor's feet from the ground.

The doctor's cries echoed from the courtyard walls and ripped into Mark's heart.

Mark tried to push against the soldier's boot but the soldier pressed down harder and showed Mark the point of his spear.

'Captain Meng!'

Meng's face darkened. He looked up at the parapet from where Colonel Fu glowered down at him.

'You will release those people immediately,' Fu roared.

Shan hesitated. He looked from Colonel Fu to Meng and back to Colonel Fu.

'Release him!' Fu roared.

Shan began to lower Doctor Falchion back to the courtyard floor but Meng rounded on him.

'You have your orders,' he snarled. 'Continue with the interrogation.'

Colonel Fu leaned out over the wall and pointed a trembling

## THE SCHOLAR'S BLADE

finger at Meng.

'*I* command here, Captain,' he bellowed. 'You will stop this *now*.'

Meng placed his fists on his hips. 'This man is a spy,' he shouted. 'He is under my charge and I will question him as I please.'

Fu's knuckles showed white against the dark granite. 'We are expecting an attack and you...' he paused, choking on his words. 'You put our only doctor to the fire.' He waved his arm and a line of soldiers appeared on the wall. Each wore Fu's jade green and each rested a musket on the parapet.

Meng's face was white. 'This is outrageous,' he hissed. 'These people are enemy spies.'

'Then their information affects us all,' Colonel Fu thundered back.

There was the scrape of heavy bolts and the inner gate groaned open. A man wearing Fu's jade-green entered the courtyard. He was slim and alongside Meng's soldiers he looked frail and out of place. He approached Meng and bowed. His voice was thin and reedy.

'Our commander orders me to escort the prisoners to his *yamen*,' he said. 'I pray you will not obstruct me.'

Meng stared into the aide's face. The thin officer paled and pointed to the muskets lining the parapet. 'Do not defy our commander,' he wheedled. 'It will not end well.'

Meng clenched and unclenched his fists then turned away.

'Release them,' he shouted and without a backward look, he strode to the inner gate.

The pressure on Mark's neck eased. He pushed himself up and looked into the face of the guard who, moments earlier, had pinned him to the courtyard floor. The guard drew his thumbnail across his throat and spat on the ground. Then he turned and followed Meng.

Tapings wearing jade-green filed into the courtyard. One of them cut the doctor's bindings and pulled him to his feet. Others flanked Mark and Tang. A spear haft dug into Mark's back and together, they all marched into the town.

# 24

Colonel Fu drew the tapestry across his door and for a while at least, shut out the garrison's troubles. He sighed and shut his eyes. When this was over he would sleep for a month. He belched and acid bile burned his throat. His guts had been in a dreadful knot since he had come to this place and now more than ever, he wished the apothecary had not fled.

What was he to do? With a regiment of men like Meng, he could take Shanghai in a day. Meng was valiant and ferocious, but he was out of control.

Fu rolled his eyes and suppressed a smile. He had to admire the woman's nerve. After the doctor's arrest, Mei had stormed into his headquarters and harangued his guards until they brought her before him.

He allowed himself some self-congratulation. His timing had been impeccable. Soon, Meng's humiliation would be the talk of the garrison. But what was he to do with the damned prisoners? The Manchu was not a problem. Fu beheaded every enemy he captured. He did not think himself cruel, Taiping prisoners suffered the same fate at Imperial hands. But the young barbarian? He was a different matter altogether. In fact, he opened up all manner of possibilities.

Fu moved to his desk, dropped onto his chair and dipped his brush into his ink tray. He had drafted the order three times but still he was uncertain. If he got it right, Meng would be finished.

If he got it wrong, then he had best open a vein and have done with it.

He stroked his moustache, how had it come to this? These days there was too much intrigue and not enough action. He smiled, he was starting to sound like the old sweats that forever fouled the mood in the billets. Was he getting old? For a while, he pondered the question.

Then he began to write.

Mark Falchion surveyed his quarters. Despite the locked door and the sentry, the room was clean and airy. They had food and a pail of water to clean the filth from their bodies and clothes. To Tang, the Taipings had issued a linen tunic with wide cuffs and a high-necked collar.

Footsteps sounded outside and the door crashed open. Two soldiers ducked under the lintel and Colonel Fu's aide swept in behind them. He regarded Mark down the length of his nose. His voice carried the high-pitched arrogance of an old-style mandarin.

'By my colonel's written order,' he whined, 'the doctor has been released.'

Mark gave silent thanks. 'Where's the doctor now?' he asked.

Annoyance flickered across the aide's face. 'I have not been informed,' he replied. 'I expect he has returned to his duties.'

'And what of us?' Tang demanded.

The aide spoke as though addressing two scullery boys.

'My colonel orders you both to attend him, now.' He rapped his fan against his hand and the two soldiers levelled their spear points. 'You will follow me,' he commanded. He turned away and glided from the room.

Mark and Tang exchanged looks, then followed. The aide led them along a bare corridor to a door guarded by two more sentries. Above the lintel was a panel of deepest crimson. Picked out in gold were the characters, 'Heaven's Warrior.'

The door opened onto a large antechamber. A carpet of russet silk covered the floor. Paintings of misted landscapes hung at the walls. Covering a third wall was a tapestry depicting a rampant dragon picked out in crimson and silver, against a background of imperial yellow.

A guard pulled back the tapestry to reveal a circular doorway. He jerked his head towards the room beyond and Mark and Tang stepped through.

In contrast to the antechamber, the room was plain. The walls were white and their only decoration was a simple cross hanging above a narrow bed. In the middle of the room was a table covered with scrolls and maps.

Folding doors opened onto a veranda where a man wearing jade-green stood looking out over the rooftops. His back was to them and his shoulders sagged as though bearing a heavy weight. At the sound of their approach, he turned and stood framed in the door. He had a strong face framed by iron-grey hair. There were worry lines around his eyes but his gaze was steady.

'Do you know who I am?' he demanded.

Mark cupped his right fist in his left hand and bowed. 'You are Colonel Fu, the garrison commander,' he said,

'And you are Mark Falchion,' Fu declared. He turned to Tang, his eyes burning. 'And this is your *Manchu*.'

'Your pardon, sir,' Mark answered. 'But Lieutenant Tang is no man's but his own.'

'It is not your place to correct me,' Fu barked. He fell silent and walked around Tang who stood with his feet apart and his fists clenched at his side.

'The lieutenant is a rare animal,' Fu mused. 'A living Manchu inside a Taiping base.'

'You speak the truth,' Tang growled. 'I am as rare as a noble Taiping.'

'Take care,' Fu growled, 'or you might not remain so uncommon.'

Mark gave a discreet cough. 'Excellency,' he said, 'in your wisdom, you have summonsed us for a purpose.'

Colonel Fu stepped away from Tang, his breathing heavy.

'Indeed, young man, indeed,' he said. He paced the room with his eyes on the floor. After several moments he asked, 'Who is this mercenary, this Ward?'

'Ward is a mighty veteran,' Mark said. 'He commands ten... no, twenty thousand men...'

Fu smiled. 'Twenty thousand, you say. Indeed, a formidable army.' He looked into Mark's face. 'But maybe you miscalculate. I estimate his force at no more than two hundred...' He held up his hand, silencing Mark's denial. 'Two hundred or twenty thousand,' he snapped. 'If he comes against me, I will crush him.'

Mark remained silent.

Colonel Fu seemed to speak to himself. 'Mercenaries are poor soldiers,' he mused. 'Their cause is empty, so at the first setback they turn and flee.' He was silent for a few seconds then his voice became brisk. 'However, they are, what should I say? Pragmatic. They are paid; they fight. Simple, no complications.'

For a while, he seemed lost in thought. 'I envy your Ward,' he sighed. 'Here, there are many complications.' He walked to the veranda and beckoned Mark to him. He pointed to the open ground beyond the town ramparts. 'East,' he said. 'If I were your Ward, I'd have come that way.'

Mark tried not to show his surprise, not only at Fu's candour but also his insight. He stood alongside the colonel.

'Why from the east, sir?' he asked, trying to sound

unconcerned.

'Out there is where my horsemen exercise their mounts,' Fu answered. He gave Mark a wry smile. 'But I suspect that's no secret to you.'

He rested his hands on the veranda buttress and spoke as though Mark were one of his junior officers. 'By now you've learned the ground's firm enough for my horses. That means it's dry enough to move men and equipment.' He knotted his brow. 'It's a big risk, though.' He pointed to the left of the open ground then to the right. 'There are waterways on both flanks and dense woodland to the rear. The area is flat and devoid of cover, it's perfect for artillery and massed troop formations. If Ward's attack fails, he'll be trapped.' Fu ground his fist against the buttress. 'First my artillery then my soldiers will annihilate him.' He turned to Mark. 'What do you think, will he take the gamble?'

'I... I do not know Ward's mind, sir,' Mark stammered.

Fu chuckled and patted Mark's shoulder. 'And if you did, you would say nothing. It's not important.'

They moved back into Fu's apartment. 'I have a proposal for you, Mister Falchion.' Fu glanced sideways at Tang. 'But it is for you alone.'

Mark looked into Fu's eyes. 'I will hear your proposal,' he said. 'But please understand, Lieutenant Tang is my comrade.'

'Hear me first,' Fu snapped. 'Western officers have a strange ritual of war. It is called *parole*.' Fu's tongue stumbled on the unfamiliar language.

'I am not acquainted with the term, sir,' Mark answered.

'It is a strange concept,' Fu said. 'Of all barbarian military practices, this is the most bizarre.' He shook his head and his brows knotted. 'Yes, most strange. If you promise not to escape or harm my men, I will return your sword and grant you freedom of the town.'

'An honourable and generous offer, Excellency,' Mark replied. 'And the lieutenant?'

Fu's eyes flashed. 'The Manchu is no Westerner. He knew the risks, the offer is for you alone.'

'Then sir, I must decline.' Mark squared his shoulders and stared straight ahead.

'Don't be stupid,' Tang hissed. 'He's right, my life is his. It's just the way of things.'

Mark stood to attention as he had seen Ward's troopers do at morning parade. 'The offer must include both or neither, Excellency.'

Fu turned and faced Tang. 'Well, *Manchu*, will you give your word?'

Tang rolled his eyes. 'Of course,' he drawled. 'I hereby swear not to escape nor harm your men.' He put his head close to Fu's and his voice became a snarl. 'Now, Taiping, bring me my sword and it had best be sharp.'

Fu whirled on Mark and pointed a quivering finger at Tang. 'You see?' he shouted. 'These Imperials are not gentlemen. Their promise means nothing.'

'I will be responsible, sir,' Mark said. 'If the lieutenant breaks his parole, you may have my head.'

'*Ha!* Do I need your permission for that?' Fu's nostrils flared; crimson spots burned his cheeks. 'Very well,' his voice was a resentful grumble. 'I will extend parole to you both. Someone will bring your weapons but your quarters will be here, in this building and next to mine. You will report to my aide thrice daily: at dawn, noon and dusk. Questions?'

'One, sir,' Mark answered, still standing to rigid attention. 'I must know your reason for making this offer.'

Fu took a sharp breath. There was frost in his voice. 'I need you to perform a service for Ward, for yourself and for me.' He looked at them from under knotted brows. 'For now, I will say no more. Do you accept my terms?'

Mark bowed. 'I do. Please accept my word. Thank you, sir.'

'You'll not thank me if this dog breaks his parole,' Fu snapped. He turned his back and fluttered his hand in dismissal.

Mark grabbed Tang's tunic and pulled him to the door.

Alone in his study, Fu growled his frustration. The Manchu was a problem but no matter, a dagger in the dark was as good as a headman's blade. But damn the boy, dictating terms like some little prince.

But would it be worthwhile? Trusting foreigners went against all Fu's instincts, but his plan could not work without Falchion's help. When Fu had the boy's confidence, he would send him to Ward with an offer no mercenary could refuse: double wages if he would bring his men into the Taiping cause.

Fu stroked his chin. The mercenaries would make a fine counterbalance to Meng's impudence. It would be a double coup: Meng would be contained and Colonel Fu would take credit for engineering a mass defection.

Ward would come, Fu was sure of it. After all, the man was a mercenary and mercenaries were nothing if not pragmatic.

With their sentry gone and the door unlocked, the room seemed almost cheerful. Tang buffed his sword with his sleeve and squinted along its edge. 'They built these towns to keep people out, not keep them in,' he said. 'Escape will be easy.'

'Did you hear nothing?' Mark sighed. 'If you break your parole, my head is forfeit.'

Tang shrugged. 'I thought we'd leave together.'

Mark sighed. 'I gave my word, I cannot break it.'

Tang blinked like someone caught by a practical joke. He let out a harsh laugh. 'Do you think us safe?' His voice was heavy with scorn. 'The colonel may let you survive the week, but I doubt he'll do me the same favour. What about the lunatic with the golden sword? And Schneider? He wants your woman.'

Mark slumped onto his cot. 'She's not my woman,' he muttered.

'Is she not?' Tang scoffed. 'I saw how you looked at her. And she at you.'

For a while, there was silence between them.

'I gave my word,' Mark grumbled.

'Yes, you gave your word,' Tang said. 'But if we want to stay alive, you'd best find a way to un-give it.'

Top Soldier Cho Lung had never seen his commander in such a state. All morning Meng had stormed around the stables, armouries and guard posts. He had inspected everything and found fault where there was none. Now it was the turn of the men guarding the eastern parapet.

Shadowing Meng was the new man, Shan. His face showed no emotion but every time Meng delivered a rebuke, his eyes gleamed.

Meng snatched a spear from a soldier and held the tip close to Cho Lung's face.

'What's this?' he demanded.

Cho took the spear and inspected it. The haft smelled of fresh linseed and its point gleamed. He took care not to cut himself on its honed edges. He looked closer, there was a small stain on the steel collar where the head fastened onto the haft.

'It might be a spot of blood, Excellency,' Cho offered.

'This spear's not tasted blood since we took Wuhsi,' Meng snarled. 'It's rust. How can I trust a man who cares nothing for his weapons?' He turned to Shan. 'Six strokes of the bamboo for this man.'

A smile touched Shan's lips. 'Yes, Captain,' he said. His voice had a rasping resonance. 'I will take care of it personally.'

But sir,' Cho remonstrated, 'it's summer, the humidity...'

'Eight strokes.' Meng snapped.

Shan's smile widened.

'The men are lax,' Meng grumbled. 'And it has nothing to do with garrison routine.'

Cho did not argue, he understood Meng's moods too well.

'You are right to remain silent,' Meng continued. 'Never contradict me in front of the troops again or I'll be looking for a new top soldier.'

Cho gave a stiff bow. 'Forgive me, sir,' he said. 'I am unused to inactivity.'

For a moment, Cho chewed his lip. 'Sir, I... I have a request,' he said.

'What request?' Meng snapped back.

'I believe Shan is unfamiliar with horses,' Cho answered, nodding towards the muscular Taiping.

'So what?' Meng answered. 'We're on garrison duty.'

'It's a quiet time,' Cho persisted. 'And training is never wasted. I can meet him later in the stables. I'll bring a few of the men and we can get acquainted.'

Meng shook his head. 'Not today,' he said. 'I have duties for Shan.' His mood brightened. 'Indeed,' he said. 'Very special duties.'

Shan placed his hand on his heart and made a shallow bow to Meng. 'Yes, Captain,' he said. 'The duties are very special.'

Meng rounded on Cho. 'Make yourself useful,' he snapped. 'Check the ammunition store and make sure the gunners haven't sold our powder to the Imperials.'

As Meng and Shan retraced their steps along the battlement walkway, Meng put his head close to Shan's and they exchanged a few words. Meng laughed, patted Shan's arm then walked alone down the ramp to the courtyard below.

The exchange bothered Cho. It was quiet and intimate. It reeked of secrets and Cho could not abide a soldier with secrets. Garrison duties were bad enough but secrets festered. Secrets caused arguments and arguments between bored soldiers were lethal affairs.

It was not like Meng to keep things from Cho and the new mood troubled him. In war it was vital to keep things simple, and the Black Dragons' command chain was perfect in its simplicity. It was Meng, followed by Cho Lung, followed by everyone else, which was just how Cho meant to keep it.

But now there was the new man; the muscular Taiping who carried a brutal *guandao* and who seemed to have the ear of their commander.

Even with the help of a few stout comrades, it would be hard to bring this one into line. For now, he could do nothing. Now was not the time to deal with the soldier called Shan.

But the time would come. It always did.

From his veranda, Colonel Fu looked over the rooftops and watched clouds drift across a darkening sky. Already, there were a few stars showing. Back home, dusk had always been his special time. Soon he would kneel by his bed, say a quiet prayer and turn in for the night.

As the sky turned from blue to indigo, Fu stepped back into the apartment. The lanterns' glow made the room seem almost inviting.

There was a scuffing noise from the anteroom. The tapestry rustled and a soldier stepped through. He carried a heavy-bladed *guandao* and wore a black uniform over a muscular frame. A light smile played on his lips.

Fu stiffened. 'Shan? Why are you here? What's the meaning of this?' he demanded.

Shan moved closer and Fu saw the crimson sheen of fresh blood on the *guandao's* blade.

'Just one sentry, Colonel?' Shan chided. 'You should have posted more than one.'

Fu cursed himself for letting his orderly care for his sword, yet he felt somehow detached, as though watching a play unfold on a stage.

Shan's eyes gleamed. He cocked his head to one side as though studying something strange and interesting. His voice was soft, almost comforting.

'You seem at peace,' he cooed. 'That is a good state to greet your maker.'

His smile broadened. His teeth gleamed white in the lantern light. The blood smearing his blade glistened. He took a step closer to Fu and moved the *guandao's* blade from side to side.

Strange, Fu thought, I have faced a thousand deaths in a hundred battles, why am I so calm now?

He squared his shoulders and closed his eyes as the *guandao* came scything towards him.

The sun had been up for more than an hour and Meng was in a foul mood. 'Is there a message?' he asked for the fifth time that morning.

'None, sir,' Cho Lung replied.

Meng slapped his hand onto the parapet. His breath hissed from between clenched teeth.

Trooper Shan looked as though he wanted to blend into the wall. His eyes flickered from Meng to Cho then back again.

Meng rounded on him. 'Did you carry out my wishes?' he demanded.

'Yes, sir,' Shan wheedled.

'Then why has there been no alarm?'

Shan could only shrug.

Meng turned to Cho. 'What is the garrison alert status?' he snapped.

'High alert, Excellency,' Cho replied. 'As it was yesterday and the day before.'

Meng paced a few yards down the balustrade. 'This is ridiculous,' he snapped. 'We should have heard.'

'Heard what, sir?' Cho asked.

'Do not question me,' Meng snarled. He span on his heel and strode to the ramp leading down into the town. He paused. 'Well?' he snapped.

'Sir?' Cho asked.

'*Sir?*' Meng mimicked. 'Follow me,' he barked. 'We must go to the garrison headquarters.' His lips curled in a humourless smile. 'Send orders for the Prussian to join us, I fear there may be a crisis.'

Meng, flanked by Gunter Schneider and Cho Lung, strode the corridor leading to Colonel Fu's apartment. Shan trailed behind them.

Except for the echo of their footsteps, the garrison headquarters was silent. Soldiers snapped to attention at Meng's passing but none would meet his eyes.

As the group neared the commander's apartment, two soldiers wearing Fu's jade-green stepped from the anteroom and crossed their spears. Without breaking stride, Meng slapped the spears aside and marched into the anteroom.

The colonel's aide looked up from his desk and blanched.

# THE SCHOLAR'S BLADE

Meng stood before him, his left hand resting on the hilt of his sword.

'Tell Colonel Fu I require an audience,' he demanded.

'*Er...* Captain Meng.' The aide stood and grabbed the edge of his desk for support. 'I fear Colonel Fu is, *um...* indisposed,' he said.

'Oh dear, I hope it's nothing serious.' Meng's tone was solicitous. He looked sideways at Shan who stifled a snigger.

'It is serious enough to keep our commander confined to his quarters,' the aide replied. His face was pale; his eyes darted between Meng and Schneider. 'I pray for his speedy recovery,' he added.

'As do we all,' said Meng. He turned away and moved to the tapestry separating the anteroom from Fu's quarters.

The aide scuttled from behind the desk and blocked the way. He tried to smile but his lips were a bloodless line. He shook his head and clasped his hands before his chest.

'Colonel Fu will be very angry if we disturb him,' he said. 'Perhaps you can return later. Tomorrow maybe.'

Meng's voice was all concern. 'How about next week?' he asked. 'Perhaps in a month or two?'

'Indeed, Captain, next week would be...'

Meng shouldered the aide aside and wrenched at the tapestry. Its rail separated from the wall with a *crack* and the tapestry thumped against the anteroom carpet. Meng stepped into the colonel's chamber.

Blood puddled the floor. Rust coloured streaks marked one wall. On the bed, a bloodstained sheet covered a reclining man. Meng lifted a corner of the sheet and feigned a wince.

'My, my,' he sighed, 'our noble colonel will be indisposed for some time.'

He dropped the sheet back into place and turned on the aide

who was hovering in the doorway. 'Who has command?' he snapped.

The aide squared his narrow shoulders. 'I was the colonel's closest confidant. I am conversant with all tactics and logistics. It is only natural that I...'

Meng glared the aide into silence. 'Typical of Fu,' he spat, 'so afraid of dissent he surrounded himself with idiots.'

The aide took a sharp breath. 'Captain Meng, this is a military garrison and you do well to remember who is senior here.'

Meng put his face inches from the aide's. 'Senior? You?' he snarled. 'You are not fit to empty my pisspot. Now get out.'

The aide's cheeks burned. 'Guards,' he called. 'Arrest Captain Meng and disarm his escort.'

The guards looked from the aide to Meng then back to the aide. Their eyes were quick and nervous.

The aide stamped his foot. '*Immediately!*' he screeched.

Shan grinned and lowered the point of his *guandao*.

Fu's guards couched their spears and stepped forward.

Cho Lung moved between them and spread his arms. His voice was soothing. 'Easy, brothers, easy,' he said. 'This is not your feud. Let the damned officers sort it out.'

The guards exchanged glances then one jerked his head towards the apartment door. They lowered their weapons and backed away.

'Traitors,' the aide howled, 'I'll have your heads...'

Shan moved behind the aide and thrust hard with his *guandao*.

The aide gave a small gasp. His eyes widened as blood smeared steel emerged from the middle of his chest.

Shan sniggered like a schoolgirl. He put his boot in the small of the aide's back and ripped the blade free.

The aide's eyes rolled and he crumpled to the floor.

'We've wasted too much time.' Meng said. He switched to English. 'Mister Schneider.'

Schneider stiffened. 'Yes, Captain Meng.'

'At last, you shall have a soldier's duty,' Meng said. 'I want the town sealed. Get to the western gate and relieve the commander. Clear any market traders from the bridge and shut the gates. From now on, you will guard our most vulnerable position.'

Schneider clicked his heels. '*Danke vielmals*, sir.'

'Cho Lung,' Meng snapped. 'The soldier, Wu Ren, speaks English. Tell him to report to Schneider.'

He looked down at the aide's body and wrinkled his nose. 'And tell the guards to drag this thing away,' he said. 'It's bleeding all over my floor.'

# 25

MARK FALCHION woke to shouted commands and the clatter of boots. He rolled off his cot and kicked the edge of Tang's cot. The lieutenant grunted and squinted against the morning light.

'What?' he moaned.

Mark was struggling with his boots. 'Get up,' he whispered. 'Something's happened.'

Tang yawned and stretched his arms. 'It had better be serious,' he grumbled.

Mark opened the door and stepped into the corridor. A dozen soldiers turned to him and levelled their spears. Their officer glared at Mark. His cheeks were pale, his lips were a thin line.

'Return to you quarters,' the officer ordered. He rounded on his men. 'And lower your weapons. There's been enough blood here.'

Half the soldiers lowered their spears. The others exchanged sullen looks. One man took a step towards Mark.

'I said, lower your weapons,' the officer barked. The soldiers scowled but moved back, muttering among themselves.

'What's happened?' Mark asked.

The officer did not answer.

Tang joined them in the corridor. 'He asked you, what's happened?' he snapped.

The officer shook his head. 'Murdered,' he sighed. 'Butchered in his quarters.'

'Who?' Mark asked.

'Who?' the officer answered. 'Who? Our commander, that is who. Colonel Fu is dead.'

The soldiers' grew more sullen, but Tang glared them into silence. He turned to the officer.

'Control yourself,' he said, his voice crisp. 'The colonel was a soldier and soldiers die. Now we must know who has taken command.'

'Who are you to question me?' the officer snorted. 'Return to your quarters immediately.'

He stationed two soldiers outside Fu's apartment then he turned and stamped away. The remainder of his soldiers followed.

Tang spoke to Mark. 'Fu must have had a deputy,' he said. 'Someone to take over should he fall.' His lips formed a humourless smile. 'But I bet he didn't expect to fall like this.' He jerked his head towards their own quarters. 'We must talk,' he whispered.

Inside their room, Tang shut the door.

'Meng's behind this,' he said. 'It can't be anyone else. Your parole agreement was with the colonel, was it not?'

'It was,' Mark answered. 'So what?'

'So, it's time to un-give your promise.'

Mark's brow furrowed. 'Yes, you're right,' he said. 'But why haven't they raised the alarm?'

Tang opened the door a crack and checked the corridor. He turned back to Mark.

'They're paralyzed,' he whispered. 'Without orders, no one knows what to do.' His lips formed a wry smile. 'If Meng seizes command too quickly, everyone will know he's behind the killing. If he waits too long, someone might beat him to it.'

Mark nodded. 'We must move quickly,' he said, 'but...'

Tang banged his fist against the wall. 'But what?' he demanded. He threw a nervous look at the door. 'But what?' he whispered.

'My... my father,' Mark stammered, 'and Mei. I won't leave them.'

'There's no time,' Tang hissed. 'Meng won't harm the garrison doctor.'

'He was willing to burn the garrison doctor yesterday,' Mark snapped back. 'Think man, he's insane. He's just murdered his own commander.'

There was a tight silence then Mark waved towards the door. 'Go if you must,' he said. 'I'll follow later.'

Tang rolled his eyes. 'Very well,' he groaned. 'We bring your father and the woman. But if they dither, we leave them. Agreed?' He frowned and his voice hardened. '*Agreed?*'

Mark nodded. 'Agreed,' he said.

He was growing accustomed to telling lies.

Doctor James Falchion spread his arms as Mark and Tang entered the apothecary.

'My boy, my boy,' he cried. 'And you, Lieutenant Tang. They told me you were free but I couldn't be sure. Mei, come see who's here.'

'Father.' Mark's voice was hushed. 'We must leave right away.'

James Falchion started to speak but Mark held up his hand. 'There's no time to waste,' he said. 'Colonel Fu's dead and Meng will seize command. We must leave before the Taipings come to their senses.'

James Falchion did not move.

'I'll carry you if I must,' Mark snapped.

'My... my instruments,' Doctor Falchion looked around as

though searching for something. 'And Mei. We can't leave Mei.'

'Nor shall we, Father. Call her.'

'Colonel Fu? Dead?' Mei stood framed in the storeroom doorway. Her face was pale. Her eyes were puffy.

She seems so vulnerable thought Mark, so alone. He wanted to reach out and cradle away her fear.

'Yes, lady,' he said. 'I'm sorry. He was my enemy but he was a good officer.'

Doctor Falchion took Mei's arm and steered her to the door. 'Come,' he said. 'We must leave.'

Mei pressed down the doctor's hands. 'What are you doing?' she demanded. 'Why must we go?'

Doctor Falchion ran his fingers through his hair. 'Forgive me,' he said. 'I'm not thinking straight.' He turned to Mark. 'Well, Mark, what's your plan?'

'*Plan?*' The word exploded from Mark's lips. 'We leave and I cut down anyone who gets in the way. That's the plan. Now come.'

Doctor Falchion backed away. 'No thank you, my boy,' he said. 'I'd rather take my chances with Meng.'

'You might get that chance sooner than you want.' Mark snapped back. He forced himself to lower his voice. 'Father, I mean no disrespect but Meng might be on the way right now and he bears no love for any of us.'

Tang held up his hand for silence. 'The doctor's right,' he said. 'Impatience serves the enemy. We need a plan.'

The room became hushed. Doctor James Falchion was first to speak. 'We can't stay here. I'm amazed they haven't sounded the alarm.' He scratched his chin and a slow smile touched his lips. 'I have it, my boy. I know a place where Meng won't find us.'

Mei's voice was urgent. 'Then you must go there, go now.'

'Yes, of course. And you will come too,' Doctor Falchion said.

'Hurry, we'll be safe with...'

'Tell me nothing,' Mei snapped. 'Just go. *Go!*'

'This is no time for a woman's folly,' Tang growled. 'Remember our agreement.'

Mark took Mei's hands and thrilled as her grip tightened on his. He put his face close to hers. Her breath was warm and soft on his cheek. A hint of jasmine lingered in her hair.

'Lady,' he said, 'now I have found you, I will not leave you.'

Mei's lips trembled. 'You do not understand,' she said. 'I cannot...'

Mark cupped his hand against Mei's cheek 'There is much I have to say to you,' he whispered.

Mei's voice was husky. 'And I to you,' she answered. She looked up into Mark's eyes then her arms were about his neck and her lips were pressing hard against his. For moment she clung to him then she released him and stepped away. She screwed shut her eyes and shook her head.

'There are things you do not know,' she said. 'Please believe me, I never told him anything bad.'

'Told who?' Mark asked. He shook his head. 'What do you mean?'

Mei lowered her eyes. 'My commander is... my commander *was* Colonel Fu.' She levelled her gaze on Mark. 'You must go now. Go to your safe place.'

She hurried to the door then paused. 'There will be a battle,' she said. 'I have... I have my duty. My comrades... they...they need me.'

For a moment, her eyes and Mark's eyes locked. She pressed her fingertips against her lips then she slipped through the door and was gone.

Tang drew his sword and strode across the room.

'Why didn't you stop her?' he demanded. 'She'll bring

the whole garrison down on us.' He threw open the door and scanned the lane. It was empty.

Mark shook his head like someone trying to understand a private joke.

'Comrades?' he asked. 'What did she mean?'

Tang rounded on him. 'Are you blind, addled or both?' he snapped. 'She is Taiping. She has taken us for fools.'

'She will say nothing,' Doctor Falchion declared. 'I'll stake my life on it.'

Tang glared at him. 'Aye. And ours too.'

For a moment, there was silence then Doctor Falchion spoke. 'There's a wine brewer nearby. He's a good man with no love for the Taipings.'

'A brewer inside a Taiping base? Never,' Tang snorted.

'The soldiers are on garrison alert,' Doctor Falchion answered. 'They've neither the time nor the men to root him out.' He fussed Mark and Tang to the door. 'We must get to the brewer's house, we'll have time to think there.'

He bundled them into the lane. They lowered their heads and hurried to the house of Yap the brewer.

Steam filled the brewer's house. It condensed on walls and over the years, had streaked them with mildew. A stone oven stood against one wall and on it, water boiled in a cauldron. Terracotta pots the height of a man stood against another wall and alongside them, bulging sacks rose from floor to ceiling. At the rear of the house, daylight trickled in through a warped door. Beside the door, a handcart stood with its tongue pointing at the rafters.

The brewer himself had a neck so short, his head perched on his shoulders like a pumpkin on a barrel. He had thick arms and the rolling gait of an old sailor. Silver stubble covered his jowls but there was no trace of silver in his hair. Some whispered that he darkened it with lampblack.

As soon as Mark ducked under the brewer's lintel, sweat glistened on his cheeks and brow.

'Hot, isn't it?' Yap the brewer said. He sidled closer to Mark.

'The secret to good wine is in the ingredients,' he declared. He scratched his belly through his tunic. 'You can't beat Kiangsu rice and sweet spring water brought all the way from Mokan Mountain.'

Doctor Falchion wafted his hand in front of his face. 'Sweet water all the way from Sungkiang's moat more like.'

Yap shrugged. 'Maybe, but after a cup or two, who cares?'

The doctor's expression became earnest. 'Do you go to the market today, my friend?'

'At the western gate? Of course, there will be men of quality there. They live upcountry and appreciate good wine.'

'Men of quality they may be,' the doctor said, 'but they must have bronze kidneys.'

Yap inclined his head to the doctor's companions. 'You and your friends seem fearful.' He squinted at James Falchion. 'I think you need more from me than wine.'

'I have a big ask, my friend,' Doctor Falchion said. 'Can your pots carry more than wine?'

'They can,' the brewer said. He touched his neck. 'But this is the only head I have and I've grown fond of it.'

'You're right,' the doctor sighed. 'I ask too much.'

Yap the brewer looked down at the floor. 'You cared for me when no others would.' He tried to stifle a smile. 'The wine must have pickled my brain,' he chuckled. 'I shall let this new batch age an extra day.'

Doctor Falchion smiled and clasped the brewer's shoulder.

Yap looked at the doctor with sad eyes.

# THE SCHOLAR'S BLADE

'You realise there is room on my cart for just two pots.'

'For pity's sake,' the doctor croaked. 'We can leave no one behind. Surely you can manage one more pot.'

Yap shook his head. 'No,' he said. 'The cart is too small and even if it were not, the guards know me. They're not stupid, an extra pot would alert them.'

Doctor Falchion nodded and folded his arms across his chest. 'I will stay,' he declared.

'No!' Mark snapped. 'If one stays, we all do.'

'You've a poor memory,' Tang growled. 'It was agreed, if they dither we leave them.'

Mark whirled on Tang. 'Then I shall dither,' he snapped. 'There's room for you. Go, save your skin.'

Tang glared at Mark and clenched his fists.

Mark squared his shoulders, his breath was harsh and shallow.

The brewer stepped between them.

'Steady, brothers,' he said. 'Your feud serves only the Taipings. There must be another way. Maybe you can draw lots...' His voice tailed away.

Mark chewed his lip. The only sound was the crackle of the fire and the water bubbling in the cauldron.

Tang took a sharp breath. 'There is another way,' he said. He laid his hand on the cart's bed and a slow smile cracked his lips. 'A laden cart is heavy and our friend the brewer grows feeble on his own wine.'

Yap's brow furrowed then he too smiled.

'Yes, of course,' he said. 'The cart gets heavier as I grow older. Maybe it's time I had some help.' He looked Tang over. 'What say you? Will you pull the cart? Barbarians don't have the strength for honest work.'

Tang threw back his head and his rolling laugh filled the

room.

'So, today I'm a coolie who must pull a wine cart,' he said. 'This way of soldiering is strange indeed.'

Yap looked from the doctor to Mark and then to Tang.

'Contraband wine, a Manchu officer and two barbarians,' he sighed. 'And me with only one head to lose.' He scratched his belly. 'I must be drunk or mad,' he said. 'Perhaps I am both. Now, help me load the pots.'

In the lanes close to the Western gate, chatter, shouts and the rumble of ironbound wheels blended into a hubbub of frustration and desperation. There were traders with goods piled on handcarts. Others struggled under bamboo yokes loaded with ironware, oils and lacquer goods. Seeking only the safety of the lands beyond the walls, there were families with their backs bent under the weight of whatever possessions they could carry.

The crowd pressed hard against the wine cart. On the cart's bed, two wine pots swayed and banged together. Lieutenant Tang and brewer Yap leaned into the cart's yoke but progress was slow. Yap wore his usual grubby tunic. Tang wore a coolie's breechclout and a conical hat of woven rattan. His upper body was bare.

As they neared the archway leading to the West gate courtyard, the crowds forced the wine cart to yet another standstill. Lieutenant Tang tried to peer over the heads of the crowd but could not see what was causing the holdup.

The crowd edged forward, then stopped, then moved again.

Tang and the brewer edged their way into the West gate courtyard but found that, too, jammed with people.

Now Tang could see the town's outer gate standing open. Beyond it, a bridge led across the moat to a bustling marketplace.

A soldier wearing jade-green stood by the gate. He held his

spear with its haft resting on the paving. His eyes narrowed as they fell on Tang.

Without thinking, Tang reached for his sword and swore under his breath when he remembered it was inside the wine pot with Mark Falchion. He looked around the courtyard, searching for other Taipings but there were none.

'One sentry?' he snorted. 'All this charade for one sentry?'

Yap licked his lips and cast his eyes about. 'One sentry down here,' he whispered. 'Many more on the parapet. *Don't look!*'

The crowd again pressed around them, forcing them to yet another standstill.

'Make way,' Yap called. 'Make way for the finest soy sauce in Kiangsu Province.'

'Hold, soy sauce trader.' The sentry stepped forward, blocking their way.

Tang pulled the brim of his hat lower and turned away his face.

'And how is your Excellency this day?' Yap fawned.

'I am well, thank you,' the sentry answered. His tone was light. 'Wait a moment for the bridge to clear.'

'I will, Excellency,' Yap replied. 'We must be careful, it's the only bridge we have left.'

'You have a new worker,' the sentry commented. 'He looks like he could do the work of ten.'

Yap sidled close to the sentry. 'He's strong, but he's a stupid lump. I employ him for the sake of his mother.' He put his finger to his temple and made circular motions.

The sentry waved them forward. 'The bridge is clear,' he said. 'You may cross.'

Yap bobbed his head and took his place at the yoke. He nudged Tang in the ribs. 'You heard the general,' he said. 'Push, you woodenheaded ox.'

Tang flashed the brewer a scowl. He leaned against the yoke and the cart eased forward.

Behind them, the crowd began to chatter, happy to be moving again. Then boots hammered on the flagstones and the chatter became a resentful murmur. Someone was shouting but the words were in a foreign tongue.

The sentry held up his hand and again blocked the way.

'Excellency,' Yap wheedled, 'I must get my goods to market before my customers head for home.'

'Wait.' The sentry's voice was uncertain. He peered over Yap's head. 'It's a barbarian,' he said, 'and one of Meng's thugs.' He craned his neck then scowled. 'It's the Prussian. I do not know the other.' He grimaced and spat on the flagstones.

They watched as Schneider cuffed aside a trader who blocked his way. His black-uniformed companion used the haft of his spear to club aside another. When they came level with the wine cart, the Prussian's breathing was harsh and his face was red. He took a moment to regain his breath then pointed at the gate and barked a command.

'What do they want, General?' Yap asked, trying to keep the panic from his voice.

'How should I know?' the guard answered. 'I don't understand barbarian gabble.'

Schneider put his face inches from the sentry's. His voice rose to a shout. His spittle flecked the sentry's cheek.

'He *commands* you to close the gate,' Schneider's companion, the soldier Wu Ren, translated.

The sentry's eyes narrowed. 'Who is he to command here?' he asked through clenched teeth.

'He's a barbarian,' Wu Ren replied, his voice like oil. 'Barbarians think we Chinese are dogs fit only to do their bidding.' He leaned on his spear and smiled, like someone enjoying a street performance.

'I'll spill his guts...' The sentry's head snapped back as Schneider backhanded him across the cheek.

'*Wah!* I bet that stung,' Wu Ren gloated. 'Do yourself a favour and shut the gate.'

The sentry stood his ground. His eyes flashed, his breathing was slow and heavy.

'Your barbarian is close to having his guts spilled,' he snorted. 'Tell him I take my orders from Colonel Fu.'

Schneider made to strike the sentry again. Then his eyes fell on the muscular coolie bent over the handcart's yoke. He squinted at Tang and his eyes widened. He pointed his sabre at Tang and roared, '*MANCHU!*'

Fear rippled through the crowd. They moved back, forming a broad circle.

Wu Ren and the sentry snapped their spears into the attack position. The sun dazzled off their spear points.

'Take your choice, Manchu,' Wu Ren snarled. 'Stand fast or die. I don't care which.'

A slow smile spread across Schneider's lips. He rapped his sabre against the nearest wine pot.

'*Herauskommen liebling,*' he called. He rested the sabre's blade on his shoulder and put his foot on the cart's wheel. 'I will not wait long,' he said. 'If you do not come out, your comrade will suffer a most unpleasant fate.'

There was a scraping noise as first one, then the second wine pot lid fell away. Mark levered himself through the pot's neck and dropped onto the cart's bed.

Schneider backed away from the cart and beckoned with his arm for Mark to step down. '*Kommen sei, leibling,*' he chortled. 'Captain Meng will want a long chat with you, *ja?*'

Mark moved to obey then he staggered and seemed about to

fall. He steadied himself against a rope securing the pot then gave its slipknot a tug. He put his shoulder to the pot and it crashed to the courtyard floor, smashing into scattered shards. Lying among the pot's remnants were Mark's *dao* and Tang's cavalry sword.

Mark leapt from the cart and snatched them up. He tossed the cavalry sword to Tang but Wu Ren snagged it with his spear. As Tang's sword clattered to the ground, Wu Ren put his foot on the hilt.

Tang put down his head and charged. He barrelled into Wu Ren, barging him aside. He snatched up his sword

Wu Ren staggered then recovered. He prodded his spear at Tang, holding him at bay.

The sentry moved closer to Wu Ren and side by side, they backed into the gate's archway where the stonework protected their flanks. Their faces were hard. Their spear points glittered.

Tang moved left, then right, probing for a way through their guard.

Mark swung round to face Schneider. He slid the *dao* from its scabbard. The sun caught the blade, making the honed steel gleam.

With his free hand, Schneider beckoned to Wu Ren and the sentry but Tang had them trapped in the archway. The Prussian's eyes flickered to the battlements.

'*Komm schnell,*' he shouted. 'Get down here, *now!*'

On the battlements, a soldier leaned on his spear and watched with indolent amusement.

Schneider turned to face Mark. He held his sabre stiff armed before him. He took a step back but the cart blocked his way. His cheeks paled; his eyes stared wide.

Mark heard his own voice, soft and low. 'I think, *Captain*, you are afraid.'

Schneider sucked in a breath. He bared his teeth. He shouted,

'*Et la,*' and lunged, driving the point of his sabre hard at Mark's chest.

Mark swung the *dao* in a quarter circle. His blade rang against the sabre, knocking it aside.

Schneider flattened his back against the cart. His eyes darted left and right.

'There is no escape.' Mark's voice was a hoarse whisper. He feinted right then flicked the blade left, slicing into Schneider's sword arm.

Pain twisted the Prussian's face. Blood spread like spilt wine, soaking his shirt. He gripped the wound with his free hand and his sabre clattered against the courtyard flagstones.

'*Falchion!*'

At the sound of Tang's voice, Mark span round and dropped to a crouch. Wu Ren's spear passed inches above his head and thudded into the cart's side-panel.

His own spear gone, Wu Ren rounded on the sentry and tried to wrest away his spear. He did not see Tang draw back his sword arm. Did not see the strength behind the throw. Did not see the Manchurian cavalry sword as it came tumbling towards him. The sword blade crunched home, shattering Wu Ren's breastbone. He gasped and fell without another sound.

Schneider's legs trembled and he dropped to one knee. He spoke through gritted teeth.

'*Nicht mehr,*' he gasped. 'No more.' He nodded towards the sentry who now stood alone. 'Kill that one and go.'

For a moment, he was silent then he looked into Mark's face and gave a harsh laugh. 'You go and I will stay.' He grasped the cart's side panel and dragged himself to his feet. '*Ja.* I will stay, my wound will heal and I will have the woman. I will have her again and again and again. Then I will give her to Meng's pet dog, Shan. And he will have her again and again.'

A chill calm wrapped itself around Mark. He stepped closer to Schneider. His words were a soft growl.

'Mei will be safe from you.'

Through his pain, Schneider leered at Mark. 'Safe? Why use such a word? She will love every moment.'

Then he looked into Mark's eyes and dreadful realisation flashed across his face.

The *dao* cut a silver arc and Schneider staggered, clutching his neck. Blood spurted from between his fingers. His eyes bulged. His mouth worked but there was no sound. He dropped to his knees then toppled face down onto the flagstones. His head jerked as though he was trying to catch his breath. Then he was still.

The sentry's eye flicked from Tang, to Mark, to Schneider's dead form, then back to Tang. He licked his lips. He sucked in a deep breath. His eyes narrowed. He levelled his spear. He took a step closer to Tang.

From the cart bed, Doctor Falchion's voice called to them.

'Put up your sword, Mark,' he ordered. 'And you, Lieutenant, stand down. The last time I saw our young friend, he'd been performing, what should I say? Unofficial spear practice?'

The doctor struggled to free himself from the wine pot. He called to the sentry.

'Come here young man,' he said. 'Help me out of this thing then tell me how mends your comrade's injured leg.'

The sentry cast down his eyes.

'Come along,' the doctor called again. 'I feel ridiculous up here.'

The sentry's cheeks reddened. He lay his spear on the ground and shouldered past Mark. He clambered onto the cart then reached out and grasped Doctor Falchion's hand.

Freed from the wine pot, the doctor slapped grime from his

shirt. 'Thank you,' he said. 'So, tell me, how is your comrade's wound?'

'It knits well, doctor. That day, you saved the life of my best friend.' The sentry shook his head. 'Doctor... what... why are you here, like this?'

'There's no time, my friend,' the doctor answered. 'Help me down from here.'

Slow realisation spread through the crowd that the courtyard was now unguarded. A man made a dash for the gate. Another followed. Then more. As the sentry and Doctor Falchion clambered down from the cart, the crowd became a wide-eyed, clamouring, shouting, crushing mass of people. They surged between Mark and Doctor Falchion, separating them and pinning Doctor Falchion against the cart. Mark reached for his father's hand but the crowd carried Mark away.

The sentry tugged the spear from the cart's side. He tried to use it as a barrier to stem the flow of people but the crowd just surged around him. Then, with the doctor hanging onto his tunic, he clubbed and elbowed his way through to Mark and Tang.

He put his head close to Mark's. 'Hurry,' he said. 'Before my officer sends soldiers from the wall.'

He pointed up to the battlement walkway where soldiers wearing jade-green were gathering near the ramp leading down to the courtyard.

'They'll have your head for this,' Doctor Falchion said. 'Come with us.'

'A barbarian and one of Meng's cockroaches,' the sentry spat. 'For this, my officer will make me top soldier. Now go, I'll tell them you fled back into town.'

'Do not be foolish, young man,' the doctor pleaded. 'For this, you will die.'

Mark raised the *dao* and clubbed the pommel hard against the sentry's temple. The sentry went down, blood matting his hair.

'He should be safe now,' Mark said. 'Come, we must hurry.' He took his father's arm and pulled him onto the bridge.

The doctor, the Manchurian soldier and the golden-haired warrior merged into the throngs bustling among the clutter of market stalls.

And then they were gone.

# 26

'EASY,' VINCENTE Macanaya called from the riverbank. *'Maingat!* Careful now. *Easy!'*

Dangling from a makeshift derrick, the barrel of a twelve-pounder field gun gleamed in the light of a dozen torch brands. A nervous recruit guided it with a rope, double looped around the muzzle and breech. Behind him, a section of Filipinos dug in their heels and hauled on the derrick-line.

'Haul her up,' Vincente bawled. 'Sergeant Ramirez, let me hear the timing,'

The sergeant filled his lungs and began to chant, '*Isa-dalawa-TATLO. Isa-dalawa-TATLO.'*

Ten days, Vincente mused, ten days and nights of non-stop recruiting and this was the best of them. They were the scrapings of Shanghai's grog shops and doss houses. There were drunks, brawlers and gamblers on the dodge from moneylenders. There were sailors plied with liquor and dumped on the Shanghai wharves by sailing masters keen to save the company payroll.

'Damn all sailing masters,' Vincente muttered. 'And damn night exercises.' And where in *Santo Nino's* name is Ward?

There was the tang of cigar smoke and Ward emerged from the night.

'How goes it, old friend?' he asked.

'Colonel?' Vincente said. 'How did you get past the sentries?'

'Sentries?' Ward raised an eyebrow.

Vincente groaned and rolled his eyes.

There was a creak from the derrick followed by a shout and the sound of wood splintering. Vincente pulled Ward clear and a rope hissed past their heads. The derrick teetered then toppled, dumping the twelve-pounder into the river.

The sergeant bellowed at the recruits. A man protested and the sergeant clubbed him to the ground with his fist.

'*Belay that!*' Ward yelled. He turned to Vincente. 'Should I ask how it's going?'

Vincente sighed and shook his head.

'Will they be ready by the sixteenth?'

Vincente frowned. 'I hope so, Colonel,' he answered. 'The Taipings at Sungkiang are veterans.'

Ward drew on his cigar. 'They must be ready,' he said. 'I'll not send men to their deaths because we didn't train them properly.'

Vincente gave a weary nod. 'They'll be ready, Colonel,' he said. 'With *Santa Nino's* blessing and Vincente's boot up their backsides, they'll be ready.'

Ward grasped Vincente's arm. 'If you say they'll be ready, old friend, that's good enough for me.' He walked into the dark, leaving only the smell of his cigar.

Vincente turned to the sergeant. '*Sarhento,*' he called. 'Get that derrick re-rigged and put men in the water. I want that field gun on shore within the hour.'

When he spoke again, it was to himself. 'Then we'll see about preparing these men to enter hell.'

At dusk, Mark Falchion, the doctor and Lieutenant Tang crouched in the reeds growing close to the waterway's bank.

'More foolishness,' the lieutenant grumbled. 'How many nights have we come here to wait? We don't know if Ward will come tonight. We don't know if he will come at all.'

'Ward will come,' Mark answered. 'And he must come soon. He's working to a deadline.'

'Why here?' Tang demanded. 'Why this very spot?'

'Colonel Fu knew why,' Mark said. 'Ward must attack from the east and this is the best place to unload men and equipment.' He flashed a rueful smile. 'I had some respect for Fu but his death serves us well. If he was alive, he'd have a strong force waiting here to ambush Ward.'

Tang gave a noncommittal grunt and turned away.

For a moment, the sky turned deep crimson then the sun dipped below the skyline and was gone. Tendrils of mist rose from the water and crept among the reeds. The air was still. All was silent but for the night chorus of cicadas and marsh frogs.

Mark slipped the *dao* from his shoulders and found a dry section of embankment to stretch out. He closed his eyes. For a moment it was as if their time in Sungkiang was just a vivid dream. Sharp and terrible, but too terrible to be real. He tried to let the fears and pain slip away but the memories were fixed hard, as if with iron nails.

*We're out!* he told himself. We're out and we're safe. Safe for now, he reminded himself, but soon, we must go back in.

And then, no one will be safe.

'They're here.'

'*What?*' Mark realised he must have slept. Lieutenant Tang loomed over him.

'I said, they're here,' Tang whispered. 'Wake yourself.'

A dark shape lay close to the bank. Mark rubbed the sleep from his eyes and squinted into the gloom. The dark shape took the form of a river steamer. Now, her paddles were still and her engine was silent.

Along *Dancer's* side railings, Filipino troopers palmed their carbines into the half cock. Men with mooring lines slipped from the deck and splashed into the shallows. A plank trundled through the gangway and onto the shore. Mark, Doctor Falchion and Lieutenant Tang clambered aboard. Hooded running lights flared at the gangway, silhouetting a figure. There was the smell of cigar smoke and a voice called out in a New England accent.

'Mark, my boy, we'd just about given you up.'

Ward clamped his cigar tight between his teeth and pumped Mark's hand. '*Darn*, it's good to have you back.' He turned to Tang. 'And the redoubtable Lieutenant,' he said. 'It's wonderful to see you alive, sir.'

Tang squinted at Mark. 'What's he saying?' he growled.

'He says he's glad you're not dead,' Mark replied. He grinned and punched Tang's shoulder. 'Don't worry,' he said. 'You'll soon change his mind.'

Vincente appeared on deck and took Mark in a crushing bear hug.

'*Santa Nino* be praised,' he cried as Mark gasped for breath. He released Mark and turned to Tang, his arms spread wide.

Tang stepped back and balled his fist.

'Vincente, take Lieutenant Tang below and kit him out,' Ward chuckled.

Vincente clasped Tang's shoulder and signalled for him to follow. There was the rattle of a deck hatch and the two men disappeared into *Dancer's* belly.

'Colonel.' Mark's voice was formal. 'May I present my father, Doctor James Falchion. Father, this is Colonel Ward of whom I spoke.'

'You've raised a fine boy, doctor.' Ward said shaking Doctor Falchion's hand. His tone became sombre. 'But now I have need of him. Lieutenant Patterson will show you the day cabin.'

'This way, sir,' a voice called. A burly man with a weathered face stepped from the shadows. Dark patches on his sleeve showed where there had once been sergeant's stripes. New officer's insignia gleamed at his collar. He flashed a grin and gestured to the deck hatch.

'Mind yer 'ead on the companionway, sir.'

Troopers piled boxes by the gangway. Others scraped sharpening stones along the edges of bayonets and machetes. Mark passed his eyes over the troopers at the railing.

'The unit seems ready for anything, Colonel,' he said.

'It's been a tough road but they're ready,' Ward answered. 'They're itching to go but there's not many of us, just two hundred. Two hundred against how many?'

Mark lowered his voice. 'Two and a half thousand,' he said. 'But they're understrength. They can't man all the defences.'

'And we have surprise on our side,' Ward said. 'What's more, the mysterious Mister Hung promises nine thousand Blue Standard infantrymen.' He frowned. 'But they won't move until we breach the defences and even then... well... they're a disheartened bunch.' He was silent for a while, then he became businesslike. 'So, young feller, tell me about our enemy.'

Mark spoke of the crisis left by Colonel Fu's murder.

'The Taipings are battle hardened,' he said. 'But they've taken the killing badly. Fu was respected; the new man's insane. He rules by fear.'

Ward gave a sharp nod. 'Good,' he said. 'Soldiers who fear their commander are slow to grasp the initiative.' He sucked on his cigar and the tip glowed red. His voice became hushed. 'How did they treat our prisoners?' he asked.

Mark lowered his eyes. 'Not well,' he sighed. 'The only survivor was Schneider.'

Ward's voice hardened. 'And?'

'His defection didn't save him.'

For a moment, Ward's breath was hard and heavy then he became businesslike.

'But let's get to the matter in hand.' he said. 'What can you tell me of their defences?'

Mark told Ward of the howitzers and of the lack of crenelated battlements. He left the town gates until last.

Ward frowned. 'Ironbound teak, you say. And we can't bring our guns to bear on the inner gate. *Damn.*' He turned to Vincente. 'How much reserve powder do we carry?'

Vincente shrugged. 'An army can never have enough powder,' he replied. 'Just tell me how much you want.'

Ward grinned. 'Excellent, we'll need plenty. Open the sail locker and set the crew to stitching haversacks.' He clamped the cigar between his teeth. 'Pack 'em tight and cut fuses for the ignitor charges. Sixty seconds, no more.' He strode to the gangway then paused. 'On second thoughts,' he called, 'make that thirty seconds.'

The hatch swung open and Tang clambered on deck. He wore a tunic of forest green and black britches tucked into infantry boots. He was bareheaded and his tunic was unbuttoned. His sword hung from a strap draped across his shoulder.

'You look like a pirate,' Mark chortled.

'Then we are a good match,' Tang snapped back. He tugged at the front of his tunic. 'Their uniforms are for dwarfs and children,' he grumbled, 'and they want me to wear green headgear. *Green.* Am I a cuckold who wears a green hat?'

'Hello, Mark.'

Mark looked into a solemn face topped by a mop of ginger hair. For several seconds he stared at Harry Jessop.

Jessop looked at the deck then raised his eyes to Mark's. 'Mark, I...'

Mark's voice was a hard whisper. 'Say nothing, Harry,' he

said. 'Just pray no one leaves you out there to die.' He turned and strode down the gangplank.

On the bank, Lo Haak stood waiting. 'This is a fine looking force,' he said. 'Where are the rest?'

'An Imperial force will join us at Sungkiang,' Mark answered. He shrugged. 'But only after we've breached the gate.'

'*Imperials?*' Lo Haak spat. 'You'd do better with a covey of women.' He grasped Mark's shoulders. 'I'm glad I killed Mouse,' he declared. 'The ancient spirit of *Kwan Yue* guided my heart as well as my hand.' His grip became tighter. 'Make sure the Taipings don't finish the job Mouse started.' He landed Mark a light punch on the chest then turned and walked into the night.

In ones and twos, sampans came to the embankment to board men and gear. Lying close by *Dancer*, impromptu rafts made from lashed together sampans prepared to receive the field guns. There was the squeal of pulleys as the first twelve-pounder swung out over the water. The Boatman cried out as the gun scraped against makeshift decking and the raft settled deeper in the water.

Mark clambered aboard a sampan. Troopers grinned and made room for him. Each had a Sharps carbine gripped between his knees. One waved a machete before Mark's face and chattered in his native tongue. Mark understood just one word: '*Taiping.*' The sampan rocked as Tang took his place. The boatman took station at the stern and leaned on his sweep.

'Sungkiang,' he called.

'*Hau, Sungkiang,*' Mark answered.

The boatman shook his head and muttered, '*Fung huan,*' as he sculled away from the bank.

Mark smiled, *fung huan*: crazy men. He slipped the *dao* from his shoulders and leaned back against the gunwale. The sampan slid into the night. The troopers chattered until their sergeant growled them into silence.

Mark Falchion gripped tight to his sword and tried not to think of what lay at their journey's end.

It was bad, Cho Lung thought, very bad. Colonel Fu was dead and everyone knew who was responsible. Would Fu's men seek revenge? He toted the odds: Fu's regiment was two and a half thousand strong, the Black Dragons a mere one hundred.

Cho frowned, indeed, it was very bad.

And what about General Kong? He would have heads for that night's work. Cho prayed his head would not be one of them. He looked into the night but his eyes were not what they had once been.

'Anything?' he asked the soldier standing next to him.

The soldier shook his head. 'Nothing,' he said. 'All quiet here.'

'Good,' Cho grunted. 'Stay alert, they will come soon.'

Cho continued to pace the battlements. Soldiers watched him as he passed but he was oblivious to them. He had always known Meng was crazy, but this? Yes, he thought, it's bad. Either the foreigner will come with his cannon or General Kong Liu will come with his provosts.

And Cho did not know who to fear the most.

A mile from Sungkiang, the sampans nudged into the shallows. In silence, men raised tripods and swung the big guns ashore. Under the quartermaster's glare, troopers unloaded cartons of roundshot, canister and grapeshot. There were barrels of gunpowder, ropes, and ladders. Squat boxes carried spare carbine ammunition. Piled alongside them were canvas haversacks, some trailing a short fuse.

Vincente massaged his backside, it felt like he had been on the little boat all night. There was some relief, though. During the last half-hour a mist had risen from the water and spread across the grasslands. He allowed himself a glow of pride as he watched his Filipinos. The dross of Shanghai's grog shops now moved with the easy confidence of soldiers.

He left his troopers and went looking for Ward. He found him in council with Harry Jessop and the bandit leader, Lo Haak. Mark Falchion was acting as translator. Ward was on one knee, studying a map by the beam of a hooded lamp. The light shadowed his eyes, making him look old.

'According to our guide, we're here.' Ward stabbed his finger onto the map. He turned and made a chopping motion with his forearm. 'And Sungkiang's a mile that way.' He stood and brushed grass from his trousers. 'The mist is our friend,' he continued, 'but unless we keep a tight grip, our boys will be spread all over this plain. Comments?'

The others stayed silent.

'Right gentlemen,' Ward said, 'order of march: headquarters on point, artillery next, then the troopers in five columns. I want your best sergeants at the flanks and rear.'

There was a murmur of assent.

'Quartermaster's stores go with the artillery,' Ward said. 'Mister Falchion and Mister Tang...' Ward looked for Mark and Tang. 'You two stick with me. Questions? No? Excellent. Douse the lamp. Where the hell's Vincente?'

'Here, Colonel.'

'Issue thirty rounds per man. And from here on, no lights, no talking, no smoking. Report back when the men are ready.'

'They've never been more ready, Colonel,' Vincente said.

'Capital!' Ward declared. He slapped his cane against his thigh. 'This time, we'll give the Taipings a flogging they won't forget.'

Gunners gritted their teeth and strained at the limbers. The carriage wheels creaked and the guns rolled forward. There was the clink of equipment and the rustle of men moving through grass.

No one spoke as the troopers moved away from the creek and into the mist.

Dressed in the yellow silk of Lady Yen's archers, Mei felt a renewed sense of belonging as she walked the parapet of Sungkiang's east wall. Her Mongolian bow was slung across her back. A quiver of arrows and an ornamental dagger hung from her belt.

A night mist had drifted in from the land surrounding the town. It shrouded the battlements and she did not see the soldier until she drew close to him. He rounded on her and levelled his spear.

'Stand!' he bellowed.

Mei fixed him with a hard glare. 'Your uniform is jade-green,' she snapped. 'But are you Fu's man or Meng's?'

'Who are you to question me?' The soldier's eyes narrowed. 'Are you Meng's lackey, sent to test me?'

Mei stepped closer to him. 'Where's your officer?' she demanded.

'Arrested,' the soldier answered. 'Anyone who questions Meng's authority is taken.' He shook his head. 'I can't have a shit without Meng's approval.'

'Meng can't be everywhere,' Mei said. 'Who's assigning duties?'

'The same person who's assigning my rest period,' the soldier grumbled.

Mei frowned. 'Very well,' she said. 'I'm attaching myself to this unit.' She grasped the hilt of her dagger. 'Do you object?' Her voice was chipped crystal.

'I don't know...' the soldier's words tailed off.

Mei peered over the balustrade but could see nothing. Then, from beyond the moat there was a shouted command. Through the mist it sounded thin and small. She leaned out as far as she could go but the mist hid everything.

From the east, there came a flat bang. Mei and the soldier dropped to a crouch. The soldier gave a self-conscious smile. 'It's only Meng exercising his howitzers,' he said.

'That was no howitzer,' Mei hissed.

There was another bang and the battlements shuddered.

'It's started,' Mei gasped. The soldier did not move. Mei grabbed his tunic and shook him. 'It's started!' she barked. 'Get a grip of yourself, get a grip of your men. Stand to! *Stand to!*'

The soldier ran along the walkway, shouting orders and kicking shapeless forms nestled against the parapet.

From the eastern gate came more explosions. Mei drew her dagger but realised how ridiculous she looked. She screwed shut her eyes and took a slow breath.

It had started.

The twelve-pounder lurched back on its carriage. Its blast hammered Mark's ears. Its sulphur smell burnt his nostrils. The second twelve-pounder fired, then the six-pound guns. With each shot, the mist twitched and curled. Ball after ball battered the gate, throwing out splinters of teak and iron.

There was a wrenching groan and a section of gate toppled into the courtyard. Men ran forward, cheering like corsairs. They laid ladder bridges across the moat. Ward was first across. Troopers swarmed after him.

From the walls came the crackle of musketry. Waterspouts erupted around the makeshift bridges. A trooper cried out and splashed into the moat. A ladder broke, dumping troopers into the water. Their equipment dragged them under.

Mark and Tang half-ran, half-bounced across a ladder bridge. Head-down, they ran for the gate and clambered over slabs of splintered teak.

They paused in the shelter of the arch. Above them, a brazier flared. Orange light danced against the courtyard's north wall where the inner gate stood, strong and menacing.

'How many haversacks do you want, Colonel?' The voice was Vincente's.

'All of 'em,' Ward snapped. 'Plumb centre if you please.'

'All twenty?' Vincente gasped.

'We've one shot at this,' Ward said. 'Make it count, old friend.'

Vincente shouldered a haversack. 'You heard the colonel,' he shouted.

Mark and Tang each grabbed a haversack. Troopers took what remained. Crazy laughter bubbled in Mark's throat.

'Here's to a long life,' he croaked.

'Can't promise that,' Vincente answered. His eyes gleamed. 'But wherever we're going, the company's real good.' He raised an arm. 'Come brothers,' he roared. '*Salakayin!*'

They put down their heads and sprinted into the courtyard.

A volley crackled from the walls. Musket balls pecked at the flagstones. A man fell. His haversack rolled away. There were more shots. More men fell. Then Mark was jamming his haversack against the gate. There was the '*thwack*' of lead on teak. Splinters sliced Mark's cheek. More troopers crowded at the gate and added their haversacks to the pile.

'Not enough,' Vincente gasped. He pointed to the fallen troopers. 'I need those haversacks.'

Mark cast his eyes over the courtyard. The braziers' glow made it a hellish place. He could not count the bodies sprawled on the flagstones. A trooper ran to retrieve a haversack. A musket ball knocked him down. Mark gulped air then he was running to the nearest body. He tugged at the haversack but the trooper groaned. His eyes flicked open. Mark dropped to his knees beside him.

'Leave him!' Vincente yelled.

Mark waved Vincente away and pulled a field dressing from his tunic.

'I said, *leave him!*' There was murder in Vincente's voice.

Mark squeezed shut his eyes, blotting out the trooper's pain. He snatched up the haversack then sprinted back to the inner gate.

Vincente scraped a match against the flagstones. Fuses flared and spat a jet of flame. '*Go!*' he roared. '*Go! Go!*'

They zigzagged across the courtyard and barrelled through the outer gate arch.

As they hunkered down against the wall, the fuses touched off the charges. Flame jetted from the outer gate's archway like a giant cannon blast. The explosion numbed Mark's ears and jarred his bones.

Vincente ran along the crouching ranks of troopers, bellowing orders. He grabbed a man's tunic and hauled him up. Troopers ran back to the gate. Mark Falchion drew his sword and stumbled after them.

Dust and smoke filled Cho Lung's throat. It felt like a span of bullocks had trampled him. Shattered bodies lay everywhere. A soldier cowered behind the buttress. Cho dragged him to his feet then staggered along the battlements, checking for others hiding in the shadows.

Musket men in jade-green emerged from the dark. Cho nodded, for now muskets would keep the enemy occupied.

Later, bright steel would destroy them.

Ward's troopers crowded at the inner gate. Its teak face was blackened and scarred. Its iron bindings were twisted and sheared but still, it stood.

Musket balls spattered the flagstones and thudded into the teak. A trooper cried out and fell. Another clawed at his back and dropped to his knees.

Then there came the groaning rasp of tortured iron and the gate collapsed into the lane beyond.

'*Salakayin!*' Vincente roared.

'*Salakayin!*' the troopers answered.

The attackers clambered over the wrecked gate and surged into a broad avenue. Mark ran with them, cheering and holding the *dao* high.

As they rounded a corner, braziers flared on the town battlements and blocking their way, ranks of jade-green uniforms waited with levelled muskets. The crash of their volley hurled a dozen troopers to the ground.

Beside Mark, a voice called, 'To me, boys. *Form line!*' The voice was Ward's. His hair was wild and there was blood on his jacket.

'Front rank *kneel!*' Ward yelled.

The troopers formed two ranks. The front rank knelt; the rear rank stood. They plucked cartridges from their belts and thumbed them into their carbines.

Taipings measured powder into their musket barrels.

'*Load and present!*' Ward shouted.

From the Taiping line, there was the clatter of ramrods.

'*Fire!*' Ward cried.

The carbines banged. The Taiping frontline crumpled. Their muskets clattered onto the cobbles.

'*Fire at will,*' Ward cried.

There was a shot, then more. The shots merged into a

continuous thunder that numbed the ears and deadened the senses. The Taipings reeled back then turned and fled up a ramp leading to the battlements.

The troopers followed, cheering. Their cheeks were black with burnt powder. Their eyes glittered. There were crazed grins on their faces.

From the ramp's head, muzzle flashes winked and muskets banged. A trooper grunted and pitched forward. Another fell, clutching his shoulder.

A Sharps replied, then another. Individual shots grew into a rolling crescendo. Gun smoke billowed and swirled between the town wall and the tenements.

There was a roar of, *'Bayonets!'* Troopers snapped steel onto their carbines.

'Up, boys!' Ward shouted. 'Up and have 'em.'

The troopers roared, *'Salakayin!'*

Mark cried, *'Shaaaa!'*

And together, they surged up the ramp.

Laughter caught in Cho Lung's throat, the enemy was coming and they were coming with steel.

His men took a step back.

'Stand!' he bellowed. 'They cannot beat you, not with steel.'

He grabbed a man's tunic and propelled him down the ramp. The man faltered and ran back.

Cho drew his sword. 'Come brothers,' he bellowed. *'Charge!'*

He did not look back because in his heart, he knew none would follow. He raised his sword. He shouted his battle cry.

And alone, he charged the enemy bayonets.

Mark ran cheering up the ramp. A lone, black-uniformed Taiping broke ranks and charged. Bayonets pitchforked him aside.

The troopers crested the ramp. A wall of spears met them. A trooper screamed, spitted through the stomach. A Taiping thrust a spear at Mark. Mark knocked it aside and cut at the man behind it. He rejoiced as the *dao* sliced through flesh and bone. Hot blood spattered his face. He wanted to laugh and scream and kill. Around him, troopers fired from the hip then thrust with their bayonets. They were laughing and screaming and cursing.

'*Salakayin. Salakayin. Salakayin.*'

The Taipings took a pace back. The troopers pumped another volley into them. The Taiping front line turned and tried to fight through their own rear rank.

Ward's troopers knelt, fired, loaded and fired again.

There was a shout from the gate tower. Mark looked back to see pig-tailed Westerners levering Taiping guns round to bear on the battlement walkway. They hammered in blocks to raise the breeches and lower the barrels.

'Fall back!' Mark shouted. 'Fall back to the gate tower.'

The troopers ran for the shelter of the tower. There was the shuddering *thud* of a howitzer as first one, then two began the appalling task of clearing the battlements.

Finally, the guns were silent. Powder residue blackened Mark Falchion's face. Enemy blood caked his sword arm. His ears sang; his mouth was parched. He felt like a drained water-skin, empty and misshapen. Everywhere, the smell of sulphur and wood smoke mingled with the abattoir stench of blood. There was no escaping it. It drifted through the alleys, it clung to the buildings, it was on his clothes and on his skin.

Now, Mark walked alone through lanes and alleys littered with Taiping dead. He came to a plaza bounded on one side by the town's western wall. On the battlements, the last embers of a burning brazier cast a flickering glow.

A cluster of bodies lay close to the wall. Most wore uniforms of jade green. There were a few black tunics. A solitary figure wore yellow.

Mark quickened his pace. His heart bounded.

*Don't let it be her. Please God, not her.*

He knelt beside the body and gently, turned it over. A gash ran the length of her body. Blood had blackened the yellow silk and was already congealing, thick and dark on the plaza's flagstones.

Mark steeled himself, afraid to look at the face. When he did, joy filled his heart. It was not Mei. For a moment, a spark of shame punished his joy.

In the shadows, something moved. Mark rose to a half-crouch and pivoted, watching, listening. Was that a footfall?

There was a shimmer of black silk as a figure stepped from the gloom. A voice spoke in English.

'Mister Falchion. I knew this moment would come.'

Adrenalin coursed through Mark.

'Meng!'

Meng smiled and raised his hands, showing empty palms.

'Easy, Mister Falchion,' he said. 'Regretfully, I do not have the time to kill you today.' He gave a mocking half-bow. 'Your Colonel Ward is bold,' he said. His voice became bitter. 'Today, the victory is his and we must skulk away through a gate he lacks the men to guard.'

Mark nodded to the dead archer. 'I suppose this was your work,' he snarled. He reached over his shoulder and slid the *dao* from its scabbard. 'You'll not find me so easy. Get ready to defend yourself.'

'You misjudge me,' Meng purred. 'That killing was not mine.' With a flourish, he waved towards the shadows. 'Allow me to introduce my new top soldier.'

From the shadows stepped a Taiping soldier. He was tall and wore Meng's all black. Even in the gloom, Mark could see the bulge of muscle beneath his tunic. He carried a heavy-bladed *guandao*. The haft was as tall as a man and the blade was broad, like a scimitar. On its trailing edge was backwards facing hook. The soldier spoke in a rolling baritone.

'I wanted the proud one,' he said. He nodded to the dead archer. 'This one would have sufficed but she was foolish.' He gave a throaty chuckle. 'She should not have refused me.'

'Forgive my manners,' Meng said. 'Let me introduce my new top soldier. I know him only as "Shan"'.

'Is this the barbarian I must kill?' Shan asked.

'It is,' Meng replied. 'Bring me his head when you are done.' To Mark he said. 'There are still some stragglers to round up, so I must leave you. Please, do not keep Shan for too long.' He turned and disappeared into the shadows.

In a display of weaponcraft, Shan swept his *guandao* in an upward cut then windmilled it overhead before snapping it down into the attack position: haft level; blade forward. In the brazier's light, the steel gleamed orange.

Mark dropped to a half crouch. For a moment, he fixed his eyes on the *guandao's* blade. He imagined it slicing through flesh and bone. Imagined the backward facing hook tearing out his guts.

Shan beckoned to Mark. His voice was soft, as though speaking to a child.

'Come little one,' he said. 'The *guandao* is mercifully quick.' Then he stepped in, fast and low, thrusting the *guandao* at Mark's belly.

Mark knocked the *guandao* aside. He followed through with cut to Shan's neck but the Taiping danced away.

Shan tossed the *guandao* into the air and caught it by the tail

## THE SCHOLAR'S BLADE

end of its haft. In one fluid motion, he swung it over his head like a giant pendulum then dropped to one knee and scythed it sideways at knee height.

Mark leapt over the blade and it sighed beneath his feet. Before Shan could regain his footing, Mark darted forward and cut hard and fast at the Taiping's shoulder.

Shan swayed back and the *dao* sliced open his tunic, etching a crimson line across his chest. The Taiping shook his head and smiled.

'The flea has a bite,' he said. 'A small bite but an annoying one.'

Then the smile fell from his lips and the battle rage twisted his face. He screamed *'Shaaaa!'* and charged.

Mark took the *dao* in a two-handed grip and swung it in an arcing parry. The blades rang together, jarring Mark's wrists and forearms. Too late, Mark saw Shan's face change from rage to triumph.

Shan twisted the *guandao's* haft, rotating its blade. He snagged Mark's blade with the *guandao's* hook, then heaved upwards and back.

Mark felt his sword wrenched from his grip. It span away from him and clattered along the plaza's flagstones.

Shan moved between Mark and the *dao*. He spoke as if comforting a frightened child.

'Do not be sad' he said. 'I promise to end the game quickly.'

Mark backed away. To his right, the western wall blocked his escape. Behind him were only shuttered windows and barred doors. He glanced to his left. An alley offered escape. He took another step back and his heel connected with a body. For a moment, he teetered then went down hard. His head slammed against the flagstones. Lights flashed behind his eyes.

Shan loomed over him. The brazier's light flickered red and

orange, turning his face into something hellish. He raised the *guandao*. Its cutting edge gleamed.

On the battlements above the plaza, something moved. There was a sound like tearing silk followed by the smack of iron on flesh. Shan roared in pain and rage. The *guandao* slipped from his hands. He clawed at something embedded in his back.

There was another tearing sound and the crunch of shattered bone. Shan sank to his knees, grasping at a bloodied arrowhead that jutted from his throat. His eyes widened, as if in surprise. For a heartbeat, his eyes stared then the light went from them. He coughed a wad of blood then pitched forward and was still.

Mark rose to his knees and shook his head to clear it. He looked up at the battlement parapet. Except for the dying brazier, it was empty.

'Mei?' he called.

There was no answer.

He ran to the wall. He looked left and right but could see no way up to the parapet. He flattened his back against the wall and scanned the plaza. Were more Taipings stragglers hiding in the shadows? How many? Where?

The area is not secure, he told himself. I can't leave her but I can't stay.

'MEI!' he shouted. Still, there was only silence.

He recovered the *dao* and forced himself to head for the alley's safety. At its mouth, he paused.

'I will find you,' he called. 'Do you hear me, Mei? I will find you and then I will say what is in my heart.'

Still, there was no answer.

Taiping archer, Ping Song-mei, stood beside the road leading from Sungkiang. She checked her quiver, it was empty. She had used her two last arrows on the giant Taiping. She screwed shut her eyes. She had killed a comrade. Was she a traitor?

She watched the remnants of the garrison file past. They walked in silence, hunch-shouldered and heavy-limbed. Some used their spears as walking staffs. Mei's eyes were gritty with fatigue. It was as if her guts had turned to stone. She backhanded a tear from her cheek. How could so few wreak such destruction? The enemy must be demons.

*Enemy!*

The enemy was a golden haired Westerner. When next she saw Mark Falchion, would it be down the length of a nocked arrow?

A pit opened inside her. *Damn you Mark Falchion! Damn you! Damn you! Damn you!*

She clenched her fists. 'I do not love you,' she whispered. She squared her shoulders and shouted at the distant walls. 'Do you hear me, Mark Falchion? I do not love you.'

Archer Ping Song-mei turned her back on Sungkiang. She was a soldier in the army of *Taiping Tien Kwoh*. Soon there would be aching muscles as she retrained with the bow. But no matter, the fight against the emperor and his mercenaries would continue.

Mei thrust out her chin. She was no traitor; she was faithful to the Taiping cause and she would kill anyone who stood against her.

But still, the face of a fair-haired, blue-eyed Westerner lingered with her.

As the sun rose behind Sungkiang, Mark Falchion joined Tang on the section of wall near the western gate tower.

Vincente was kneeling beside Ward, who sat propped against the battlements. His face was pale and his shirt was bloodied. An orderly pressed a field dressing against his shoulder. At Mark and Tang's approach, Vincente rose to meet them.

'The colonel's caught one in the shoulder,' he said.

'Have you taken command?' Mark asked.

Vincente gave a barking laugh. 'Did you hear that, Colonel?' he said to Ward. 'Do you feel like handing over command?'

Ward beckoned them forward. 'What's the cost, Vincente?' he croaked.

Vincente read from a small notebook. 'Sixty-two dead, one hundred wounded.' He shut the notebook. 'Sorry, Colonel.'

Ward gave a heavy sigh. 'A bad do, old friend.'

To the north, the dawn sun winked off massed spear points as a column of Imperial infantry marched towards them.

'I see our gallant allies are arriving.' Vincente grumbled. 'They're taking care not to obstruct the enemy's retreat.'

'I could have done with them when we were clawing up that ramp,' Ward said. He looked up at Mark and Tang. 'I'm glad you two have become friends.' He winced as the orderly swabbed his shoulder. 'You're a good team,' he said. 'I'll make sure you stick together.'

'What did he say?' Tang muttered.

'He says we have served the emperor well,' Mark answered, 'We must continue our duties together.'

Tang nodded. For a moment, a smile touched his lips then it was gone.

Jessop joined them. 'The town's ours, Colonel,' he declared. 'There are pockets of resistance but the main body of enemy is retreating towards Chingpu.' He turned to Mark. 'For what it's worth Mark, I'm glad to see you on your feet.'

As Jessop turned to leave, Mark touched his arm.

'I was in the courtyard,' Mark said. He lowered his eyes, hunting for the right words. 'There was a wounded trooper. I wanted to help him... but...' He looked into Jessop's eyes. 'I left him Harry, I left him to die.'

'I know old fellow, I know,' Jessop said. 'It's hard. We'll speak of it later.' He smiled then made his way down the ramp leading into the town.

Mark spoke more to himself than to anyone. 'Is it over?'

Vincente answered. 'Over? No Mark. The Taiping's prize is Shanghai; their prize is modern rifles and artillery.' He shook his head. 'The prize is too great. The Taipings will regroup and they'll be back.'

'Who will stop them?' Mark asked.

Vincente played a match over the tip of a cigar. He blew out a stream of smoke and his eyes glittered. 'Who? You of course,' he said. 'You, me, the colonel, Harry Jessop and all the others. *We* will damn well stop them.'

Mark gazed over the battlements. Somewhere out there, a woman marched with the Taiping army. Her face drifted before him. Her eyes and lips filled his head. He banged his fist against the parapet. *Enough,* he commanded himself, banishing her from his thoughts.

The journey back to the Soochow colleges starts now, he told himself. And the road will be a hard one.

# Historical Note

In 1644, the Manchurian army seized Peking and toppled China's Ming Emperor. The Manchus established the Ching dynasty but the Chinese people never accepted their rule. Over the next two centuries, there were many rebellions.

The strangest, yet most successful rebel group was a Christian cult called *Taiping Tien Kwoh* or the Kingdom of Heavenly Peace. Its founder was Hoong Hsiu-chuan, a failed civil service candidate who claimed to be the younger brother of Jesus Christ.

Born into a modest farming family, Hoong despised the Manchurians and declared God had demanded their overthrow. Preaching a mixture of evangelism and politics, Hoong developed a huge following. In March 1853, he led a rebel army into the ancient city of Nanking from where he conducted a rebellion that claimed at least twenty million lives.

Hoong Hsiu-chuan employed two thousand women to run his palace administration and he elevated some to great prominence. There were also sightings of women in the Taiping army's front ranks. However, he imposed strict discipline on his household women, ordering severe beatings for minor offences such as frowning or the late delivery of towels.

By 1860, the rebellion had stalled and the Taipings decided to force arms deals from Shanghai's foreign traders. In the spring of that year, the Taipings marched on Shanghai with orders to seize the city's Chinese quarter but to leave the foreign settlements alone. It was a masterstroke: the foreign powers had no mandate to defend the Chinese quarter but the threat to their interests was clear.

As the Taipings marched, the colonial powers dithered and into this picture stepped Frederick Townsend Ward.

Ward came from a prosperous New England family but at the age of nineteen he went in search of adventure. He prospected for gold in California, rode with the Texas Rangers, was a mercenary in northern Mexico, served with the French army in the Crimea and sailed aboard clipper ships plying the China seas.

He arrived in Shanghai in 1859, just before his twenty-eighth birthday. His easy charm won him friends amongst the Chinese business community. When the colonial powers failed to meet the Taiping threat, a coalition of Chinese businessmen and Imperial officials asked Ward to raise a mercenary defence force.

Ward's first objective was the Taiping stronghold of Sungkiang. He recruited two hundred men; mostly Americans but also some Europeans and a handful of Filipinos. He chose Vincente Macanaya as his *aide de camp*.

The first attack was a fiasco, but Ward convinced his backers to give him another chance. He promoted his best men to officer rank and discharged the rest. In just two weeks, Ward and Vincente raised and trained a force of two hundred Filipino troopers.

Their next attack fared better and Ward took Sungkiang for his headquarters. Both sides suffered heavy casualties. Ward's sixty-two dead and one hundred wounded was eighty percent of his force. Taiping casualties are unknown but estimated to be a full third of their strength, which numbered thousands. Ward was himself wounded at Sungkiang but before seeking medical treatment in Shanghai, he arranged for the care of his wounded troopers, established his headquarters and oversaw the deployment of Imperial troops sent to garrison the town.

Many other players in this story were real people: Sir John

Michel commanded British land forces and Admiral Sir James Hope, know to his men as 'Fighting Jimmy', commanded the Royal Navy's China Fleet. Chaloner Alabaster was a linguist with Shanghai's British consulate and wrote several accounts of Ward's battles. Colonel Ikedanbu paid the price for his overconfidence at Jintian. Yang Fang headed the Takei Bank and H. Fogg and Company supplied most of Ward's military and logistical needs.

I based the mysterious Mister Hung on Li Hung-chang, a brilliant military and civil administrator. In later years, he risked his career and maybe his life by saving many Westerners from the excesses of the Boxers, an anti-foreign movement sponsored by the Empress Dowager.

Nanking's porcelain tower was built in the fifteenth century. However, after the Taipings captured the city, they removed the internal flooring to prevent it being used as an observation platform by attacking forces. In 1856, they destroyed it completely.

Those familiar with Chinese names will see I have abandoned the modern form of romanised Chinese, called *pinyin*. Instead, I've used a style common during the mid-nineteenth century. So, today's Nanjing becomes old fashioned Nanking and names like the Taiping ruler, Hoong Xiuquan, becomes the more reader friendly Hoong Hsiu-chuan.

In researching this story, I owe much to two remarkable books. The first is Jonathan Spence's *God's Chinese Son*, the story of the Taiping ruler, Hoong Hsiu-chuan. The second is *The Devil's Soldier* by Caleb Carr, an account of Frederick Ward's defence of Shanghai. Both volumes are thoroughly enjoyable and I heartily recommend them.

Sadly, neither of these excellent works mentions Mark Falchion or Lieutenant Tang who are, of course, my own inventions. Neither do they mention a Taiping archer called Ping Song-mei. However, when Hoong Hsiu-chuan made his triumphal entry to Nanking, he had an escort of thirty-two women. All sat astride horses and carried yellow parasols. I like to think their commander would have been a formidable woman and that amongst them was a teenage girl fleeing the life of a *mi-jeh*.

Taiping ambitions for Shanghai did not end with Ward's victory at Sungkiang. Soon, Mark Falchion will have both old and new enemies to challenge him.

# About The Author

**Chris Emmett** served with the Hong Kong Police for twenty-eight years, worked on the Hong Kong-China border during the Chairman Mao era and did three tours with the paramilitary Police Tactical Unit. While in the Narcotics Bureau, he was part of the team that arrested the owner of Hong Kong's most popular newspaper for dealing in opium and heroin. His first book, 'Hong Kong Policeman,' was published in 2014 and Inside the Lines was published in 2019. The Scholar's Blade is his first novel.

Milton Keynes UK
Ingram Content Group UK Ltd.
UKHW040054200424
441418UK00007B/228